THE FINAL
CHASE

Published in the UK in 2023 by DR Enterprises

Paperback ISBN 978-1-7399182-8-6
eBook ISBN 978-1-7399182-9-3

Cover design and typeset by SpiffingCovers

Editing by Jessica Chapman

THE FINAL
CHASE

DOUGLAS
ROBERTS

Lieutenant-Colonel Bernard Utting OBE
Commissioned into the Royal Engineers in 1940, decommissioned
from the XIV 'forgotten army' in December 1945.

Chapter 1

The Last Airfield

April 1945

Building an entire airfield from scratch, including many outbuildings, hangers, and a control tower in less than ten weeks is never easy and it helps if you're not being shot at. Lieutenant-Colonel Bernard Stock of the Royal Engineers was grateful that the Japanese had not found this new location – yet. How could their air force miss this one? It was to have two parallel runways, was to be the longest yet, and should have been visible to every Zero within 10 miles. Perhaps it was the exceptionally high trees that surrounded this valley or the pervasive mist that rolled off the top of the ridge masking the western end of the 3,000-foot clearing: one runway half a mile long. Or perhaps the Japs had decided that no one could possibly build an airfield on the side of this particular mountain.

Whatever the reason, Stock, as always, had risen to the challenge given to him by the brigadier the previous month. Without any misgivings, and a confident smile, he said it could be done. "But Christ, what have I let myself in for this time?" he thought to himself on his way to start Airfield Number 22 – that was how many he had personally built, some out of the dense forests of Burma during the Fourteenth Army's campaign against the Japanese. "And only ten weeks to get one of the two runways serviceable – bloody hell!" But then again, he thought to himself, if it had been easy, they wouldn't have summoned him to do it. 'The impossible we do at once, miracles take a little longer' was the motto of the Royal Engineers, and he wasn't about to disappoint them.

The orders had come down directly from General Slim to Brigadier General Henry Alfredson, Stock's immediate superior officer. There were rumours about a bigger glider that had to be towed behind a more powerful Dakota together with a much larger bomber coded B29, that needed all of the long runways, and Stock had to make sure it wasn't about to become a giant hedge trimmer to the lofty vegetation.

Two weeks to go before Runway N22a had to be operational, and Stock still needed more labour over and above the 8,000 coolies he had already subpoenaed from the local population. The four D8 bulldozers that Division had given him were inadequate and needed the constant attention of the always-ready Sergeant Forbes. The fuel had been watered-down by the locals, and the new filters only fitted when squashed into the canister with a 10 lb sledgehammer. Six new D10 bulldozers were supposed to be arriving last week, and they would have been just about capable of scything through the pulpy trees that had taken up residence in this part of the forest. But their arrival was not to be, as their transporters had been strafed by the Japanese air force ten days ago. Which was why Stock needed more coolies.

Indigenous coolies were the happiest of people, if kept well-fed, had access to their families, and were not eaten by the numerous tigers that had been drawn to this human feast.

"Sahib, Sahib… there is another man-eater that has moved into the forest," said Corporal Bherti, waking up Stock one morning. "It must be killed before work can begin today." Stock groaned at the thought of having to wait in ambush with a goat for the latest threat to his dream of producing 'the impossible'.

He found Burmese goats especially smelly this time of the year, and their two-toned bleating was enough to want to stuff rifle wadding in each ear but then he would not hear the tiger's approach. He'd given each goat a name. Alphabetically, this one he would call Gertrude, if only to whisper to it to be quiet in the middle of the night or bleat at the right time. For some reason, these goats liked being whispered to, but it was probably Stock's breath that eased the itching of the lice-ridden ear that soothed it. Stock needed Gertrude to bleat loudly today so that she would attract the tiger sooner rather than relying upon her dreadful odour to sift through the trees to the highly sensitive nose of the tiger. Stock would have to clean himself up as well after working half the night on one of the D8s that had developed a nasty hiccup.

As a precaution, Stock had kept his 12-bore shotgun with a lethal charge under his camp bed ever since one particular tiger two weeks ago had come sniffing around his tent. This was becoming tedious to him, and Stock had better things to do than rid the area of local teeth, but not one of his 8,000 coolies would venture out of their compound until he returned from the edge of the jungle with a tiger in tow. Stock had thought of getting one of the tigers stuffed so that he could produce it at the drop of a hat, but that would involve the local taxidermist who, no doubt, had numerous cousins working on the airstrip who would soon get to hear of the stuffed tiger; maybe even recognise it. No, Stock would have to shoot this tiger as well, and hope this would placate his coolies, at least for a few more days.

Corporal Bherti fetched Lieutenant Geoffrey Marston who usually enjoyed accompanying Stock on these hunts and alerted Private Floppy. No one knew why he was called 'Floppy', but having been Stock's Batman since Airfield Number Nineteen, he was used to being the first to 'flop' to the ground whenever anything like machine gun fire threatened the peace and quiet. The fragile-framed Floppy was also an ex-game keeper, had a knack for knowing which way the wind was blowing, and had developed a keen sense of where it was best not to lurk for man-eaters.

"Come on, then, get the green shells from the box on the side there, and don't forget the drawstring and wadding this time." Stock's mood was quickly turning to frustration with this time-consuming exercise. "Meet me by the Mess Tent in five minutes," addressing Floppy. "No – let's meet in ten minutes. I need to clean up a little first."

He had considered training Floppy to shoot tigers, but not every ex-gamekeeper could handle a 12-bore with a lethal charge shot, and it was more likely to blow Floppy off his small feet and just frighten the tiger than to achieve a clean kill. It was important to Stock that a graceful animal such as these magnificent royal Bengal tigers, should not suffer, indeed not just these tigers, but any animal. He had grown up on a Norfolk farm and hated to see what the suffering animals went through on their way to the slaughterhouse. His siblings had no such qualms, and even his father sometimes seemed indifferent as to how the animals suffered, just as long as they were slaughtered quickly. 'How different we are now' Stock thought, but quickly returned to the problem at hand.

It would be quite clinical, Stock thought, but it was easier at night, and he really was not looking forward to this morning's kill. At night, he could detect the tiger's approach from the blood-red reflection of the tiger's eyes in the weak flame that flickered from the oil lamp on the end of the bamboo pole above the goat. Aim right between the red eyes and pull the trigger, and as quickly as possible, then scamper up to the safety of a tree, unless he was already in one, which he usually was. It took a little while for the smoke discharge to clear, and only when Stock was sure the tiger was dead would he venture back down. In Stock's experience, a wounded tiger's reactions were even quicker when alerted to a missed or wounding shot, and twice as dangerous. A daylight kill was rather tricky as there was no reflection in the eyes to aim at but, instead, only the hazy camouflaged fur and protruding ears to act as a guide as to where the centre of the head was.

By the Mess Tent, Floppy already had the 12-bore crooked under his arm in the hope of being chosen to execute the beast, and had a mournful look in his eyes, as though this might convey his attitude of capability to Stock.

Stock's voice was rather terse. "Good morning, Geoffrey. Corporal, what can you tell us about this tiger? Where was it last seen, and is it a female, as usual? Is it pregnant, how old is it, and is it alone? Oh, and I presume it hasn't eaten anyone yet!

"Sahib, it is not a female, but an older man-eater, with a large scar below its right ear. I think it has been in a fight, and perhaps cannot see properly out of its right eye, which is why it is now hunting us instead of its usual meal. He will be angry and hungry, but now very wary and even more dangerous. We last saw it over there, behind where we left last night's tools." Bherti pointed towards a pile of rammers and forks quite some distance away from the Mess Tent.

Stock's mood was not improved with the production of Gertrude by Bherti's sister who trawled an obviously reluctant goat behind her on a piece of twiney string that looked as though it was about to snap at one of the many knots in it.

"Sahib, this goat is a good milker, and will only cost forty rupees" said Bherti, hoping to be able to pass on a rupee or two to his sister.

Stock's eyebrows raised a little. "If it's a good milker, then we can pay you the usual twenty rupees.". Stock was used to this ritual of bartering. "But tell your sister her family can have the goat when we are finished, alive or dead."

This was just about as good a deal as Bherti was going to get from Stock, but he hoped for a little more. "Yes Sahib, but this one is old, and has tough meat on it, and it will not feed her family for more than three days."

Stock really did not want to spend time bartering, but knew he had to keep in with Bharti's sister who seemed to have an endless supply of goats. "Tell her she can have a half day's field rations as well." 'That ought to do it' thought Stock.

Bharti's almost incomprehensible colloquial Urdu with his sister was difficult for Stock to keep up with. He had forced himself to attain some knowledge of the language, at least the most basic syllables and phrases, but not to this extent.

Bharti's sister looked very happy, and Stock could now get on with planning how best to deal with the latest threat to his coolies.

Turning to Lieutenant Marston to discuss how they would approach the area, Stock was interrupted by Floppy's sudden galvanising into motion into what seemed like a crouching monkey in readiness to make one of his sudden 'flops'. Stock was used to this, and suspected some form of enemy to appear, but as they both looked in the direction of what was obviously an engine, a Jeep appeared on the dusty track that led from the western edge of the airfield. Floppy's keen sense of self-preservation relaxed, as did his ears.

The approaching Jeep picked up speed as it found the even surface of a partly smoothed runway, sounding overjoyed to engage top gear with the engine note taking on a deeper echo against the arena of trees. As it neared the hunting party, the driver looked rather grim-faced, and probably had every right to be, since the Jeep had just come from the side of the area where the tiger had last been spotted. An open-top vehicle was probably not the best mode of transport in the vicinity of a man-eating tiger.

The passenger's features became familiar to Stock, who recognised Major Charles Grears from Brigade HQ; He too was not smiling but hanging on to the windscreen bar and seat with both hands even as they skidded to a halt by the party.

It was obvious to Stock that they had spotted the tiger on their way in and decided to take this opportunity to needle his friend.

"Good morning, Grears. Going hunting with that machine gun? That's not how it's supposed to be done, you know," he pointed at the Maxim mounted on the rear of the Jeep. The thought crossed his mind that he may be able to train Floppy to use a steadier form of gun on that nasty set of teeth, but it didn't last long.

"My God, Stock, but there's a tiger nestled just above that rock behind those trees. Can't you…?" Grears then spotted the 12-bore in Floppy's hands, and it dawned on him that any further comments were totally wasted. It also dawned on him that Stock had got another jibe at him and at his own expense. Climbing out of the Jeep and getting over his initial surprise, he saluted, although he knew it probably wasn't absolutely necessary as he and Bernard knew each other well. 'This looks official' thought Stock returning the salute. Lieutenant Marston's salute was textbook.

"And how can we help a lost staff officer today?" Yet another small jibe, but Stock's tone concealed his concern that the Brigadier had sent Grears to check up on his progress.

Grears' hand dropped to the crease on his trousers. "I need to have a word with you - alone." 'This is very official' thought Stock. Grears' driver had wandered off and was rolling a cigarette while kicking up dust from the runway, but Marston's presence dictated that he would need to be ordered to leave.

Stock's nod to Marston was as good as any order, "I'll talk later with Private Floppy and Corporal Bherti about how best to approach the tiger." He gestured to the others who wandered off towards the Mess Tent, sister, and goat in tow.

"I presume Brigadier Alfredson is getting worried about the runway being_"

"No, no, no," Grears interrupted, taking Stock by the elbow, and walking him in the opposite direction from the Mess Tent. "It's nothing to do with that. The brigadier sent me here. You are to report to him straight away at brigade HQ on the other side of the Irrawaddy River." Grears paused. "I have been ordered to take over from you."

It was like a butcher's knife had been drawn across Stock's stomach. "You're relieving me? But why?" Stock was momentarily speechless.

It had occurred to Grears that he could have quite easily have rubbed Stock's nose in it, as he knew what finishing this airfield meant to Stock as well as to the Allies. Having had a long, if not tedious, journey by jeep down from brigade over the past four hours, he had had plenty of time to consider the best way of breaking the news. Grears was not the most tactful of men, and his plans to let Stock know in a gentlemanly manner now went up in smoke.

Major Grears had broken the news the only way he knew how,

"There was a bit of a flap on this morning, people to-ing and fro-ing, and getting the brigadier out of bed that early, always keeps us on our toes. He didn't say much, but he told me to come and fetch you now and that I was to take over from you."

Stock was still taking stock of his predicament. He often played with words when under pressure, but no more came, but his thoughts drifted amongst the reasons behind the order. Why? I'm the only one who can get this airfield finished in time… Brigadier knows that. Grears won't cope… He can't even shoot a pistol straight, let alone kill a tiger. Brigadier wants me to….??? It can't be a mistake, otherwise Grears wouldn't be here.' Stock's thoughts were now concentrating on Grears.

"What exactly did the brigadier say?"

"Just that I am to put you in that Jeep and get you to brigade immediately."." Grears had now got over his embarrassment of being the bearer of bad news. "I am to stay here and finish the runway and take temporary command of your battalion. He's the brigadier's driver, and he'll take you there," he said, gesturing towards Pearson, who was now looking under the bonnet of the Jeep. "Left about 2.30 this morning, but there don't seem to be any Japs about, so you ought to be alright. He's a good driver, but he didn't half give me a shock when he swerved to go around that bloody tiger's rock."

The silence between them was broken by Gertrude's distant bleat, and Stock's thoughts turned to what the brigadier would want with him. "Did he say anything about what this is to do with?"

"Uuuummm, no, but I suppose it's your family connections with Brigadier Alfredson. He did say I must talk to you alone and he didn't tell me anything more." Grears looked around. "You'd better let me know your schedule for this place and get going. He's really anxious that you should be back at HQ as soon as you can be."

The reality of Grears' news now fully sunk into Stock, as he turned to look at what he had achieved over the past three weeks. Turning unadulterated jungle into an extensive forward airfield, right under the Japs' noses, when finished and operational, was always the most gratifying part to Stock. He just would not get a chance to see it this time. Anyone could clear jungle, but to turn the space into an airfield capable of taking heavy aircraft was totally different. Locating the willing coolies, paying them the equivalent of a halfpenny a day, feeding them and their families, resolving disputes, and, yes, even protecting them from marauding tigers. Soil compaction, drainage to cope with heavy rains in the monsoon season, siting the latrines and repelling as much malaria as possible, keeping the machinery running… The list was endless and very taxing to even the best Royal Engineer. Then of course there were the Japanese, who quite rightly took extreme umbrage at an enemy airfield being created, often just behind their lines. Stock had personally shot down and killed the pilot of one Zero that had happened across one of his earlier airfields. He had suffered mortars and infantry attack, and even an uprising by unsympathetic coolies. Even though it was his job in the war, he still maintained great pride in being a professional sapper and seeing his creations completed.

Stock was an optimist, and now the butcher's knife no longer had such a sting, but it would remain there until he found the reason why the brigadier had ordered him back to HQ. That at least was something to look forward to, wasn't it?

Strapping his ready kit bag into the Jeep and instructing Pearson to take the longer perimeter road to avoid the tiger, he chuckled at the thought of Floppy taking on a fierce man-killer. 'Looks like he's got his wish. Hope he survives. And hope he manages to keep the locals off the menu'.

Chapter 2

Headquarters

The tedious journey to Fort Hertz, the Brigade HQ on the outskirts of Putao, was mercifully uneventful. As he approached the pre-colonial two-storey building through the humid afternoon sunshine, from the sentries' reactions it was obvious to him that he was expected. Another unit of engineers had obviously been busy, as the electrically powered ceiling fans were turning just enough to disturb the ever-present squadrons of flies that circled the adjutant's office.

A sergeant ushered Stock into the relative cool of the outer office, where a staff officer was hunched over a desk. "Aah, there you are, sir. The brigadier's waiting for you. Over the quad and through the door at the far end.".”

One of the two sentries on either side knocked and immediately opened one half of the double doors into Brigadier Alfredson's sanctorum. The other preceded Stock to announce him. To Stock, the reaction from three of the people in the room could not have been timelier. In perfect synchronisation, they all snapped their gazes in his direction. 'What the hell is going on here?' he thought. If Stock's thoughts were confused by this summons before, they were clearer now. It was official, very official, as Alfredson's first words were: "Stock, glad to see you made it safely."

Those few words in themselves said more to Stock than a thousand others, as he and George Henry Alfredson had known each other from their school days. Not only that, but Stock's elder brother Richard had married into the wealth of the Alfredson family which helped create a cohesive atmosphere whenever the two families had a get-together. Their shared love of the games of rugby-football, cricket, even croquet, and other such British sporting pastimes had bound them to each other like brothers. Alfredson's initial address to Stock meant that whatever was to come next would not only be official, but probably bloody dangerous as well, but it was not the danger aspect that worried Stock.

After Alfredson's initial welcome, his face broke into a smile, but only for a standard, polite two seconds, as if to indicate that their friendship still stood firm.

"I believe you know Major Deeks?" Again, was this an offering of friendship? "This is Mr Corston from Intelligence, and Colonel Haruko of their eighteenth division."."

Apart from the distant garrison noises from the nearby barracks, the dull silence penetrated Stock as he tried to fathom what a smartly dressed Japanese staff officer was doing here. Officialdom… It took Stock an extra second or so to come to attention and salute. "Time is rather short, and we need to take action immediately. Come and sit here, Stock," said Alfredson ushering to a seat next to Colonel Haruko. No explanation had been offered as to why Haruko was on his own, or how he got here, and certainly Stock was not about to ask.

Stock's inquisitive second glance at Haruko showed a well-presented, middle-aged man. Extraordinarily, he was well over six feet tall. Coming from a nation of 'Nips', he would have had a clear and commanding view over those surrounding him anywhere he went. Well-built and without excess fat, his physical superiority seemed to back up the level stare that he now returned to Stock.

Haruko's lips hardly moved, but he spoke in almost perfect English, "I think it best if the Brigadier continues."

Stock's attention now reverted to Alfredson who gave an almost imperceptible nod as if to say that that was the end of introductions, his eyes reverting to his large leather-embossed desk in front of him.

"What I have to say will be known only to us present here, General Slim, General Keisuke, and his immediate staff." He briefly looked up and nodded in Haruko's direction. "In other words, not a word to anybody about this." He paused for a moment to give full effect to the gravitas of what he had just said. "Am I clear?" This was Alfredson's way of letting Stock know that he was now in the same privileged, if not very awkward, position as the others. "In case you're wondering, the Chinese are not involved at this stage so don't go letting the cat out of the bag on that front."

"Keisuke is a very influential man and even has the ear of the emperor. He's learned of our latest weapon - the atom bomb - and what it can do and, from what I've been told, by all reports, it can wipe out entire civilisations. I can't imagine it doing that, but it must be very powerful indeed. I know very little about it, other than the Americans are hoping to test it shortly. Keisuke and a few other like-minded generals do not want to see their way of life destroyed and realise that, as they are losing the war. They are considering negotiating the surrender of their north-east armies. If we can persuade Keisuke to capitulate, it will probably mean that most of the other Japanese forces in the area will consider doing the same, and at the very least it will create tremendous demoralisation throughout the entire Japanese army. If this happens, gentlemen, I think we can say that the war on the mainland really will be over very soon.

"Colonel Haruko here has been sent by Keisuke to General Slim to offer a negotiated settlement. For certain political reasons, namely the American and Chinese factors, I have been asked to handle the negotiations at this stage.

Alfredson quite rightly paused for breath.

"I have sent for you both, Deeks and Stock, as my most trusted senior officers, to accompany Colonel Haruko here back to his army HQ to relay General Slim's acceptance of their surrender, and to prepare details of the hand-over of personnel and arms." Alfredson lifted and dropped back down onto his desk two files to indicate that most of the details had already been worked out and were within.

Stock unconsciously blinked for almost too long, taking in the enormity of the situation. His thoughts almost betrayed the mixed emotions that 'pin-balled' around inside his head. Victory, we've done it. No more Japanese. Go home soon. Not quite yet. Must go behind enemy lines again. What's in those folders? How can I do this? Where exactly are we going? Why is Haruko on his own? Why me? Yes, why me?

Alfredson's voice instinctively lowered. "The consequences of the Japanese high command discovering this before we have had a chance to take over from Keisuke are all very clear, which is why speed is of the essence. Not only will it delay our victory, but it obviously puts him, the colonel, and a certain number of their staff in the most dangerous of positions." Alfredson's attention focused on Deeks and Stock. "You'll be leaving with the colonel and Mr Corston by one of our Beauforts from the airstrip here in just over an hour." He glanced at the large round clock on the wall above the door. "The quartermaster will have your equipment ready, but I'm afraid if you have any questions, the colonel and Mr Corston here will be able to answer some of them in the plane. Thank you, gentlemen." Alfredson's raised voice summoned one of the sentries outside, and the door opened.

Deeks and Stock, in unison, stood to attention and saluted, while Haruko bent his large frame into the traditional Japanese 'half-bow'. As they filed out towards the veranda, Alfredson's voice beckoned Stock back, "Errr, Stock, as you were the last here, I'd like to fill you in on what you missed earlier. Come back in for a minute, would you?" He once again beckoned to a chair, but a closer one than before. The door closed, and Alfredson crossed his legs as he reclined into his own chair.

After an awkward pause that allowed Stock to get comfortable, "Listen, Bernard, I know this is not what you are used to and is a far cry from those airfields, but there's a bit more to this than what I have told the others, and I need someone who I can absolutely trust. Besides which, you are senior enough to carry this off. In fact, I have promoted you to a full colonel on my staff as of today since this will give you adequate seniority. Besides which, I'll not have you salute to the likes of Haruko." He gestured to what Stock guessed to be the staff officer outside on the veranda, "Whitman has your new uniform."

Promotion is always quicker during a conflict, and Stock had not expected his next step up for several months, if indeed before the war ended. "If this is a permanent promotion, sir, will I be returning to finish my airfield in time for…?"

Alfredson interrupted with his raised hand, "Hold on, Bernard, I am not sure you'll be needed there anymore, as we have another project on the drawing board coming up. Right now, I need to tell you more about General Keisuke's offer, but not in front of those gentlemen. I don't trust any Jap, and especially Haruko, but in this instance, we have little choice." An old-fashioned look crossed his face. "Haruko is just a cat's-paw, but he has doubtless been given very specific orders by Keisuke, and I doubt he knows what else is behind all this.".

Stock's already surprised logical mind was now grappling with more inferences. "You mean to tell me that there's no bomb and it's all a big hoax and that."

Alfredson's usual mode of interruption with his hand stopped Stock once again. "No, no, no, that's all true, and Deeks and Corston can manage that part of the equation. You will be tagging along with them. On the face of it, you will be in charge of the negotiations, but you will need to delegate the surrender details to Deeks primarily. You won't have much time either, because if Keisuke's corps commanders get wind of what's going on before it is a *fait accompli*, well, I suspect it won't happen at all, and you and your party will find yourselves in very hot water.".

Stock knew Alfredson was referring to the rumours about how the Japanese treated their prisoners-of-war, and it was probably one of the more primeval fears that kept the men of the Fourteenth Army on their guard. The probability of surviving capture by the Japanese was considered slim at best, and if Stock was captured right in the heart of one of those Japanese armies, with their knowledge of what he and his party were attempting to do, Stock would be tortured to reveal more than he knew.

"This comes from Winston Churchill himself and not even General Slim has been told all the details, so this part is very privileged information. Not even the courier who brought me this message this morning knows, so you have to keep this to yourself. And there's no written orders to go with it. Winston and I go back a long way, nearly as long as you and I've known each other, so I can understand his decision to ask me to help."

If Alfredson's tone had been serious before, his wider eyes now concentrated on Stock as if to relay the importance of what he was saying. A feeling of numbness crept over Stock, and he decided it best not to say anything. What could he say, anyway?

Alfredson's tone hardened even further. "It turns out that the king's nephew, Ignatius, has secretly been engaged to Keisuke's daughter, Akiko, since before the outbreak of the war. Not only that, but Keisuke's eldest son is married to the emperor's daughter." He paused, not for effect, but to catch his own breath as if the words themselves were enough to bring the war to an end. "Winston needs to make sure that the two of them never meet again and has asked me to intervene." He waited a while to allow Stock to take in what had just been said. "Akiko is visiting her father at the moment at his army HQ, and you are to bring her here, to me."

Alfredson did not interrupt while Stock closed his eyes for a long time. A blink was not sufficient. Time to think, think, think. If the king's nephew and Akiko did meet and marry, then Keisuke's son would become part of the immediate accession to the throne of England. And if he did become King, there would be - Bloody Hell - a Jap on the British throne. Stock snapped open his eyes to find Alfredson glaring at him as if it were all his fault. 'By Christ, but this could be a mess. If we win the war, we could have a Jap king. If were to lose the war, we would definitely have a Jap king. No, it's unthinkable. We can't allow it... *I* can't allow it. What would happen back home? Strikes, riots, Civil War! The consequences are too horrible to contemplate. I've got to help stop it.'

Stock's sharp intake of breath relayed to Alfredson that he now understood the gravity of the situation. His heart sank as he realised that it was going to be up to him to carry this off. Hang on a minute, I'm not trained for this…. But before he had the time to ask himself 'why me?' for the second time in less than 24 hours, he realised that this could never be trusted to someone outside the most reliable circle, and his connections with the great and the good had placed him in the right place at the right time… from their point of view. Trust. He was being entrusted to capture, kidnap, and return the daughter of an enemy general, who was about to surrender his army. What were the chances of Keisuke surrendering, then, if he knew of Stock's mission? His own quick death would be a blessing if he got caught, rather than being captured… This is very, very dangerous. Stock let go of his breath and frowned at Alfredson.

"I knew you would realise the all-round consequences," said Alfredson, handing Stock a tumbler of whisky that he had not noticed him pour out while he had his eyes closed. "Here, take this. It may be your last for a while." Alfredson turned back to his desk and read from a piece of paper. "Winston's words: *I cannot stress strongly enough the importance of keeping this information from the enemy. Should he discover this clandestine relationship, it would destroy the royal family, and possibly the British empire if it ever came to fruition.*" He finishes with "*We must succeed at all costs, and I repeat at all costs. I have every faith in you, my dear friend. Yours etcetera.*"

Alfredson sat on the corner of his desk as he returned the piece of paper to his top drawer. "You are to go as I cannot. I don't know the other officers as well as you, and besides which General Slim would forbid me to accompany Haruko. Whatever else, I cannot disobey that order. If I were to fall into the Japs' hands…" He left the sentence unfinished, as the consequences were plain. He was commander of the oversized brigade and the troop dispositions had to remain secret. His absence would more than raise suspicions that something else was going on. "Not only is your loyalty beyond question, but you are one of the few men I know who is capable of outthinking your opponent at the drop of a hat." He was referring to their several clashes on the rugby field and the bridge table, as well as Stock's ability to be one step ahead of him most of the time.

It was a depressing moment for both men.

Stock finished the tumbler and leant forward to put it back on the desk; He was indeed ahead of the brigadier, or so he thought. "Am I to assume that Akiko will come willingly if she knows that the king's nephew has asked for her? Oh, and what does she look like?

Alfredson straightened and stretched over to his other top drawer and handed Stock a small photograph. "She's the one on the far right of the picture. Taken just before the war with the Japanese imperial family and, yes, we believe she will come willingly. I am afraid I cannot give you a love letter in case you are captured, but His signet ring was sent with the courier and ought to persuade her that He is waiting for her here. I don't know how Winston got hold of it, and it is not my place to ask, even if I could. It's up to you to convince her to get on that plane."

Stock's mood deepened further. Having to lie to a woman in love would earn him her scorn, if not a knitting-needle in the neck. "What's to happen to her once I bring her back here?"

Alfredson paused and looked down before replying, "Please don't ask me; I don't know. I don't think Winston would want me to know in any case." The implications depressed Stock to unknown depths. The silence was now an invisible barrier between them, all except their eye-to-eye contact. Their common ground was only that they were doing it for King, Country, and Empire. He mused further and reflected that he had not been given either an order or been volunteered to do this. He was flying into the enemy's camp, where he would need to be very careful what he said to whom. He was going to lie to the only two friendly companions accompanying him, one of those a life-long friend. Lie to an enemy general. Deceive his staff. Somehow contact a general's daughter and find out if her sympathies really were genuine. Lie, deceive, and ultimately betray her. A woman scorned…

"I'm afraid I've no written orders for you and the other two may be reluctant to help you, so this may come in handy, but only as a last resort, you understand." He handed Stock a small, folded piece of paper which he now opened. *Provide all assistance. GA.*

"Well, I think you had better be on your way." Alfredson held out his hand, rather than accept a salute from Stock. "Goodbye, Bernard. No 'best of luck, old chap' as it was clearly inappropriate; they both knew that there was no 'right thing' to do here. Stock mused on the Engineers' saying once again: 'The impossible we do at once; miracles take a little longer'. What did this qualify as?

Their firm handshake broke the spell of the invisible barrier and re-cemented their relationship as the best of friends. Stock's spirits lifted a little as he walked towards the double doors. He would think of something to save Akiko.

Chapter 3
Springfields

Today

We all know about OAPs. They're our Grandparents who shuffle around in threadbare slippers and saggy cardigans with missing buttons. Three-quarters deaf, with misaligned glasses, encrusted dentures, gnarled hands gripping warped walking-sticks, tripping over whatever is available at the time. They have a permanent stoop from either looking down to focus on what they are about to trip over, or from craning their scrawny necks to cup an ear to hear what is being said to them. These are the dull and all too often forgotten people in our lives. Dull because their world has been shut off from them by either sight or sound, or both, and their capabilities of interacting with the latest news has become such a burden that they simply don't bother to do so. Their memories are faded and mixed up, and most of what they have to say has all been heard before. We all do our best to humour them with the same old repetitive remarks, and in the end, as they already know what we are going to say, they don't bother responding any differently. These are a burden on our lives, and much as we love them, as soon as is socially acceptable we wheel them off to a 'Home', where they meet others who have met the same fate.

This is a pity, because these folks have seen it all before, and their memories span generations, but they are incapable of relating their experiences to us 'youngsters'; Even if that youngster is a newcomer to the Home at the relatively young age of 75, or a great-great-grandfather yet to reach the ripe old age of 110. "I remember at Queen Victoria's funeral… or was it her marriage to Prince Albert…?" The fact that these two events happened several decades apart has melded into one, and by the time they have decided which one of these glorious state occasions it was, the rest of the story has been forgotten. It's not that they cannot take in the latest information, it is that their weary brains cannot digest it. Some call it Alzheimer's disease, others call it whatever is the latest scientific name to be produced by the health authorities. Whatever it is called has the same effect, and their vast knowledge, accumulated over the past century, is locked inside their heads.

Of course, some grow old gracefully and still have most of their own teeth as well as their own ears and eyes working in perfect unison. They have some wonderful stories to tell, and we sit on the edge of our chairs waiting to find out what comes next, and it's not normally a fart.

Bernard Stock was one of the former. His once proud frame now spent most of its days in a well-cushioned armchair, in front of a TV with the volume turned right up just in case the others at the back of the room missed anything. As though addressing a crowd of a million listeners a long way away, but not shouting, the pretty young girl presenting the news would rattle on about the latest murder, economic panics, cutbacks etc., and finish up with a heart-warming story. She announced that Tiddles the cat had been rescued from the jaws of death by the fire brigade. The video showed a tearful young girl looking up at a leafy tree while a fireman on the extendable Ladders had frightened the wits out of the cat with an extended arm. The film clip didn't show it, but as they left in their 15-ton firetruck, it had run poor Tiddles over. She would no doubt be reprimanded for the hint of a smile that crossed her face. Bernard was not totally dead from the neck up, and he was still capable of understanding most of what went on around him, and a smile creased his face on hearing the fate of the poor animal, but he couldn't remember the name of his cat.

He had been in Springfields House 'retirement' home for some months, but his state of mind excluded him from the luxury of realising this; he was incapable if discerning that sort of timespan, and to him it could have been days, but it really did not matter. Nor did it matter that he was content if only he was capable of knowing what true contentment was. What did matter was that he was safely ensconced in a cushioned armchair which he was unlikely to fall out of, and this was the main concern of the staff who patrolled the Day Rooms on the lookout for anyone erring from their set position. God forbid that they should try to get up and go to the loo unaccompanied; the non-slip floor would certainly be responsible for catching the edge of a slipper, even if it was on the correct foot.

Springfields House was a big Victorian-type mansion set in several acres, and because of its size and grandeur, had been saved from demolition, but instead converted into an up-market Home for the Elderly. It once boasted its own vegetable garden and orchard, with a small army of gardeners, cooks, servants, and butler, all housed in a suitable annexe. In its heyday, its semi-circular gravelled 'in and out' driveway would have been filled with horse-drawn carriages and, later, expensive motor cars. This led directly to the pillared entrance on the north side, and facing south towards the sun were landscaped gardens leading down to a large pond, adjacent to a 9-foot wall separating the garden from the coaching house and stables. At the end of the walled garden, lay the outskirts of the village of Yeasting, and the young boys from the village looked forward to every autumn with glee, as they helped the head gardener pick the best apples. They tended to eat nearly as much as they picked, but he didn't mind, as long as there was enough left over.

With the fading of the once proud family that owned Springfields House and the rise of inheritance taxes, it was inevitable that it would soon go to seed. Due to lack of maintenance, it was with relief to the last surviving relative of that family that it had been sold at auction in the late 1980s to a developer who intended to turn it into flats. The unfortunate developer had neither the permission from the local Council, nor the business acumen to survive the property downturn, and eventually went bankrupt in the mid-1990s still waiting for the requisite permission. The Council, however, was in need of somewhere to house the growing population of OAPs, compulsorily purchased it and gave itself permission to convert it into a suitable Home.

This was ideal for the expanding population of Yeasting in Sussex, as the large garden was designated for new housing, the coaching house and annexe converted and modernised into flats, but the main house was split into two parts. One part was for those who could still just about fend for themselves but had few relatives who could spare the time to see to their daily needs. They were free to come and go as they pleased and were often seen in the village, in The Comrades Club, or at whist drives. They were a credit to society and welcomed by the shopkeepers in the village.

The other part was for those who were on medication, and for the safety of everybody, locked in behind security doors. These were a hazard to society and given half-the-chance, would have wandered off down the road, only to fall into the river, or step out in front of the bus. One had been arrested for indecent behaviour, having escaped, and used his walking stick to lift the skirt of a woman waiting at the bus stop. Another had actually managed to board a coach for Brighton and had found his way to the aquarium and into the penguin enclosure. Sitting partly in the water, he related his youthful sexual exploits to one of the mesmerized penguins face-to-face and was eventually arrested after being complained about by an upset family. Not having any identification, nor being able to even remember his name, this resulted in a lengthy process of determining who he was, and where he lived.

When this sort of incident happened, the staff at Springfields were harangued, and on occasion sacked. Which was why they could relax a little, once they had everybody sitting in an armchair, gazing into middle space in the direction of the television set. Little attention was paid to the other part of the Home, as there was rarely anything to attend to, but occasionally one of the patients would reach an age where he would be considered too vague to be left to his own devices and moved from the 'open' part of the Home to the 'secure' part.

On entering Springfields through the twin pillars and double oak doors, one would be confronted with a tall, efficient-looking, over-sized desk, behind which sat a receptionist-cum-nurse. Behind her was a partitioned wall with the usual posters on health & safety, trying to persuade the whole world to try to give up smoking or alcohol etc. It seemed that this was the sole purpose of the wall, but it did in fact prevent a direct view through the long hallway onto the gardens behind. One of the doors off the hallway led to the manager's office, which had once been the billiard room. This too had been sub-divided to enable the accounts manager his own quiet but cramped space. To the right was a corridor that led to the 'open' part of the Home, and immediately to the left a pair of Georgian wired security doors which accessed the 'secure' area. This part of Springfields was nicknamed 'The Clink' from the sound the doors made when they automatically closed shut and were electronically controlled either by a button behind the receptionist's desk or by entering a 4-digit code on the panel from the secure side. It was therefore, in theory, impossible for anyone to pass through these doors without either entering the code or with a push of the button from behind the desk.

All visitors were required to sign a leather-bound register that was on top of the front desk, whether they be just visiting or delivery personnel, and the faded sign behind the receptionist reminded one of such. Not being a purpose-built Home with a separate entrance for goods, it was often a little inconvenient for visitors to have to sidle their way past a stack-trolley of food being delivered, or boxes of medicines piled against the side of the desk. This was one of the 'bugbears' of the administrator, who reminded the Council at every opportunity to do something about it.

A shift system for employees on a 24-hour basis, coupled with visitors and delivery drivers throughout the day, meant that there was a sporadic flow of people in and out of the building and, whoever the receptionist was, needed to keep a beady eye on comings and goings. Depending upon who was behind the desk at the time, the regular delivery drivers would avoid signing the register, either to be just annoying or because they couldn't be bothered. In any case, the register that was supposed to provide an accurate record of who was where and when, was anything but.

The staff at Springfields were quite happy with their lot in life, as most of them lived in or around Yeasting, and many merely had to walk to work. They considered themselves safe from the ravages of Council cutbacks, as they thought they knew that their jobs were of such vital importance. Sporadically, there was a long waiting list of potential patients, some of whom never made it, and consequentially their attitude was rather relaxed. They all knew their jobs and were eager to please, with the ulterior motive of having got the 'inmates' out of harm's way in the Day Room in front of the television they could then nip out for a cigarette, or join in the poker school in their own 'mess' room, which doubled up as a stores area, until one of the Matrons, or worse still, the administrator came snooping around. They had their own alarm system for detecting the approach of the administrator. They had clubbed together one Christmas and given him an expensive pair of latex-soled leather shoes, which squeaked just enough on that part of the corridor to give themselves time to look industrious when he eventually did enter the room. He never did catch on why that part of the floor seemed the cleanest in the building.

In Springfields, the administrator was at the top of the pecking order, answerable only to the executive of the Council. His assistant ran the day-to-day items of the Home, as well as being the accounts manager. At permanent loggerheads with the assistant was the head Matron, who considered her patients more valuable than the meagre amounts of money the Council were providing. There's always one, isn't there, and Doris was it. She ruled the Home as though it was an extension of her own personal ego, was always right and always had to have the last word, right or wrong. Under her were three other Matrons, six sisters, and twenty-two trained nurses. Right at the bottom of this seemingly well-organised Ladder came the maintenance man, and his apprentice, although nobody could ever remember the Lad's name. These two lowly employees were responsible for the upkeep of what remained of the spacious gardens, as well as keeping the inside of the Home spick and span. As head of maintenance, Ron was proud and very diligent, and especially enjoyed tending the lawn and rose beds as though they were his own.

It was in this serene atmosphere that Bernard's family had reluctantly decided that Springfields would be an ideal setting for him to spend his remaining days. Bernard did not know he had a choice, but soon melded into the monotony of the daily schedule and became one of the 'secure' inmates. He had to be in the secure wing as, when living at home, he often forgot which room he had just come from, or why he was going to another room. Matters got worse when he was found by a neighbour searching in a field full of bullocks, looking for his car keys, even though they had been taken from him some years previously. Locking him in his bungalow was not an option either as one evening he decided he would visit the local pub but, upon finding his front door locked, he climbed out of the window by putting a stool up against the wall. This was some feat, considering that his hundredth birthday was in sight, and he needed a walking stick to go any distance. Fortunately, the landlord of the Frog and Hopper Inn recognized him and phoned to alert his family - not before giving him two large whiskeys. This had been the final straw for Bernard's family so in the summer, they had easily convinced him that he was going to a new home, just for a while.

Thus, Bernard's daily routine consisted of him being woken at 8 am, washed and brushed, and assisted in getting dressed into his day clothes before being accompanied to the breakfast conservatory, and then onto the day lounge for a day-full of TV. Occasionally, the staff would create a game to break up not only their boredom but also that of their patients. A giant game of Scrabble would be produced until one of the more awkward patients would upset their cup of tea on it, or another fall out of their chair in the excitement. Other games would be 'remember-the-name-of-the person on your… left or right?' but this only led to arguments as to who was who. Throughout the day the same debate between the same two gentlemen would often be repeated from the day before. Feeding time at lunch was a painful experience for those who had forgotten their teeth, and a necessity for others who needed to be spoon-fed, which was why soup featured quite regularly. Tea-time however was totally different. It seems that however old one is, and however severe the onset of Alzheimer's disease, participating in the English custom of drinking tea is never forgotten, except for the odd argument about who gets the last piece of cake. Bedtime at 9 pm could not come soon enough for some of the staff, and the ritual undressing of unwilling bodies into their pyjamas marked the end of another day.

Visiting hours were designed so that relatives could visit their loved ones in a dignified repose; between 10 am and 8 pm, but the background whiff of Dettol could never disguise the glorious surroundings or the purpose of Springfields.

Bernard was lucky. His only son Roger had married Susan, both of them now in their mid-40s, and had produced twins, an unusual combination of a boy, Tom, and girl, Ann, who were now at that inquisitive age of 10 years old. Roger and Susan had little option but to move to Yeasting on the Surrey/Sussex border because that was where they ran their bed & breakfast business.

Susan had inherited the B&B from her Parents some 15 years earlier after they had both been killed in a plane crash. At the time both Roger and Susan had been working for a firm of shipbrokers in the City and intended to get engaged and marry. The naturally untimely death of her parents catalysed their plans and clarified their future, as neither of them wanted to stay in London to raise a family. The relatively sedate village of Yeasting beckoned them as though their future had been determined by the Gods from the moment they had been born. Not only was the B&B an ideal business for them to fall into, but they both enjoyed the prospects of what it entailed. It also gave them the opportunity to persuade Bernard to live with them, under their watchful eyes, in his own detached bungalow next door that came with the business. It took several years and a bit too much bullying from Roger, but in the end there was little choice as his advancing years began to take their toll on him.

Close enough to London's Gatwick airport to have a regular supply of guests toing and froing, Yeasting was set in an unspoilt part of the South of England with rolling countryside views towards the South Downs in the distance. It was at the end of a British Rail branch-line and just off the main road from London to Brighton and enjoyed the unusual luxury of not being disturbed by the noise from the airport. Quite naturally, where there's a church, there's a pub, and the triangular green that separated the two was the home to the village cricket club. The ancient stocks that belonged to a more sinister age were nearer the pub than the church. Their sprawling Bed & Breakfast, called The Twinings, was adjacent to the Frog and Hopper Inn, and they had set about renovating it to a sympathetically high standard as soon as possible after the funerals. It wasn't quite the perfect picturesque village scene, and one would not have been surprised to see thatched roofs, but there were none. It was the comparatively ugly one or two shopfronts that spoiled that scene but, as the shopkeepers would have been the first to point out, it was their own livelihood that came first, and neon lights on plastic fascia signs above their doors shone out through wind and rain.

Bernard was not a burden on them, at least to start with, and indeed he perked up once he became familiar with his new surroundings. He would be delighted to receive some of his old friends on their way to the airport, and most took the opportunity to stay over in one of the B&B rooms next door. The adjacent pub provided a superb location for entertaining, often well into the small hours of the morning, and it was seldom that Terry, the Landlord of the Frog and Hopper, declined to stay open 'after hours' as he thoroughly enjoyed the tales and banter that Bernard brought with his friends. The best stories came from the rugby crowd, and in particular from one of Bernard's more frequent visitors, Digby.

He and Bernard would corner the bar and later ease themselves into the creaky padded wooden chairs next to the blackened fireplace, also not too far from the bar and certainly within earshot of Terry.

"Cold! This isn't cold. You should have seen what Bernard was wearing when we played those bloody Scotsmen in Aberdeen," said the indignant Digby to one of the complaining locals who had wandered into their corner of the pub. He didn't need to shout as his booming voice carried anywhere he went. Digby focused on the approaching Terry on the other side of the bar. "Now that was cold. The ground was so frozen you couldn't make a ball stand on end. It was hard as a billiard table and Bernard here had managed to persuade the managing director of the local woollen factory to let the whole team have fleece jockstraps. He said he was going to present them to the Scottish team, once we had beaten them, but their bloody scrumhalf ripped off Bernard's shorts to expose his underwear. The Scots were so surprised, and rolling around in laughter, calling us all sorts of Sassenach names, that we scored… right under their posts. Oh, we… *gave them a bloody good hiding, we gave them a bloody good hiding…*" this to the tune of 'For he's a jolly good fellow', fuelled by the several whiskies they had both enjoyed.

Bernard's laughter cracked open his mouth as he recalled that he had also lost one of his front teeth on the rock-like field that day. "Don't give me all the credit. It was your idea we had to make them look like pansies, but I must admit I did enjoy those warm jockstraps."

Digby's eyes revealed that it had indeed been a team effort between them. "Yes, .and we set fire to one of them in the bar while it was still on their skipper." His raised voice by now had half the pub joining in the fun. "And you went and put the bugger out with the soda siphon." Another round of '*Oh, we gave them a bloody good hiding, we gave them a bloody good hiding…'*

These were very happy times for what remained of Roger and Susan's older family, but all too soon Bernard's friends themselves became too old to travel or had passed away, and his contact with his past began to dwindle into distant memories. Phone calls from his army days also dried up and did not carry the same personal weight.

Some quarter-of-a-mile away from The Twinings, a little way up the hill past the doctor's surgery, Springfield House separated the original village from the new houses that now threatened to encroach on the wooded region.

"We can't let him look after himself any longer," repeated Susan for the tenth time in as many weeks. "What's he going to do next? Drive off in someone else's car? He can hardly manage to get his own breakfast, and his laundry is really getting me down. I can't put up with it any longer."

Roger had heard her arguments almost on a daily basis, and in his heart knew they had to put his dad into a home. It would probably finish him off, but then again, 99 or thereabouts was a good innings. If only he could have made a 100 in his own home. Roger considered himself quite practical about Bernard and, after the initial realization that this would be the only course to take, had let Susan unconsciously say out loud what he too was thinking. It was no good playing the Devil's Advocate any longer and, after the last incident with Bernard's escape from his bungalow, Susan had booked an appointment with Mr Green, the accounts manager at Springfields. The typical blustery winter morning weather did nothing to lift their spirits as they walked hand-in-hand up the lane towards Springfields.

Susan tried levity. "Look on the bright side. It's not even 10 minutes' walk, and we can take the kids to see him after school."

"Now hold it," said Roger, yanking Susan's hand to a sudden halt. "If you think I've got the time to spend every afternoon taking the kids to see Bernard, then you've got another think coming." Roger was now becoming angry at the thought of being dictated to by his wife, on a 'Stock' matter. In the same instant, their eyes levelled at each other, and he knew he had to give in; Susan knew that look. She also had the sense to know when not to push Roger too hard.

Susan took Roger's other hand in hers as they both tried to fathom each other's inner thoughts through each other's eyes. After a few precious moments, and without a further word, they each turned to continue their lonely walk up the hill.

"Let's try to make a regular visiting day. Say Wednesdays. Both kids get home earlier from school then, and that won't get in the way of Ann's music lessons. Just for half-an-hour." Susan knew her concessional comment would get Roger's approval, and, in any case, she knew she would see more of Bernard than just that.

Roger mused for a short while. "Yeah. Sorry about that, and of course you're right. Let's see what Mr Green has to say." This as their feet started to turn the gravel on the entrance.

Both oak doors were closed, probably to keep out the cold, and there was no obvious bellpush anywhere, only a heavy-looking brass lion's head that was the knocker. Roger loved knockers. With excessive force, he brought the outer ring crashing down onto the lion's chest just once. He was rewarded with a playful 'whack' from Susan, which he knew was bound to come. The 'knock' didn't so much as echo, as reverberate, probably to the annoyance of everybody within earshot, which was why Roger liked knockers. "A-hah," said Roger, pretending to notice for the first time the round matching brass door handles on each door. The right-hand one opened easily and led onto an inset coconut mat which they both duly wiped their shoes on.

"Mr & Mrs Stock?" a young female voice questioned. Roger looked ahead, and then around, and then up for the source of the youthful-sounding voice. "Hello - over here," said a hand appearing from behind a stack of white cardboard boxes on top of a wooden desk a few feet in front of them.

Roger led Susan around to the right-hand side of the desk and saw a petite brunette, half perched on a swivel chair, cradling a phone between her ear and shoulder. Her hand now beckoned them to wait while she finished her phone conversation.

"Ok, Saturday'll be fine. Thanks, Bye." Swivelling around to face them, "Sorry about that. I'm Natalie", holding out one hand whilst her other replaced the phone back on its keep.

"Good morning. This is my wife, Susan, and I'm Roger. We have an appointment with Mr Green," said Roger, taking her manicured hand first, before Susan did likewise.

Natalie smiled and stretched her other hand towards the phone once again. "I'll just let him know you're here." Her dexterous hand found the oversized phone system in one easy go, whilst looking between Roger and Susan, suggesting that whatever pose she cared to take, she always knew where it was at any one given point in time. After a couple of flicks with the end of her forefinger, she had the phone system working for her at the speed of light. After a short while, one of the lights turned from red to green indicating that there was now an open channel.

"Roger and Susan are here to see you," she said, talking into the intercom.

"Miss. Banks. How many times have I told you not to refer to potential clients by their first names? That's my job." The bored-sounding voice at the other end paused. "Now, if you are referring to Mr & Mrs Stock. Please let them know I'll be right out." The slight background hiss and crackle of the intercom silenced, and at the same time, the light returned to red.

Natalie's composure did not alter; she was obviously used to this kind of admonishment. Instead, rather resignedly she smiled at the Stocks "Mr Green will be out shortly."

"Thanks," said Roger, returning her smile and, looking around for somewhere to wait, sauntered towards the two utility-type chairs next to a stack of magazines on a low table. He never made it those few feet.

The same oak door they had entered just two minutes ago

suddenly swung open, right into Roger's path, followed by an overalled man reversing a 2-wheeled stacking-trolley across the coconut mat, right up to the desk.

"Morning, Naty. Where can I put this lot?" he said over his shoulder. Without giving Natalie a chance to respond, he shifted the trolley to unload the wooden-slatted crates that contained fruit and veg.

"Right here ok?" This, right in front of the desk.

Natalie's hands and face peered over the cardboard boxes on the desk. "Just at the end, Joe," she said, causing Joe to shift his stance to move the trolley towards one end of the desk and unload the several crates in one go.

"There you go, Naty. Here's the chit."

To the Stocks standing there, this seemed exactly what it was; a regular delivery and handover of foodstuffs destined for the kitchen, and the slick operation had taken place in just a few seconds. Young Joe leaned over to pass a limp-looking piece of blue paper with one hand, turned, and readied the now empty trolley to leave. As he did so, he caught Roger's leg with the end of the trolley.

"Ow. Shit." Said Roger hopping-back out of the way.

"Oops. Sorry, Guv," said Joe briefly looking at Roger. "Didn't see you there." It was difficult to see how Joe could have not noticed two other people in the now confined space between the doors and the desk but, before any further words were said, Joe had wheeled his trolley through the still-open door and returned to his van outside.

"Obviously off his trolley," remarked Susan, quickly closing the door to keep the gusting rain from swamping the coconut mat further.

Natalie had come around one side of the desk to sympathise with Roger, who had pulled up his trouser leg to see if there was any permanent damage. "Are you alright?"

"I'll live," replied Roger, now rubbing the area that would soon become a bruise. "Bloody idiot needs his licence looking at. Does he always do that to people around here?" looking at Natalie, as though she could do something about Joe.

"I'm very sorry. He hasn't done that before, but he's always in such a rush, I supposed it had to happen sooner or later." This was no consolation to Roger, who had decided to move smartly away from the front doors just in case Joe returned.

Susan patted Roger on the shoulder and gave Natalie a wink "It's ok. He's got another leg."

Roger was taken aback that Susan had taken a line out of his own phrasebook. "Bastard can't drive a trolley, let alone a van."

Natalie hurriedly backed away to answer the beckoning phone from behind her desk just as Mr Green appeared around the side of the partitioning and stopped in his tracks at the sight of the boxes on top of the desk and the tower of crates that were almost level with the top of the boxes. Natalie wisely decided to answer the phone before Mr Green could direct his wrath at her. After a moment, he turned his attention to the Stocks.

"Good morning. I'm Mr Green, and welcome to Springfields House." He paused, seeing the look on Roger's face. "Is everything alright?"

"No, it bloody isn't." Roger was now leaning against the wall and standing on his uninjured leg, rubbing his other against the damaged shinbone. "I've only been here one minute, and already feel like I ought to be an inmate. Your delivery man just ran over my leg with his trolley. The Git needs talking to." Roger instantly felt better, having had a chance to vent his anger on someone with a bit more sympathy than Susan.

Susan interjected with one of her gracious smiles, to calm the situation down before it got heated. "Hello, Mr Green. I'm Susan Stock and this is my husband, Roger.

Not surprisingly, Green was caught off balance between their two totally differing attitudes but managed to proffer an acceptable handshake to them both with Roger on two feet by this time. "Please. Follow me," he said and managed just one step towards the gap to the side of the partitioning before remembering that he needed them to sign the register. Almost deftly, he angled his direction towards the near end of the desk where it usually lay on top. "Would you mind signing in?" he said, spinning the big book around and groping over the far edge for the attached biro that was string-bound to its spine. Susan did so for both of them, fearing that Roger, in his current frame of mind, would be more likely to name themselves 'Mr & Mrs M. Mouse', living in 'A Hole, Sorry, YUK'.

The Stocks followed Green down the elegant wood-panelled hallway, past the bottom of a double-width, sweeping staircase, and through one of the doorways on the left. Green quietly closed the door behind them.

"Please sit yourselves down", offering his hand towards the two chairs 'this side' of the desk. Two chairs had already been positioned in anticipation of their arrival and the thought crossed Roger's mind that more than two would have been superfluous. Even one on some occasions, as those visitors who sat in these chairs would have been there for just one purpose. "Can I offer you tea or coffee?" said Green, hovering by the 'teas maid' machine.

"Not for me, thanks," replied Susan.

Green's attention swapped to Roger, who was considering asking for a medicinal Scotch instead. "No, thanks, I'm fine now," he retorted.

"Right, then," said Green, heading for his own chair on the 'other side, a little crestfallen that Roger would not be partaking in his peace offering of refreshment.

"I'm the assistant manager here," a stress on the 'I'm' as though he had to prove it by saying so, "and Mr Howard is the Administrator, but he's away on holiday at the moment, otherwise he would have met you himself. I am sure I can answer any queries you may have. But let's talk about Bernard. He's your father, isn't he?" he asked, looking at Roger who had by now forgotten all about his bruised leg and had remembered the real reason why they had come to Springfields. Susan had given the basic details over the phone a few days earlier.

Green had diverted his eyes towards a buff folder he was now opening, soon to be marked 'Bernard Stock. 24th April 1910'. His pen now poised in anticipation of need. It was also a cue for Roger to let him know more about Bernard.

"Yes. He'll be 100 next April. Not this coming April, but the year after. He can still move about with the help of his stick, but it's his forgetfulness that's the worrying thing, and sooner or later he's going to hurt himself."

Green had heard this all before, but still managed to look interested. "Go on." Questing for a different story from the usual ones.

"Just this morning, we caught him scrambling his eggs with port, instead of butter, and the other day he'd cornered a 'Daddy Longlegs', and was trying to kill it with his stick, instead of the flyswat, but all he managed to do was knock a row of glasses off the shelf. There was broken glass all over the floor, and if he'd fallen on that..." Roger had no need to finish the sentence. Green was writing.

Susan continued where Roger had stopped. "We think he may be beginning to lose control of his bowels. It doesn't happen regularly, only on the occasion when he has a few. But we've had to lock him in, particularly at night, as he tends to wander off. It's almost as bad as having a child at a Fun Fair."

"No, it's worse than that," Roger butted in. "He's an adult and people don't pay any attention to old folks wandering across The Green on their own. But a child on their own would attract attention. He needs someone to keep an eye on him the whole time, and we can't do it all of the time, and it needs to be somewhere he can't escape from. I hear you can manage that here."

"Is he on any medication at the moment?" asked Green, preparing another form from the file. "I'll need his consent to access his medical files from the Doctors'... I presume he is registered there?"

"No, he's not on any regular medication, but he occasionally visits the Surgery for some liniment for his stiff hips. He's surprisingly fit for his age. I think he's under Dr. Foster. Do you know him?"

Green replied that he did and proceeded to go through Bernard's medical history with them. Roger thought to enlighten Green further. "You know he was in the War," referring to World War II. This did not surprise Green, as several of the patients had come from that era, although they were beginning to thin out now, due to their age. "He was a colonel in The Royal Engineers, in Assam most of the time, I think. He did get captured just before the end. When I was little, I sometimes got woken up by his nightmares. He had some great stories to tell us, and I think he got jaundice once, and malaria as well. He doesn't talk much about the last part, but I think he almost died in a Japanese POW camp."

Roger's pause reflected the seriousness of what had happened to Bernard, and it was not lost on Green whose grandfather had been a lowly corporal in the infantry and had been killed in France.

"Well, I think that's just about all I need to know about Bernard for the moment. Perhaps you can ask your father to sign this form," said Green, handing Roger a white envelope over the desk. "I'd like to show you around now, and I'll explain how we look after the patients as we go, but I have to say that we have a waiting list, and I can't say with any certainty as to when a room might become available. Perhaps in the next few months, but it all depends upon our current patients."

He paused before breaking the bad news, which he had kept until last.

"I am afraid that from your description of Bernard that he will have to have his own room in the secure wing. Because of the extra security needed and the fact that he sounds like he will soon need help being constantly looked after, the monthly charges will be a lot higher. If he were in our open wing, where he would be free to come and go whenever he liked, we would require just £1,100 a month, but as we will be responsible for him for the rest of his life, in circumstances where we are held to account for his well-being, I have to tell you that the monthly rate is nearly double: £2,000 a month."

This was always an awkward moment for Green, and the Stocks were no exception, as he could see them calculating the annual cost. "Medication and other services such as hairdressing, dentist, chiropodist, etc. are extra, and will be added on to the monthly account."

Roger and Susan both knew that Bernard was a wealthy man and to most people these costs would have been prohibitive. It would not, however, be a problem for the Stock Family, but even so, if he lived in Springfields for several years they could see that their legacy would be noticeably dented.

Green's well-timed spell of silence, allowing potential clients to assess their future financial implications, was followed by yet more unsettling news that had on occasion un-nerved some.

"May I suggest that you discuss this with your solicitor as you will probably have to seek an enduring power of attorney? In Bernard's condition, his current state of mind can only deteriorate, and unless you have control over his affairs, then the State will appoint someone who might re-locate Bernard to a Home elsewhere. It's not my place to advise you on such matters, but I thought I would bring this to your attention before it gets too late. You see, if Bernard refuses to hand over his power of attorney to you, he will still have complete control over his own affairs and may alter his Will to exclude you. I've seen it happen before, and the first thing the relatives know is when their solicitor tells them that an entire estate has been left to Battersea Dogs Home, a local church, or some other charity. Do you have a solicitor?"

This last part was galling for Roger and Susan and certainly unnerved them both. They exchanged questioning glances, in the hope that the other had come across this before. "Errrrm yes, we have our family solicitor in London, but he hasn't mentioned this to us before," said Roger, being the first to recover from the potential consequences. "But surely if he's made his Will, he can't change it when he's in here, can he?"

"I'm afraid it's worse than that. You see, although he is under our care and we can restrict his movements, in the eyes of the law he is still considered an individual in his own right. As such he can in theory check himself out of here, catch a plane and spend what's left of his money on a yacht in the South of France. But the biggest worry would be if that he became so insensible, or 'of unsound mind', the State can and has done so in the past, appoint someone to administer his affairs on his behalf. That someone is then at liberty to decide that this is not the best place for Bernard and move him to a home in, say, Cardiff AND that person would have control of all Bernard's finances, and may decide to sell his house, and invest the money in an account in, say, Guatemala."

Green paused for a suitable time yet again, but longer. "It's not a nice position to be caught in, and I can see you ought to take the necessary steps before much longer." It was clear to him that this was coming as a complete surprise to the Stocks, as indeed it had to others before them.

"Perhaps you can contact your solicitor later today after I've shown you around?" Green's cue indicated that there was no more bad news and that it was time for the Stocks to consider matters closer to hand. He slid his chair backwards enough for him to stand, subconsciously encouraging them to do likewise rather than ask further questions about a matter he might not be empowered to fully answer. "Please follow me," he said, opening the door.

The administrator's office that Green had been using in his absence was well-insulated and pretty much in the centre of Springfields House. Few sounds penetrated its walls, and it came as a bit of a surprise to see through the French windows at the back of the hallway that winter had returned to the outside world. Angled rain attacked the windows like demonic lemmings going the wrong way.

"Let's not look at the gardens first," commented Green, hoping to lighten the atmosphere. "I'll show you around the open wing later if you like, but I think you'll be more interested in seeing where Bernard will be staying." Before turning towards the front desk, where Natalie could be heard speaking on the telephone, Green pointed in the opposite direction. "This is the administration area; the kitchens and stores are down there. Behind the staircase are the 'open' day dining rooms."

He continued past the partitioned wall to a control panel adjacent to the security doors and pressed a wall-mounted button which also connected with Natalie's desk-mounted one. The door automatically swung open to a floor-stopper at 90 degrees, and he waited while the Stocks passed through before joining them. Immediately, the door silently closed behind them. "You can see that we take the security of our patients seriously here. Nobody can get past this door without releasing it first. There's a smoke sensor in case of a fire that opens them as well." Pre-empting their next question.

He took two paces towards what turned out to be a well-disguised lift behind one of the oak-panelled doors and pressed a code into the brass panel next to it. "Upstairs are the bedrooms."

Waiting for a lift is one of the most boring tasks in life, but we all tend to stare at the door, willing it to open before we can concentrate our minds elsewhere. After a few brief moments, the door began to slide open, and the automatic shuffling and etiquette of 'who goes first' took place. Out of the lift shot a stainless-steel tea trolley, as though propelled by an aircraft-carrier launcher. Not only was it accompanied by the extra loud rattle of cups and saucers etc., that go with crossing a cattle grid, but also an un-natural 'brrerring' noise. Roger was horrified to see that he was standing directly in its path and quickly hopped out of the way. Not quickly enough. It caught his leg just below the knee and came to a dead stop.

"Aaaargh!" shouted the unbalanced Roger, not having time to swear, as the pain shot up his already bruised shin, and it was enough to cause him to shudder into Susan while trying to clutch at his leg.

Whether or not it came to a stop because it had made solid

contact with Roger, or if it was because the person shoving the trolley had yanked back on the rail at the other end, was not clear, but the effect was still the same. Half-empty cups, saucers, spoons, sugar cubes, and other assorted accoutrements that go with a used tea trolley continued their journey forwards, unencumbered by the now static trolley. A mixture of cold, sugar-laced tea, the dregs from discarded cups, and half-used milk jugs, ended their journey by either bouncing off Roger or spilling onto the oak flooring around his feet.

"Bloody Hell. What's that trolley doing all by itself?" cursed Roger, looking into the recesses of the lift for the person responsible for its speed, but he could see nobody.

Susan was more surprised than Green and continued her efforts to support Roger who was now furiously rubbing his shin again. Green, however, had a horrible, sinking 'déjà vu' feeling, and, after looking briefly at the couple struggling to stay upright, leaned over the back edge of the trolley, only to look down on the culprit. Ron's Lad!

Not only was he small, but indeed small enough to be a dwarf, although he had few of those features. Everyone called him 'Ron's Lad', and his face had a very 'boyish' look about it, but his five o'clock shadow that seemingly never altered betrayed his manly status. Nobody knew where he came from, some suspected he lived with Ron in the old annexe and nobody had ever seen him reading or writing, and few heard him speak. He now cowered behind the errant tea trolley, having ceased his impression of a Formula 1 car out of the blocks, and sheepishly looked up into Green's angry face.

Green had caught him on several previous occasions obliviously speeding the tea trolley from one room to the next and had warned him on each of those occasions to stop doing it. Ron's Lad now gulped, having seen the consequences of his rapid trolley service, looking at the hopping Roger between the middle and top shelf of the trolley.

"I've told you about this before," admonished a genuinely angry

Green." Don't you listen to what you're told? You're a wretched nuisance, and I'm not putting up with it any longer. In future, you're to stick to cleaning the corridors. Am I clear?" He waited for a response from Ron's Lad, which ended up as a very slight nod. "Now go and get a mop and clear this lot up." Green was aware that he could not say or do much more in the company of visitors, and now turned his attention to Roger.

"Are you alright?" he asked the now upright Roger for the second time in as many hours.

"I'm not used to this. Do you breed them here or did they see me coming today?" Roger was trying to be polite, and would have said more, but for Green's quick response.

"I really am very sorry. You can see he has trouble seeing where he is going." This took the wind out of Roger's sails; belittling dwarfs was considered politically incorrect these days.

"He'll be ok," said Susan, being her diplomatic self again. "And he's still got another leg." Roger saw the funny side of Susan's quick wit, and stuck his tongue out at her, making sure that Green wasn't looking.

"Please. Shall we continue?" said Green moving the trolley out of the way and ushering them towards the lift. "We have four floors, the top one for our 'in-house' staff, the other two for our patients. As the layout is about the same on both of these, I'll show you the first floor."

The door slid back to reveal a polished beech floor, with anaglypta paper walls up to a chest-high dado rail running the length. It was not a long corridor, but wide, with one end leading to the staircase behind another set of security doors. In the other direction were doorless frames leading to other narrower corridors, off which were the bedrooms. Green appeared to pick one at random.

"Each room has been designed to cater for the needs of the elderly. For example, the legs of the beds are recessed to prevent the stubbing of toes. There's a desk for them to sit at if they wish, and drawers below for them to store their belongings. We do not encourage them to bring any valuables in, not because of theft, but so that they don't lend and lose them. I'm sure you can see what I mean." Indeed, the Stocks quickly grasped why.

"There are emergency pull cords beside each bed, and in the en-suite bathrooms." Green motioned to an open doorway, and paused before continuing, as his next point was usually the 'clincher' to anyone who was still in any doubt as to the suitability of Springfields. "We like our patients to retain as much dignity as possible while they are with us, but unfortunately, some of the more incapable need help with their ablutions. Our trained staff tend to them here in their own rooms when they wake in the mornings, and again before they go to bed. By the time they are accompanied downstairs for their daily routines, they can continue without the embarrassment of being unsuitably dressed in front of visitors. We also have a dedicated room on the ground floor for other 'mistakes' during the day."

Roger and Susan were impressed with the layout of the spacious room, as well as the delicate way Green was phrasing himself. It was very clean and tidy, with high ceilings as befitted a building of its era.

Green pointed to the wide sash window. "The glass has been replaced with toughened, and its opening restricted so that no one can accidentally fall out." He opened the bottom half, which banged to a 'stop' some inches from its starting place. "I think you will find that Bernard would soon feel at home here."

As they filed out into the corridor, Roger looked down the far end and spotted a 'Fire Exit' sign. "Is that necessary? Surely some can't walk, and I presume there's an outside staircase?"

"We need that for building regulations, besides which our in-house staff would be on hand to help anyone in the event of a fire or any other such emergency. Let me show you the Day Rooms," said Green, back tracking to the lift.

On exiting the lift on the ground floor level, they were led to the end of a longer corridor and around the corner to a wide archway into a room that was being prepared for lunch. Part of the room had the same high ceilings, but at the far end, it lowered into a conservatory area.

Back along the corridor, Green opened one half of a set of doors to reveal the Day Room. It was an initial shock to Roger and Susan to see so many very, very old people sitting, doing nothing. Two gentlemen were poised in such a position that it looked like they were debating some serious issue, each waiting for the other to make the next comment which never came. Another was mumbling to himself. At least three were asleep, mouths wide open, their faces pointing up to heaven. Most were sitting in their chairs that had been arranged in a semi-circle around a television set in the far corner. Three, however, were holding a lively debate by the French windows. One gentleman nearest to them, whose skull-like appearance pervaded his facial features, seemed to be looking directly at them. His eyes were so far sunken into their sockets that it almost defied belief. He never blinked, perhaps in the desperate hope of not missing a single second of the rest of his shortening life. Behind the open door sat a young nurse at a table. She smiled at the Stocks as they entered but did not say anything.

Before Roger and Susan could fully take all this in, their next shock was the smell. That unique smell of dying. You don't come across it anywhere else in the world, except in an old age pensioners' home for those who are about to breathe their last breath. It's a stale smell. Not like a library, nor like a room that has been sealed for months. It's a smell of decay, but unlike that of plants, and it seems to carry with it the memories of those within the room. It doesn't waft, nor come and go, and even if the room had been empty, it would still linger as though time had decided to let it rest in peace. It is not a smell one ever forgets.

Green was well aware of the impact on the unsuspecting and started his well-rehearsed oratory about what went on in the Day Room. Neither Roger nor Susan took any of it in at first but followed Green out of the room when ushered to do so. It was as though they had just been in and out of a time-warp, but instantly, they returned to 'the real world', with its recessed bright lights shining down from the ceiling above.

They were led back through the security doors by Green who had punched in the code on the panel. Natalie was still on the phone as they shook hands and promised to get in touch.

Roger wished they had brought an umbrella, while Susan wished they had come in the car.

Chapter 4

The best day of our lives

With the driving rain and their hurried return to The Twinings, speaking was not a real option, other than to curse.

"Bloody weather." Roger's socks had got wet, and they had crammed themselves through the back door together. Susan had the better of it as she had been wearing her lapelled coat, but Roger's suit was definitely looking bedraggled. "Bloody weather," he repeated, squirming his arms out of his sleeves. "I'm getting out of these wet things," he said, already halfway up the staircase. He ended up taking a quick shower and started to feel a lot better until he ran the loofa across his forgotten shin. "Aaaaargh…"

Twenty minutes later, he found Susan leaning against the kitchen work-surface, staring into middle space while clutching a mug of tea. She'd had more time to muse over the morning's revelations than Roger.

"We can't put him in there. He'll go mad." Her voice had a distinct resignation about it.

Roger slowed mid-step en route to the kettle. Now was the time and place to discuss Bernard's future, and before they knew it, it was mid-afternoon, and the kids could be heard outside returning from school. Susan rushed outside to meet Mrs Johns who had, no doubt, accompanied them as she quite often did.

The 'Pros and Cons' continued over the next few days, not quite at every opportunity, and the frequency of these debates lessened. They were reminded on a daily basis every time one or other of them popped next door to see Bernard. They were both secretly praying that Bernard would get better, but in reality, they both knew that

Green's comments were all too true and that sooner or later they would have to face the inevitable. Later, please let it be later.

The later came sooner. One morning, on her way back from taking the kids to school, Susan let herself in through Bernard's front door. There was no response to her habitual greeting, and it was with horror she discovered a small pool of blood on the bathroom floor. A dotted trail of blood lead outside through the back door. She followed it along the garden path as far as she could, before the lessening dots became lost in the muddied footpath that led across the green and towards the church.

Beside the graveyard, she found the north entrance door to the church half-open. Inside, it was as quiet as a church; after all, it was one. She followed a fading trail of damp dots on the flag-stoned floor that led to the Registry Room behind the organ. That was where she found Bernard, leaning heavily on his stick, leaning over an opened tome. Her hushed intake of breath made him look up.

"Mary, I can't find our wedding certificate. Have you seen it? Mary, you are looking beautiful today."

Susan quickly recovered from her surprise and relief at finding Bernard. He obviously thought she was Mary, his wife who had died several years earlier. "Come here and help me find it. It's here somewhere," he said, turning another page in what was probably the marriage register.

Susan then saw that Bernard's greying black hair was matted with blood which had streamed down his arm and onto the walking stick, ending up in a trickle past the rubber end-stopper. She realised that this was where the dots had come from. Thinking as fast as she could how best to handle the delicate situation, she walked over and put her hand on his. "It's ok, Bernard, it's safe in the house." She hoped her lie, passing herself off as Mary, would not be detected. "We put it in your chest, remember?"

Bernard straightened, and his long stare penetrated Susan. "Well, we had better get it straight away. We will need it for the Lord Mayor's show tomorrow."

Susan struggled to keep up. It was as though he was living a dream, and she was in it. "Yes, Bernard. We'll go and get it straight away." Her only thought at that moment was to get Bernard back to his bungalow, and so she clasped his hand in hers and side by side they made their way out of the church and back across the green.

Bernard gently stopped and turned as they reached the footpath past the lychgate. "It was a splendid day, wasn't it?" he said, looking up at the steeple that housed the clock. Susan realised that he must have been referring to his wedding day. She hadn't even been born then, but it brought back her memories of when she and Roger had got married in this same church.

"Oh, yes. It was wonderful."

Only the birdsong in the background broke the stillness and for a brief moment, she forgot that it was Bernard, not Roger, who was standing next to her. Her blinkered emotions got the better of her as she pictured the idyllic scene with confetti flying and happy guests cheering as her new husband held her arm in his. Tears of joy welled up in her eyes and goose pimples ran down her arms. She smiled, and kissed him on the cheek, suddenly realising that she had become part of his dream. The happiest of moments soon passed, and while one part of her wanted to share that common moment again, another part jerked her back to today as the Postman wheeled his bicycle into view.

"Come on. Let's get back."

After she had cleaned Bernard up, and made sure he was happy having his breakfast, she discovered that he must have slipped and hit his head on the basin in the bathroom. She also discovered that that amount of blood quickly turned to glue, but she returned to The Twinings and faced Roger.

"I think we had better ring Mr Green," she said, before she related Bernard's latest adventure, missing out the part when they had stopped to reflect on their perfect day. "I'll do it if you like?"

Roger looked down for a few moments and nodded.

A short while later as she reached for the phone, she found her hand shaking. It was like carrying out a death sentence, she thought. Instead, and very unusually for her, she opened the cocktail cabinet and poured herself a small dark rum - neat.

"Mr Green? Good morning, I am Susan Stock, and you showed us round about a fortnight ago." Green could hardly forget the 'day-of-the-trolley' incident. "We'd like to confirm a room in your secure wing for Bernard as soon as one is available."

"Well, Mrs Stock, I hope you will forgive my presumption, but I had already put his name on the waiting list as soon as you left. I hope you don't mind. How is he today?" he asked, prompting Susan to give the suspected reason for the phone call.

"He caught his head on the basin in the bathroom and wandered off again this morning but he's alright now. How soon do you think it might be before a room is free?"

"At the moment, he's third on the list, so I suppose it may be one or two, or possibly three months. I really couldn't be more specific than that, you understand."

Chapter 5
Decision Day

Just over a month later, it was with genuine sadness that Susan received a call from Mr Green. A room for Bernard in the secure wing had at last become vacant and would be available when they were ready. Perhaps this coming Friday? Susan said they would bring Bernard over mid-morning after the kids had gone off to school.

Since her walk across the green with Bernard, Susan had spent more time with him, and after school nearly every afternoon would take the kids to see him for half an hour or so, before chivvying them back home to do their homework. In the past, the kids would only see Bernard once or twice each week for fleeting periods, but Susan had decided to get them and Bernard used to seeing each other on a more regular basis. She pitied Bernard for what he was about to have to go through and considered that daily visits by her and the kids would help the transition.

She had bullied Bernard to respond to the kids' questions about his past, and it was not long before the kids took up her quest, on her behalf.

"Go on, what happened next?" or "Tell us the one about…", were the two most used phrases coming from Tom and Ann, sometimes in unison.

Bernard, normally sitting in a modern armchair beside his old military desk in the front room, initially had to be prompted by Susan as to what to talk about, and he often took so long getting through a particular story that Susan would have to call a halt for the day. The kids soon looked forward to every afternoon and created their own form of prompting.

"You were going to tell us about the Zeppelin yesterday and where you hid. Go on. What happened neeeeext?" they cried.

"Well," Bernard racked his memory back to the First World War when he was a child, half their size. He talked slowly, as he needed time to recollect what indeed happened next.

"Had I told you how big it was?"

"Yeeeess."

"And did I tell you how close it was?"

"Yeeeess"

"And did I tell you about the sheep running in all directions?"

"Come on, Grandpa. You were about to hide in the cellar," volunteered Tom, eager to find out the next bit.

"Oh, yes," said Bernard shifting his weight to the other buttock.

"You were just about to go down there," piped up Ann. "But you said it was dark."

The memories came flooding back to Bernard. "Your Great-Aunty Matilda was pushing us through the cellar door, and a gust of wind blew out the candle. Uncle Guy and I were petrified, and we stood stock still at the top of the steps. Neither of us had been down there before, as we were forbidden to ever go down there on our own. Have you ever heard of The Bogey Man?" he said quietly lowering his tone of voice as though he may have been overheard.

The effect on the kids was predictable. "Nooooo?" said Tom, half frightened to ask. "Who's The Bogey Man?"

Bernard was now struggling to remember exactly who The Bogey Man was. It was so long ago, and his long stare at the kids only heightened their senses.

"Well," another pause. "He only comes out when it is very dark, and he lives in the darkest corners of the cellar. He sometimes goes up into the loft as well, but only on the darkest of nights. He waits for children, just like you, to come towards him. As you get nearer, you can hear him moaning 'Wrhooooorah' very quietly. The closer you get, the louder he becomes. Wrhoooooorah. Then you can hear him breathing." Bernard now started to shrug his shoulders from side to side in imitation while rasping his own breath. The kids' eyes were definitely getting bigger. Susan too, standing by the fireplace, was starting to get the creeps.

"Nearer and nearer he comes. You can feel the ground shake with every step. You can hear the rustle of his body as he positions himself. His great body ripples and his long arms come out." Bernard's hands and arms now slowly extended in a grappling position above the kids' heads. "He gets ready for the 'bear hug'. His moans get louder… And louder. Wrhooooooraaahhh. There's only one thing you can do. Run. You turn and run as fast as you can before his great hand can get you." Bernard suddenly dropped his arms and grabbed one kid with each hand.

Sitting on the rug in front of him, the kids had no chance of escape, and their petrified screams pierced the room. Even Susan jumped a little. Despite their struggles, Bernard managed to pull them both towards him, and gave them a combined bear hug.

"Wrhoooooooooraaahh," he roared and then laughed as much as his old age allowed.

"But what's he look like?" shouted Tom, eventually breaking away from Bernard. Ann was jumping up and down in excitement. "And how did you get down to the cellar?"

Susan was aware that this would be a good time to break, before the next part of the story tomorrow. "Tom, Ann, come on now. Homework time."

The kids voiced their natural disappointment but headed off to the porch to get their shoes.

She had taken one of these early opportunities after the kids had gone home to broach the subject of moving to Springfields and had been surprised by how receptive Bernard had been to the idea. She did not feel quite so guilty as, after each visit from the kids, Bernard would soon fall asleep in his chair as though wearied by his recollections. By the time she had received Green's phone call, she felt she could tell Bernard that it had all been arranged and that he would accept it.

In the meantime, Roger had obtained Bernard's signature on the Home's 'requisition for information' form and had also been in touch with their Family's Solicitor, John Boyd.

The day before Bernard was due to move, Roger and Susan had spent several hours ferrying and arranging some of his chattels into his new room at Springfields. They decided against taking him to the pub next door on the Thursday night to avoid Bernard's embarrassing ramblings in public. One moment, he was perfectly normal and lucid, and the next he would drift off into some unknown narrative. It was indeed time for him to move to Springfields.

Bernard fell into the daily routine quite easily, and on his more alacritous days, enjoyed the company of some of the livelier 'inmates'. He soon discovered that the gent in the room opposite his had also been in Assam during the war. Captain Cyril Perry's platoon had been surrounded and then captured by the Japanese while on infantry patrol. They shared several common interests, and, on occasions, Perry would enjoy the company of Tom and Ann when they visited almost every other day. Either Roger or Susan would accompany them, but as the year wore on and the evenings got longer, the kids would sometime be allowed to walk hand in hand together from home to Home.

There were a few others with some sporadic bright spark of life left in them and two other military personnel, but they usually slept most of their days.

Roger and Susan promised themselves to go through Bernard's bungalow in the summer, but it stayed empty.

Chapter 6
The High and the Lowly

Roger Parsons was a bachelor and a bit of a stickler. He was also the Administrator of Springfields House. He had had just a few short years left before retirement when his last employers had sold their business. King and Barnes brewery in Horsham, West Sussex, had been in the brewing business since 1906, but with the passing of the head of the family it was now being sold to a rival brewery. It was subsequentially closed and demolished. Roger Parsons had been in charge of distribution to their large chain of pubs dotted around the south and east of England. He had nearly moved to the West Country to buy his own pub with his redundancy money. There were several to choose from at the right price due to the changeable English weather of late.

His nephew worked in the Health Department of the local Council. Upon hearing that his uncle was kicking his heels, he had suggested he applied for the role of administrator at Springfields House which was about to open. With the job came generous pension benefits so, with little hesitation, he applied.

His was the last post to be filled, which meant that he had not had the luxury of choosing his own staff. He later found out that another had had that privilege, but at the last minute she had deferred to her husband's request to take another job nearer to where they lived. He also found out that the Council had been desperate to appoint someone at very short notice, and when his over-qualified portfolio landed on the Chief Executive's desk, he had been offered the job without even an interview.

Within an hour of arriving at Springfields for the first time, he discovered he had less than three days before the first patient was due to arrive. Fortunately, the secure wing had been completed on time so that side of things could be put on the backburner for the time being.

In the next hour, he discovered that he was well overstaffed, due to the unsecured wing not being totally ready, but at least the staff were at hand, but also that nobody had considered ordering any food or drink for the future incumbents. The telephone system didn't work, the lift was yet to be signed off as being safe, and no reception desk had been ordered, although there was a receptionist. There were a hundred and one other things that needed urgent attention, and he quickly turned on Mr Green, blaming him for all the deficiencies.

It was not fair on Green, as he had been led to believe that the appointed female Administrator had had all those problems in hand. His protestations to Parsons fell on deaf ears. Parsons was used to a well-oiled industry that relied upon efficiency in the private sector to survive, not the laid-back 'pass-the-blame' attitude that pervaded a local health authority.

As the first patient was arriving, he was haranguing his staff. Under his gaze, they were scurrying here and there to prepare the bed linen, clearing an endless supply of boxes out of the way, and assembling the reception desk, which they were not really qualified to do. Ron and his Lad were the stars of the moment, and they seemed to be in more than one place at a time than was humanly possible.

Parsons had had visions of greeting the first patient personally under the twin pillars and ushering them round a spotless facility that anyone could be proud of. What happened was quite the reverse and turned out to be a catalogue of disasters. There was no umbrella to offer any rain protection from the ambulance to the doors. The gap between the pillars was piled high with soggy half-empty crates and boxes, so much so that they had to wait over a minute while these were moved to one side to allow passage. The desk was being built right in the entranceway, and all sorts of wires snaked in different directions across the floor. Parsons was fuming. He knew that at least one bedroom and the Day Rooms were ready, but he wasn't too sure about the kitchen.

Skipping over the wire-strewn floor as if in a minefield, he failed to realise that the 'slippery when wet' sign had not even been deployed, and duly landed heavily on his side. At least it was a good place to break his hip, surrounded as he was by nurses, but he had to wait more than an hour before someone had used their mobile phone to summon back the ambulance that had just left.

There had been complications with Mr Parson's replacement hip surgery, and it had taken several months before he had been able to return to Springfields. Even then it had been only for a short visit. He had shrewdly considered that if he kept himself on the 'sick list' long enough, he would eventually be made redundant, and with it would come a healthy redundancy package. He therefore exaggerated his situation and enjoyed all the privileges while staying as far away from Springfields as possible.

It therefore fell to Mr Green to assume the role of Administrator until another could be appointed. That had been well over a year ago. After the incident with the trolley, Mr Green had decided to fully take on the mantle and started to mould his surroundings to suit himself, rather than on someone else's behalf. After all, why shouldn't the Council appoint him when the time came?

He had called Ron and his 'Lad' into his office and let them know in no uncertain terms that trolley racing through the building was to stop immediately, deliveries should not be left unattended by the front desk, and that the passageway to and from the kitchen was to be kept clear of all unsuitable objects. He continued with his list of shortcomings. While Ron had agreed, his 'Lad' had merely stood there, nodded, and grunted.

He continued with each member of staff, in pecking order, pointing out some deficiency or other, or just providing a reminder of what was expected. Even some praise was merited here and there.

He saved the most awkward until the last.

Doris was a matron from the 'old school' and still insisted on wearing her old-style Matrons' cap which, instead of being open at the top, folded itself from the front and over the head to drape down behind the nape of the neck. Everybody wilted when she lashed out with her tongue, including Green, and it was impossible to order her to do anything. One could only suggest in the politest of terms.

"Good morning, Manager," she reminded him of his status as she entered his office after the briefest of knocks on the door.

"Good morning, Matron." Her mere presence demanded formality on every occasion and first names were certainly not tolerated. Green was seated behind his desk but did not bother offering her a chair, knowing that she would stand in any case. Probably so that she could look down on him.

"We need to discuss certain items this morning. No doubt you have heard about the incident with Mr & Mrs Stock?"

Very little escaped her attention. "Don't you mean incidents?" Her nonchalant way of correcting others kept them firmly in their place. "I hear you have spoken to him and Ron. Did you dismiss the Lad?" She did not have to add the words 'and if not, why not?'

While she clearly 'ruled the roost', both Green and Doris knew that she did not have that authority. It suited her to let others get on while she told them what to do. Green shuddered to think of the consequences of her being the administrator; in theory, when he was away, she was in charge.

"I didn't think that kind of incident merited his dismissal, and as for the delivery driver, well, there's little I can do about that." Green found himself defending his actions once again, to his 'inferior'.

"The Lad's a nuisance and ought to go, but it's your decision." Inferring that Green was liable for any further such incidents. "And talking of boxes, when are you going to get the Council to let us have proper access to the medical supplies? It's no good them sending them to us in good condition if we can't get them into the refrigerated store straight away." She was referring to the white insulated boxes that seemed to decorate the top of the reception desk most of the time. "I've had to return two consignments just this month. You really must do something about it." Her tone indicated that he had been a naughty boy by ignoring her earlier demands.

"I have been and will do so again as soon as I can. I believe the chief executive is due to call in next month, and it will be the first thing I bring to his attention." Green didn't want this part of the conversation to continue any longer. "Now, can we discuss the condition of the two new patients?"

Their deliberations of the inmates continued until Doris felt she could satisfactorily sign off the register of patients for that week. She returned to the problem of boxes.

"We have a consignment of Razadyne II arriving next month, and I have been reading the Fisher Centre's information pack on it. It's the new wonder drug for the Alzheimer sufferers and needs to be stored at a constant 3 degrees, but if not then it's useless. We have got to have a better method of delivery."

Green had also seen the memo from the Council which emphasized not only its temperamental condition but also its expected effects which were supposed to be very impressive. One day, Green would be able to get one step ahead of Matron, but not on this occasion. He had been saving this piece of information for the last part of their meeting in the hope that she had not had time to familiarize herself with it but, once again, she had beaten him to it.

"I'm afraid we won't have a new entrance by then, but I'll issue a memo to the reception staff. I must say that if it produces the results that they say it will, then we may not have a need for the security wing for much longer. It's supposed to work wonders on long-term sufferers."

"We will see about that," replied Matron sceptically.

Meanwhile, down the hall in the staff room there came a raucous cheer. Ron had won on the horses again. As per the norm, just before the lunch duties, some of them gathered around the small tv set to egg on Ron's latest bet. He was surprisingly good at picking a winner, and those who were interested had clubbed together and formed their own syndicate. Nothing serious, but the almost daily £1 bet from each of them went into the pot, and the winnings saved for the Christmas party. Its finances were already very healthy, and next Christmas was a long way off. It had been a 12-1 bet that had paid off.

Natalie poked her head around the door "Keep it down. Matron's in with Mr Green." This had the immediate effect of complete silence. "Can someone get the new boxes? Quickly." She disappeared back to her desk.

On her way past the administrator's office through the opening door, she heard Matron getting her last word in with Mr Green and decided that she had better move the boxes out of sight herself; Before Matron saw them. They would all be in trouble if she found them there again.

Natalie deftly trotted around to the front of the desk, opened one side of the outside front doors, returned to the desk, picked up the top two white insulated boxes, retraced her steps, and placed them carefully on the ground outside the other front door. She then returned and repeated her porter duties a further two times, closed the big door, and quickly sat herself down on her chair, trying to look as diligent as possible. Just in time too as Matron appeared from behind the partitioning. Natalie was praying that she would not be going outside and sighed in relief as Matron strode past on her way to the open wing.

Green was beginning to develop a tic.

Spring was in the air and Ron started to spend too much time in the back garden, leaving his Lad to keep the inside clean and tidy. The Council had told Ron that he was going to work in Springfields and would live alone in the Annexe, but when he moved in, he found someone else there; a lad had already taken one of the two bedrooms. Ron didn't mind and assumed that this was what the Council had decided, so didn't pursue the matter.

Of very short stature, only coming chest-high on a normal

person, Ron's Lad - as he was now known - looked no older than a seventeen-year-old, but even he didn't know his own age. He had the kind of face that one could not easily categorise, but it was a kindly-looking face and one that made people automatically almost feel sorry for him. He was also rather shy and unassuming. It had taken Ron a few weeks before their first conversation produced any results, and Ron had sworn that he would not tell a living soul.

The Lad had admitted that he had come to England on a small boat, escaping from the civil war in Yugoslavia, where he had been tortured. He had lost both his parents and had come to England, as he had heard them say that he had an uncle in Surrey. He did not want to be found as he had heard that people like him were sent back to their own country, and he did not want to be tortured again, so had developed a natural aversion to strangers.

He had been wandering around the South of England like a nomad, doing odd jobs for people, and one day had come across the newly refurbished annexe. He had started to clear up what remained of the untidy building site adjacent and attend to the garden at Springfields. Nobody had blinked an eye, including the newly appointed Mr Green who had assumed that he was one of the staff.

He was intelligent and a hard worker but - perhaps due to what he had endured in Yugoslavia - had some unusual idiosyncrasies. If one wanted a garden fork, for example, the next day he would produce three different types; the two that one didn't choose would disappear. No job was too difficult, and never took very long. On one occasion he had overheard a desperate Mr Green pleading with someone over the phone to remove the nesting crows from one of the chimney pots but when the RSPCB had arrived, they found Ron's Lad in the back garden clutching a nest full of hatchlings. It had been a complete mystery how he had got them down, as there was no evidence of a ladder anywhere and the chimney pots were inaccessible from the attic.

He had always loved the detailed side of nature and had acquired a mini zoo of reptiles and snakes that he kept in a bathtub in his room in the Annexe. He had nurtured most of them from birth, and of an evening time, he would croon over them, but occasionally one or two would disappear only to reappear again a few days later, hunger being the most probable cause. It was not unusual for him to collect indigenous lizards from the long grass at the edge of the orchard, and he would hide them in his shirt or deep pockets throughout the day until he finally had a chance to return them either to their own homes or, if he thought they needed help, to his bathtub.

Everyone liked Ron's Lad except Matron. Any sort of request would be met with varying kinds of smiles, depending upon the request. Demands or orders would be met with a grunt-cum-nod. He did talk to people but only those he trusted or had known for a while, especially Ron. He liked to talk with the folk in the secure wing, knowing that they were not a hazard to his continued existence at Springfields but didn't like being overheard by some of the staff. When they were sitting in their armchairs, he didn't have to bend down to their eye level, and whenever he had spare time, he would lean against an adjacent armchair and listen with rapture to the stories that came from a bygone era. In short, he avoided anyone in authority when he could. He also had a wicked sense of humour and would delight in anonymous practical jokes. If someone had upset him, or he thought they deserved some kind of retribution, he would devise some way of getting his own back depending upon the severity of their 'inconsideration'. So far, nobody had thought that the occasional strange happenings were anything but 'just one of those things'.

As he was the butt of Matron's attention, she was his main target. On one occasion he had managed to swap the sugar for the salt in her teacup. He changed her egg timer so that her eggs were either under or overdone. The most embarrassing moment for her had come when she discovered someone's underwear hanging on a branch in the driveway on the way in one morning, only to discover it was hers.

He got on well with Natalie but knew she liked to slip her shoes off when sitting behind her desk. In a bad mood one afternoon, she had told him off once for not helping her move some files. He had glued one of her shoes to the floor.

Mr Green was the easiest, and it had been easy to swap one teaspoon for another, fresh out of the microwave. The howl that followed had been most gratifying.

It didn't take him long to come across Bernard, whom he considered one of the more entertaining inmates. Cyril and Bernard had their favourite corner in the Day Room, and nearly every day they would reminisce, in between cups of tea, pill-taking, and dozing off. Ron's Lad was only too eager to refill their cups in order to keep them awake, and he would often need to prompt them into remembering. He soon got used to their vagaries of time and place, and it didn't matter to him that they often confused people. The one definite thing that they both remembered was the fact that they had been up against the Japanese during the war, and it was clear that they had both suffered, as he had in his youth. It was probably this common experience that drew him to them.

The fact that one was a colonel and the other a captain did not cause any friction. What occasionally did was the different roles that each had played: one an Engineer, and the other a 'foot-plodder'. Their common beef with each other was traditionally that one would not be able to keep up with the other: one had transport, while the other had to walk; one would be ahead of the other, preparing the ground, while the other would be catching up. Inter-regimental rivalries and ribbing of each other's modus operandi, on occasion, spilled over into raised voices, and denials of accusations. When these heated arguments attracted the attention of the nurse, Ron's Lad would make himself scarce.

Chapter 7
Tea for Two

Some two weeks later, Green's memo about boxes was sellotaped to Natalie's desk. She reminded every passer-by of its importance until something more urgent cropped up, like the ringing of the phone. For a while, the reception area became an easily navigated passageway between the secure and open wings of the House and, for a while, Springfields became a smooth-operating home for the elderly. No tea trolley incidents, no mysteries, and nobody died. The chief executive of the Council came and went, and Spring was definitely here to stay. In fact, it was becoming monotonous and would have stayed that way, had it not been for one particular animal: a ferret.

It used to be called 'The Domino Effect', but these days, it is called 'The Butterfly Effect'. Whatever it is called, the eventual outcome is determined by the merest and most trivial of incidents, apparently unconnected to even the most observant. The end result can only really be described as 'an act of God'.

Occasionally, on Jo's delivery rounds and if he was ahead of schedule, he would stop off mid-way through and visit his brother, who liked to collect unusual pets. The latest acquisition was a pair of ferrets. Not knowing how to handle them correctly, Jo had been bitten through to the bone on one of his fingers. He had left it over the weekend before going to the hospital to have his very painful, and very swollen, finger attended to. The doctor's concern was that he may have contracted a form of TB, and ordered that Jo be kept in for observation.

In Jo's place, an agency delivery driver had been given the task of making the medical drops for that week and was unaware of the protocols that go with these delicate supplies. Arriving at Springfields House, he encountered Ron's Lad coming around the corner of the building, dragging a hose with a sprinkler attached.

"Where do you want this lot, mate?"

Ron's Lad didn't want to stop right there and take the boxes off him, so he just paused, grunted, and motioned to the front door with a nod. The agency driver dragged the stacked trolley full of white boxes behind him instead of pushing it in front of him. He failed to notice that the load was rather unstable and, before he could correct himself, they toppled over onto the gravel driveway still someway from the front doors.

"Sodding boxes," he swore and bent over to carry the boxes one by one to leave them side by side outside the front door. Just as he turned, he got wet. Ron's Lad had turned on the sprinkler. "Oi! Pack it in." He wanted to thump that little runt, but Ron's Lad was nowhere to be seen; he had 'legged it', having turned on the hose from around the corner. Ron's Lad would see to the boxes once it was safe to do so.

It was a busy day for Ron's Lad. As well as his tasks in the Home, Ron had asked him to help in the gardens and had also asked him to go down to the local hardware shop to get some slug pellets. It wasn't until late into the afternoon that Ron's Lad remembered about the boxes outside the front door. En route to the kitchens, he mentioned them to Natalie. Once she had disentangled herself from the phone cord, she popped her head outside, hoping there would be just one or two boxes. Instead, she found eight, most of them saturated by the sprinkler. She then went in search of either Ron or his Lad to get them stored out of sight, and this too took some while. She found both of them in the staff room having a cup of tea.

"Are you two going to shift these boxes, or what? It's nearly knocking off time, and they've got to be put away before anyone sees them."

"In a minute, luv. Just putting our feet up," said Ron in between biscuit mouthfuls.

Some five minutes later, Ron and his Lad got wet, so the sprinkler was turned off. At least the newly planted lavender wouldn't wither from drought. As Ron bent down to pick up thc first box, he noticed that the labels usually attached to each box had become un-glued by the 'downpour' and had collected in the adjacent grated gully. Along with the boxes, a large envelope with the consignment notes had also become saturated.

Ron was aware of the consequences of what Mr Green and Matron would say if they saw this. "Hey, quick. What are we going to do about this lot?" as his Lad returned from around the corner. "I can't even read what these labels say, let alone which box they should be on."

A thought entered the Lad's head. "Are they all the same?"

Their eye-to-eye contact, and a nod of their heads, confirmed what they now both thought, and Ron, looking over his shoulder to see if they were being observed, bent down, and started to open one of the soggy boxes; his Lad did likewise. The boxes fell apart very easily, but they soon confirmed that all the medicines were the same.

"Right, quick, let's get them inside before Matron comes. You get the wheelbarrow." Ron could see that the boxes had outlived their usefulness. While his Lad nipped off around the corner, he picked up the limp envelope, knowing that it would contain the storage instructions. He couldn't get the papers out, so folded it in half, and stuffed it down the back of his trousers. Even getting wet underpants was preferable to being found out.

Ron's Lad returned with a 'brrerr ing - bdaarrrrrrah', spitting gravel from the tyre of the wheelbarrow. 'Eeeeecchhhhhhhh', as he skidded around to a halt next to the boxes. He was enjoying himself. An old-fashioned look from Ron said more than a thousand words, and he quickly started to load the medicines into the wheelbarrow. It took two loads, and while his Lad manned the wheelbarrow Ron acted as lookout by going ahead to make sure that nobody other than Natalie saw what they were up to.

Ron had decided to stash the medicines in one of the cupboards rather than the fridge as he couldn't retrieve the instructions and placed the envelope on the radiator to dry out. Once it had dried out in the morning, he would be able to find out what it said.

"Not a word about this to anyone. Understand?" Ron's Lad grunted in assent on his way out with the wheelbarrow and went to remove the rest of the evidence floating in the gully. Ron went over to Natalie who, for once, was not on the phone, but still standing where Ron had left her a few minutes earlier keeping a lookout by the open wing.

"Listen. If Matron finds out what we've just done, we'll really be in for it, so not a word. OK? I'm drying out the paperwork now, and I'll let you have it in the morning. It's safe enough overnight in one of the storage cupboards."

Natalie tip-toed back to her desk and assumed her usual pose. "OK," she whispered. "But make sure it's first thing before Matron gets in. As long as I can get the consignment papers with them by the time she checks it, she'll never know." They both knew what they were doing was wrong, but something similar had happened once before and nothing had come of it. "The night staff are due in soon and if they don't discover it, there shouldn't be a problem." Natalie then updated the medicines register to show that they had received them that day.

As good as his word, the next morning, before most of the day staff had come in, Ron extracted the now crinkly papers from the envelope. Quite a lot was illegible and some of the print had transferred from one side of the page to the other where it had been folded. As luck would have it, he could pick out that the medicines should be stored in a fridge, so set about taking them from the cupboard and putting them in the large fridge in some of the dedicated trays. He then put the consignment notes under one of the trays.

Nobody would know. He left the counterpart delivery note on Natalie's desk in the tray marked 'MEDICINES IN'.

Nobody did know, except when Matron came in and took the

delivery note from the tray. She wrinkled her nose in disgust.

"Look at the condition of this note," she berated Natalie while reaching for the medicines register. "I can hardly read it. When did it come in?" Natalie kept quiet, waiting for Matron to read it for herself. "I've been waiting for this." Her tone then changed. "Did it go straight into the fridge?"

"I think so, Matron. I know it's in there." Natalie hoped that the mention of it being elsewhere would take Matron away to that same place.

"Why can't you look after the paperwork properly? What happened to it?"

"I…I spilt my tea, and some of it went onto the papers. But the medicine's in the fridge." Natalie was saved by the bell as the phone rang and she quickly answered it. Matron went off in an apparent huff in search of the new medicine thinking about Razadyne II; The latest wonder drug that reportedly transformed lives. Would it be the liquid or the powder form they had sent her? How many doses? What did it look like? What did it smell like? What did it taste like? How long would it take to have an effect? These and other like questions resurrected themselves as she bustled her way down the hallway to the stores. She had already had clearance from the Council's health authority to administer it, and the Doctor had left it up to her judgment as to whom would receive it. In truth, the doctor had been glad to pass on the responsibility.

The third fridge she opened revealed several trays of nondescript white sachets; it was in powder form, then. She found the consignment notes. Not only had they clearly suffered the same aqueous fate as the delivery note, but these were hard and crinkly and almost illegible. She stood there, peeling the pages apart, trying to decipher the typed information, fury rising in her that Natalie had got them wet. She would have strong words with her later but for now she continued to separate the pages and came to the dosage page. Here it was.

'To b m xed with warm ater, d oroughly stir d. o be aken before r fter meals. Dos ge 15 mg. Daily.

Ke refr rated. Stor elow 3C. Do not mix h alc hol. Be t befor Nov .

On her way back to her office in the open wing, she cursed Natalie again, who was fortunately not at her desk. She would find her later, but right now her thoughts centred around Razadyne II. 15mg. That was quite a lot, but then again, it was a new drug. She already had her own list of patients who she had decided would be taking it, and mentally calculated that it looked like the health authority had sent her almost a year's supply. Although it was bound to be safe, having been passed by the World Health Authority, she decided to play it safe and would try it first of all on some of the healthier patients. Just in case. In fact, why not start right now? Those two new arrivals would do. That new colonel and the captain, what were their names? Stock and Perry. After all, if anything went wrong, they would be the most likely to survive. She'd administer it herself - with a cup of tea.

A short while later - and to the great surprise of the rest of the staff - Matron was wheeling the tea trolley around the Day Room. Nobody had ever seen her belittle herself by stooping to such a menial task before, and they naturally steered clear of her. If only they had known it, they could have all been stark bollock naked and she wouldn't have noticed. Her mind was so set on the next few minutes. She found Stock and Perry in their usual chairs.

"Good morning, gentlemen, and how are you both today?"

Stock didn't, but Perry recognized her straight away, "We were just discussing the merits of travelling by sea, and how the gentle rolling motion of a ship can help send you off to sleep. It depends…"

Matron interrupted; she didn't have time to join in their fantasies. "Gentlemen. I am offering you a cup of 'Matron's tea'. Now, how many sugars do you take?"

Not being the regular dispenser of tea, she didn't know any better, and she soon regretted having raised the question of sugars and giving anyone a choice.

Perry was obviously on one of his better days, "I think I'll take one…no, perhaps two please, Matron. I'll say, this is a rare sight, you handing out the teas. Is it your birthday?"

Stock was still considering the question and frowning in great thought. "Aren't you that Petty Officer I saw in Bombay? In the adjutant's office on the docks? You remember, Cyril, she had great legs." And he craned his neck to inspect the bottom half of Matron's legs that protruded from below her skirt.

Matron was pouring from the china teapot which contained the Razadyne and had to consciously control herself. She hadn't done this sort of thing for a very long time, not since her early nursing days, and remembered why she had delegated others to carry out this tedious task. She didn't want to engage in their conversation, but also wanted to make sure that they drank all of the tea, so with clenched teeth she drew up another chair and started to make polite conversation.

"I'm sorry to disappoint you, Colonel, but I have never been to India. I hear it is hot there this time of the year." She hoped to distract Stock's attention away from her legs, which she now crossed at ankle level. "Do you suffer from the heat?"

Perry was still with it. "Hot! Hot doesn't describe it properly. Bombay has its own type of heat in the summer; it gets to over a hundred. So hot even the flies hide. It's the smell from the cows at midday that gets up your nose. They aren't very hygienic and leave their droppings all over the roads."

Matron was beginning to cringe and decided to steer the conversation towards tea drinking. "Do you keep cool by drinking tea?"

"Of course. We all used to take tea in the afternoons, in the Club."

Perry lifted his cup. Matron's psychology was working, but Stock was not responding, and she was just wondering how to get him to take his medicine, when Perry continued. "By Jove. This is an excellent cup of tea. Bernard, you really must try this. It reminds me of that Oolong tea we had trouble getting more of. It's got that… mmmmm. Not sure what it's got, but… mmmmmmmm…"

"Go on, Colonel. Try it," said Matron, pushing the cup nearer Stock. Stock at last looked at the cup, slowly lifted it to his lips, and sipped, paused for a moment, and sipped again. Maybe it was the taste, or perhaps the aroma, but whatever it was, it received his approval, and invoked his own memories of pleasant afternoons taking tea on the back lawn of 'the Club'.

Perry continued his ramblings in between sippings, "We used to have tea served on the terrace at 3 o'clock every day in Rangapara, and even in the field, we had…"

Matron wasn't listening, but instead watched the pair of them ingesting their hidden medicine. The wafting aroma did indeed smell encouraging, so she poured herself a cup from the urn, which did not contain anything but tea.

She beckoned the day nurse to come over.

"Can you dispense the rest of the tea to the others, but not out of the teapot? Only the urn." She noted that most of the others were looking their usual sheepish selves while some were apparently staring at the tv and the mid-morning news advising anyone who was paying attention that a Japanese delegation was to visit Buckingham Palace to celebrate the armistice marking the end of WWII this coming August.

The nurse nodded and wheeled the trolley away from Matron.

Perry was still on the subject of tea "Probably all because of the water." he paused. "Is there any more?" His cup was empty. Matron had made enough for two cups only, but now felt obliged to tip the last few drops into Perry's cup. She noticed that Stock was coming to the end of his cup also, so took it from him. She decided to be ingratiating.

"I'll make some more for you, but not until later." Thinking that they would not notice the difference between 'later' and 'tomorrow'.

She left the Day Room with a rare smile on her face. It had been easy, all except the part about her legs. She'd check up on them before bedtime.

It must have been soon after lunchtime that the Razadyne started to take effect. Not that either Stock or Perry were aware of what was happening, but somewhere in the recesses of their minds re-connections were taking place. For Stock, nearly a century of memories started to organize themselves into chronological order. For the first time in many weeks, he could look at a clock and understand what time it was: almost teatime and almost time for a visit from his grandchildren. Oh, yes, they had been asking about the farm. He was still very vague, and it seemed that just an instant had passed before Tom and Ann came bounding in still in their school uniforms.

"Hello, Grandpa," Ann spoke first, while Tom pulled up a footstool for them both to sit on. "We've been learning about rivers today and went on a trip on the bus. I've got some pussy-willow. Look." She pulled out a bag of the furry buds from her satchel and put one on Bernard's arm of his chair. "They're lovely and soft," she said, tickling her own cheek with another.

Not to be outdone, Tom dug around in his pocket and produced a small plastic jar of muddy-looking water. "I've got some tadpoles, and we're going to dig a pond in the garden when we get home, and then we're going to have frogs and I'm going to get a goldfish as well."

Bernard thought back to his days when he was their age. He used to love making dams from the several ditches that flowed across the farmland, and the wildlife that proliferated in them. "I got in trouble once."

He immediately had their attention. Grandpa getting into trouble - whatever next?

"When I was about your age, your Aunty Jean and I had just discovered a pond full of tadpoles just like those there," he said, pointing at Tom's jar. The kids were in rapture at what he had done with them. Bernard in his usual slow, considered manner let them hang on his words. "We had been told to clear some fallen branches from the fence next to the pond behind the house, and underneath we found that besides the pond was another very small pond, and it was alive with tadpoles… Tiny incy-wincy little ones." His voice pitched up several octaves at the same time as pinching his forefinger and thumb almost together to show just how small they were. "We got a bucket from the yard and filled it with water and tadpoles then took it into the kitchen where we got the magnifying glass and watched them wiggling about. When the cook saw us, she told us to take them away, and do you know where we put them?"

Tom and Ann shook their heads in unison.

"Can you guess?" He let them think a while longer. "Come on, where do you find water in a house?"

"In the toilet," blurted out Tom.

"In a jug of water," said Ann.

"Noooooo," Bernard was enjoying himself again. "We put them in the water tank in the loft where we could look at them whenever we wanted to. We didn't have any torches then, but we got some candles from the dining room, and had our very own place where we could look at them."

"Wasn't it too dark when you weren't there?" asked Ann. "How did they grow?"

"Well," Bernard tilted his head back a little and laughed. "Ha, haaa. Your Great Aunty Mildred called us into the drawing room later and we had to stand to attention in front of her. She asked us if we knew anything about tadpoles. Now, you know I've told you to always tell the truth?" he paused for their forthcoming assent, which came with nods. "Well, at first, we kept quiet, but Aunty Jean said we had found some in the pond, so I agreed. We were very frightened of Aunty Mildred as she used to clip us round the ear if we misbehaved.

"What happened to the tadpoles?" piped up Tom.

Bernard let them wait an eternity before answering, "They came out of the taps."

The predictable giggles from Tom and Ann brought a wide

smile to Bernard. "And they kept coming out of the taps for days, and Aunty Jean and I were sent up to the loft to empty all of them out. It took us ages, and I think there might be some there today because we couldn't get rid of them all." More laughter from the twins, but Tom was sceptical.

"Didn't they grow up and become too big to get down the pipes?"

"Oh, yes," said Bernard, now worrying about his exaggeration being found out. "But those that we didn't catch grew up in the loft and eventually escaped and they had baby tadpoles, and for years afterwards there were always lots of frogs around the farm."

Just then, Susan walked in and made a beeline for the small group. "Hello, kids, I thought I'd find you here. Good afternoon, Bernard."

"Mummy," in unison from the twins. Bernard slowly looked up into the eyes of his daughter-in-law. Susan wasn't expecting much of a response from Bernard but, instead of the vague, far-away look she had come to accept recently, his eyes seemed to be more focused.

"Hello, Susan, and how are you today? Are you going to be getting a goldfish bowl, or will you be digging a pond?"

Susan was momentarily non-plussed at two questions from Bernard in as many seconds. Lately, the conversations they'd had had been more one-sided with her asking one question at a time and allowing Bernard adequate time to consider a response. She looked at the twins and saw Tom jiggling his jar of tadpoles from side to side, and instantly understood why Bernard had asked the latter.

"I think we might be better off getting a goldfish bowl because if we put them in a pond, you won't be able to see them grow so easily."

"Can't we get both? said Tom excitedly.

"And I can grow some pussy willow," retorted Ann, not to be outdone by Tom.

"We'll see when we get home. I'm sorry to take the kids away from you, but they have tests coming up soon and they both need to knuckle down to their studies. Don't you?" she glared at the Twins. Tom was initially more reluctant than Ann to get up, but there was obviously no way he was going to be left on his own with Grandpa.

"Bye, Grandpa," they chorused almost in unison. "See you tomorrow." As they both started to shuffle away, Bernard let them have a piece of advice.

"Goodbye, children. I'll tell you more about the farm tomorrow, but let's keep the story I told you just now a secret for the moment."

Tom and Ann felt privileged to have been let in on one of Bernard's secrets, which is exactly how he meant them to feel.

Susan ushered them out of the Day Room.

Left alone again, Bernard's thoughts wandered back to when he was a young lad, and he dwelt on the fond memories of his siblings. All the fun they had enjoyed, being outside surrounded by acres of farmland. He now recalled sitting on the hind quarters of one of the enormous draught horses that they had used to plough the fields; even when he stretched his legs as wide as they would go, they still did not come anywhere near straddling the animal. His father, grandfather, or uncle would be at the tiller while he just sat and watched the world go by, back and forth, back and forth. He had tried to pay attention at the time but there were so many distractions, and he knew he would be asked how many furrows had been ploughed when the field was done. He recalled being admonished when he got the answer wrong, but he remembered now – it was.67.

"If you furrow them too close, the wheat will grow too tall, and if there is a strong wind, it will be flattened. If you make them too far apart, you will not get the most out of the field." This sort of knowledge was given to him so that one day he would be able to pass it on to his children.

There was the time when his sister had been the May Queen of Dereham, and he found himself thinking about how he and his brother had shinned up the pole the night before and shortened some of the bunting strings that the girls would use to dance around the pole; they had also half-cut some others. The well-rehearsed first dance produced the desired effects with the girls bumping into one another, falling over, and tangling the strings. Bernard chuckled to himself as he pictured the anguished look on the surrounding faces, while some, like he and his brother, just stood and belly laughed. Was it that year or another, that they had put some of the tadpoles in the jelly mix while the cook's back was turned?

Before he realized, they were being summoned out of the Day Room to supper by Ron's Lad, who paused to look at Bernard a little longer than normal. When it was Ron's Lad's turn to get the inmates to supper, he would go around the room, to wake some of them, and if necessary, ask one of the nurses to help. He sat down opposite Bernard, trying to guess what was going through his mind, as this was definitely out of character for him.

Bernard was staring into middle space with a wide grin.

"Colonel? Colonel?" This time he leant forward and gently shook his arm. Bernard reacted by slowly turning his head towards the voice and focusing on Ron's Lad. "Are you alright, Colonel?"

Several seconds passed before Bernard managed to bring himself back to the present time and day. "Oh, yes. I was just remembering my dear sister, and what fun we used to have. I wonder if she is still alive."

"Colonel, it's time for supper and it's time to go through to the dining room."

Bernard began to ease himself out of the chair but then perched on its edge. "Here, have you got some of that toothpaste on you? My dentures are coming loose again, and your special mixture seems to be the only decent one that works for any length of time."

Ron's Lad beamed and reached into his pocket for a nondescript, white tube while Bernard retrieved his upper plate from his mouth with his thumb. "Wonderful stuff, this. What's in it?"

"That would be telling but it has all sorts of uses, and not just for dentures." Bernard had a quizzical look on his face, egging on Ron's Lad to divulge more. "Well, it's not just a glue, you know. It's real toothpaste, and I clean my teeth with it." Bernard still waited for more while applying a small amount to the top of his plate. "You can use it for cleaning your glasses, for example, or even to make brass plaques shine if you polish it with a damp cloth. And it is also a filler once it has had time to harden. You know the basin taps in your room? On the top is a white disc with the letter H or C so that you know which one is hot or cold. They come loose sometimes so I just put some on the underneath of the disc and put it back, and it never comes off again unless you want it to. Much cheaper than proper glue and easier to clean afterwards. Here, let me show you." He took Bernard's glasses off his nose and spread a little of the paste on each lens. He then got a tissue from the nearby table and began to polish.

Bernard was still adjusting his dentures to a snug fit. "How did you find all this out? Sounds a bit like Potty Putty."

"Oh, I experimented when we didn't have any glue about and found it's useful for all sorts of things. You can even write with it, and I had to put some in a leaking radiator once. It worked." He handed Bernard's glasses back to him. "Here, try these."

Anyone who wears glasses knows how easily the lenses become smudged and how awkward it can be to get rid of a smear that seems to creep back around behind the part that has just been cleaned. Particularly after a meal. These were now crystal and Bernard's reaction was all that Ron's Lad could have asked for.

"Hey! I can see a lot better now. Can you let me have some so I can use it myself?"

After a short pause, Ron's Lad beam expanded. "Here you are, then," he said, handing Bernard the tube they had just been using, but don't tell the others. Shall we go?"

The room was now almost empty, bar the last shuffler making his way through the door.

Supper was uneventful. Bernard was in a reflective mood as he sat with three others around a square table. He hardly said a word, but then again, conversation between patients was always a bit thin on the ground, and especially so at mealtimes. Eating and talking at the same time is particularly difficult if your dentures don't fit properly as they have a habit of ending up in the soup.

For the next few days, Matron's concern over her two guinea pigs was quite genuine, and to begin with, she would have one of her nurses check their temperatures and blood pressures etc. every morning and enter them into their respective medical history folders: no change. She did, however, notice that they were spending more and more time together and their chat was definitely more animated than recently. She chose to join them again one morning.

"And how are we today? Tea?" She had come prepared with her 'Matron's brew' on the trolley and set about being 'mother' without waiting for an answer.

"I should say so," retorted Bernard.

"Yes, me too, but no sugar for me today. It detracts from the flavour. And very little milk, please." Perry shifted his frame nearer the edge of the chair so that he could reach his cup more easily. "Have you noticed that, Bernard?"

"You are quite right, Cyril. I'll take the same thank you, Matron. By Jove, you look happy this morning. Have you had some good news?" Bernard had noticed a smile on Matron's face, but Perry was concentrating on taking his cup and saucer without spilling a drop.

"I'm just pleased that you find my brew so satisfying. It's not everybody that appreciates it as much as you two gentlemen." Rather than treat them like demented old fogies, she had decided to try a more human approach and it seemed to be working. "Biscuits?"

Both Stock and Perry were busy taking their first sips of their daily not-too-hot tea, saucers in one hand, and cups in the other. Perry managed a negative shake of the head, followed by Bernard's agreement via sign language. Matron just looked on in amazement and wondered if there were any addictive qualities that came with the medicine. She made a mental note to re-read the information sheet.

"Coffee. Downfall of the British Empire. Did you know that?" volunteered Perry. "They say that with the advent of coffee came the downfall of the British Empire, and it stands to reason why, really.

You see, when coffee was introduced from Africa in the early 1600s, the coffee shops restricted it to men only, but it was in the latter part of the 1800s when women were allowed to frequent these shops and they could buy it over the counter, that demand really took off. The best coffee came from Brazil. Our East India Company, or, as it was known then, The Honourable East India Trading Company, owned acres and acres of prime tea growing land all over India, which they had franchised out to British Naturals. When demand began to drop off, the prices naturally fell, and the Company had no need to retain such a large military presence in India. I believe it all came to a head in the Great Stock Market Crash of 1929." He paused to take a slurp of his tea. "One of my uncles came back broke from India."

Bernard considered this for a moment. "I disagree. Tea was only a minor part of the Company's assets. Its operations covered a whole range of commodities, and not only from India. The plantation owners bought their land from the company and managed to do very nicely. I met several of them on occasions whenever I returned to Headquarters, and they were certainly not going bankrupt even though there was a war on. Just because the company did not own the coffee plantations in Brazil did not mean they were not trading it. They were just too slow to take advantage of the emerging coffee market and did not invest in the rootstock early enough."

Bernard now sat forward on his armchair. "No, the real downfall of the British Empire came with Coca-Cola's availability to the masses. With it came the American way of life and ethos that was pervading America at the time - and still is. Their iconic glass bottle represented a 'throw-away' society which eroded the longer-lasting values of The British, and, in particular, taught the young that anything could be replaced for relatively little money. They grew up not having to look after their possessions and treated everything as cheap. We helped keep this country safe because we know the value of our way of life, and these little buggers who run today's society think they know better. They're wrong.... wrong."

Bernard's voice had risen to well above the norm as he thumped his stick down in agitation. Perry nodded in assent. "You're quite right, and as often as not our efforts are not appreciated, but they'll drink anything today as long as it's cheap. If you really like the taste of something enough, you'll keep drinking it, and like it or not, Coca-Cola seems to fit the bill. Coffee definitely comes into that same category. I read in this morning's paper that…"

"It can't possibly come into the same category. One is a traditional beverage, the other a modern-day placebo. Now, if we…" Bernard continued, but Perry was having none of it.

Matron just sat there in awe. Just a few days ago, such a conversation was unthinkable, and certainly, there had never been any thumping of sticks to emphasise a point. The alacrity with which they put their points of view across was as pertinent as it was ferocious, but most of the other patients were totally oblivious. The Razadyne was obviously working and working very well.

She leant forward, trying to get their attention. "Could I ask you, gentlemen, to keep your voices down?" She waited for the silence, but it never came. Then she had an inspiration. "More tea, gentlemen?" As if a wand had been waved, Stock and Perry stopped interrupting each other and looked at her.

"Yes, thank you," Perry was the first to respond and silence reinstated itself in the Day Room, for the time being.

Stock and Perry had a disturbed night's sleep, Razadyne being the culprit. It was working its chemical magic and remaking those connections that had been degenerating in recent years. It was affecting Stock more than Perry, and throughout the past few nights, Bernard would wake up from his half-slumber and recall his past in greater and greater detail. He talked in his sleep. If anyone had been in the room with him, it would not have made any sense, but to him it made all the sense in the world.

Bernard was beginning to reawaken.

Chapter 8
Breakfast

Spring is a wonderful time of the year, and not just for humans, nor is it just a phenomenon found just in sunny Surrey. The mere word 'spring' conjures up activity of all sorts and is probably one of the most apt words in the English language. Fed up with the inevitability of the cold and wet winter months, plants as well as animals emerge from nature's hibernation. Whether or not we humans realise it, our own biochemistry is affected in some way or another, which is probably why some bright spark decided to coincide the cheeriness of Christmas time with the longest night of the year. Everyone looks forward to spring, and subconsciously our spirits lift with the lengthening days, and we begin to make optimistic plans to enjoy ourselves in the forthcoming sunshine. We 'come out of our shells', 'spring clean', even the clocks 'spring' forward. For the birds, that earlier and earlier each morning sing their 'dawn chorus', and for the animals that have spent their time surviving in burrows or under a carpet of leaves and come out of hibernation. Even the grass is greener. Stock and Perry were coming out of their own form of hibernation too; getting up a little earlier each day, ready for breakfast without being reminded, and even with their own teeth in place.

They sat down across one of the tables in the dining room. "Fancy some bread?" asked Perry, fiddling with his cutlery.

Stock eased himself onto the chair with the help of his walking stick. "Only if it's fresh."

Perry leaned across to the long table next to them where the breakfast paraphernalia had been laid out since the previous night and fingered the nearest slice. "Fishbait," he said disdainfully. "And I suppose the butter's going rancid again. Make good toast though. Want me to make some?"

Stock thought the offer over. "It does not do justice to the jam, which is not bad, but it is useless unless there is something decent to put it on. I think they have bread deliveries every other day, so I think I will wait until tomorrow. Are those flakes the same as yesterday's?"

Perry leaned over once again. "Same bowl, but half empty. Must be. I don't like those flakes. Somehow, they tend to find their way under my upper dentures, and if the milk's not as fresh as it ought to be it makes it difficult to clean them properly afterwards." Perry looked dejected and started playing with the salt and pepper pots.

Stock's eyes lit up. "How about some proper breakfast? Bacon, eggs, and decent fried bread?"

"How?"

"The Frog and Hopper. Caroline provides an All Day Breakfast. At least she used to." Perry could not believe his ears, his mouth opened wide enough to almost fit a slice of fried bread into it. It took him a few moments to see that Stock was smiling but was serious.

"I'd love to, but how?"

"I know Caroline well, and I am sure she will give us a good breakfast. Come on, it is only a short walk down there." Stock shifted his weight and grabbed his stick.

"Hang on a minute. How are we going to get out of here?"

"Trust me." Stock rose and began to head for the corridor that led to the security doors. He turned back to Perry and said, "Keep up." As the junior of the two officers, Perry automatically fell into step behind and as they approached the locked doors, Stock peered around to see if they were being observed, but it was earlier than when most of the staff arrived for work, and nobody was about. "Watch this."

Stock pressed four digits on the keypad next to the doors and was rewarded with a 'Buzz' as the magnetic lock released. "Come on."

Perry just stood there until Stock turned before the door swung to and pulled him through by the sleeve. "How did you do that? Where did…?" He was silenced by Stock's abrupt response.

"Not now, later. Come on, quick." They both hobbled in a straight line for the front doors. Nobody was at the front desk and without any sideways glances, Stock opened one half and went out, Perry right behind him.

"I'll tell you later, but now we need to go down that road before someone comes." Stock pointed the way with his stick and set off at a respectable pace with Perry in tow. Rounding the next corner, Stock stopped, a little out of breath. "We are out of sight now so there is no need to rush, but it's down the end of this lane about a quarter of a mile or so."

Perry was still non-plussed by what had just happened and was still trying to get to grips with reality. "I can't believe this; we're free. We've just escaped from - from home. How did you know what buttons to press and how do you know which way to go, and how?"

Stock rounded on Perry. "You are full of 'How's' this morning. You know, you have really just got to trust your superiors from time to time." This was the first occasion that Perry had been reminded that he had been just a captain, and now it was Stock who was the full colonel. Perry had not considered his military rank for several decades and it was an issue that had certainly not presented itself in 'The Home'. "It is perfectly simple. I just watched one of the janitors when he passed through the doors and thought I would keep it up my sleeve. As for where we are, remember, I live in this village." Stock could almost see the cogs of thought going around in Perry's mind, and let it sink in. "Now, shall we have some breakfast?"

Perry just nodded and followed Stock in line. A snail would have been proud of their pace along the pitted, narrow tarmacadam lane, but Spring was in the air, and for anyone it would have been a very pleasant time of day to take a walk. Although it was nearer half-a-mile and they had to stop a couple of times for Stock to put his foot back in his slipper, it took them nearly 30 minutes to reach the green that was overlooked by the Frog & Hopper. Nobody had seen them, but if they had it would have been a comical sight. Both were dressed in their shabby dressing gowns and slippers, with sticks, hobbling along apparently aimlessly. Had it not been for the surrounding vegetation and overhanging branches concealing their presence, they might have never made it.

All Day Breakfast started at 7 am and the Frog & Hopper had built up a good reputation amongst the local van delivery drivers, and even some of the truckers, who occasionally diverted from the main London to Brighton Road, just to get a good quality breakfast. Cafes are affectionally known as 'greasy spoons' and Terry's wife, Caroline, was aware that some preferred their first meal of the day without a puddle of grease on the bottom of their plates. She used extra virgin olive oil but insisted on using salted butter, especially when cooking the mushrooms, and was very proud of her reputation. It had been her idea from the outset when buying the pub with Terry to offer a quality breakfast service, and it had been paying off for several years now. She ruled her own kitchen and would be the first up in the mornings, allowing Terry to sleep off the excesses of the previous night if necessary. After all, it was Terry who was normally the last in bed, having got rid of the last few hardened locals.

She was just retrieving the crate of milk from outside the side door, left by the milkman sometime in the wee hours of the morning, when she spotted a couple of old folk shambling across the road towards her. Being out of the ordinary, she waited until they were closer, and her frown turned into a smile when she recognised Bernard Stock.

Once they were within earshot, she said, "Well, well, what a surprise. How the devil are you?" Stock waited briefly for Perry to catch up, as well as his breath, and it took them both a while before either of them was capable of any sort of conversation.

"I think we need to sit down," said Stock, and without any further invitation, he went through the side door closely followed by Perry. Caroline brought in the milk crate and in automation put it on the countertop on the far side of the kitchen, just in time to see them disappearing through the swing door that separated it from the main bar. Her curiosity impelled her to find out what was going on and she found the two gents settling into chairs in Stock's favourite corner, next to the fireplace.

The cushioned chairs in the pub were lower than what they had been used to in Springfields. Stock let his weight take him the final few inches, and even with the aid of his stick he let out an "Oooooofff" as he landed; Perry managed it more easily.

Caroline let them regain some sort of composure as they were both clearly in distress from their physical exertions. "I must say, Bernard, you're the last person I was expecting to see, and who might this be? Let me get you some water first."

They both gratefully accepted the pints of tap water while Caroline stood and tried to figure out what they were both doing here at this time of the morning.

It was Perry who recovered first "That's the most welcome drink I think I've ever had and thank you." Stock was regaining his composure as he returned his glass to the table "Not up to Terry's standard measures, though." The glint in his eye was not missed by Caroline.

"Now, I'm just trying to figure out if you two gents are on day-release, or if they've kicked you out of Springfields." The smile on her face said it all, but she was certainly bemused by their presence, and in their state of dress.

Perry deferred to Bernard. "We have come to offer some intelligent conversation to a beautiful woman whose intellectual talent is sorely missed."

Bernard's compliments had the desired effect and Caroline's bemused expression erupted into a hearty laugh. "And you've lost none of *your* smooth talent, have you? And, oooh, it's nice to see you again. You really are looking more like your old self. But go on, tell me what's happened. Why are you here?"

"One could scour the countryside and still not find the welcome and ability of a woman such as this." Although this comment was addressed to Perry, Bernard was orating to mid-air with his flattery, but he now focused on Caroline. "Captain Cyril Perry and I have come to taste the delights of your home cooking. Do you think you can oblige us?"

Caroline, quite naturally really for a woman, was once again under Bernard's spell, but it still took her a few seconds to fathom exactly what was going on. "You've escaped, and you've walked all the way down here for breakfast. They don't know you're here, do they?" She let out a great "Yesssssss! That's it, isn't it? Ha ha!" and turned to the bar counter for support which helped prevent her from doubling over with mirth. "Ho, ho." Laughing like she hadn't done so in ages. "And all you really want is breakfast. Ha, ha-ha-ha...." Laughter tears were beginning to form. "This means you really do like my Roly-Poly. He, he, he, he." By now she had two hands on the countertop (remembering the comments Bernard had made in the past about her finest cake). "Well, ha ha ha... I haven't got any ready. Ho ha he..." Her voice rose in semi-hysteria.

Stock and Perry were thoroughly enjoying the moment of her antics and waited for her to abate enough to respond. She eventually pulled up a chair opposite and balled her fingers into her eyes to contain the tears of joy; her shoulders were still oscillating, and she was pressing the palms of her hands onto her face so that only her nose protruded. She was now realising that these two had 'legged-it' from Springfields just to have a decent breakfast; she was still terribly fond of Bernard and overjoyed that he was still living up to his reputation.

Regaining relative composure "Ok, ok. You two gents stay there. I'll get you some breakfast." Rising from her chair en route to the kitchen, she asked, "What are your appetites like these days? No, don't tell me, I think I can guess. You wouldn't have come this far unless you were starving. Hang on a few minutes." Her laughter re-asserted itself once again and seemed louder from the echo in the kitchen.

"She's very perceptive," announced Perry once she was out of earshot, "and seems to know you rather well. Care to let me into your little secret?"

Stock then told Perry about the last few years of his life living next door to the pub. "I am afraid I may have misled some of the locals with some of my stories, but it never does any harm, and I like to leave a certain amount to their own imagination and let them deduce the rest. They think I am some sort of Bulldog Drummond type of character. I have tried telling them that my stories are true, but somehow, they only half-believe me. Instead, the exaggerations have become some sort of local legend. It is like the fisherman's catch of the day. What started out as an eighteen-inch-long cod in the cold and sober light of day, by the end of the night and after a few whiskies ends up a four-foot monster.

Perry conceded this point, "I know what you mean. I was racing this chap on another Bantam 125 along the perimeter of an airfield once. We were lucky if we reached 45 miles an hour, but somehow, as far as I know, I still hold the record top speed of 68.

Stock continued, "There are, of course, some genuine mistakes. In Assam, I put in a requisition for 2,000 twelve-inch iron staples for holding railway sleepers together along the edge of a runway. What I actually received was 20,000. When they arrived, the duplicate form had been folded vertically in two and the damp had copied the 000s onto the adjacent page, so that 2,000 looked like 20,000. The rest came in useful, as I paid the locals with them instead of Rupees. They used them as pins for building their mud huts."

They could still hear Caroline in the kitchen chuckling to herself and the wafting aroma of bacon & egg drifted through the pub silenced Stock and Perry momentarily. A particular smell is one of the senses that the brain never forgets throughout one's entire life. This primaeval asset of a human will invoke all sorts of memories even though several decades may have passed, and both Stock and Perry subconsciously started salivating in anticipation. Not in the same way that a hound will do but enough to raise their spirits even further. It had been a long time since either of them had enjoyed not just the taste, but the smell. Stock surveyed the slightly dusty atmosphere in the window-washed sunlight that pervades most pubs first thing in the morning and smiled to himself; It was one of his favourite memories.

"Here you go, you criminals," Caroline chuckled as she reappeared with two plates, and leaned over to the adjacent table to fetch the tray of ready-prepared knives, forks, salt, pepper, etc. "The fried eggs are sunny side up, not like the rubber ones you're probably used to up at Springfields, and I'll bring you some tea in a sec."

"I can't remember the last time we had fried eggs, and they certainly weren't this colour," commented Perry as he looked down at the bright yellow yoke.

"Corn-fed!" shouted Caroline over her shoulder.

A pot of tea on a small tray appeared; Stock and Perry were rather occupied with tucking onto a delicious typical English Breakfast and hardly noticed Caroline. All three did however temporarily stop whatever they were doing when the front door of the pub opened and in walked a short, dark-haired, moustached man. The mere fact that a door from the outside world had opened reminded them that Stock and Perry really ought not to be doing what they were doing: enjoying themselves. This minor anxiety passed almost immediately as it was not someone from the Home who had come looking for them, but Syd, the parish groundsman. His job was to maintain the local hedges, ditches, and lawns, and was a regular at the pub.

"Morning, Caroline. Nice one again," he commented as he sauntered over to their table. "Good grief, it's the colonel." His recognition taking just a few seconds. "Sorry, sir. Good morning, sir. 'Ow are you? I thought you had gone to Springfields." It took him a few moments to realise that their state of dress was not quite what one would expect. Syd had also tended Stock's hedges from time to time. Strictly speaking, his job precluded him from taking on private work, but Stock's hedge abutted the lane, and Syd knew he would be looked after by the colonel if he made a good job of squaring off. Syd also knew his place when in the presence of the colonel and had the utmost respect for him.

Caroline was less formal and took the opportunity to blow her own trumpet, "They've legged it from Springfields to get a proper breakfast and naturally came here. The usual?"

"I understand, sir." He glanced over at Perry with an inquisitive expression, but not daring to ask who the other gentleman might be, preferring to be told.

"Thank you for asking, Syd, and I must say it is a pleasure to see you once again. And how is that lovely Wife of yours?" Her name escaped Stock, but his endearing question brought another smile to Syd's leathery face. "This is Captain Perry, and we are both enjoying one of Caroline's wonderful breakfasts. Would you like to join us?"

To Syd, being asked to share a meal with the colonel was indeed an honour and he sat himself down. "Thank you, sir. Lyn is very well and still running our launderette. Please excuse me, but I need to clear out the west gully this morning and I put on my working clothes." His apology was rather superfluous considering his companion's attire, but nonetheless, Syd felt he had to offer an apology for his moth-eaten jumper, which had a waft of creosote about it. He still wasn't entirely convinced about Caroline's explanation of their presence and, not being as 'sharp' as Caroline, felt the need to enquire further. "Are you enjoying Springfields?

Stock was plying his plate with more salt in between mouthfuls of egg-stained fried bread. "Come to think of it, I would have to say that the food could certainly be better; this one is most definitely the tastiest meal we have had since I can remember. What do you think, Cyril?

"Uuuummmmm. Not so sure about the tea though. It lacks the punch of Matron's, but wonderful mushrooms. Might be something in the water." He continued eating rather than talking.

During Syd's Army days in the '60s, he had experienced the rations they had been given, but when it came to making tea, he agreed with Perry's summing up. There was a definite art in straining tea. Too much and the taste could turn bitter, too little and it tasted like yesterday's.

"Will you be attending the Anniversary March again this year, sir?" This to commemorate the D-Day landings on 6th June 1944. Stock carried on breakfasting without batting an eyelid; this may have been either because of the total change in conversation subject, or because Stock's cognitive powers were still rather weak.

The comment was overheard by Caroline returning with Syd's plate. "Oh, please say yes. It was so much fun a few years ago for the 50th." Her giggles were returning to interrupt her narrative, but turning to Perry she managed to continue, "We had both the German and the French Mayors over from the twinned towns, and what started out as a very pompous occasion almost turned into a riot. Bernard here was sat in that very same chair discussing the merits of French wines over those of German wines - you remember, don't you, Bernard? - you were trying all sorts of wines and managed to get everybody pissed. Ha-ha-ha-ha...."

Stock paused his mastication and tried to remember, remember, remember. Yes, that was it. The Mayor from Viligny and the Burgemeister from Groult, together with their families, had been invited by the Town Councillors to commemorate the 50th anniversary of the Normandy Beach landings, and once the parade and speeches had finished, they had all repaired to the Frog and Hopper. Although Stock had been in Assam at the time, he had also been one of the evacuees from France in 1939. Although he had only been a Second Lieutenant at the time, as one of those 'channel-hoppers' this qualified him as having fought the common enemy. It had been a very hot day and, as one of the more prominent residents of the village, Bernard had been one of those who had been asked to officiate. It started out quite innocently with Bernard insisting that the best thing to cool one down was a pint of British beer; The kids had ice creams. The conversation had veered onto the subject of wines and, while Stock did not consider himself an expert, his post-war travels had given him a good grounding. He appreciated the qualities of a fine wine and in his 'cellar' next door, he had built up a fair selection over the years.

They eventually got around to a wine-tasting session, but not the type where one used a spittoon, even though the French mayor and his wife added a little water to each glass of red - a Frankish trait. The mayor from Groult was crowing about German champagne, even though nobody had either heard of such a drinkable item, or even had any to try, and then the insults started. Stock's impish humour had only fuelled the quickly developing row, and national pride now emerged from the imbibed representatives. Stock had thoroughly revelled in the contretemps and his provocative comments only managed to raise the volume of expletives from the continentals.

The 'discussion' had started at the bar but then it spilled over into the beer garden at the front of the Frog and Hopper and managed to involve the English mayor's wife, who happened to be a buxom Belgian, and whose family owned a brewery that produced some of the famous and very strong Trappist Monks' beer. The flailing gesticulating arms of the Frenchman managed to knock an ice cream cone out of the hand of one of the German's children onto the shapely legs of the German's wife. She let out a scream and rushed off to the Ladies' toilet, not caring that she had nudged someone's elbow, spilling their glass. Only the dog was happy, lapping up the fallen ice cream, but matters then got a little out of hand. Shouting and finger-poking between the German and the Frenchman reached hair's breadth from a fully blown fight. The German had got hold of one of the pub umbrellas to fend off the attack, and the Frenchman had picked up a metal tray and was using it as a shield. The conflict was only broken up when Caroline squeezed herself between them with a platter of canapés. Her landlady skills at averting 'trouble' managed to calm them down as she ushered them back into the bar and sat them both down in the corner next to Stock. Her withering look implored him to keep the peace.

A little food helped soak up the alcohol and, as the afternoon hazed into evening, as did the conversation, aided by the inevitable after-dinner liqueurs. The Entente Cordiale remained intact until well past midnight.

Stock was only sure that it was springtime but could not put day and date together, and did not know how far off the 6th of June was, but in response to Syd, "If I am asked, I would not mind helping again. One likes to contribute." This almost brought Caroline to her knees, but she eventually went off to attend to other customers that were beginning to fill up the pub.

Their breakfast continued with reminiscences, and it was Perry who first started to feel sleepy, his eyes shutting in contentment. Caroline glanced over at this peaceful scene, and as Syd got up to go, she asked him if he wouldn't mind taking them back to Springfields in his van, rather than have them walk back up the hill.

Nobody at the Home noticed Syd's van pulling up outside, nor Stock and Perry making their way stiffly back through the front doors. Although Natalie had been at her desk moments before, one of the Nurses had asked her to help her find Stock & Perry, whose absence had been noted at breakfast. It was easy to re-access the secure wing, as from the reception side it was merely a matter of pressing a button to release the magnetic retainers. It was some 10 minutes later, when panic was beginning to set in among the staff, that they were found in the Day Room fast asleep in their favourite armchairs.

Chapter 9

Auntie

Sir John Corston was nervous. Competent, but still nervous about having to give this television interview. As Senior Minister at The Home Office, albeit not for very long, he was responsible for the entire department and he considered himself good at his job, but this latest instruction directly from Downing Street had made him nervous. He had never had to appear on national television before, only local, but obviously the Prime Minister had decided that someone in his position of seniority was required, and this definitely fell within his department's remit. He was surprised that the Home Secretary or even the PM himself was not making the announcement, but his was not to reason why, only to carry out his political masters' demands. He had followed in his father's footsteps by joining the civil service straight from Oxford and, through well-established connections, his rise up through 'pay grades' and a series of timely events had pushed him to the forefront of promotion, which now placed him at the top of the career ladder. Whether or not he agreed with the political decisions which came from those elected to government, it was his job to see that those decisions were actioned, and he had a very well-oiled department at his disposal. He could either expedite or delay, appoint or disappoint, influence or command almost everything that came 'from above', but this latest directive required immediate attention.

He was required to announce to the nation that there was to be a series of ceremonies across the UK to celebrate the anniversary of the end of World War II, which would in particular be attended by the Japanese emperor and his family as well as the highest officials in the Japanese government. In a meeting with the press secretary from No.10 earlier that morning, it had been made very clear to him that this was more than just a political coup, and that it had taken over three years to bring all those governments and related factions from around the world together in one place to commemorate the Japanese surrender over sixty years ago. It would also include an apology from the Japanese emperor for the treatment of POWs, and a further announcement of new car factories to be built in the Midlands, securing thousands of jobs for the future. Lastly, there was to be the creation of a new annual national holiday across the whole of the United Kingdom called 'Peace Day', to be held annually on the first Monday in August. The aspirations of many of the world's leaders in setting this up was that Peace Day would become an annual worldwide event that would encourage cessations of hostilities on a global scale, a very tall order indeed. News of this importance was not likely to stay quiet for very long, and it had been agreed that it should go public at 12.00 Greenwich Mean Time that day.

Sir John had initially been elated upon hearing the news, but very quickly realised that most of the work that came with it was going to fall squarely on his shoulders. The current government had a long track record of making announcements that were intended to raise the morale of the populace, but in reality, rarely did any of their announcements amount to anything significant, and he was well aware that the majority of voters now scorned the government for doing so. The only difference, in this case, was that the creation of a new national holiday would be welcomed by almost everybody, apart from those in his department.

He was grateful that No.10's press secretary had provided him with prepared narratives he could present to the cameras; only after he had made the announcement would the prime minister follow up with his carefully prepared statement, and his own interpretations. It had been explained to him that things were being done this way around so that they would appear to be non-political, but Sir John knew that in reality it was in case proceedings went wrong, that it would be him and his department that would take the blame.

The British Broadcasting Company, affectionally known as 'Auntie', had its Broadcasting Centre just north of West Kensington, and it seemed that the word had already 'leaked' out as when he arrived at the BBC there was a plethora of reporters blocking his access to the front doors. Sir John wished he had made alternative arrangements, and his "no comments" did nothing to ease his passage, but once inside the safety of the foyer, the hushed atmosphere prevailed, and a sense of normality returned to him. He went through the usual pre-broadcast formalities and was given a warm welcome by his chat show host, who glibly led him onto the subject that he had come to announce.

"Yes, the rumours are true, and I am delighted to officially announce that we are finally laying to rest any such spectres of hostilities that may have been harboured by some since the end of the Second World War. There will be a worldwide Peace Day on 1st August which we hope will encourage global peace and help to stabilise those areas where there is current conflict.

His host was itching to interrupt and took the slightest opportunity in Sir John's pause for breath, "But surely this will be seen by the Arab world as just another Western-led gambit to retain its dominance over the rest of the world?"

"Not at all. The Heads of State of all those nations that were involved will be in attendance for the main ceremony, including those from the Arab nations. After all, the war did encompass the Middle East and they will be sending their emissaries also. The President of France, the Chancellor of Germany, the Italian Prime Minister, the President of the United States." He was padding out this part of the announcement a typical diplomatic ploy that left less time for awkward questions later.... "The New Zealanders, the Australians... In particular, we are expecting His Royal Highness, the Emperor of Japan including his Prime Minister and some of his cabinet, and we are expecting him to proffer apologies on behalf of the Japanese nation regarding the treatment of allied prisoners of war.

The producer of the program was on the ball, having had a previous intimate relationship with the host, she was more than ready on this auspicious occasion. She deftly switched cameras away from Sir John to him. The small LED red light underneath the lens came on. "The treatment of British POWs in particular has been striking a chord in the heart of this nation for decades. What difference will this apology make?"

Sir John was ready for this one. "This will open the way for even more trade negotiations between not only Japan and the UK, but also our partners in Europe, and the United States of America. Indeed, we expect this to usher in a new era of world trade." He was well aware that there was a dangerous link between the morals of an apology for wrongs, connected with the capitalism of trade, but this link could not be avoided, whichever way it was put.

Sir John continued to read relevant passages from the script he had been given, depending upon the order in which his host presented the questions. The one subject that was dwelt on the most was the new national holiday, and he was grateful for this, as it meant that he did not have to touch on the subject of where in the UK the new jobs were going to be created. That was best left to the politicians anyway.

Once away from the television cameras, he was ushered into a recording studio that frequently doubled up as an interviewing studio, later to be broadcast through the various radio stations, and he went from studio to studio throughout the afternoon. He told similar stories there, but radio interviewers were not as restrained as those on camera, and he had to utilise all of his diplomatic skills and refer several times to the official script. The treatment of POWs could be a very touchy subject, even after more than half a century.

The costs of another national holiday were already being berated by a representative from the Confederation of British Industry. The expense of another public holiday would mean that industry as a whole would suffer 'x' million man-hours lost, and that did not include the number of employees phoning in sick the day after, as was the general habit. The two union spokespersons were at loggerheads over the matter of where the new car factory was going to be built. The Welshman was trumpeting about the vast amount of skilled labour in Swansea who had been out of work since the steel industry had all but shut down there, while the Yorkshireman droned on about the historic car-making industry in Birmingham. The mixture of the two totally differing accents contrasted in such a way that it caught the attention of the 'Garage Music' sect listening on the radio waves, and a lampoon of their argument was already winging its way across the internet.

From nowhere, hearsay about a brand-new town being created in the north-east to service the new factory which would be powered entirely by wind farms had the environmentalists up in arms. As usual, they could not agree on any cohesive direction, and the two women representing two differing factions from the 'Green' lobby were raising their voices to such an extent that the producer had to turn down the 'output' control on the console.

"You cannot sustain a whole town and a high-usage factory that runs 24 hours a day from just wind power. What happens when there is not enough wind? Are you expecting to persuade the pigs to fart in the right direction at the right time? You have to back it up with traditional gas or coal-fired power stations, and that is counterproductive." This from the stubby-looking blonde.

The brunette replied in a condescending manner and with a little more tact. "Yes, you can. You simply store the electricity in cells in an underground bunker until it is needed. We just have to build in a factor to allow for when there is a lack of wind. Besides which it can be backed up with wave power."

The blonde was furious. "And I suppose you want to put those massive wind turbines along one of Britain's most beautiful shorelines. You'd ruin it. This is coming at just the wrong time. We're trying to have that part of the coastline designated a world heritage site to protect the birds migrating from the Arctic to the Mediterranean, and this is their only stopover point on a 3,000-mile journey. They'd never make it without that stop. And what about those long blades? They'd chop half the population of those birds in two. No. You can't do it. Only a moron would think of that. And what about the newts!"

"Are you calling me a moron? It wasn't me who thought of that. It was your uncle who..."

"He's only my step-uncle, and it wasn't him. It was whatshisface you went out with last Easter.... the fat git."

"Don't you call him fat."

The interviewer had by this time led Sir John out of the studio, and was calling security on the phone, just as the blonde grabbed hold of the boom mike to whack the other over the head.

Officials from the two main unions that cover the UK's rail network had somehow managed to persuade one of the producers to interview them live during the afternoon chat show. Bob Hawk from the National Union of Rail, Maritime and Transport Workers (RMT) was arguing with Terry Noman from ASLEF, The Associated Society of Locomotive Engineers and Firemen (Sheffield) about the best way to create a brand-new rail link between the new town, Leeds and beyond. Unusually between themselves, they managed to find common ground and agreed that there was little necessity to have a direct link to London. Their weak bond of cooperation became stronger when the interviewer read from a slip of paper he had just been handed that apparently there would be no rail link with the new town, only a bus service. To Bob Hawk, whose roots lay with The Society of Wheel-Tappers and Shunters (SWETS) when he was just a lad of 13 years old, this news, if indeed true, was a real slap in the face of what he had agreed with the Transport Minister just last year. The air turned blue as he slated the government's two-faced attitude, on the one hand encouraging the public to get out of their cars and into the trains, and on the other, passing up the chance to create a new branch line, which would be more likely to force motorists off the road. Terry Noman who had recently been re-elected as General Secretary of ASLEF by the narrowest of margins, felt that he also needed to speak up for his members' interests, and added to the condemnation of those "lazy, over-fed twats in Whitehall". For the first time in decades, the leaders of these two Unions shook hands and jointly declared that there would be industrial action resulting in the direst consequences unless their demands for a brand new rail link were included in the plans for the new town.

The BBC phone-in line operators had their tea break cancelled to handle the extra calls, and the volume of emails managed to 'crash' the server's mainframe.

Somewhere en route between the Radio 4 and the Radio 2 studios, with the number of people rushing to and fro, an exasperated Sir John lost his 'chaperone', but somehow managed to find his way into one of the broom cupboards. Silence at last and hidden behind the closed door he could discern the bustle. From under his jacket, he retrieved and switched on his mobile phone and contacted his secretary. "Jefferies, you've got to get me out of here. Find someone who knows a back way into the 'Beeb' and tell them to have a car waiting. Not an official-looking car, but one of those Rovers. It's dreadful in here and they won't stop asking questions. Yes, yes, I've conducted the interviews but there's still a couple that I haven't, so you'll just re-appoint for tomorrow, and with a bit of luck all this excitement will have died down a bit by then. Yes, back entrance, say 10 minutes. It's going to take me that long to find my way out of here."

He closed his phone, leaned up against the wall and shut his eyes for a few seconds. He was just thinking of to whom he could delegate tomorrow's job of carrying out the interviews, when the cupboard door burst open, smacking him in the mouth, and causing him to drop his phone which scuttled under a rack of towels. He instinctively covered his face with his hands.

The 'chaperone' had arrived. "Ahha. Here you are, Sir John. Got lost, did we? Don't worry, you're not the first. In fact, this is where we find quite a lot of our missing guests, but you're lucky you've got me. Not everybody around here knows where to look, but I do. Bit of a rabbit warren this place, but when you've been here as long as I have, you know where to look... I say, have you got a nosebleed?"

Sir John was examining the red stain on his right hand and reaching for the handkerchief in his top pocket with his left. His face was aghast not only from the pain of having his nose possibly broken but from the very 'camp' voice that came from his 'chaperone'. It took him a few moments to regain his composure.

"Sir John? Sir?

"It's alright... I think I'll live."

"Now, if you'll follow me, please, we have Studio 12b free for just a short while before...."

sir John's interrupting hand rested firmly on his shoulder. "I need to return to the office straight away, and I am sure a fellow of your knowledge of the building can show me the rear exit." This was more of a command than a comment, but it was also music to the chaperone's ears, who at first misunderstood what was required of him until Sir John added "Now please" nodding his head towards the door.

His embarrassment was lost on Sir John who did not realise what effect his double meaning had had. He was about to protest 'But, Sir John...' when he caught the look in his eye and decided to accede by proceeding through the door into the corridor that had by now evolved its own 'two-way' system of human traffic. He led Sir John through ever narrowing and quietening corridors to a slightly grubby lift with a worn linoleum floor, which descended and opened up onto an internal staircase with a green 'Fire' sign posted on the wall. Just a few feet away was a similar sign screwed on not quite level and nearly in the centre of another door. They were just heading for this exit when they heard a rattle of keys on the other side and saw the door open to reveal a smartly dressed man stepping over the threshold as if he were going about his daily business. He looked up, startled to see two men staring at him.

Sir John's chaperone was the first to recover. "Hello. Who are you?

The man hesitated. "I am 'ere to see Geoff, ...in Current Effairs. 'E told me to come over this afternoon." The look on his face was not convincing and his Gallic accent did not help either, but he continued, "About the latest on the car factory." He looked down at his wristwatch. "I must 'urry," and sped off past them up the staircase, leaving the exit door open.

sir John's curiosity surfaced. "That cannot be normal, can it? Who was that chap, have you seen him before?"

"Well..., it's not that unusual as we often escort people in and out of this door to avoid the Press at the front door, and then we can either nip through the gardens to Frithville or turn right onto South Africa Road. I didn't know he had a key, though. I expect your chap will be waiting in Frithville."

"Yes, but who was he?"

"I've seen him before, and I think he's from the French Embassy, but I'm not sure. I don't think he works here."

The few seconds of silence between them allowed Sir John to consider the implications of a French official having direct access to the BBC...AND a contact in Current Affairs. He made a mental note to pursue the subject once he was back in his office. "Right, which way now?" His chaperone ushered him through the door and pointed slightly to the left towards Frithville Gardens.

Sir John was still contemplating the repercussions of a foreigner obtaining British information from what was arguably the best news service in the world as he walked back to his office. In fact, he was fuming by the time his secretary, Jeffries, found him at his desk, and the poor chap took the brunt of his expletives.

"How the hell does bloody Monsieur Frenchman Frog obtain a key to the back door of the BBC when we have to make an appointment just to go to the reception desk? You know what this means? This means that whatever news the BBC has picked up on, the bloody French get to hear about it before we do. That's not on!" He was almost shouting, and his blood pressure was definitely rising. "They managed to wrongfoot us on the immigration issue last year, and now we know why: they knew what our press release said even before it was released and beat us to it by issuing their own only minutes before. Summon the Director General of the BBC immediately and tell him I expect answers." Jeffries went to obey his master's command and started out of the room. "No, wait a moment."

Sir John had managed to calm down just a little, now that he knew who was going to receive the sharp end of his tongue.

"Wait, wait…" Jeffries closed the door and returned to his station in front of the desk, while Sir John closed his eyes in thought. He also placed his hands over his nose as if in prayer, but only momentarily. "Aaaargh." As he very swiftly remembered his swollen nose.

"Jeffries, how do *you* make an appointment with the BBC?"

"Well, Sir John, this morning I asked our departmental PR Officer to make the appointment you have just had. I imagine he would either delegate one of his fellows or make the appointment himself. Would you like me to enquire further?"

There was a pause while Sir John took this in. "Yes, please, and then ask the fellow who made that appointment to come and see me. I think we may be able to turn this to our advantage. Let's see if we can't get our own key.... eeeh?" A smile crossed Jeffries' face as he retreated towards the door.

Chapter 10
Revelations

The arrival of General Cecil Bristow at Springfields did not cause anything more than a cursory stir; mainly because he was being admitted as a patient, but he was the most senior officer to have become an inmate. Another bed had become vacant two days earlier and Mr Green had been quick off the ball in phoning the next on the list so that the room was empty for as little time as possible, and he could therefore maximise the earnings of the Home. He was wheeled in, accompanied by the usual family type eager to make an aged relative happy, but primarily to be rid of the mundane caring responsibility.

Apart from Bristow's infirmness in his legs, there appeared to be nothing much the matter with him, but it soon became apparent that he had been placed in the 'secure' wing for good reason. He had a habit of talking to himself a lot and seemed to be holding conversations with nonexistent others around him at unexpected times of the day and night. These conversations would often start with a 'barking' exclamation and his voice was more suited to that of a sergeant-major on a parade ground; and was deep with it.

"WHAT!" on one occasion startled one of the passing nurses collecting the lunch trays, so much so that she almost jumped out of her skin and dropped a tray full of crockery and cutlery. Any patient who had slept through the 'WHAT' was certainly now not asleep after the shattering crash of the dropped tray. When 'the others' were not around, he would engage the staff in rhetorical conversation. "Cleaning up again, eeehhh? Good show, keeps the mosquitoes away. Using Dettol again, I see? Marvellous, good field tactics. Use what they send you. ATTENTION." Causing one of the cleaners to jolt upright from the crouched position under the newspaper table.

It wasn't long before Stock and Perry met Bristow. Sitting in their 'snug' corner of the Day Room, the three of them were creating quite a scene. All military men, all from the same field of operations, all about the same age, and often speaking over each other recollecting their tales in the army. That is until one or two of them dozed off, much to the relief of the staff, but even then, that didn't always stop Bristow.

"Stock, ummmmm, Stock? I say, were you the fellow involved in that polo match at Shilong who managed to geld the maharaja's pony with his mallet?" The general was trying to place Stock.

"Never played polo in my life, but I am rather good at rugby, golf, and tennis, and I do like a game of cricket. Back in England, I captained the 1st for Bury St. Edmunds for a while and led the East Dereham lawn tennis club in the same year."

"Bit of a sportsman, are you? How about you Perry, what's your forte?"

"I'm afraid I'm not much of a sportsman and certainly not in his league. I prefer cycling and sightseeing."

"ROT." Making a few of the patients look around. "Bloody bicycles. Got run over by one once. Chap hit me right on the knee and I haven't been able to straighten it properly since. NO. Man's got to have a proper sport, like Stock here. Now polo, that's a man's game, taming your mount as well as your opponents. I remember…" So, it went on, but Perry had lost concentration and Stock had shut his eyes.

A few days later in the Day Room, Stock found himself waking up in front of the television set without the company of either Perry or Bristow. He sat bleary-eyed for a few moments before finding his glasses in his lap on top of the newspaper he must have been reading before he had dozed off, and it took him a while to regain his bearings. He looked around to see that the room was occupied by just two others, asleep with their heads lolling against the wings of their chairs. The volume on the TV set was on the loud side as usual, but it was the early evening news and since Stock had been under Matron's medication, he had been taking in more and more information, not that he could always make sense of it.

The pretty newscaster was reporting on the announcement of the new 'Peace Day' and the screen switched to reveal Sir John Corston in front of a bank of microphones.

"Sir John Corston from the home office is with us now, live from Westminster. Sir John, we all know about your earlier announcement of a new public holiday, but please tell us more about the long overdue apology that the Japanese emperor will be making." The tone of his monologue was patronising, and Stock had started to pay attention to the name 'Corston'.

"I have here with me First Secretary Keisuke from Japan's Foreign Ministry." The camera panned out to show a respectable-looking Japanese gentleman, complete with pinstripe suit, standing off to one side and slightly behind Sir John. "He and I will be discussing details of the emperor's visit in August and the wording of the proposed apology in respect of the treatment of those prisoners held in camps by the Japanese during World War II. This will hopefully be the final chapter of that terrible conflict between our two nations. The national holiday on 1st August will be called Peace Day, and for the first time in history, will bring together."

Stock's attention was now fully focused on the television, and he gripped his armchair with his wrinkled hands. Memories began to flood back. He had not heard those names for a very long time indeed, and it invoked a 'déjà vu' moment. His mind whirled with words and pictures in random order. Corston...Keisuke, yes, and, Deeks,

Keisuke was ushered up to the microphones by Sir John to say a few words. His English was faultless. "His Imperial Majesty, the Emperor of Japan, has asked me to convey his greetings to the people of the British Empire and to assure them that the era of previous hostilities can now be consigned to the history books. He looks forward to the honour of addressing your Nation and to join with him in celebration of a new chapter of cooperation between the Japanese people, and the peoples of Great Britain." Accompanied by a smile, he gave a typical slight Japanese bow to the camera to signify the end of his speech.

The television returned to the newscaster and although Stock was looking at it, he saw nothing except images from Burma. He wasn't sure if he recognised either Sir John or Keisuke, but they looked familiar, and yet... He just sat in his armchair staring straight ahead until the nurses came to take him up to his bedroom.

"Come on, Colonel. Time for bed, ...Colonel, Colonel?" Stock finally managed to half focus on the nurse gently shaking his arm and trying to help him to a standing position. "Are you alright, Colonel?" His eyes were glazed, and the nurse was beginning to worry and was just about to summon more experienced help, when at last, Bernard faced her.

"Yes, bedtime."

His movements were automatic with the nurse struggling more than usual to change him out of his day clothes and into his pyjamas. By the time she had him in bed, she was still rather concerned that Bernard had hardly said a word in answer to her running comments. "Mind the door, here's your toothmug for your teeth..." etc. She was considering asking Matron to come and look at him but really didn't like to risk Matron's scorn at her inexperience. Besides which, she still had one more to put to bed.

So, Bernard Stock descended into a disturbed sleep and dreamed of things from a very long time ago; Things that in his old age he had totally forgotten. Web-like jumbled reflections skitted along threads that only led to more threads of disjointed images. Time was irrelevant. In fact, everything was irrelevant to everything else as his subconscious integrated impossible scenarios with each other. Incognisance of who was doing what, or with, to whom, where and why, interlaced with sounds of music, voices, and other non-descriptive echoes, emanated out of haphazard sequence.

He was back on the farm with his school friends, trying to save the fields from flooding, but the sun was shining. His school friends were all just sitting on a big horse, joking with each other as he tried to get them to hold the other end of the brown string that would stop the onrush of green water that was becoming impatient. A tentacle of water picked him up and threw him into the mouth of a great white whale, and then he was sitting next to Captain Ahab on the beast's tongue that rippled them to and fro. He had to get out and he found himself climbing up the tonsils to the waterspout and was expelled in a great cloud of steam that gently lowered him onto an empty grassy field. He was alone, but from nowhere, his legs were grappled by a man dressed in a rugby shirt and a very dirty scrum cap. Then there were other players all around him, shouting and pointing in different directions. "It's up to you now." He turned to see Alfredson's hand firmly on his shoulder, but he was looking the other way. "THERE'S the enemy." Stock turned to see that the opposition consisted of an army of Japanese, dressed in traditional Samurai uniform; Thousands of them crammed into one half of the pitch and they were all screaming their war cry in his direction. In their centre was Akiko. Akiko! He had to save her from the hordes. Head down, he charged into the crowd of warriors to get to her, but their bamboo swords were beating him through an ever-lengthening gauntlet that terminated at a great wooden stage on which Akiko stood alone. He couldn't reach the rope she had dangled down, however high he jumped and jumped.

Stock fell out of bed, and immediately woke. 'Where the hell am I?' It was dark all around him except for a thin wedge of light coming from underneath the door, and it was quiet with it. Nobody was shouting at him or telling him what to do, so he just lay there, trying to make sense of his dreams yet all could picture was Akiko, her beautiful face and delicate skin. 'Who was Akiko? He was married to, to... Mary. No, she had passed away, so who was Akiko? Alfredson, yes, that was his name. If only he could place him.... and Akiko. Who was she? Where was she?'

Thoughts circled his mind just as a scuba diver sees fish circling high above him, and each fish was like a different memory, but they weren't all swimming in the same direction. It was so peaceful and courteous, their bright colours reflecting their scales in the shafted sunlight as they gently drifted from microbe to microbe. They seemed to sense his affinity with them. Except some fish now started to dart here and there, and suddenly there was a predator in the arena, then two, then more. With nowhere to hide, the panicked fish fled in confusion, vacuuming the space behind with their tails. Stock felt sorry for them and wanted to help in some way, but he was rooted to the spot, standing on a sandy bed next to a cave entrance. He cried out and instantly, as if of one mind, the fish turned and darted past him into the shelter of his cave. He could see them more clearly now as they gathered around him, sucking at the tips of his fingers as though they held food. As he looked at each one in turn, it was as though they were being released from a spell, dissolving into faces and names, and finally Stock could talk to them, and they could talk back. He was shaking with joy, and they shook too. He was shaking, no, being shaken awake.

"Colonel, Colonel!" A nurse had come to help Stock out of bed and found him lying on the floor. A small pool of blood had stuck his hair to the floor. She pulled the emergency cord to summon assistance and was relieved when she saw Stock open his eyes. She noticed that he held a curious smile on his face, but her concern was where the blood had come from. The duty sister arrived with another nurse in tow and, taking in the situation, she knelt down to assess Stock's condition without moving him at all in case he had sustained unseen injury. Stock surprised them all by raising his head, pulling his hair off the floor, and sitting up, albeit with the nurse's help.

"It is nice to see you all, and how are you this morning, Sister?"

"More like how are you?" Her eyes darted from one side of his head to the other, trying to locate the source of the blood that had coagulated down one side of his face. She found a bruised cut just above his right ear. "Here we are, not too serious. Looks like you fell out of bed and hit your head on your toothmug." She picked up Stock's mug and teeth lying next to his bed. "You must have knocked this over in the night." She turned to one of the nurses. "Help me get him up onto the bed, and then go and get a medium-sized dressing, a sponge, warm water and some antiseptic cream."

Once safely on the bed, Stock grinned a toothless smile. "I say, it is not every day that one has the pleasure of three girls trying to get me into bed. Will you be staying?" This raised smiles all around and the sister's knowledge of Stock convinced her that she would not have to call out the doctor immediately, but she would mention it to him when he called later.

Matron had dedicated a nurse to ensure Stock made it to breakfast without any mishaps and to keep an eye on him until the doctor had examined him mid-morning. She guided him to where Perry was sitting. "Good morning, Cyril....the colonel had a fall in the night." Gesturing to Stock's bandage around his head. "But he's alright now and I'm here. Just in case."

"Been in the wars again?" said Perry looking up from his meagre-looking breakfast. "Or did you get hit by one of Bristow's mallets?"

Stock eyed Perry with a kind of look that required a smart answer. "If I told you that I had three exciting girls in my bedroom last night, I doubt you would believe me.

This got Perry thinking and his initial expression of melancholy soon turned to envy, but he soon twigged that they must have all been Staff. "Tripped over in the rush, did you? Forgot to tie your shoelaces. No, don't tell me, it was the terrible twins." He was referring to two of the staff who were actually sisters, and unsurprisingly, looked similar.

"Sorry to disappoint you, but I must admit to having merely fallen out of bed. Head's a bit sore though. Here, what is for breakfast today?" Stock was eyeing up a new-looking bain-marie that had made an appearance on the serving table for the first time.

Stock's dedicated nurse sitting at their table went and had a look under the cover. "Kippers," she beamed. "Would you like some?"

"What? No rubber eggs left?" joked Perry. "In that case, I'll try one. You too?"

"I cannot remember the last time I had a kipper. Go on then." Stock suspected they would be the same sub-standard as the rest of the food, but with the taste of the first mouthful, it was as though he had stepped back in time. To him, they were wonderful, and he relished the necessity of picking out the bones between mouthfuls.

There were, however, consequences to the kippers being offered to the inmates that only transpired later that morning. Matron did not miss the opportunity to get the upper hand on Mr Green in his office again. "Whose idea was it anyway to serve up kippers? All of my nurses have spent the entire morning extracting kipper bones from dentures, and most of the patients are endlessly coughing because they have swallowed too many bones; They're stuck in their throats. Where did they come from?"

"For your information, they were a gift from the general's family, together with the silver-plated bain-marie. Apparently, kippers are his favourite and they insisted that we take a weekly delivery to keep him happy. Besides which, not that it is your concern, it means we can cut down on other foods and help reduce the food budget. They are healthy and high in the essential minerals that particularly help those with dementia."

'One to me,' thought Green.

Matron was not having this so easily. "We can't have the staff wasting their time like this. If this were to happen on a daily basis, then we would have to take on extra staff every time to slap backs and save the patients from choking. That can't be efficient. You'll have to find another way to keep the general's family happy." Over to you thought Matron. She loved putting Green in a sticky position.

"I can't tell the family that we don't want the kippers and you're telling me that we can't serve them. We can't keep them from the general, so what are we going to do with them? …. How about we give them to the staff as part of their daily diet and deduct the 'cost' from their wages?"

"No, that won't work. Not everybody likes kippers, and I am sure the family would find out sooner or later. Besides which, they leave a fishy smell about the Home." The ball's still in your court thought Matron, inwardly smiling.

Green really didn't want to be left alone with this problem, and while he wanted to come up with a solution before Matron, he didn't want her to just walk away from him, leaving it entirely up to him. "I know. I'll request that we have them delivered already filleted. Leave it to me. I'll ring the family." Gotchya. He reached for the phone to signify that it was his decision that had been made.

Matron didn't have an answer, but still needed to get the last word in. "Very well, but it will have to be on a trial basis." Thus, leaving the door ajar for further confrontation on this subject.

"I need to tell you," she phrased it to infer that what needed telling came from a higher authority than her, "that Colonel Stock fell out of bed last night and bumped his head." A patient wandering around with a prominent bandage on their head could hardly be concealed. "He seems perfectly alright to me, but he did cut his head and I'll get the doctor to check him on his rounds. In fact, he's probably already here." She abruptly got up and bustled out of Green's office.

She caught up with the doctor on the first floor emerging from one of the patient's rooms and started to explain Stock's situation.

He held up his hand. "It's all under control," he announced. "And there's nothing to be worried about. I've already seen him in the Day Room. It's nothing more than a slight bump, and all he has is a slight headache. As he's on Razadyne, I've asked Sister to give him the mildest medication possible, and she told me you have some children's Calpol in stock."

"Yes. That ought to do it. Just for today, though?"

"No. Daily for the time being. I'm a little surprised that he noticed he had a headache as most patients don't. He does seem to be very perky at the moment. Just keep an eye on him."

She found Bristow, Stock and Perry huddled in their favourite corner and stopped short in surprise. They were playing cards on the coffee table normally reserved for magazines etc.

"BLAST YOU, STOCK." Bellowed the general slapping down a card in the centre of the table. "You seem to have an uncanny knack of knowing what I have in my hand. How did you know I only had the Jack left?"

"Ahhhhh. That's a trick I learned in Rangapoor. I had only just arrived from England as a captain and when I reported to General Forbes at HQ, the first thing he asked me was if I played Bridge. I did not even have time to salute before I was drafted into their evening session. I was partnered by the chaplain-general and we were up against the general and another colonel. I did feel a bit lowly being just a captain, but we managed to trounce them. The chaplain taught me that one," Stock trailed off into middle space, reflecting upon the occasion.

"Yes, but how did you know, Stock? Stock?"

Matron decided to intervene just as the morning tea trolley appeared in the room, and took over from the auxiliary nurse, checking that her special pot was on the top tray. "Good morning, gentlemen. Tea? Are you playing Bridge?"

"Ummmm... dummy Bridge, but not very well," remarked Perry. "Stock here is thrashing us both. Lucky we're not playing for money, even a penny-a-thousand. He's had us every hand so far. Ah, yes, please. Two lumps for me today, please."

Matron was about to ask the general first, in deference to rank, but proceeded with Perry's request first. From what she had just seen and heard, it was apparent that Stock had not suffered any side effects from his bedside fall last night, although his bandaged head reminded her of Pudsey Bear from Children in Need. A few blood spots were dotted around unevenly, and she made a mental note to ask one of the nurses to change it.

Stock wandered off to the toilet and was just returning when his grandchildren came bounding down the corridor. "Grandpa...

yeeeeaaahhhh..." and hugged as far up his body as their arms could reach.

"Hello, children and where have you just come from?" Stock grinned one of his 'toothless' smiles as he relished the time about to be spent with his Grandchildren.

Ann was the quickest. "We've just walked along the lane from home, and Mum said we could if we were careful."

"And look what I've found," replied Tom, pulling out a hairy caterpillar from inside his shirt. "It only eats plants, doesn't it?"

Stock thought for a moment "Wellllll., let me think. In Burma they were a lot bigger and, here, wait a minute, let me sit down." He turned towards the Day Room and decided to head for a set of unoccupied chairs rather than rejoin his contemporaries. Stock 'oofed' the last few inches into a threadbare armchair with the help of his stick, which he now wedged between the swab and a cushion. "Come here, you two." Holding out his arms so that they perched facing each other on his knees. "Now, show me this chap you have." Tom dutifully complied by producing a 3" green hairy animal that arched and searched for an alternative hold. "He looks rather handsome, doesn't he? Have you got a name for him?"

"Mum says that all caterpillars are called Cecil, but I think that's silly." It was certainly silly coming from Tom, as the gap between his two front teeth exacerbated the 'S's'. Tom produced a few beech leaves and put them in the path of the constantly moving 'Cecil'.

"You were going to tell us about the really big ones," said Ann, fidgeting with the leaves, much to Tom's annoyance.

"Wellllll...." Stock needed time to think of a story that would be both plausible yet entertaining, but he had indeed encountered some very odd insects. "In the deepest part of the jungle, the local villagers called them 'Outpour'. If it was a little chap, it was just 'Optou'" Stock's voice pitched up a couple of octaves, but if it was a big feller it was 'Oooooooptou'." His voice now dropped to the bass level and Stock held his index fingers together and moved them apart until they were about as wide as his body. Tom and Ann's eyes grew in size as Stock's fingers separated. In Stock's experience, all insects had been called 'Ooptou' and the flying ones had another similar name, but he couldn't recall that right now.

"Thooooousands of them would dangle down from the creepers, moving from tree to tree and looking for their brothers and sisters, finding their next tasty leaf to chew, and the more they ate, the bigger they became, and the longer their hair grew. Some of the largest had stinging hairs, and some were even poisonous. Their favourite hiding place, though, was in your boots." It was time to make the kids jump and he gathered them closer to his face, lowering his voice so that they had to crane their necks nearer to him. "When you were asleep, they would come along the floor of your bedroom and climb up the side of your boots." Stock was now creeping his index fingers along their shoulders and down their arms, caterpillar-style. "They would topple over the lip of your boot and tumble down inside and curl up for the night, snug and warm. When you got up in the morning and put your feet in your boots, it would make them jump so much they puffed up to twice their size and tickled the bottom of your feet." He had managed to 'caterpillar' his fingers down their legs towards their feet, and now used his nails to tickle the inside of their ankles.

The kids jumped and squealed in unison, which had the effect of producing one of Stock's grins. He loved to make his grandchildren giggle and squirm with delight, and so much so that on this occasion Ann developed the hiccups. The first one prompted a surprised hand in front of her mouth, with oversized eyes to go with it, which made Tom laugh even louder, and he slid off Stock's leg onto the floor in uncontrollable fits. He had completely forgotten about his prize caterpillar, which by now was legging it towards the nearest skirting board.

"Hic." And Ann was off again, so Stock prodded her with his stick. "I can't help it. It's his fault. Hic."

This mirth attracted the attention of a passing Ron's Lad, who took in the situation at a glance. He took a glass from the trolley, filled it with water, and went over to Ann. "Try drinking this from the other side like this… .and don't forget to hold your breath at the same time." She grasped the glass with both hands and craned her head over the glass to suck from the wrong side. The inevitable happened, and water cascaded down onto Tom, who promptly stopped his cackling and stood up to shake off the few drops of water that had actually managed to reach his skin. "Urrrrrgghhh. That's horrible."

Ann was looking at Ron's Lad as she handed back the glass. "You can breathe now," he said after a short while, and she let out as big a 'phew' as she could before sucking in again. She waited… and waited… and waited. "Hey. It works. No more hiccups."

"Hey. Where's my caterpillar?" Tom was burying his head into the back of his shirt and ended up almost taking it off. His fruitless search ended as Susan entered, having decided that the children had probably had long enough on their own.

"Hello, Bernard. Thought I'd let the kids go ahead on their own today. Hope they haven't been too much trouble." This classic rhetorical statement is probably one of the most overused, with precisely the reverse effects.

Ann reacted first. "Grandpa was just telling us about caterpillars. Really big ones." Holding her arms out wide at full stretch. Tom was half looking around the room for his missing one but didn't want to say anything in case it got him into trouble.

"I am afraid I'm going to have to take them away from you now, Bernard. It's their music practice time."

Stock had been sitting quietly happy while things and people had been coming and going, and now managed a nod at Susan.

"Come along, kids. We must go. Now. Say goodbye to Grandpa."

Hugs and goodbyes left Stock sitting on his own, so he merely shut his eyes and drifted off to sleep. Just as he did so, he remembered the time when he had found a scorpion in his boot and involuntarily twitched his right foot.

None of the staff paid any attention to him, or any of the others who were asleep in their chairs, but the volume of the TV was turned up for the racing results and left up. The midday news came on, and once again, the main topic was the forthcoming visit of Japanese dignitaries. Stock could not help but hear this news, although the TV screen was just out of sight. With nobody else to talk to, or to interrupt his train of thought, Stock's mind was focusing more and more on those events that had been so elusive. His bedtime, with the help of one of the nurses, turned into an automatic reaction, his thoughts firmly set on remembering what really happened, and left alone he was able to concentrate enough to recall the correct order in which matters had occurred.

Chapter 11
The Definition of Happiness

The local Council had in place its systems to ensure the safety of those living within its borders as directed by the central government, which among such matters included the wellbeing of its increasing ageing population, and they were obliged under statute to ensure that there were no Health and Safety issues that might endanger the lives of every person from birth to death. When it came to the old age pensioners who needed nursing care, the financial director of Horsham Borough Council was well aware that this represented a growing and significant financial burden on the borough's coffers, and he had always been on the lookout for ways to reduce the allocation of monies earmarked. The Health and Safety Executive (HSE) was a law unto itself and had on one occasion caused the evacuation of the Council Offices when one keen employee thought they had found some white asbestos in the Ladies' toilet which turned out to be nothing more sinister than cotton wool. Their funding came from the Council, and there was a never-ending argument between the HSE and the financial director. It was found to be far cheaper to employ a just-out-of-college female 'know-it-all' graduate than retain an experienced older operative. Whereas the older person would expect to be employed for life and build up a very healthy pension upon retirement which the Council had to pay for, a young female, for example, would not need to be sent on any refresher courses, and would probably meet a young man, get married and become pregnant, not necessarily in that order, and consequentially leave the Council's employ without ever having built up any significant pension rights and thus save a significant amount of money. A young lass also had a salary of less than a third of someone else who had been at their post for over twenty years, so it made all the sense in the world to the financial director to utilise the younger female generation to help him meet the demands of the central government.

This was almost just the type that Horsham HSE had taken on in mid-June, and such were her impressive results to date that Miss Eve Newbury had joined straight from Durham University at the tender age of twenty-one, without waiting for the results of the final exams she had just taken, or even taking a summer holiday. She had been raised in poverty mainly by her mother - since her philandering father had long since vanished - not far from the Yorkshire seaside town of Scarborough and had lived among the lower echelons of society witnessing the foul behaviour that came with drunken youths, swearing, fighting, and vomiting as they exited from the nightclubs in the early hours of the morning. She had been bullied at school as the 'studious' type and it had disgusted her that society, in general, was quite happy to see teenagers leave school and immediately sign on for unemployment benefits, only to waste their weekly allowance on getting plastered and engaging in sexual activity on the streets with someone who was drunker than they were on a Saturday night; and then brag about it the following week until the next Saturday came along. It was probably the sight of all that vomit that had turned her into a dedicated vegetarian. Well before leaving school, she had determined to raise herself above this level of existence and had diligently studied rather than waste what little money she had on weekends out or holidays and had been accepted on the HSE degree course. Eve was expecting to obtain one of the few 'Firsts' from Durham which was why Horsham Council had offered her the job back in January, but her blinkered life had so far kept her to within less than 80 miles of Scarborough, and she had had difficulty within herself, not just accepting a position so far away but also getting there on public transport for her first job interview.

Now, as one of the six women that made up Horsham's HSE

department, and very unwise to the ways of the real commercial world, on her first day she had been handed a batch of assignments by the team leader. Unusually for Horsham, this was a mature woman who was due to retire shortly. Only known to herself, Mrs Patricia Weeks was well past her retirement age, and in order to get a job in England, had somehow managed to lie about her real age when her family had re-emigrated from New Zealand. One would have to be very sharp indeed to be able to pull the wool over her eyes, as many of the local businesses had found. She was one of those 'prim and proper' women who kept very much to herself and her family and was respected by all her colleagues for her efficiency but unsurprisingly, nobody could ever remember when she had first joined the Council.

On Eve's first day at her new job, after she had gone through the usual 'settling in' procedures, she had been handed a pile of files which Mrs Weeks had put on her desk.

"You're expected to get through about two cases a day and make regular site visits as per the schedule here," she explained, indicating to a prescribed sheaf of papers on the top. "And as it's your first day, you can come with me later to Springfields. It's an OAP Home out in the countryside, and God know how they manage to stay off our blacklist, but they do. I'll leave you to let them know we're coming.... say at 3 o'clock?"

Their twenty-minute journey to Springfields was by taxi, as it was the Council's policy that they were cheaper than supplying cars to their employees, and all the while Eve had had to sit there and listen to all the do's and dont's, managing to take in only a fraction of the pearls of wisdom while offering the occasional "um" and "I see."

"The problem with Springfields is that it is one of the homes that caters for private patients as well as our own Council patients. If it were dedicated exclusively to Council patients, it wouldn't even be there but in a new building somewhere else, like the one next to the hospital off the high street, but we need the beds and that's why it is there. Now, Mr Green....you did speak to Mr Green about our coming, didn't you?"

An "Um" and a nod from Eve managed to interrupt Mrs Weeks.

"Now, Mr Green is only there as an administrator on a temporary basis until Mr Parsons recovers, and I personally don't think he is quite up to the job, so don't let him give you any of the usual old 'flannel' about things being on back-order or pending, because he's been warned before, and if necessary, we'll issue the 14-day Notice. Take note of the access points and remember the latest legislation regarding handrails. The kitchen ventilation, ..."

Eve was struggling to keep up and was relieved when they finally arrived. Natalie ushered them straight through to Mr Green's office as she, along with the rest of the staff, had all been warned about their impending arrival. Any visit from the HSE every three or four months tended to instil a sense of foreboding among the senior staff, whereas the kitchen porters and ancillary nurses really couldn't care less; what went on at that sort of level really didn't concern them.

Mr Green and Mrs Weeks had crossed paths before, and after the introduction of Eve was made, she set out their agenda for their visit. "I'll go through the safety records, while Eve will inspect the buildings. Can you allocate someone to show her around?" Green was quite expecting this and would have considered asking Matron just to annoy her, but this was her day off, so he asked Natalie to ask Ron to carry out this task.

Ron's Lad had wisely opted to keep a low profile, as on a previous occasion Mrs Weeks had told Green to 'keep that grotty looking urchin out of the way'. After she had left, he had been told by Green that as he wasn't on any official records, he couldn't be seen at Springfields and that if he was found by her again, he might be taken into custody. He had naturally taken an instant dislike to Mrs Weeks. As Ron was going to be with Eve, the Lad thought he would keep an eye on Mrs Weeks, just in case, by eavesdropping through Green's open window.

Mrs Weeks was given the spare desk in Green's office and had the run of the filing cabinets that lined the walls, while Green went about the rest of his normal daily routine. He occasionally popped back in to answer the inevitable questions.

"I've been going through your maintenance log and the last time I was here there was a shifty-looking character who you claimed was not officially on the payroll. Is he still here?"

Green was not one to tell a bare-faced lie. "He occasionally comes and goes, and we use him from time to time whenever he appears."

"Well, that's not acceptable. You couldn't tell me his name before because you said you didn't know it. Do you now know who he is and where he comes from?"

"Sorry, I still can't help you."

"Under HSE Directive 14, nobody who does not have contractual liability insurance and is not directly employed is allowed to offer his or her services, and furthermore..."

Green all but switched off as new directives were being issued all too frequently and then updated even more often.

"If you can't let me have his name and address, I have to ask the immigration service to investigate, and I'll issue the notice when I get back to my office."

"I'll see what I can find out by the end of the day." And they continued their discussions on other matters.

This was a bit too uncomfortable for Ron's Lad; action had to be taken. He didn't know anything about Mrs Weeks, nor her strengths and weaknesses, but after all, she was a woman, and all women had a phobia of something. An idea crossed his mind, and he left his hideaway in the shrubbery and headed for the cellar, where he prepared the scene. He then took up position in the hallway behind one of the curtains that led to the French windows and waited for Mr Green to leave his office. It was a long shot, but he had to try something, and besides which, if successful, it would be rather ignominious. He didn't have to wait long for Mr Green to leave his office, and making sure nobody else was about, crept quietly to the partially closed office door and started scratching with his nails at the wooden skirting board, much like a rodent would do when gnawing, softly at first. This indeed attracted Mrs Weeks' attention who looked towards the doorway and when it continued, got up to investigate, naturally coming to the conclusion that there may be a rat on the premises.

Ron's Lad was quick off the mark, and he soundlessly nipped over to the opposite end of the hallway to the cellar door, which was accessed from under the main staircase. Just in time he was out of her sight and continued his impersonation of a hungry rat. Mrs Weeks stood stock still by the office doorway and at first didn't hear the direction of where the gnawing sound was coming from and was about to turn away, when she distinctly heard it again. Her curiosity was now in full swing as she felt certain that there was at least one rat, and if she could at least see it, then it would be a feather in her cap when it came to writing up her report. She had come across rats before and was distinctly unhappy with them; it made the hairs on the back of her neck stand up, and Ron's Lad had quite rightly guessed that she would be frightened by them. In his experience, most people were.

Ron's Lad had positioned himself halfway down the cellar staircase, so that he could quickly disappear down the bottom, all the while scratching at the wood panelling that covered the entrance to the cellar stairs. He could see her reflection in the French windows, and when she came close, he swung himself around the stairs to underneath the steps and continued to scratch, but this time a little louder.

Having been built at the height of the British Empire, this was a proper cellar which divided into several full-height rooms and included a Buttery, an extensive wine rack room, a meat hanging room, a coal cellar, and a room for smoking and curing. An archway-shaped door led a narrow corridor to a chamber that housed the access to the round bricked well, which was at a lower level than the rest of the underground. Electricity had been installed at some point in the house's history, but only some of the dim dust-covered light bulbs worked, casting eerie shadows around blind corners. Nobody except Ron's Lad had been further than the first room, and there were all kinds of clutter and rubbish that made an ideal nesting place for rats. In fact, there really were rats down there and Ron's Lad had one of the babies in his annexe, but they had seemed content to stay in their den and had not disturbed the human occupants of Springfields. There was also the inevitable plethora of spiders' webs, that pervaded the flaking white-washed walls in this damp atmosphere, and he was careful not to brush them aside as he retrieved the penknife from his pocket, and almost casually scratched it against the stone wall, emulating what he hoped would be the sound of a rat to Mrs Weeks; it succeeded.

Only two of the light bulbs worked, as he had removed some of the others a few minutes ago, and it was with trepidation that Mrs Weeks took her first steps down the stairs, all the while treading quietly so as not to disturb the wildlife she had come to witness. She had second thoughts as she reached the bottom, trying to decide whether to turn left or right when the scratching led her towards an unlit room through a wide sturdy doorway. On the one hand, she wanted to return to the sunlight of the rest of the world and just call in the exterminators, but on the other hand, she really wanted to catch sight of whatever it was that was making the noise, and thus have the vermin exterminated.

Her eyes were still adjusting to the gloom, and she could make out the outline of old iron pipes that came and went through walls and ceilings, some of them intertwined with sporadic light-seeking ivy. There was an old grandfather clock set at an angle in the far corner and a series of rusty knives and hatchets hanging from even rustier beam-mounted butchers' hooks. The floor was littered with discoloured straw, discarded wires and mouldy cardboard and wooden boxes which she picked her way between to follow the sound. She had to duck her head through an archway, her face coming into hidden contact with decades of matted cobwebs, and as she involuntarily tried to take a step backwards, her front foot didn't find the ground where it was supposed to be. This was the entrance to the Well Room, and she tumbled down painfully onto her knees, knocking her head against the round brickwork of the well. She passed out.

Ron's Lad had adjusted much better to the gloom as he saw her outline in the doorway, and although he hadn't meant to have her pass out, it would suit him perfectly. So far, he hadn't been seen and she was none the wiser. He made sure she was not bleeding or too uncomfortable and gathered a few armfuls of straw and strewed them over her body, then topped that off with copious quantities of spiders' webs across her face and added some shredded cardboard boxes to keep her warm. He then left the Well Room but closed and jammed the door firmly shut; it was totally dark in there.

He had not meant for her to become disabled in this manner, just frightened enough to leave quickly without jeopardising his position. It was time he kept an eye on the other woman.

*****

Ron and Eve were getting on fine, and she found him to be a very pleasant man. They had started at the top of the building and so far, she could not see anything that did not comply with the regulations, all except an emergency light that was flickering. She had taken in Mrs Weeks' advice and was saving herself for the kitchen, and when they eventually arrived there, she immediately spotted the inadequate ventilation fan.

"I think this was pointed out to you last time," she said, glancing down at her clipboard that held a record of faults.

"That it was, and I have asked Mr Green to hurry the new one along on several occasions. Can you bear with me a while longer and I'll promise to have it replaced as soon as possible?"

Perhaps it was Ron's honest approach or her inexperience, but she conceded the point.

"You see, if you close the kitchen down, it will mean that we will have to bring in meals from outside, and that will cost the Council dearly. Just give me till the end of the month." His plea fell on fertile ears.

"Ok. But just to the end of the month". She glanced around the rest of the kitchen. "That EXIT sign above the back door, it looks too small to me." She got her tape measure out and asked Ron to find her some steps so that she could reach it. "Yes, it's the old imperial size and ought to be metric. I'll make a note on here."

"That's easily fixed. I think we have a spare in the store cupboard, and I'll do it right after you have gone."

"OK. Now can I have a look outside?" They went through the back door under the exit sign and into the back garden. The crazy-paved patio led directly onto an even lawn, shaded by the overhanging leaves of a walnut tree. Several patients were sitting in the provided chairs not doing or even looking at anything in particular, one of them was being tucked into a blanket by one of the staff.

"This is a lovely setting. You must enjoy working here," she asked rhetorically.

"Oh yes. It's not too stressful, except sometimes in the Winter when the ice freezes up the pipes." They continued to walk down the pathway so that Eve could turn around from a decent distance and look at the rear elevation.

"What's that building there?" asked Eve as they approached the two-storey annexe that protruded above a yew hedge.

"Oh, that's where I live. It's quite small. Do you want to see?"

Eve nodded, happy to be invited into this friendly man's world, and he led the way around the side of the hedge and held open the front door for her. It was a typical entranceway to a working man's abode, the threshold having a thick cocoanut mat on which sat a pair of Wellington boots, a scrubbing brush, and a pair of well-worn shears.

"Me and my Lad live here, and it's just right for the both of us."

Eve didn't know that his Lad was neither his son nor that Mrs Weeks was on his case. He showed her around the living room and kitchen pointing out mementoes from his past and was about to show her upstairs when one of the nurses cried out from outside the front door.

"Ron...Ron. Can you come? Mrs Chambers has fallen out of her chair again and I need your help to put her back in it."

"Ok, I'll be right with you." He turned to Eve. "Please help yourself, while I look after Mrs Chambers. She's always falling out of her chair but doesn't seem to mind. Back in a few minutes." He left Eve to explore what little there was of the upstairs, not considering for one minute that she would venture into the bathroom.

She gingerly pushed open one of the two doors at the top of the stairs and saw laid out in front of her one of the neatest bedrooms she had ever set eyes on. The centrepiece was a traditional patchwork quilt, perfectly aligned, covering the single bed, with a pair of 'grandad' slippers just visible underneath. A headboard with a matching cover was wall-mounted underneath a plain wooden shelf, on which there were several ornaments, and a bedside cupboard supported a lampshaded light. The dappled sunlight played over the quilt and carpet and reflected onto the lightly flowered wallpaper, and completing the perfect scene was a mirrored pine sideboard with drawers below. No wonder Ron was content, she thought as she closed the door behind her and crossed the top of the staircase to one of the other doors.

Smiling broadly and in a serene mental frame of mind, she opened it. There was quite a bit of resistance and she soon realised that it was a self-closing door, so pushed harder and staggered two paces into the room, the door closing hard behind her. She froze.

In direct contrast to the other room, her first impression was that this was the ugliest and most untidy space she had ever seen. The bed was nothing more than a sleeping bag on the floor which seemed to move, and what looked like a bathtub had plants growing out of it all the way up to the ceiling and mostly covering the Velux window....and things moving about on the walls and.... and, reptiles tasting her scent with their forked tongues. She was petrified, literally, of lizards and snakes, which now seemed to all be converging on her position. As a child, her mother had taken her first to their doctor and then to a specialist who had declared that she suffered from ophidiophobia; an in-bred phobia and complete dread of any reptile. It seizes up the brain and produces an inordinate fear that blocks logical thinking, as well as raising the heartbeat and blood pressure to unsustainable levels. She didn't even have the power to move her hand to the door handle just behind her, let alone turn it, but stood rooted to the spot with wide, terrified eyes. Even if there was just one snake behind a thick glass pane twenty feet or so away, she would have had difficulty controlling herself, but this was her worst nightmare. Her brain did the only thing that it could; it shut down, and she fainted amongst all of those things she feared and hated most.

Ron returned a few minutes later and called out for her from the bottom of the stairs, but when he didn't get a response, he shut the front door and left.

*****

The duty of organising the relatively simple task of afternoon tea in Matron's absence was allocated to one of the kitchen porters who on more than two occasions had recently observed her adding a white powder from the third medicine fridge. As far as he was concerned this was now the norm, and nobody had told him otherwise. He had just finished filling the large urn with boiling water and now had the door open to the third fridge where the Razadyne II took up most of the shelves within. He did not have the mental agility of anyone more than the average kitchen porter but understood the basic instruction of 15mg daily. To him, logic suggested that this would be per patient. He multiplied the number of patients, plus some for the staff and visitors, by 15 and filled the measuring jug up to the calculated amount, added this to the urn and gave it a good stir before adding the normal number of tea bags. Waiting a few minutes for the concoction to brew, he then gave it another stir for good measure, since in every instance the tea bags always took up the space at the very bottom of the urn. The finished product on the tea trolley was now more concentrated than Matron's usual brew and he wheeled this through to the Day Room, where a nurse took over from him and started dispensing it.

For some reason, there were fewer visitors that day, but it didn't take long before one of them returned from the patio requesting another two cups - one for her and the other for her mother. It was a similar story with the patients who would normally have left at least half a cup of lukewarm muddy-looking tea, and requests for more were soon coming thick and fast.

The military crowd were enjoying the fine English weather with their tea under the shade of the walnut tree but not altogether getting on with each other. The argument was over the latest front-page news in the Telegraph about the role of the church in the face of the overwhelming immigration of those of different religions. The debate had started off harmlessly enough, but Bristow, Stock and Perry could not agree on anything much and as the discussion became more and more heated, so did their tempers. At their time of life, old doctrines and beliefs were firmly entrenched and none of them wanted to alter their perceptions and therefore have to re-align their thoughts with modern thinking. At least they all had one thing in common which was that they were Christians, but this didn't occur to them at the time, and all three of them fought their corner, often having to raise their voice to be overheard by the others; Bristow had the advantage here in that his voice was naturally louder than the others.

Stock was waving his stick in Bristow's direction across the table. "These bloody people, they don't know how lucky they are, and you, you bugger…" His stick sent a cup-and-saucer flying onto the patio where it smashed into a hundred-and-one bits.

"Don't you 'Bugger Me'. It's people like you who are to blame, you damn communist," bellowed Bristow, his voice carrying throughout the garden for all to hear.

"Communist! Me? A communist? By your definition, your ethos can't perceive the meaning of the word and if it weren't for your braying voice, nobody would even listen to you."

Bristow's rage spilt into a physical reaction as he stood up as fast as he could. Tipping over his metal chair, he leaned over to hit Stock with his fist but tripped on one of the table legs, which sent the rest of the tea-set scuttling onto the patio. Stock had also stood up, and then Perry, as Bristow was ranting at the top of his voice, spittle flying from his mouth; all three of them squared up to each other, but Mr Green and another male nurse had come running out and they restrained Bristow as he lashed out at anyone who came close. His bellowing and violence shattered what final decorum usually goes with an OAP home, and he was led away inside by two struggling nurses.

Stock and Perry had managed to contain themselves, turned to look at each other and then just sat down as if nothing much had happened.

"Can we have some more tea, please?" Piped up Perry to Mr Green who just stood there wondering what had just happened.

"Of course." In automation, he went off to the tea trolley in the hope that it would be a calming measure to the remaining warring factions that now seemed to be at peace with each other.

"Looks like you hit a sore spot there."

"The man is an ignoramus," Stock mused. "Lucky I was not under his command. I doubt we would have got on back then either."

Green returned with two more cups and pulled up a chair to join them. "What happened?"

"He couldn't stand losing an argument so tried to hit Stock here."

"We were having a delightful discussion and airing our own points of view, but he was trying to force his own doctrine on us and lost his temper."

"I agree, but he's nothing more than a big bully really when it comes down to it."

"Do you think he's really the violent type?" Green was wondering if he ought to recommend that Bristow was relocated somewhere more suitable, something he was reluctant to do in view of his family's connections.

"Maybe. But give the fellow a chance. After all, it may just have been the heat of the day that really got to him."

Stock was less forgiving, but eventually Mr Green thanked them for their help and went off to catch up on Mrs Weeks' progress. There was no sign of her, but the empty desk had half-open ledgers and he assumed she was in mid-workings and had gone to the toilet, so he turned his attention to his own tasks. Several minutes later, Ron knocked on his door.

"Errrr, Mr Green. Have you seen Eve?"

His eyebrow rose as he looked up at Ron. "Not since you and she went walkabout. Have you seen Mrs Weeks?"

"No."

"Can you go and look for them?"

"OK." And off went Ron. He returned some ten minutes later with the news that neither of them was on the premises. Green frowned. It was baffling that Mrs Weeks should leave without a word. He looked over at the vacant desk.

"Where did you last see Eve?"

"I left her in the Annexe, but she's not there now."

Green paused to consider the situation. "I can only guess that they were called away on an emergency. Has anybody seen them?"

"No."

"Oh, well. No doubt they'll be back at some point." He returned to concentrate on one of the open files in front of him. "Oh. Can you attend to the mess on the patio? Some broken crockery. Bristow lost his temper and broke some."

"Yes, sir." And off went Ron.

*****

Ron's Lad was concerned. In between odd jobs, he had kept returning to the cellar to listen out for the sounds of Mrs Weeks recovering, and in the dingy gloom he could hear and make out rats and other smaller creatures going about their business. It wasn't until the early evening that he heard a moan from behind the door and it took another minute or so before the first shout followed by a scream of terror, then another, and another as Mrs Weeks blundered about in the total darkness. She was not to know that the only person who could hear or help her was just a few feet away. Not that that person was likely to help her very much and it was all that Ron's Lad could have asked for. He was not a cruel person, but Mrs Weeks had to be stopped, so he let her screams continue until they lessened into wails, and then sobs, and finally moans interrupted with crying. The situation now presented Ron's Lad with an ideal opportunity, and he left her to go and find some used clothes from the laundry and returned with a torch. He considered that she was probably now so scared to death and that she might soon very well be just that if he didn't do something. He hoped that she would be a quivering heap of her former self and likely to be biddable. The creaking door as he opened it produced no reaction from her, and the torch light found her huddled on her side, next to the well. Her mascara had run, her hair was dishevelled from where she had clawed at it with her hands, and her eyes were transfixed. 'This will do nicely' thought Ron's Lad, as he quickly exchanged her clothing for the smelly urine-stained nightdress. By the time he had finished, she looked exactly like one of the other patients, and making sure nobody saw him, he led her out of the cellar and upstairs to one of the empty bedrooms and tucked her into the bed. He closed the door and left, leaving her still sobbing and moaning gently to herself. Ron's Lad hoped that with any luck she would not be able to recollect anything, and he went back to Mr Green's office, found her handbag under the desk, and placed it in the well room just in case.

*****

About the same time that Mrs Weeks was emerging back into consciousness, having packed up for the day, Ron headed for the annexe. As per norm, he called out for his Lad but when there was no response, he investigated the upstairs bathroom and found Eve unconscious full stretch on the floor, a millipede just appearing from under her skirt. He was initially so shocked and horrified that it took him a while before he lifted her into his arms and carried her across to his adjacent bedroom and laid her gently on his bed. He brushed away her silky hair from her mouth and noticed that her face now had faint red blotches on it, and looking further down, so did her legs. He flicked away a woodlouse that was meandering across her blouse and called urgently to her again and again. At last, her body responded and, surfacing from oblivion, she screamed.

It took him a while to calm her down, and he helped her with a glass of water from the flask beside his bed as she sat up.

"It was horrible. I can't stand snakes and they bring me out in blotches. I think I must have fainted. I didn't know they were there. What are they doing there anyway?"

"Oh, don't worry about those, they're my Lad's and they're harmless. You see, they're his pets. Are you feeling better now?" He had noticed that the blotches were disappearing.

"Yes, thank you. You must think I'm a bit silly fainting at the sight of spiders and snakes." She explained her phobia that had been diagnosed since she was a child and how she grew up in Yorkshire and Ron admitted that he too had a phobia. "I don't like moths much. I don't know why as they're gentle creatures and I get on well with caterpillars, it's just the little flapping noise they make that makes me shiver. My Dad used to say that they were only good for feeding the birds and we had hundreds of mothballs around the house. Perhaps I inherited it from him. I don't know."

They carried on talking for a while, and it may have been the shifting of the shadows from the waning sunlight or the slight drop in temperature, but Eve looked at her watch and gasped. "Crikey, look at the time, I had better go and find Mrs Weeks," she muttered as she dismounted from the bed.

"Oh, she's gone ages ago. Suddenly left without telling anyone. How did you get here?"

"By taxi."

"Come with me. I'll call you one. Where do you live?"

Eve had to look into her handbag to confirm her address, as she had not yet memorised it. She had rented a one-bed flat just outside Horsham as it was cheaper than in the centre.

"I'll tell you what," said Ron. "It's not too far from here and I'll walk you home. That is if you're up for a walk. Shouldn't take much more than twenty minutes. If you like we can stop by the pub on the way. Have you had supper yet?"

Ron collected his bicycle so that he could ride home quicker, and they didn't hurry down the leafy lanes but instead enjoyed each other's company in the pleasant evening atmosphere.

Eve was happy.

So was Ron.

Ron's Lad was also happy.

Mr Green was almost unconcerned, but happy that Mrs Weeks had gone away.

Stock and Perry were happy.

Bristow was in no condition to know if he was happy or not.

In fact, everybody was happy in their own way except Mrs Weeks who just lay on the bed shaking like jelly, her brain functions reduced to the minimum.

Chapter 12

Flight

April 1945

Dressed in a brand-new uniform of a full colonel, Stock was escorted in a Jeep by one of the brigadier's staff to an airfield where a Beaufort Bomber waited, presumably, Stock thought, chosen over the much-loved Dakota because of its speed. The others were already inside and waiting for him. He had not even stepped out of the Jeep before the pilot fired the first of the twin engines.

Emerging from the brigadier's office, he had been confronted by a very smart sergeant, whose ram-rod straight salute would have done justice on the parade ground. "If you'll follow me, sir." He about turned and marched down the length of the veranda, not waiting for any acknowledgement from Stock other than his belated salute. Stock followed the sergeant across a grassed area to an adjacent building where a door was held open for him. "Whitman will look after you now, sir. He's the brigadier's batman. I'll be outside if you need anything, sir." The sergeant closed the door firmly on his way out.

"This way, sir." This from a corporal who had emerged from one of the several doors and ushered Stock into a sparsely decorated room. Stock had not really had time to take everything in and it now dawned on him that he really was a full colonel as he surveyed a new uniform hanging from one of the rails that ran down one of the side walls. "I understand that time is a little short, sir, so if you'll allow me…." He approached Stock and began to unbuckle his Sam Browne that supported the heavy pistol around his waist and helped him out of the harness and the rest of his rather tired uniform. "I've prepared this new one from the brigadier's description of you, sir, so please excuse me if it is a little out in one or two places."

The main difference between his new and old uniforms, apart from the spotless starched material, was the red stripe down the outside of each leg which denoted his rank as that of a senior officer. It wasn't out in the slightest and Stock paused to consider that Alfredson had taken the trouble to check on his size although he probably already knew it. The mere presence of the perfectly fitting uniform also gave away the fact that Alfredson must have known about this for more than just a few hours as did both the sergeant and corporal who knew exactly what to do. Stock stood to attention after donning his new cap as the corporal used a black-bristled brush to flick away the few remaining dots of dust. "There you are, sir…. good as new." He finally produced a swagger stick, but Stock rejected this as they only got in the way. There was no mirror, but with the addition of an extra 'pip' on his shoulder epaulettes, he felt like a full colonel.

Without any noticeable warning or signal, the sergeant re-appeared, and, as if to confirm Stock's promotion, ram-rodded to attention while still holding open the door. It was clearly Stock's cue to exit and thus he found himself in the Jeep a few moments later.

The assembled passengers were sitting opposite each other on jury-rigged canvas seats towards the front of the aircraft. As he pulled himself in, Stock noticed with reassurance that the bomb-bay doors had been covered over with a tarpaulin and strung in a lattice pattern with rope tethers from each side. He also noticed that Deeks was now dressed in his 'civilian' uniform. They all looked towards him as his shadow darkened the small hatch, and he had to cling onto the bomb racks to reach one of the two remaining seats; he chose to sit next to Haruko, bearing in mind Alfredson's earlier comments. "Congratulations on your promotion, colonel." Stock eased himself into the short seat at the same time that the pilot chose to start the second engine. Stock's experience of these bombers was that they were very noisy inside and almost impossible to hold a conversation in. Why then had Alfredson suggested that he and Deeks would be briefed more fully during the flight? Were there some things that Alfredson did not want Stock to know about?

"Long overdue," was all he could manage.

He looked over at Deeks and Corston, the former straining his head so that he could understand what Corston was saying to him. Deeks looked worried. Perhaps he ought to have insisted on sitting next to Corston, who was, after all, the Intelligence man and ought to know more than Deeks did, but it was too late now. Feeling that he ought to at least try to find out more, he was about to ask Haruko exactly where they were going to land when the engine noise rose, and the pilot manoeuvred towards the runway. Not one of mine, Stock mused as the plane bumped roughly over a drainage gully. Any attempt at conversation now was pointless as the engines were opened to full throttle for the take-off. Deeks looked even more worried. Perhaps he is frightened of flying thought Stock.

Without the burden of a heavy load of bombs, the pilot had no trouble in gaining any kind of altitude quickly and with levelling off came a comparative drop in engine noise, but shouting was still the only real option.

"Where are we landing?" Stock thought to keep the questions to a minimum.

Haruko turned to face Stock's ear, "The airfield just north of the Waskipi River." Before Stock could ask the next obvious question, he continued, "My adjutant is expecting us."

Stock only vaguely knew that the river was to the north-east of where, only yesterday, he had been building his own airfield, and he knew better than to ask further or even look out of the window for some sort of landmark. Even with a map, the jungle all looked the same from the air, but a competent navigator would use the glint from the several watercourses that crisscrossed below while taking bearings from other landmarks such as the occasional peak that protruded through the green far below.

Stock scrutinised Haruko for several moments as in his experience a good look into the face of one's opponent for any length of time sometimes revealed true intentions, but on this occasion, he was met by a fixed smile. There were a hundred and one questions he wanted to ask but that was impossible.

"You will see once we land," was all that Haruko could manage to convey to Stock. He had to assume that Haruko had specific instructions from his General Keisuke and that when they had landed there would need to be a covert meeting almost straight away. Stock had noticed now that the timing of the flight was all important, as he was temporarily blinded through an observation port in the fuselage by the almost setting sun. An enemy plane being spotted by an eager anti-aircraft gunner would ruin all plans, which was probably why the plane was now descending to nearer the treetops. Out of the setting sun, and with very little time to react, was probably the best way to deal with those on the ground and it would also be hard for an enemy fighter to spot. He assumed that the pilot had also been briefed, but to what extent? If he was to rescue Akiko, could he rely on the pilot to carry out his orders for a sudden take-off? In the dark? Even if he did manage a sudden take-off, would they be able to make it back across the river to friendly territory? Even if he did manage to pull off what was effectively a kidnapping, would he be able to persuade Deeks and Corston to leave immediately with him? Would there be an opportunity for them to leave immediately, without raising suspicion? In fact, come to think of it, almost anything immediate or done quickly in the enemy camp would raise suspicions. He would need another method and rose to go and speak to the pilot while they were still airborne.

Stock raised himself from his wobbly seat and made his way towards the cockpit where it was relatively quiet. There were two pilots at the controls. He tapped the shoulder of the man in the left-hand seat and was rewarded with a positive glance from him.

Where to start? "How far to where we are going?"

The pilot briefly glanced across at one of the gauges. "About another half an hour." Then a more thorough look at Stock, weighing him up. "You're the colonel, aren't you?" Rhetorically. "I've been told to follow your orders, but they didn't tell me exactly what's going on other than we are going to take the Jap colonel back to an airfield. I've already worked out it's behind enemy lines and was hoping you would be able to fill us in."

Stock was relieved that he didn't have to ask too many awkward questions and that the pilot had been told just enough. More evidence of Alfredson's efficiency. "I am afraid I cannot tell you too much, but we may need to take off again very quickly, so try to leave her parked into the wind." Stock's knowledge of aircraft was not quite non-existent, and even though he could not fly one as a builder of airfields he was intimate with wind directions, take-off, and landing distances etc. "Can you find your way back again in the dark?"

Not unsurprisingly, this last question produced a grimace from the pilot, as few had flown over this part of enemy territory, and probably none during the hours of darkness. "I'm sure we can manage to end up going in the right direction." This being a typically superior-type comment from one RAF officer to another land-bound officer. "Smith here is rather a good navigator, even if he does sometimes forget to put his boots on the right way around. Isn't that right, Smithers?" There was an obvious bond between the two pilots.

"There wouldn't have been any delay at all if someone hadn't swapped my boots for some about five sizes too small." It was aimed at the senior pilot, who ignored the jibe.

Stock was glad to have these two chaps not just on his side, but also clearly ready to follow his orders. "I might need to hide someone else on board on the way back without any of the others knowing. Can Smith here be ready at the back hatch?"

A moment of thought before Smith answered, "No problem at all. I'll have a tarpaulin ready for you."

Stock considered his next statement carefully. "We may need to take off without the others. Any of them."

This time, Smith didn't answer, leaving it up to his superior. The pause lengthened, and Stock hoped he wouldn't have a rebellion on his hands, and he held his breath for quite some time.

"Whatever you say, sir."

Stock returned to his seat and the cacophonous roar and began to plan how he would find out where Akiko was, and then excused himself from the proceedings to speak to her. He leaned over to Haruko's ear, "Less than half an hour."

"I know," came the response.

Of course, you would know, thought Stock. I have to broach the subject of Keisuke's daughter with him; it may be my only real opportunity. Perhaps he could use the 'hostage pawn' strategy, and suddenly he knew how. Somehow, he would make an opportunity before they got off the plane.

The Beaufort droned on into the dusk with an occasional small change of direction, but without another word being said, each man obviously caught up in their own thoughts. Stock considered further how this unreal scenario might have come about. 'It can't be a trap, I don't know enough about the overall operations in this part of the jungle, and neither does Deems. They could be after Corston, he's in intelligence. No, it's too elaborate, surely. It can't be a delaying tactic; this wouldn't make any difference. Perhaps...' Stock's wandering hypothesis came and went until Smith appeared at the cockpit door. Haruko got up and made his way forward and disappeared into the cockpit and, shortly after, the Beaufort made a dramatic turn to the right and the engine roar lessened a little. He leaned forward and beckoned to Corston who did likewise.

"I need to talk to Haruko before we get out. Can you and Deeks get out first, and give me a few minutes with him?"

Corston mouthed OK and sat back in his seat as the plane twisted and bucked the other way, the engine noise all but disappearing. Then they were on the ground, the three of them looking at each other in apprehension. They had arrived.

While the plane taxied, Stock got up and met Haruko coming

out of the cockpit. This is a most awkward place to hold a plan of action discussion, he thought, but at least there is little chance of being overheard.

"We do not have long, and I need to go through a few things with you," he said as Haruko straightened up. "We will not have a chance once we are in the company of your fellow officers, and I need to know a few things before we all discuss the proposed capitulation."

"Colonel, it's all been worked out by General Keisuke, his Adjutant, and myself before I left here. I think you are only here on behalf of your Brigadier to formalise the terms from a military perspective."

If he knows about Akiko, then he's not letting me know thought Stock. He had to take a risk and reveal more of his reason for being there, but he had already noticed the ring on Haruko's finger. "Where is your family at the moment and where is the general's family?" For the first time, he could see a change in Haruko's normally placid visage. "General Alfredson is concerned that if this coup does not go to plan, then your families will probably not be safe. There are likely to be consequences and one of my duties is to make sure they get away safely."

"There is no need to worry on that account. We have decided that our families are of little consequence compared to the alternative. Do not concern yourself about them."

Damn, thought Stock, but I've got to find out where they are. "I appreciate that, sir, but I need to know in case they are used as a lever against you, and, in particular, the General. Hostages if you like. It would be better if there was less of a chance to jeopardise this surrender."

Haruko's normally inscrutable face now frowned a little. "We do not like to think of this as surrender. It is a very sensitive point with General Keisuke, which your colleagues are well aware of." He gestured to where Deeks and Corston were sitting. "You must not call it surrender. That may make us reconsider our position. We think of this as a truce."

Bloody hell, thought Stock, but this is far more complex than he dared to think, and he was relieved that Deeks and Corston were going to handle that part of it.

Haruko continued. "You are quite right to concern yourself with our families though. They are not in danger, but they are here in the general's headquarters. You may be introduced to them later but do not annoy the general with these questions."

Stock had to have one more go at finding out their exact location, but perhaps now was not the time nor the place without giving away his hidden agenda. If Keisuke's HQ was adjacent to this airfield, then there was a chance he could spirit Akiko away, but if it was some miles away, then that would make it far more difficult.

"Colonel, it is not just from the Imperial Staff that there may be danger, but from elements within your own force once they discover what has happened. It would be for the best if you could arrange for me to meet with them as soon as possible.

"Shall we go?" As the Beaufort came to a stop, Haruko did not give Stock any chance to pursue the matter further as he made towards his compatriots. Corston, still seated, was looking at Stock in a quizzical manner.

Smith had opened the hatch and standing to one side saw an efficient team of Japanese soldiers carrying a set of steps to meet the fuselage. Haruko led the entourage and as Stock brought up the rear he turned to Smith. "Do not get out but be ready." Smith would normally have walked around the aircraft and inspected it as a matter of course, but not on this occasion.

Stock emerged from the plane into the near darkness of a new night. He could see Haruko already talking to a group of Japanese some thirty feet away in the gloom, broken only by dim light emitting from a field marquee a short distance away. His senses were heightened by the potential danger and, even before he reached the last of three steps, he could smell the distinctive odour of his enemies: the body sweat that came from different food, a whiff of distilled rice alcohol, the machine oil that went with their rifles, the raucous whiff of tobacco, and he could feel their presence. He straightened as he reached the ground between two pairs of armed soldiers who were not in the saluting pose and walked over to the others. The darkness was so intense that he could not see the runway they had just landed on, nor if there were any other tents or structures nearby. He was trying to locate some sort of landmark so that he could find his way back and was at last rewarded by a tell-tale radio mast that looked to be planted just behind the marquee. He became aware of an anomaly. There was absolutely no human noise. The creatures of the jungle were preparing themselves for what creatures do on a nightly basis: hunt, kill, feed, and survive.

"In here, Colonel," Haruko addressed Stock, although his comment was aimed at the party members. "These soldiers are loyal to me, but it is safer inside." He led them past another pair of sentries into the marquee which, Stock soon realised, was Haruko's own HQ and a good deal larger than its outside had initially portrayed. Canvas tarpaulins suspended from bamboo poles divided up the space, and they were led through a mini maze to Haruko's inner sanctum where a radio operator was scarcely visible behind a bank of equipment, and a secretarial type hunched over paperwork. Another pair of sentries stood like statues on either side of the entrance. A hazy head-height layer of tobacco smoke and paraffin fumes stretched across the dull interior, intensified by the humidity, and a series of candles set in water bowls laid out to attract the armadas of mosquitoes and other flying insects to their watery grave added to the obnoxious atmosphere.

Haruko almost sauntered over to his operations desk where a jaundiced-looking junior officer was waiting behind his readied chair, and he barked a short order aimed at the radio operator, who galvanised himself into activity. "The general knows we are here, and we shall join him immediately."

He turned to the junior officer and dispensed more orders. "Hai," accompanied the terse half-bow and he turned sharply away to a flap in the rear of the marquee which he now held open. "Gentlemen, follow me."

Haruko disappeared through the same flap, ducking down for head clearance. Following, Stock and his colleagues found themselves outside once again and just ahead of them, a string of dim electric bulbs led to and across a narrow ravine, spanned by a narrow rope and bamboo walkway. Yet more sentries paired the entrance to this bridge which danced unpredictably as they crossed it. Stock could not see the bottom in the darkness, but a tiny glint not too far down showed that there was water running in it. Setting foot on firm soil and following Haruko along the flickering and sporadic line of bulbs, he could now hear the background sound of an engine, then the tinny sound of oriental music from a radio, then voices, lots of them. In less than three minutes and cresting a small rise across a cleared compound, they could see a relatively brightly lit multi-storied pyramidal stone building and, off to one side, several other structures were just about visible in the gloom. Haruko led them up the steps and this time the sentries snapped to attention as they passed.

There was no door through to the massive entrance and they entered a cavernous lobby, surrounded by tall pillars, decaying ornate furnishings and statues of mythical creatures. Creepers, moss, and other tendrils pervaded throughout what was once an ancient temple of some importance, but Haruko did not pause to look up, as the others did, but continued directly across the uneven flagged ground towards a galleried archway at the far end. On his way across the enclosed courtyard, Stock noted that on at least one level there were guards patrolling the inner balconies. He was looking for some indication that Akiko and the more important families, including the general's, had been billeted within these walls. There was a glimmer of light.

Under the archway, Haruko led them off to the right and into some sort of antechamber, paused for them all to catch up in front of a wide door where a pair of sentries 'clipped' to attention. "Wait here." He turned and used his weight to open the heavy door into what the others saw as another large room and watched Haruko as he in turn brought himself to attention and completed his half-bow. What was said was out of earshot, but Haruko turned to them. "The general will see you now." He stood to one side as they entered. Stock was the last. Their path was half-blocked by a Japanese staff officer who greeted them with the same half-bow.

"I am Major Tadao, and I am your intermediary and interpreter. You will sit on this side of the table." His staccato English was not as good as Haruko's and carried a strong oriental accent with it. He led them smartly further into the room towards the right-hand side of a slab of a long stone table where three plain wooden chairs had been pulled out in preparation.

As Stock sat down, Haruko joined his compatriots on the other side. There were four of them, but one sat well back from the others in the shadows of the vast room, half in and half out of the edge of a curtain. Only the bottom half of his legs were directly in the light, and one could hardly make him out. Tadao, whose duties included introductions, continued, "You will tell the general who you are and what you do here." He looked pointedly at Deeks who was furthest from Stock.

"Major Deeks of the Royal Logistics Corps." He wanted to add more and then thought the better of it as Major Tadao commenced his translation.

"I am John Corston, attached to Brigadier General Alfredson's headquarters from the Foreign Office. I am here to see the smooth transition of protocols on behalf of His Majesty's Government." He patted a rather small leather attaché case that he had just placed on the table in front of him. "I have here with me the documents that will provide the handover of military powers from General Keisuke to General Alfredson, which will be ratified by Colonel Stock here." He had diplomatically avoided the term 'surrender', and looked over to Stock to signify that it was now his turn.

"Colonel Stock of the Fourteenth Army, sir." He had nearly blurted out his old rank and was glad that Corston had given him an official role, and a reason for being at the table.

The interpreter rattled on. After a short pause and a nod from Keisuke, he continued, "The Honourable General Keisuke does not extend a welcome but assures you that while you are here you are under his protection." While the latter part of this statement was self-evident, the former was a reminder of the typical two-edged sword that had become synonymous with the Japanese. Keisuke now spoke for the first time. The soft timber of his voice was unexpected and seemed to carry naturally, almost reverberating off the cavernous walls. It was as though there were two of them talking in almost perfect unison, and even though his mouth moved, his words appeared to emanate from behind his head. He was seated upright with his forearms resting on the edge of the table, his fingers concatenating. His steady eyes did not waver from Corston's, and his first words were eagerly awaited, even though they were through Major Tadao.

"Never in my wildest dreams could I foresee this day when I would be sitting across the same table as my enemy, and talking about what we are about to discuss. For generations, both of our countries have been seeking to expand because of one of the most basic human instincts that is in every one of us: greed. The advent of modern machinery has shrunk the world and brought us crashing together head-on, like two bull elephants each trying to dominate the herd. If one of us does not turn away before the final blow, then one of us will be mortally wounded. I have carried out my Emperor's wishes for many years now. From China to Indonesia, I have blindly pursued his dreams of Empire to rival that of your King's without any thoughts of failure. Blindness is an affliction of the weak and I am now beginning to see that the politicians who advise our Emperor are themselves afflicted and baring their own fangs of greed. My Emperor commands my total loyalty, and I will still carry out his every command, but through my intimacy with him I have detected a change. The orders that come from high command no longer carry his personal thoughts, but those of others, and it is clear to me that his ideals have been compromised."

He paused, waiting for Tadao to catch up, but the slight downturn in his voice was betraying his emotion.

"I am not a greedy man and I have no thoughts for further advancement. Indeed, I am most grateful for the chances that have come my way to place me here in the position I am in, and it is mainly because my Emperor has decided such. I therefore owe him my life and I would sacrifice it if he commanded. I wish I could be with him now. To assure him, to help him, to tell him 'Command me and I will obey'. But I am here, in Burma, many miles away at his behest, and I miss his presence."

He had remained quite still throughout his oration, almost oblivious to Tadao, but he continued.

"I write to him almost daily now, and perhaps this is a sign of my weakness. I assure him that I will succeed, but this is becoming more and more difficult when your forces are pushing us backwards and strangling our supply lines, so I can no longer lie to him."

He paused to swallow.

"I understand that people refer to your Fourteenth Army as 'The Forgotten Army' but I think this also refers to us. We seem to be in our own private war in this jungle, all of us cut off from the rest of the world, except for the occasional direction from above that tells us to beat you, quicker, and in the next breath denies us the troops or equipment to do so. These are the people who dare not come here to see the reality of this place and are the same afflicted people who tell the Emperor that we will succeed, and they are wrong. They tell us that we are carrying out tactical withdrawals in the Pacific Islands so that we can draw the Americans into a trap and destroy them. The food and oil shortages at home are so that our troops can enjoy the very best we can offer. They tell of our victories here in Burma but not of the losses, and it is they who are deceiving our Emperor. Even with his divine powers how can he be able to foresee the future that is not reality? What is now happening to Germany, I do not want to see happen to Japan, and for the unafflicted, this is what is happening."

Keisuke now sat forwards resting his elbows on the table. Nobody else moved and his lowered voice now carried a warning.

"I have heard that America has developed a super bomb that can destroy an entire country with just one blow. I have heard that it will soon be ready, and I have heard that it will soon be tried out on Japan. How can an educated man ignore this threat?" It was a rhetorical question and he briefly cast his gaze on Stock, presumably because he was a military man and not a civilian.

Stock saw a man with whom he empathised. His verbal display of loyalty that probably his own staff had not even seen, portrayed him as someone who you would want on your side if the going got rough, and it seemed now that the choices Keisuke faced were as rough as they were going to get. Stock wondered what he would do if the tables were turned and shuddered at the thought.

"We all know the purpose of your being here, but you will not succeed unless you can convince me that what I have said is true."

The two-edged sword had reared its head again and the two choices were very polarised. If Corston denied the existence of the bomb, then there would be no surrender. If he admitted that it existed, it could mean an early end to the war. It could also be a ruse to obtain the information that Keisuke lacked, and he would be responsible.

Corston was very uneasy at being put on the spot and the long silence that followed was almost deafening with repercussions. Diplomat he may have been but perhaps this was beyond his capabilities. He did not have the authority to reveal this kind of information, and in any case, all he had heard himself was also just a rumour. He needed non-existent time to think this through, but it was his turn to speak, and he was not sure if he could say the right things that would convince Keisuke.

Stock could see what was going through Corston's mind. It was the same as his. But Corston was probably just the type of politician that Keisuke distrusted, and anything he said might not be believed. Keisuke had previously looked at Stock just once, but that would have to be enough.

"I believe I can convince you," Stock's voice cut through the atmosphere like an arrow.

There was an aghast look on Corston's face, which quickly dissipated when he realised that he had just gained some time.

Keisuke tilted his head slightly, separated his arms and lowered them to the table as he changed his stare to Stock. It was not a staring contest, but more of a search for an insight into each other's thoughts. An invisible probe that could determine the outcome. "Perhaps you can, Colonel."

Stock's assessment of Keisuke while he had been talking revealed that he was probably not a man who would be easily convinced, nor someone who would take precipitous action. He considered that Keisuke's oration had been well thought out and mulled over for some time. Alfredson had told them about the bomb and Stock hoped the lies he was about to tell Keisuke would not be detected. He would have to gamble.

"General, I have to assume that you know who I am and what I have been doing." He paused for any sort of reaction but there was none. "The airfields I have been building have mainly been of a standard length, but I was called away before I could finish the last one. It is a double runway to be almost three times the normal length and reinforced to take B29s."

This was too much for Corston, giving vital tactical information away to the enemy. He almost screamed at Stock, "Colonel, how can you...."

"Be quiet, Corston." The bite in Stock's voice silenced Corston immediately. He didn't even look at him but continued his stare at the general opposite.

"Additionally, I have had to build larger camouflaged bunkers with walls strong enough to hold oversized gantries for lifting very heavy bombs. The fuel depot is partially underground, and the tractor sheds are also oversized. Mine is not to reason why." He did not add 'mine is but to do or die' as per the saying. "But it is clearly designed to take the largest planes, carrying the heaviest load possible. I understand that the bomb is very powerful indeed and what other possible purpose would a forward airfield such as this have, other than to provide facilities for just this weapon? For the first time, I have had to construct overhead refuelling arms that are clearly dedicated to heavy bombers and mid-air refuellers."

He waited for Tadao to catch up.

"I am not an aviation expert, but I believe this airfield may be within striking distance of the more Southern Japanese Islands and certainly forward enough to act as a refuelling and rearming base for such a weapon. I was ordered to have this airfield operational at the shortest possible moment, and certainly by the end of May." He added. "I was hoping to complete it two weeks earlier but that is not going to happen now."

At least part of what Stock had said was true and, as his latest airfield had not been discovered yet, he hoped there would be enough doubt in Keisuke's mind.

Once Tadao stopped speaking, Keisuke continued to hold Stock's gaze for a long while before responding.

"Colonel, if you are the man who I think you are then I must congratulate you on being so efficient. You have been a thorn in my side for some time. Your airfields have been the one single item that has been responsible for our need to angle our lines to suit. We have been unable to stop General Wingate from producing his heavy guns so far forward, and so quickly. As soon as we discovered and destroyed one of your airfields, another would crop up, even behind our own lines. You are a brave man. I must agree with you that your latest project seems untactical for this theatre of operation and I must consider this further. After all, this may be but a smoke screen."

Stock could see the logic behind Keisuke's thinking, but he still had more to add. "I think if I were in your position, I would also be sceptical, but before we left General Alfredson's headquarters, he spoke to me in private. The others had left the room, and he told me that you would probably demand some sort of proof of the bomb. I am afraid that I cannot offer you any proof, but it does demonstrate the gravity of this situation when a general discloses this kind of delicate information to an inferior. He authorised ONLY ME to let you know about the bomb." Stock paused for a short while and added, "Colonel Haruko can confirm this happened." Stock also hoped that the looks on both Corston's and Deeks's faces would back up his story. They did.

Keisuke leaned forward to look down the table at Haruko who nodded in assent. Surely, thought Stock, he must at least acknowledge that all the evidence led to the one conclusion that was sought. Stock now noticed that Keisuke's previous upright posture had slipped and that his shoulders were slightly drooped. Was this in response to recognition of what he had suspected or just weariness? Difficult to tell. Perhaps just more straw on the camel's back would do it.

"General. I dare not presume to know your thoughts, but when an enemy colonel from the deepest parts of the jungle sits in front of me and tells me that he knows one of the best-kept secrets of the war, I think I would be wise to heed that knowledge. From your own network of informants, you have heard of this bomb and its destructive power. The question I think you must answer is 'Is everybody wrong?' If the answer is no, then, in your own words, one must not be afflicted."

The deep silence seemed to intensify the depression that was creeping over Keisuke, and Stock almost felt pity for the once proud General whom he could almost feel had now conceded. He proved correct. Keisuke must have known this moment had been coming even before he had contacted Alfredson.

"I am in command of over 80,000 soldiers who would die for their Emperor if I commanded them to do so. Faced with what you have told me, I will not give that order, nor will I give the order to surrender. That is the ultimate dishonour. I know you are preparing an assault up the Khandi Valley soon and I think we know with which regiments. No doubt they will be using one of your forward airfields?"

Stock needed only a moment to remember how long ago he had been in the Khandi Valley. "Quite possibly," he responded.

"We are of course preparing to repel them especially as this thrust will threaten our last main supply line." He paused for a while to reflect. "But all this is insignificant compared to the power of your bomb which now threatens to destroy our entire way of life and my thoughts turn to an honourable solution. Not just for ourselves, but for..."

Keisuke continued with a monologue that went on for almost half an hour. Despite the intensity of the moment, Stock was not the only one on his side of the table who was having trouble concentrating, and his thoughts turned to the problem of how to locate Akiko if indeed she was here. Surely, she would be housed in the same building as Keisuke? Very possibly she was in this very one. He knew very little Japanese, but he had to assume that she spoke English. He slipped his hand into his pocket to finger the signet ring that Alfredson had given him and hoped that its mere production to her would say a thousand words. When he did find her quarters, he had to assume she would have at least one, if not two, female attendants, but thought it unlikely that they would share the same bedroom. He had noted that the outside of the temple had numerous balconies, particularly on the second and third levels, but getting up there, and more particularly, getting down again was a problem. Access to those levels was going to have to be made from the inner verandas and he would somehow have to detach himself from this party. Which door would lead to Akiko's quarters? If he at least knew that he would somehow find a way out and back to the plane. One other matter that had crossed his mind, but he could no longer defer, was what if she refused to come with him? Could he knock her out and physically carry her to the plane? He was still putting off making that decision.

Stock re-focused on the discussion between Corston and the general who had been putting the interpreter to full use for the past hour, but Stock felt that the timbre of their voices betrayed more and more discord. He butted in.

"Sir, may I suggest that we adjourn to consider the proposals so far."

It all went very quiet while Keisuke looked squarely at Stock. "Colonel, I think that perhaps you missed your true vocation. Your diplomatic corps could use your services. We will continue in one hour." As Keisuke stood, followed smartly in unison by Tadao and Haruko, Stock, Deeks and Corston did likewise, but in the English fashion and not together. The fourth Japanese officer in the background silently got up and disappeared further into another room without being seen. 'Who is he?' thought Stock. 'Possibly Kempeitai, the Japanese secret police?'

As Keisuke and Haruko marched off, Tadao addressed them. "Do not go from this room."

Chapter 13

A Holiday

Today

"You're going on a holiday," commented one of the nurses condescendingly in response as they escorted Bristow to his bedroom.

"Holiday. What for? Never been on holiday in my life. Why would I want to go on holiday?" Bristow had calmed down a little as they entered the coolness of the building but was still rather belligerent.

Most of the staff tried to avoid Bristow whenever they could due to his spiky personality. Two male nurses that now accompanied him up to his bedroom had had little contact with him and were not familiar with his idiosyncrasies, other than his reputation of startling everyone with his booming voice.

The older nurse tried a more diplomatic approach. "More of a rest, really, but we're taking you back to your room. Do you want to go to the toilet?"

Bristow shook his head while shuffling down the corridor between his two chaperones. "Can't remember going on holiday before. What's it like?"

The younger nurse persisted with the holiday idea. "I always go on holiday whenever I can. It helps me relax and I think you ought to try it. I remember."

By the time they reached his bedroom and sat him in the armchair most of the steam had gone from Bristow and he had returned to his normal self. Listening to the young chap rattle on in his dulcet tones had somehow placated him and, in any case, he was feeling rather tired. The senior Sister's visit a few minutes later, as was required whenever one of the patients became violent, was almost unnecessary as he was starting to drift off to sleep, but she directed one of the nurses to stay with him until supper time.

Bristow was on holiday.

*****

I'm not going on holiday, was Roger's depressing thought for the morning, at least not a proper holiday. In recent years and with the kids at the right age they had rented a three-bed cottage near Kingsbridge in Devon in the remote village of East Portlemouth for a fortnight each Summer. Perched nearly 300 feet above the sea on a steep cliff, it had wonderful scenic views overlooking the Salcombe Estuary from where they would enjoy watching the comings and goings of the many types of mainly sailing boats. Most years, depending upon the weather, they would hire a small one themselves and the kids had grown up under the illusion that there really was a type of boat called a 'putt-putt'. The previous year Roger had put his name down and paid for a seminar in Blackpool dedicated to the smaller bed & breakfast fraternity. Susan had suggested that it would present him with an opportunity to keep up with the latest developments and legislation in the B&B world. It had been postponed due to the heavy snowfall in January and he had just opened a letter notifying him that this had been re-scheduled for this August. It was only a three-day seminar and perhaps they could all go while he attended what he had already paid for while Susan and the kids could enjoy the seaside delights of Blackpool. Some holiday, Roger thought again as he looked forward to the proper holiday the following month in Devon.

They couldn't both go as they had already some confirmed guests for that week so Susan had made the decision that she would stay behind with the kids while Roger would go to the seminar by himself.

"Going by train makes more sense and once you get there, you're not going to need a car anyway. It's probably going to be a boozy affair and you'll probably forget where you left it in any case. Even if you did find it again, you'll probably manage to lose the keys." She took delight in reminding Roger of the time when he had gone on the very alcoholic Easter cricket tour to Yorkshire and had returned by coach with the rest of the team, forgetting that he had driven up. When he did return to collect the car, he had found that he had left his keys back at home and he had spent the best part of three days just going up and down the country just to get his car back.

"Ok. I give in. But I won't know anyone up there and it's not like the rest of the team are going to be there egging me on."

"It won't be long before you come across someone you know, and you'll end up in the bar afterwards and forget where you came from. Go and enjoy yourself. I can manage here fine."

"As long as I don't have to eat that 'icky-thump' stuff for breakfast. He was referring to the black pudding made from congealed pig's blood and offal that made an automatic appearance on every breakfast plate in that part of the world.

"I'm sure you'll live." Susan was unsympathetic in her retort as she walked out of the room to go and prepare one of the bedrooms. "And make sure you take your phone charger with you this time. Anyway, it's not for a few days yet so you've got plenty of time to find it." Roger started to mutter to himself but then froze, as he really couldn't remember where he had left his own phone a few days ago.

On her way through the hall, Susan answered the cordless phone as it rang. "Twinings B&B."

"Susan. I'm so glad I got you and not Roger. How are you?" It was unmistakably her school friend Victoria; nobody else greeted her on the phone like that and in any case, her unique cheery voice gave her away, so she never bothered to introduce herself. She had married Simon, an established but up-and-coming banker, a few years ago and still lived happily with him in a small mansion on the outskirts of Winchester. She and Susan still met two or three times a year at some 'Do' or other and they got on like a house on fire, fuelled quite often by an excess of alcohol. Her only slightly annoying trait was that she couldn't stop talking and was oblivious to this when it came to butting in. She didn't give Susan much of a chance to answer. "We've just got back from The Canaries. Spent a week out there at Gordon's villa. You remember Gordon don't you, you know, the one…"

It took a while before she paused enough for Susan to get a word in, but she eventually got to the point of her phone call. "Listen. Simon's up for promotion and he may be appointed to the Board Of Directors, but it looks like he's going to have to be at work the whole of next weekend. Well, not really work as he's been invited up to the Chairman's country estate near Cheltenham and he thinks he's going to be offered the position. I told him you can't turn that down so bugger off and get your promotion. Here, if he gets it, it means more champagne. Hee. Hee."

Susan was delighted at the news as tall, dark, handsome Simon was one of her favourites. She sat down on the bed in the room she was supposed to be preparing, since every time Vicky rang it took at least half an hour.

"Now, this weekend, we're celebrating the new holiday and I organized a spa hotel and an Ann Summers evening. Can you come?" Hee. Hee. At the innuendo. "So far, I've got Erica, Paula, Janie, and Lotty, and there's space for two more. Do say you can make it. They've got a new range of rabbits and the woman I've been in touch with said that I was to make sure that everybody there has a very open mind, and you were one of my first thoughts. Oh, do come. Hee hee…"

Susan had heard about these Ann Summers evenings and had secretly always wanted to join in on one but had never had the courage to ask if anyone was having one. Vicky was still talking but Susan was only half listening to her description of the sexual delights that the Ann Summers woman was going to bring along. She realised that it was the same weekend that Roger was going to be away, and she was thinking of who she might be able to get to babysit for the night; perhaps Sarah from the village?

"Well, Roger's off to a seminar at The Grand in Blackpool that night and we have some guests to attend to as well as looking after the kids, and…"

"Don't let these trivial things get in the way, come over and enjoy yourself. You'd best stay both nights, one at the hotel and the other here; I'll have a bed for you as you're coming furthest, oh, and don't forget to bring a change of outfit or two. I've heard that these evenings can get a bit messy. We need to get to the spa early as I've booked the whole day and it's all on Simon's firm. Hee hee."

Susan made her mind up and decided she would definitely go. It was not that she needed much persuasion, and the timing was more or less about right, but she thought she had better not tell Roger, at least not this year. Sarah was delighted to be asked to babysit and look after the B&B for the night and Susan said she would let her know the exact timing etc.

*****

The Reverend Huw Lister was the vicar of the local church, and it was incumbent on him to attend Springfields whenever one of the patients was about to pass away. He had received a phone call from Mr Green a short while ago, even though he was preparing to leave for his annual holiday later that day.

"You're too late," said a bored-looking Natalie before he had even crossed the threshold of the front doors. "Mr Watts snuffed it about an hour ago and the doctor's been and gone."

He paused in his pace as he approached Natalie's desk, half-considering whether or not to just turn around, but as he now had time on his hands perhaps he could spend some of it with some of the others who were not looking quite so healthy. He came across a lonely Stock in the corner of the patio reading the Financial Times. "Good morning. Do you mind if I join you?"

Stock lowered one corner of the pink paper enough to see someone who was obviously from the religious fraternity and beckoned him to a matching chair next to him.

Huw introduced himself as the Vicar of St. Margaret's. He was a fifty-five-year-old bachelor who had covered three local churches for the past ten years or so and was quite content with his occupation. "I've seen you once before, but I don't think you've been here very long, have you?"

Stock was in an ebullient mood and weighed up if it would be better to give a short answer or a cheeky one; just to test the man's sense of humour and to see if he was worth talking to.

"That depends upon how long one has to live." This brought a smile to Huw as he sat down. Stock continued "I once had a friend who used to count the number of days he had left. When I first met him, it was in the region of 10,000 and thirty years later he still maintained that he had 5,000, and that was the day before he passed away. How many have you got left?"

"I've never counted." His arithmetic relating to the inevitable outcome was not one of the foremost thoughts in his mind. "It wasn't that long ago that the biblical 'three score years and ten' seemed a bit of a luxury but with today's modern drugs, it's a bit on the lean side. You're obviously enjoying your days." Probing Stock as to his age.

They continued talking about the lighter things in life and Huw was delighted to find someone in the Home who could not only keep up with him without him having to repeat himself but also provide him with mental exercise. One of the nurses emerged through the French windows with two cups of tea and some biscuits perched on the saucers. "Here you are and there's only one sugar for you, Reverend, as you told me last time that you were trying to cut down."

Stock was grateful for the refreshment in the gathering warmth of the day. "I was on a cruise liner once; my Father had taken us all to see the Norwegian Fjords in RMS Majestic, I think it was, and it held about a thousand passengers. The captain took my brother and me to see the marvels of the control room, what we would now call the bridge. It was directed from that one little control room at the top of the ship with its thousands of tonnage of weight, and if anything went seriously wrong with that little office, some thousand souls might perish. It occurred to me then, and again now, how like we are to that ship. Your brain is that control room directing your actions so that your actions can only be what your brain decides. From that viewpoint, it becomes very clear that our brains might be studied and attended to. You know what happens to muscles which are not used, don't you? They become useless and wither. The same thing happens to the brain."

Huw was enthralled by the logic Stock was displaying, and so far, he couldn't fault it. He wondered where Stock was going with his story, so he let him continue without interruption.

"Why some people seem cleverer than others is because they are using all of their brains constantly, but the majority of people only use one-eighth, and there are some whose brains have gone rusty through disuse. The astonishing thing is that the more you think the more you can, and therefore the brain has no limitations. Select problems and study them, impersonal problems. Not those that make you dwell on yourself; that often leads to depression, but, for instance, how would you increase sales if you were Mr Branson or if you were in charge of the government? How would you make the country more prosperous? But the poor old brain cannot successfully produce or exercise alone; it needs lubrication and nourishment." He paused to sip his tea while Huw took in what Stock was saying, not noticing that Stock was giving his own brain what it needed but was prompted.

"These vital things," said Stock, indicating his hovering cup, "are supplied to it by you, but not only in the form of physical things. It requires the right thoughts to feed it, to stimulate it and the right action results. You cannot do anything without the right thinking. The chicken-hearted throw up the battle before it has had a chance to be interesting while the courageous get the fun of the fight and the fruits of victory. That courage is necessary in all walks of life. For example, it takes courage to walk alone into a crowded hall for the first time and the same sort of courage to defend one's principles when all are against you. Courage has a sister: staying power. And that is what the British race is noted for. Clinging to the reins of a runaway horse when all others have dropped behind when one desperately wants to let go."

Stock leaned forward, arching his hands together and resting his elbows on the table. "So, you must decide to adopt courage and its sister staying power before your life is through. You will want them at your service for whatever reason, so you had better get to know them both. If you can stick it out when everyone had fallen behind and stay there until your heart is bleeding with despair, you will win."

He sat back, taking his cup in hand as he did so. "On its own, the brain can do some very useful work for you by producing original ideas. I have never accepted the fact that because a thing has been done one way in the past, it must continue that same way. I have always tried to find a better, quicker, more efficient method. That is how ideas and inventions which have revolutionised the world have come about."

Huw was agog at the profound statements that emanated from the centenarian in front of him. He had trouble keeping up. These were not the ramblings of an old fogey but carefully considered thoughts. "You've obviously had plenty of time to think things through and it shows that you have endured suffering at some point in your life. It's an optimistic view of life that you are portraying, but what about your regrets?

"One only really remembers the more enjoyable moments of one's life when asked a question like that, even then when one is in an introspective mood. I am sure everybody can reflect on moments of horror that we choose to ignore. I know I do. I was just reading about the results of a new wonder drug that has been granted approval by NICE, it says here." Stock looked at the page he had been reading a few minutes earlier. It has all the attributes of being able to roll back the effects of Alzheimer's disease thus enabling us all to remember our childhood.' Would you choose to remember just the fond memories and suppress those moments of anguish? That surely is utopian."

A worried look came over Huw's face as he felt he was clearly in the presence of a sage whose mind was every bit as active as his, and perhaps more so. He hadn't been expecting this kind of retort to a simple question and he shifted himself more upright in his chair. This was someone whose opinions he could value. "I'm inclined to agree with you, but we're not given the choice these days." He waved his hand. "This establishment's sole purpose is to keep you alive as long as possible and if that means giving you a drug to do that, then so be it. You're right though. When I think back to when I was small, the first thing I remember is looking up fondly at my parents and being in the company of my older brother, but if I think hard enough, I can also remember the way he died on the farm, under the wheels of a tractor. It's not something I care to think of first. I was lucky enough to have missed the war, but I presume you must have seen some of the horrors, and from what you have just said you are able to inhibit those memories in preference to others."

Huw thought he could see Stock struggling with his inner self; a fight between those good and evil thoughts. What has he done? Is this to be some sort of confession? Stock closed his eyes cutting off their eye contact.

"I shot down a Japanese Zero once above one of my airfields. He must have been lost and discovered us by chance. We were well out of the way." Stock was narrating in a sombre voice. "He circled us a couple of times so he could see the layout. The machinery and fuel were off at one end and the village was at the other end. He chose the village end and started shooting it up. Again, and again aiming at the fleeing villagers. All I had was an old Lewis gun mounted on my

Jeep, but I managed to shoot him down and he landed quite close. I had not seen the enemy this close before and, as I got nearer, I could see he was covered in his own blood and trapped in his seat. I think I must have hit him in the shoulder because he was clutching at it with his other hand, screaming in agony. Fire was starting to run back from the engine, and he was choking on the fumes that emerged from the cockpit as I climbed onto the wing. He looked directly at me with hate in those bloodshot yellow eyes, crying from the thick acrid smoke, and it felt like I could see right into the foulness of his inner soul. He shouted venom and spittle at me in defiance. I was not only angry at what he had just done to all those unarmed Coolies, their wives, their sons and daughters, those who had been loyal to me and looked to me to be their provider and protector. I was vengeful."

Huw could see that Stock's hands were gripping the arms of the metal-framed garden chair. "He could not get out of his seat even though he tried, and I just stood there looking down on him asking why? Why had he killed those Coolies when I was his real target? My airfield, my equipment all safe, but he chose to take the lives of those who could not fend for themselves. What gave him the right to pick on them and not me? He was a bully, a coward, and had no right to live any longer." Stock paused. "He was dying anyway and now it was up to me to decide how he was going to meet his death. I could leave him to burn, or die from his injuries, so I drew my revolver and shot him."

Insects overlooking the pair of them lightly buzzed in the heavy air under the shade of the walnut tree. Stock opened his eyes and there was fire in them. "It was a mercy killing and that is the only way I can live with myself. You see, everything has a right to live from the smallest ant to the biggest elephant, but it is only the nature of humans that decides otherwise and has dominance over all around it. It is mother nature's way of saying the strong survive and the weak perish. I remember a few seconds before I had decided to shoot him and put him out of his misery, that it was the right thing to do. I think that was the most harrowing moment of my life. Something that one never forgets but chooses not to remember."

Stock was silent while he reflected upon one particular moment in his long life. He had told a few others of how he had downed a Japanese Zero but not anybody else before about his feelings on the matter.

This was not the first time that Huw had been given such an insight into someone else's darkest emotions. From the way it had been described to him, he did not feel that there was any need to offer any mitigation, but he felt he had to say something. "I too think you did the right thing, and I don't think that any considered reason anybody can come up with would class what you did as being evil. Everybody has God on their side when it comes to war, but at the end of the day, it is all about what we truly feel in our own hearts. A matter of good against evil....eh?"

Stock was glad that this religious man was not preaching to him but instead seemed to share his own ideals. "It may surprise you to know that I am not a confirmed Christian."

Huw raised his eyebrow and was indeed surprised, but let Stock continue.

"I do not believe that there is a God....or Gods... I can see you are perplexed, and I am sorry if I disappoint you, but I am just one of nature's creatures like the ant or the elephant but at least I can control my own convictions without outside influence. Can you?"

Huw sat back and crossed his legs. "That's a very difficult question. What outside influences were you thinking of?"

"You mentioned good and evil. I prefer to justify my own thoughts and actions and live with the consequences of the power of good. Yes, there is evil there, but I still wake up every morning and believe in the power of good. The power to help others and one's fellow man. The power to overcome difficulties. The power not to become, as many in the world have, but to decide to rise above those who struggle to get ahead in this world by purely selfish means. I have the right to decide my own destiny but at no cost to others. I can decide what is right and wrong in my own mind without being told how to do it by some ecclesiastic, and I can sleep soundly at night, knowing that I am at peace with myself."

"I remember the words of the first verse of just one hymn, and then only because my brother-in-law was captain of a minesweeper during the War. When we attended his funeral, we sang about the sea as it was his love, but I will not sing it for you now and I am sure you will not want to hear my rusty voice. I have forgotten who wrote those words, but you too will recognise the hymn."

<blockquote>
Eternal Father strong to save
Whose arm hath bound the restless wave
Who biddest the mighty ocean deep
Its own appointed limits keep
Oh hear us when we cry to thee
For those in peril on the sea
</blockquote>

"I loved that man, and that night I sat alone in my room and mourned his death, considering the meaning of those words and it helped me clarify my place on this earth and whether I ought to look to God for comfort or elsewhere. It implies that He is omnipotent yet cannot control the limit of the ocean and it follows that on a wider aspect, the whole world. Why would He create such a thing and then leave it to its own devices and why would He listen when we cry?" Stock was staring at an earwig scuttling its way towards him across the top of the table. "If I were to crush that earwig, do you think God would listen? And if he did listen....to whom? The earwig or me?"

"Up to that point in my life, I had been taught to trust God and I decided then that it was only His principles that needed trusting, not the interpretation of others. I draw my strength from my own understanding of the power of good."

Huw was gracious enough to accept this man's argument but in his own mind he was firmly convinced of the preachings he advocated to others. On the other hand, he had to admit that Stock's outlook on life had merit and he didn't have to rely on God to provide succour - he had his own. "What will you do when your thousands of days are up? Will you turn to anyone?"

Stock brushed away a wasp that was hovering above his right arm. "Those Coolies looked up to me as though I was their God. Before I entered their world, they worked in their own paddy fields every day with their Families and had an innocent way of life. They were poorer than church mice, but they were content and always smiling, and the most trivial event would occasion a cheer from them. In the short time I was there I had given them a glimpse of another way of life, one that they had never experienced. I organised them to build better irrigation and toilets, gave them medicine, taught them another language, and opened up their minds to what was beyond their valley and their own comprehension. I paid them a pittance of forty rupees a week to build an airstrip and all the while I supplied them with more food than they could eat, and it did not take them long to look on me as someone to look up to. To them, I had been sent to look after them and their trust in me was absolute. It was a bitter blow to me that I could not save those who had been killed by that Zero, and I learned many things that day. They had turned to me as their God to look after them and I failed, so in turn, why should I look to a God who has so far promised that I shall live forever, yet my life on this earth has a finite date?

"No. When my time is due, I do not think I will turn to anyone other than myself and I shall do so convinced in myself that I have been a good man. Perhaps my ancestors are waiting for me, perhaps not. I do not know if they are there looking down on me now or if they exist at all, but if they do, I will join them knowing that I have done the right things in my life." He closed his eyes again as though this was his final decision, but he needed the rest in any case.

Huw just sat there looking at a man who had spent a lifetime building up his own convictions and, even though it was probably his duty, he could not even fathom how he would go about converting those cast iron ideals. Ideals that were based in common with those of Christianity, yet founded on experiences from just one lifetime, and yet would that be the right thing to do to someone who was nearing the end of their days? He felt that there was more to come from this man and that he had hardly scraped the tip of the iceberg and decided to remember what Stock had said about the power of goodness in his next sermon. The crinkled lines on a sleeping Stock's face exuded an air of serenity and to Huw, portrayed the perfect depiction of one who was at complete peace with themselves, so he just sat there for several minutes looking and wondering if he could attain the same when it came to his time.

It was time to go on holiday, but he resolved to return to continue their conversation, so he got up and went to go inside, but paused by the French windows as a worrying thought crossed his mind. What if Stock converted him?

Chapter 14

Uniform

The mixture of Razadyne II and Calpol had slipped through the experimental net as the results of such an unlikely concoction had not shown up in the trials, and certainly not in the likes of Stock. Concentration in a blinkered sort-of-way was becoming increasingly easy, but still, the connection of time and place was elusive. He had no way of knowing that his mental and physical afflictions were caused merely by old age and most of the time he didn't realise that he was in a Home, only that he was home. The characters of people around him changed haphazardly, and even their faces took on the appearances of those from his distant memories. A well-trained psychoanalyst, even with the help of a frontal lobotomy, would not have been able to discover either the cause or symptoms.

Over the next few nights and as often as not while he was sleeping in one of the day chairs, Stock tried to make sense of his troubled dreams. His mind became more and more active from the daily tea, but however hard he tried, he couldn't put the events into chronological order. One minute he was living out a dream when he was cruising among the Norwegian Fjords playing deck quoits with his parents, and the next minute he was back in his hometown, building a brick wall with his favourite trowel. He remembered one of his favourite tricks he used to play on a newcomer navvy on one of the sites. He would announce that they had to mix a load of mortar very quickly, and while directing the gang, announce that they needed some 'wet cement' and he'd send the poor youth off to the stores to ask for a bag of 'wet cement'. Old Bill in the stores was wise to this, and the poor breathless lad would return to the site having carried a hundredweight of nothing but water for some considerable distance, the further the better. They all stood around laughing seeing the look on the lad's face as he realised that his task was as fruitless as taking a bag of sand to the desert.

But his thoughts kept returning to Akiko, and Deeks, and Corston, always interrupted by getting up in the morning, having breakfast, lunch, tea, supper, going back to bed. As though in a trance with automation taking over, his higher brain functions were concentrating on, on, on, something he felt he still had to do.

The prompt finally came one lunchtime in July, once again from the ever-intrusive TV reaching out to Stock sitting in one of the easy chairs. The same pretty newscaster was hosting an hour-long, in-depth program about the new public holiday on 1st August just a few days away. The announcement about Peace Day earlier in the year had caught the attention of the entire world, and those governments who had previously put this down to a G8-led plan to boost their own economies had jumped on the now overcrowded bandwagon. Even the warring factions in the Middle East were taking it seriously, despite the French attempting to have the date changed at the last minute to coincide with their own Bastille Day. London would become the centre of the world just for one day, as almost every national leader would be in attendance for the ceremony to be held at The Cenotaph.

A relaxed Sir John Corston was once again in front of the cameras at the BBC. Relaxed because this time those dissenters from the previous occasion had melted away ahead of the onrush of goodwill that pervaded every aspect of the expected occasion. After a few short film clips from the two world wars, the camera switched back to the studio.

"Sir John, I understand that your father was in the Far East towards the end of the war. Did he have any stories to tell you, and how did you feel about his return after so many years of absence when you were growing up as a child?"

"Indeed. For some of the time he was stationed in Assam as a liaison officer between the British and Americans. I don't remember much as I was only a small child then, but I do remember his homecoming. Our family, along with hundreds, no thousands, of others were on Southampton docks when they disembarked and I remember looking up at an enormous ship, seeing the entire side full of troops waving to us. It was the first time I could remember meeting my father and it was a tremendous thrill being picked up and hugged by him."

"And what of his recollections of the war did he tell you about?"

"He wasn't in the front line but spent most of his time flying around the Far East theatre of operations, but he did tell me he was actually behind enemy lines in Burma on one occasion. He described the squalid conditions that the troops had to bear, particularly during the Monsoon when it rained incessantly."

She briefly looked down to her desk where a series of typed questions helped prompt her. "We've all heard about the apology for the treatment of allied prisoners-of-war that will be forthcoming from the Japanese Emperor. What difference do you think this will make to the few of those who are still alive?"

From Corston's perspective, this was the most delicate of subjects concerning the entire proceedings, which needed to be handled with the greatest of care. In fact, the entire 'raison d'être' hinged upon the apology being offered, and without it, it was possible that there would be the direst of diplomatic consequences worldwide. It was generally felt that it was now too late for the Japanese to withdraw the offer of their apology, but it could still not happen if the wrong thing was said at the wrong time. Time to earn his vast diplomatic salary.

"The difference will be of great significance, not just to those who still survive the war, but to those families whose parents, uncles, brothers, and so on, continue to feel their loss. Even after all these decades, there remains an element of anguish."

"Is your father still alive, Sir John, and do you retain any animosity towards the Japanese?"

"No, he passed away some years ago, and I am just grateful that he managed to return safely from the war."

"I presume you will be at the Cenotaph ceremony, Sir John, but what will your role be there?"

"I am in a rather unique position as it was my father's side of the family who had links with the Japanese back then, and I have continued and nurtured those links since before my father retired from the civil service. I will personally be escorting the Japanese delegation headed by Mr Keisuke, from The Guildhall to The Cenotaph where the Queen and the other heads of state will carry out the formalities, including the offer of the apology from Emperor Akihito of Japan."

"Thank you, Sir John. We also have in the studio...."

She turned towards another gentleman, but Stock knew what he had to do, and it was now all clear in his own mind how he would do it. He would go to The Guildhall. He would rescue Akiko. He would return her to Alfredson. He would carry out his duty to King and Country.

First of all, though, he needed his uniform, and the mere thought of wearing it once again made him raise his head and put his shoulders back with pride. He had last left it hanging in his wardrobe and could see himself putting the cover over it: his hat in the cardboard box on the shelf above. The only problem he had was remembering where that particular wardrobe was, so he shut his eyes in an attempt to picture its location. Putting one's uniform away for the last time can be a very emotional moment, being the end of a chapter in one's life, the end and culmination of a career. It had had that effect on Stock at the time. Like that of a small boy selling his model train set to afford the latest Scalextric set, or a teenager selling his trusted bike to move up to a second-hand, well-used first car. He could see inside the room, and the sill under the window decorated with a half-empty ashtray of buttons, pins, and paper clips, framed by a pair of brown and white patterned curtains. Through the window was a man pushing a noisy lawnmower over the grass in the dappled sunlight.

He stopped briefly, ran a handkerchief across his brow, and turned to wave at the window, before returning to his enjoyable chore, and Stock recognised him as his son, Roger, and instantly felt at peace with himself. He wanted to go out there and help him, join in with him, and reassure him that he loved him, but he was interrupted by something pulling at his sleeve. Looking down he saw Goldie the retriever tugging his arm gently with his teeth down to canine level. The pulling became stronger, and Stock felt himself jerking, jerking.

"Grandpa, grandpa, wake up." Both Ann and Tom were in front of him, but it was Tom who was doing the shaking, while Ann was mini-jumping. Stock turned from dream to reality, and somewhere between the two states of mind, he made the connection that the two little 'uns in front of him were his grandchildren and that they lived just a short walk away, next door to where he lived, where his wardrobe was., where his uniform was. He could not understand what he was doing in Springfields, when his home, his life, were just around the corner.

"What have you done to your head? It looks funny. Hee hee." Jump. "Hee hee." Jump. "It looks like a Turman."

"Not Turman...Turbun." Tom's pronunciation emphasised the ... 'bun' part.

Stock was not quite 'with it' having just been woken but was now 'coming round' after his short nap.

"Just a fall," was all he could manage.

"We've been to the seaside," squeaked Ann with excitement in between landing back on solid ground occasionally. "And it was very, very windy and Mummy lost her hat. Hee heeee"

"Yes, and we found a cave with lots and lots of crabs in it, but I found these shells," said Tom, not to be outdone with the latest news. He reached into his pocket which seemed to be deeper than his arms were long and produced a handful of small snail-like empty shells. "Look at these." Offering them to Stock in his cupped hands.

He dutifully held out a hand to receive Tom's treasure, who tipped them into it. He could smell the sea air that came with them and focused on their differing shapes and colours, recalling when he had been to the seaside as a small boy and probably been just as excited. "How did you catch all of these?"

"We were in the rock pools next to the cave and there were thooooousands of them, and some of them were moving, and I found the biggest," said Tom, reaching further into his pocket to produce a fair-sized flatter shell. "And Dad says you can always hear the sea in it if you put it up to your ear. Here, listen." He shoved it against Stock's ear.

Ann bent over to listen as well, and as she did so knocked Stock's hand holding the shells, which now mostly scattered themselves onto the floor. Tom immediately bent down to retrieve his mementoes, and while doing so discovered one had sprouted legs and was running under Stock's chair. "Look, this one's still alive." Both kids were now grovelling around the floor trying to find others that might also be alive.

Stock was laughing to himself and eventually had the company of his grandchildren back, although they seemed more interested in looking closely into every shell to see if there were any others that had managed to cling to life, by tapping them on the table.

"Did you have any ice cream?"

"Raspberry."

"Chocolate."

"Did you know, your Great Uncle Guy never had ice cream until he was fourteen years old."

The look on their faces betrayed the answer, "Why not?"

"When we were your age, we went to Clacton-on-Sea, and we were each given one small ice cream tub with a wooden spoon, but do you know why Guy never touched his?"

Head shaking from the kids.

"He said, "I've never tried it, so I don't like it.""

Silence for a moment from the kids as they tried to comprehend Great Uncle Guy's words, and it was Ann who reacted first.

"But how did he know he didn't like it if he hadn't tried it?"

Tom immediately took the opposite view. "Because he hadn't tried it to find out, Silly."

"What happencd when he was fourteen?"

"He must have tried it."

"And did he like it?"

Stock was laughing at the common conundrum of 'which came first – the chicken or the egg'. He went on, "I would always eat his when we were given any, but one day, he just grabbed my tub and ate it all in one go. And do you know what?" More head shaking. "He ate so much ice cream that day that he was sick, but I think it was really the candy floss that made him sick."

"What's candy floss?"

"It's that sticky stuff on a stick, and I love it," said Tom smugly.

"Why haven't I tried it?"

"Oh look, here's another one that's alive." As one of the shells tried to escape the tabletop and landed on Ann's shoe. With a hop, skip, jump and a loud "Eeeeek" she danced out of the way as the mollusc legged it in search of much-needed water.

Susan had arrived at the same time as the kids but had been talking in the hallway corridor with Mr Green. They both now craned their necks around the doorway to see what all the kerfuffle was about; neither of them spotted the winkle as it disappeared under the skirting board. Susan finished her conversation with Mr Green and came over to join the rest of her family.

"What's been going on, you two?

"Nothing." In unison, but with a guilty look crossing Tom's face more than Ann's, as he assumed his mother would frown upon him bringing livestock into Springfields.

"You're looking well today, Bernard, apart from your new hat. Can you remember what happened?" Susan had walked behind his chair to inspect the hidden injury.

"Not really. Just woke up on the floor."

"Mr Green tells me it's nothing to worry about. How do you feel?"

"Had a headache a while ago, but that is gone now. They gave me something horrible for it. Reminded me of those pink prawns we used to pinch from Finches sweet shop."

Susan had spotted a handful of shells interspersed with sand grains on the table next to him and understood what had been happening. She knew Bernard better than to ask him if they had been pests and would never begrudge him those precious moments with his grandchildren.

"I've just been speaking with Mr Green, who is organising the annual outing to the County Agricultural Show in Hassocks tomorrow. He thinks you are ok to go, and I thought you might like to get out and enjoy a bit of fresh air, so I've put your name on the list, and apparently, some of the girls from Virgin Airways are coming along to help look after you. I think you'll also be visiting one of the local Harveys pubs, but I can't remember the name of it right now. You're ok with that, aren't you?" She was a bit apprehensive of Bernard's response, as this would be the first time he would be going on one of these trips, but she hoped that the mention of a pub visit ought to easily sway him.

It did.

"It's either the Spotted Dog or Cat, or maybe it had a stripe in its name, I can't remember, but the coach is leaving after breakfast, and you'll be back soon after teatime. Oh, and I'm off to Winchester for a couple of days to see an old-school friend. You probably don't remember Victoria. She came to our wedding, but I don't think you've seen her since.

Stock was not really listening, but subconsciously he took it in. He was thinking about what he had to do, and a thought crossed his mind. Yes, a day out.

"Do you want me to leave the kids with you a while longer? I need to pick up the dry cleaning before it shuts. Kids, another fifteen minutes only, and don't tire Grandpa out. He's got a busy day tomorrow." Nodding of heads.

She leaned over and pecked him on the cheek before leaving.

She had not even left the room before Tom was back on his hands and knees searching for the 'one that got away'.

To Stock, this was a God-sent opportunity, and he called Tom and Ann over to sit on his knees. "I have indeed got a busy day tomorrow. Can you two keep a secret?" he almost whispered.

More nodding of heads.

Have you ever been to London?"

Shaking of heads

"Would you like to come to London with me?"

Nodding of heads

"But don't say a word to anyone. Not even your mother. It will be our secret adventure, and I'll treat you to candyfloss."

"Yeeeaaaahh." And Ann started mini-bouncing on Stock's lap.

"Now shhhuuuuussshhh," said Stock in hushed tones. "Come back here after breakfast in the morning, but not a word to anyone."

"Can I bring my seashells? I've got more at home, and I can put them in my backpack."

"And can I bring my new handbag and skipping rope?"

"Of course, you can." Stock paused for a moment. "If you have got a camera, you can bring that too so that you can take some photographs."

"I got a new camera for Christmas," piped up Tom. "And it's got a really powerful zoom on it." He was now thinking about photographing his collection of seashells.

Stock cast his mind back to when his father had told them they were going on a tram ride for the first time the next morning, and how excited he felt. Why he remembered it had cost 'one and tuppence' he couldn't remember, but he didn't sleep a wink that night. Even now he could almost feel the pain from the 'thick ear' he'd received from his mother for not doing up his shoelaces properly, and how his brother Guy had laughed at him. But he too got a 'thick ear'.

"I think you had better get home now and remember, it's our little secret. Not a word to anyone."

"Yeeeaaaahh," screeched Ann, bouncing off Stock's lap, as

Tom swept up the remaining shells off the table into his hand and back into his pocket. "Bye, Grandpa. See you tomorrow."

Stock knew his own teatime was approaching, but before he became ensconced with Perry and Bristow he had one more task to perform. He got up out of his chair with the help of his stick and wandered off down the hall, towards the main reception desk. He knew how to get through the security doors but didn't want to alert the staff to the fact that he could, so he waited in a chair by one of the windows and it wasn't long before one of the day nurses paused en route to the kitchen.

"Good afternoon, Colonel, looks like you're waiting for a bus. Where are you off to?"

"Hello, Stephanie, and nice to see you again. I am waiting for Ron's Lad. Have you seen him?"

"Oh, yes. He's just outside watering the lawn."

"Can you ask him if he can come and see me?"

"Will do. Just let me drop these trays off in the kitchen. What do you want him for?"

"Dentures," replied Stock, grimacing.

Stephanie disappeared through one of the wooden doors, but Stock decided to stay put so that he could have a word with Ron's Lad in private when he came through. He passed the time trying to picture exactly what he had to do and was rather grateful that Tom and Ann would be with him. He felt up to the task probably through ignorance, as he couldn't foresee the enormity of what lay ahead. But then again, this was exactly the kind of situation that he had thrived on his whole life, and just because the unknown was in front of him, only made him react to resolve whatever it was. Overcoming problems and obstacles was what motivated him and, although now motivated, he was also misguided but not only just from his own narrow perspective.

He was brought back to life by the appearance of Ron's Lad who left a trail of water across the polished floor from his dripping trouser bottoms. "Hello, Colonel. Stephanie says your dentures need some of my special paste."

"No, it is not that, but I would like you to do something for me. I need to get a few things from my house, but I do not want to worry anyone. Would you mind pushing me down there in a wheelchair?" He could see the quizzical expression on the Lad's face, so continued, "I wanted to get my old uniform for Peace Day and surprise the others, but it is a bit too far for me to walk there and back with a suitcase."

Ron's Lad considered this request. Nobody had said he couldn't, and after all, he'd only be doing what some of the other Staff did on occasions – take the old folk out for a country 'walk' down to the Village.

"OK. Back in a minute." And he abruptly wheeled about in search of one of the numerous wheelchairs that were kept at the end of the corridor.

Stock had hardly had time to take in the suddenness of the acceptance of his request when he saw Ron's Lad returning, seated in an electric wheelchair. It was a robust type that had a joystick mounted on one of the arms and was approaching at high speed.

"Bbbrrrrrrrrrrr...Aaarrrrr...Eeeecccchhhh," as he brought it to a halt in front of Stock. "Jump in, Colonel."

Jumping was not an option, but Stock did as he was told as quickly as he could as Ron's Lad pressed the keypad on the security doors a few feet away and returned to take up his position in charge of the handles behind him.

"Don't know how good the battery is but this one also pushes easily." As they sailed through into the reception area. They got as far as the open front doors when they heard a cacophony of noise followed by a high-pitched scream from behind them. Ron's Lad glanced over his shoulder to see that Stephanie had fallen over on the slippery floor where a few moments ago he and his dripping trousers had been standing. She had been returning to the Day Room with a tray full of crockery in readiness for teatime and assumed that as she had passed there a few minutes earlier it wouldn't be slippery.

The cleaners were not in sight and there was no 'slippery when wet' sign out, so there was no reason to suspect that it would be.

Ron's Lad decided he and Stock ought not to be caught anywhere near the scene so continued down the ramp in short order. "If you push the joystick forwards it will make us go faster." And as Stock took control of the machine, he put his feet on the two anti-tip tubes that protruded from the back.

Stock knew the way and was learning fast how to guide the machine. He was enjoying himself retracing the steps he and Perry had made not so long ago; although it wasn't exactly a fast journey, it was considerably quicker than if he had had to walk, and he vaguely recalled some of the various cars he had driven in the past.

Before he knew it, he was drawing up alongside the hedge that abutted his house and steered the machine into the pathway through the open gate that led to his front door. "Here we are." Letting go of the joystick also seemed to act as a brake.

Ron's Lad had often passed Stock's house en route to the village but never realised to whom it belonged. "Nice lawn," he said lightly, scrubbing one of his shoes across the blades. "And no moss."

Stock had dismounted and now bent over to retrieve the door key from under the upside-down frogged brick to one side of the porch. He was glad it was still there and was relieved when it turned in the lock. The door opened nearly all the way until the bottom jammed against one of the uneven tiles just inside. "Come inside and make yourself a cup of tea. I won't be long." And he headed off through his sitting room towards his bedroom door on the other side.

He opened the door slowly, still not certain that this was where he had pictured his wardrobe, but sure enough there it was. An elegant 3-door walnut wardrobe with a mirror on the inside of the middle door. It would creak a little when opened fully and was adjacent to the same window through which he had pictured Roger. He leant his stick against one of the handles protruding enough from the adjacent chest of drawers and opened the middle and right-hand doors together. There, just where he had left it all those years ago, was his uniform covered with a transparent plastic cover. On the shelf above and perfectly positioned was the box that housed his peaked hat with a red band around it, and directly below on the shoe rack were his gaiters and boots in a transparent plastic bag. He pulled open the top drawer of the in-built row of drawers to reveal his Sam Browne and swagger stick, next to which was his webbed holster with his service revolver still in it. Next to these was a Kukri in a black leather holster, presented to him by the men in his regiment.

Stock just stood and stared, taking in the flood of memories that wafted out of the time capsule, his mind whirling with the familiar odour that accompanied him, and he unconsciously reached out and steadied himself against the top of the chest of drawers. He eventually opened the second wardrobe drawer and took out a rectangular black box, took two paces backwards, and slowly sat down on the edge of his bed. His hands were shaking just a little as he opened the spring-loaded lid to reveal a row of medals embedded into the supporting velvet. There were five of them with a corresponding set of Miniatures and Ribbons and he rubbed his thumb over each one in turn, starting with the OBE on the left.

"Colonel? Colonel?" Ron's Lad stood nervously in the doorway; he'd never been asked into someone else's house before, and he spotted Stock sitting worryingly still on his bed. "Colonel." No response so he walked quietly forward and shook him gently on the shoulder. "Colonel."

Stock gently closed the lid on his medals as though he was putting a child to bed and turned to look at Ron's Lad, not tears in his eyes, only a far-away look of one who no longer cares what fate will do to them.

"We really ought to be going back., They'll be missing us soon."

"Yes. Just give me a minute but hang on. Can you get a case from under the bed, yes, the brown leather one." Ron's Lad retrieved a rather beaten-up small suitcase with two straps and brass buckles towards each end.

"Thank you. Can you wait for me?" Ron's Lad reversed himself out of the room and went to wait outside while Stock packed his uniform, Sam Browne, and all the other items that went with them. He was just closing the doors, when he glimpsed the outline of his military dispatch box, almost the size of a shoe box, in the bottom right-hand corner, the key still in it. He opened it and, from within a grey sock, pulled out several rolled-up banknotes. 'Yes. I'll need some money,' he thought to himself as he put the sock in one of his shoes in the case and closed it. The removal of the grey sock exposed a small, ungummed envelope and his hand shook slightly as he emptied a gold ring into his other hand; it was the same ring that Alfredson had given him. The immaculate deep red ruby set into the outline of a lion's head winked back at him and reinforced the memories of the first moment he saw it. "We must succeed at all costs."

Ron's Lad was dutifully waiting for him ready to push-start the wheelchair. Stock replaced the key under the brick before re-seating himself in the wheelchair. Ron's Lad was quick off the mark, and they scraped through the narrow gate and turned right up the slight hill towards Springfields.

"I think we ought to get in through the back way. There's less likely to be anyone about there at this time, so turn left just after the main entrance and I'll show you the where." Ron's Lad continued to direct Stock right up to the kitchen door and jumped off as they reached it. He took a quick glance through its opening and beckoned Stock inside.

"Shall I take this up to your room for you, Colonel?" he asked, referring to the case.

"Yes, please, and perhaps you could put it in the bottom of the wardrobe."

As Ron's Lad turned to go, Stock added, "Thank you for your help today, I enjoyed it." But he was gone. 'And so should I be' Stock thought as he headed out of the kitchen and back into one of the corridors through one of the 'secure' doors that opened with the touch of a button from his side. He was feeling quite exhilarated but weary as he 'sticked' his way to the Day Room where tea was being served. There was now a small bright yellow 'Slippery When Wet' A-board in the corridor.

"Ah, there you are, Stock," boomed Bristow from the depths of his winged chair. "Been trying to keep up with the lasses again, eeeh? Can't imagine you catching more than one at a time though, heeeh heeeh." Turning to Perry seated next to him. "Had the local colour queuing up at the door when we were stationed in Pashwada, but that all stopped when we… when… whe…

It was clear his memory was fading so Stock interrupted before sitting himself down in a similar chair. "When your wife joined you?" he volunteered.

Bristow couldn't make his mind up if Stock was laughing at him or with him.

"I had a wife once," Volunteered Perry. "Lost her one day in Margate when she got on a fishing boat instead of the foot ferry, but she did come back with a nice piece of haddock which we ate later. Come to think of it, she never did tell me how she got it."

"Who was it who said, 'Life without women is life without love' or was it 'life without love is Life without women.' I can never remember which way around it goes. How about you, General? Have you ever been married?"

Had any of them been able to even remember that they may have had the same conversation the day before was irrelevant, as they were interrupted by the rattle of the approaching tea trolley being pushed by Matron.

"Talking of women," Bristow commented as he spotted Matron.

She was immediately on the defensive, having overheard Bristow's comment and brought the trolley to more of a halt than it deserved. She suspected his remarks would be up to their usual derogatory standard and braced herself for another session of abuse. Before Bristow could continue, she got the first word in, while 'being mother'.

"Well, gentlemen. You're all off to the County Show tomorrow and the weather forecast promises to be excellent. The coach leaves at 9 am sharp, so the nurses will be getting you up a bit earlier than normal. Should be a wonderful day out."

While Stock was in 'the know', Bristow and Perry were both non-plussed.

"What show?" quizzed Bristow.

"Which county?" asked Perry.

Stock was wondering if he would fit into his uniform.

*****

The kids were jumping for joy on their way over to the village hall across the green, their faces painted in as many bright colours as were in the box. Susan had watched them go from behind the boundary hedge and only turned away once she had seen that Melanie had spotted them from outside the kids' party venue; Mel's youngest would be nine tomorrow. She was excited at the prospect of the evening at Vicky's and normally she would have let Melanie know that Sarah would be collecting them later that evening but felt no qualms as Sarah was very reliable.

Dusk was approaching when the birthday party ended. Melanie handed out party bags to those who were leaving. "I'll see you across the Green," she said to Tom and Ann as they exited the foyer, and off they trotted. Before Melanie could accompany them, they were already well en route towards The Twinings, and she watched them until they were nearly home before attending to the few others. She glanced back a few moments later to see Tom and Ann disappearing down their drive and never gave a second thought to their safety.

"Grandpa said we weren't to say a word to anyone about tomorrow. So, we had better not tell Aunty Sarah, had we?" said Tom as they were halfway across the Green.

"But who's going to put us to bed?"

"Look. Don't you want to go to London tomorrow?"

"Yes. I'm really looking forward to a day out with Grandpa. He's such good fun," she laughed. "Ok, but how are we going to get in without Aunty Sarah seeing us? She's bound to ask us questions and if we don't come back, then she's going to ask even more questions."

Tom thought this one out for a minute. "I know what. Why don't we just creep in and go straight to bed and when she comes to check if we are in bed, we can pretend to be asleep."

"But what about our bedtime story? You know I can't go to sleep unless Mummy reads us one."

"I'll read us one," volunteered Tom. "And besides which, I need to pack my backpack. I've got those new walkie-talkies I was given for my birthday, and I've been dying to try them out. Do you know if Mum got new batteries?"

"In the hall drawer, I think."

"Come on then. Let's go in through the back door." He took one step further before adding, "Quietly. Take your shoes off."

They tip-toed across the driveway and around the side of the house towards the path that led from The Twinings to Grandpa's and Tom gingerly opened the always unlocked half-glazed back door, hoping it would not squeak. It didn't, but the cat meowed instead in greeting. Tom couldn't see Sarah, but he heard the tv in the guest's drawing room and hoped that any sounds the staircase made would be covered by it. He stopped briefly to open a drawer and took out a ten-pack of batteries, before leading Ann up the stairs.

"Quick. Get into bed in case Aunty Sarah comes."

They covered themselves with their duvets hardly daring to breathe for a full five minutes before Ann whispered, "What about brushing our teeth?"

"She's bound to hear us if we go to the bathroom. We can do that in the morning."

"What about my story?"

"Wait a sec," said Tom. He groped for his bedside torch and the big hardback Riverbank Tales book. "What chapter were we at?"

"Fergus had just fallen into the canal."

Tom read about the fictitious canal boat and the friends that manned it until he started to fall asleep.

Chapter 15
The Right Connections

What was going on in Springfields could hardly be called a bustle, but it came as close as it was ever going to get. The staff were quicker than Mr Green and it had been a bit of a scramble to see who could book part of their holiday to include the Peace Day weekend celebrations first. At the time, Mr Green had not realised that this new public holiday was going to fall on the same weekend as the annual outing to the County Show, and he was now short-staffed. Even with the help of the Virgin girls, some of whom had also decided to take their holiday time elsewhere at the last minute, he did not really have enough staff to accompany the patients on the outing as well as leave some behind to attend to those who were not able to go.

It had only dawned on him a few days prior as he came to prepare the duty roster, but he was too proud to mention the problem to Matron, so he had 'press-ganged' both Ron and his Lad into doing tasks neither of them had been trained to do. Maintenance could be put on hold for a day as well as the daily office works, so he had put himself in charge of the coach party but needed to be accompanied by Matron with her medical skills in case one of the patients needed assistance as they often did. Ron would be in charge of the kitchen and his Lad would ferry the meals, tea trolley, etc., to and fro, but Ron's additional task would be to answer the telephone; Mr Green was gambling on the hope that this weekend there would not be many calls. One of the junior sisters and two trainee nurses would make up the skeleton staff to 'hold the fort' for the twenty or so inmates left behind, but in any case, Hassocks was not too far away, and he had left his mobile number sellotaped in a prominent place on the reception desk.

It was not a lottery about who came and who stayed behind. Mr Green had presented his list of those going to Matron based primarily on the incontinence status of a patient; colostomy bags were definitely out.

The patients being left behind were of little concern, and they carried on in their own world oblivious to whatever else was going on around them. The others, however, more than made up for this. Having been woken up earlier than usual by the few busy staff and told to get themselves dressed as best they could, but to take a few personal items for their one and only 'Day Out' of the year, confused most of them. Endless questions muttered at passing nurses who needed to take on octopus-like simultaneous tasks, coupled with their own inadequacies in being able to coordinate their dress code, and all under the pressure of time, portrayed to Mr Green a scene from an ant's nest. People going in all directions at different speeds with their own agenda did not help him. Of course, he was directing the human traffic by marching up and down, clipboard and pen in hand, ticking off his checklist of who needed to be where and when, but soon discovered that ticking a box did not necessarily mean that the job had been done. On several occasions he found himself ticking boxes more than once as patients who had been directed to go and stay in the Day Room simply wandered out again in search of something. Either a cardigan or a matching pair of shoes and, inevitably, their own walking stick and the right set of dentures all had to be located and fetched. And then there was the final loo visit for all.

It was worse than handling a class of small children who would at least be able to hear what was being said to them. A good half of the patients were almost deaf and misunderstood what was actually being asked of them. Some were partially sighted and unused to being led along unfamiliar corridors and placed, albeit only temporarily, in different rooms. Matters got worse when the security doors, not being used to the extra demands being put on them, jammed themselves shut. Through the glass, those on one side trying to get through could see others on the other side also trying to get through in the opposite direction, and it was Ron who eventually turned off the power to enable the doors to be opened. Meanwhile, some of the patients caught on the wrong side of the door without their chaperone had aimlessly dissipated throughout the rest of the building, and some even found themselves outside which was quite an unnerving experience for one fellow who thought the front lawn was part of the hockey pitch and proceeded to 'dead head' the geraniums with his stick.

The general, having coerced Perry to tag along, led him to the remote wing where the female patients were housed and was having himself a whale of a time, having surrounded himself with a 'hareem' of girls, some of whom were paying attention to his stories. If Green had had more hair, he would have considered tearing some of it out, and he eventually escorted Bristow and Perry back to the waiting coach. There he found that only three of the five Virgin girls had arrived, but at least the coach looked almost full which could only be a good thing as it meant that the patients were where they should be.

Throughout all this mayhem Stock had got himself dressed into his full uniform and for the main had sat quietly on a stool in the reception area awaiting the arrival of his grandchildren. He was just beginning to worry that they wouldn't be coming when they appeared through the wide-open front doors, bright and cheerful as always.

"Over here, you two scallywags," he called out as they almost sailed passed him en route to the normal Day Room. Tom's school backpack was clearly very heavy for him and was bulging to such an extent that he hadn't managed to do the zip all the way up.

Ann's bright pink handbag was also open, and part of her skipping rope dangled out of it, almost reaching the floor. "Hello, Grandpa. Wow. Is that your uniform?

He was indeed quite an imposing figure even though the uniform fitted quite loosely. He had not had to spend much time cleaning it the previous night as it had been well preserved in his wardrobe.

"Cooooor. Look at those medals." Tom was fingering the half-a-dozen on Stock's chest. "What's this one?" Raising the OBE.

"I will tell you all about them later, but I think we ought to get on the coach."

"Are we going on that bus outside?" Tom was eager.

Stock helped himself up with his walking stick. Not too many people were on the coach yet, and Stock chose to go to the back where he hoped Tom and Ann, being relatively small, would not be spotted. The coach driver had been coerced into rounding up the errant patients from wandering off down the road as the Stocks embarked through the side door.

"Guess what we had for breakfast?"

Stock hadn't the faintest idea.

"Pop Tarts....and they were hot, out of the toaster."

"I had chocolate."

"And I had raspberry." Evidence of which adorned her dress.

It was some quite time before Mr Green weaved through the trip-hazard of sticks protruding into the aisle, ticking off names on his clipboard, while the driver directed the loading of the wheelchairs into the baggage compartment below.

"Come on, Grandpa, what's the biggest medal for?" reminded Tom.

"That is the Order of the British Empire presented to me by the King." Both kids were crowding to look closely at the words 'For God and The Empire' circling the polished medal.

"Don't you mean Queen?"

"A long time ago, before you were born - before your father was born - King George the Sixth was on the throne and he presented this to me himself.

"This one looks pretty," piped up Ann as she prodded the end of a pointed star.

"That one is the Burma Star and was awarded to all of us who served in Burma."

*****

The BBC was overloaded and was raking it in. Every foreign outside broadcaster needed to obtain a licence to transmit, and that transmission then had to go through the BBC's satellite uplink network and, in turn, needed the approval of the Home Office. It thus fell within the jurisdiction of Sir John Corston's department, and he had had to create an entire dedicated sub-department to oversee every aspect of the inaugural occasion of Peace Day. He had directed his secretary, Jefferies, to put forward names of those senior enough to head the new sub-department, and he quite naturally turned to one of his old schoolmates and closest friends, Arthur Wickes, whose first task had been to provide a name for the newly formed piece of governmental machinery. Thus PAWD(s-d) was formed and was immediately frowned upon by those who had long since lost their sense of humour, but for those who had been seconded to the Peace Around the World Day (sub-department), it was a breath of fresh air in a somewhat stale Government.

PAWD was not over-endowed with personnel and was primarily in existence to carry out the smooth running of a world-class diplomatic event. Wickes had been on the phone to his contact in the BBC requesting him to search their vast database for the most senior officer who had served in the Far East who was not only still alive but 'kicking'. This was a much quicker method of finding out than by putting a request through the normal channels to the Ministry of Defence, whose nose was well-and-truly out of joint in any case as they had not been asked to create this department themselves.

"Do let me know who you find; we may want him in London if he's able."

The man at the BBC was struggling. He had trawled through mountains of documents, contacted the regimental commanders of current battalions, the Fleet Air Arm, Navy and Submariner services, the Royal Air Force, and tracked down the respective relatives who had had fathers, uncles etc., serving in the Far East during WWII.

The response was usually along the same lines: "I'm sorry, he passed away last year." Or "Oh. He's in a home now but you won't get any sense out of him. He's over 100, you know."

'The Fishtail Club' never actually formed but was an unrecognised group of flying officers who had been shot down at sea and had been rescued. There was apparently one fellow remaining who had gone through this ordeal - twice.

"Yes, he's living with us at home, and he's got all his marbles. In fact, his mind is very active, and he does The Times crossword every day in just a few minutes." Hope of someone at last. "He's very asthmatic with his one lung, though, and can hardly speak."

This was not what he wanted to hear, but he finally got a positive answer through The Burma Star Association and was directed to Springfields Home where, he was assured, there would be two officers: a colonel and a captain. There was also a general in that area, but the chap thought it would be a waste of time interviewing a deranged man and, as far as he knew, these were just about the last surviving officers from the Fourteenth Army. The chap thought that Colonel Stock would be his best bet as he had spoken to him earlier in the year.

An entire outside broadcast unit consisting of an enormous pantechnicon, two other lorries and a van plus a prominent 'Face' in his own car from the BBC, complete with a make-up department was dispatched from London and arrived at Springfields not long after the coach pulled out of sight. Meanwhile, the phone at Springfields had been ringing non-stop in an attempt by the desperate BBC man to speak to someone about Colonel Stock. He had taken a gamble in sending the OB unit before confirming that Stock would be the person to interview, but he was now under pressure to deliver what had been demanded of him.

Ron's Lad was passing the reception desk on his way to the

utility room, his hands full with bucket, mop, disinfectant etc. He had just come from clearing up a particularly incontinent gentleman who had managed to soil just about everything in sight as he had shuffled his way from chair to chair, and Ron's Lad was eager to rid himself of the foul-smelling chair covers.

"Hello."

"Do you have a Colonel Stock staying with you?"

"Yes, we do."

"Is he still alive?"

"If he wasn't alive, he wouldn't be here, would he?" Ron's Lad's logic was infallible. "Who is this?"

"I'm Ted Johns from the BBC, and I want to speak to Colonel Stock."

"Well, you can't." Ron's Lad thought that if he kept his answers as short as possible, the chap would go away.

"Why not? You said he was staying with you."

"That's right. He is."

"Well, why can't I speak to him?"

"He's not here."

"But you said he was with you."

"He is and he isn't."

Ted Johns pulled the phone away from the side of his face to look into the ear-end to try to understand the contradicting voice at the other end, but it didn't help. "Is there someone else I can speak to?

"No." As far as Ron's Lad was concerned there was no more to be said so he put the phone back down and continued with his unsavoury task.

An exasperated Ted Johns heard the phone line go dead and wondered what sort of establishment Stock was staying in. According to the voice at Springfields at least he was alive and was also known there. He called the OB Director's mobile phone and passed the information on, hoping that they would have more luck.

The OB 'Face' and director was Camp, not only by name but

also by nature. Everyone knew it and everyone was fed up with Nicholas Camp whose condescending attitude was only surpassed by his annoying voice. His schooling at Harrow where he had been boarded by his Parents had brought him into contact with some of the future rich and famous, and the only reason why he was tolerated at the BBC was because of his links, and he was a right know-it-all. His first success that brought him to the attention of the BBC hierarchy was when he had managed to set up an interview between Sir Donald Frist and the Sultan of Brunei, who was not only the world's wealthiest man, but who had up until then refused all approaches from the media worldwide. Camp's price for this had been permanent employment with the BBC as a Director, where he felt he could influence the rest of the world with his ethos of life. On a typical day, he would be seen prancing about the corridors of Broadcasting House sporting an oversized spotted pink cravat, which didn't quite cover his hairless chest underneath his very open shirt. Chequered grey and yellow trousers terminated at the bottom of his legs where a pair of moccasins adorned his feet.

That morning, however, he was not in the best of moods, having cut his little toe when trimming his toenails, and nothing else was going right for him.

The pantechnicon blocked the narrow lane outside Springfields and out strode Camp across the gravel car park directly up to the front doors. He didn't pause as he put one hand out to open the one side that was clearly the one that opened. Only it didn't and he body-checked into it. He was not used to doors that didn't open since most of his work entailed large city-centred offices which were permanently unlocked during the day, or even opened for him. He was face to face with the belligerent-looking lion's head knocker as though it ought to automatically knock for him, but as it didn't, he slammed the ring thrice against the striker and took two paces back down the steps to try and look through the adjacent windows.

Meanwhile, his crew had exited their mini-van and had started to retrieve their equipment from the mobile studio, strewing it across the front lawn. Frustration had set in by the time one of the nurses opened the right-hand door, which should have been locked in any case but wasn't.

"Yes?"

Camp barged passed her and was confronted by an empty reception hall and desk. He spun around on the nurse. "Where's everybody, and where's Colonel Stock?"

"I, I'm not sure." She was only a young trainee and not used to dealing with people who carried such an air of authority.

"Well go and find someone higher up the food chain., NOW."

"I'll just go and get someone," she stuttered and went in search of someone older.

Camp's assistant and a few of the others had now entered the building, loaded with the various tools of their trade as they had been told that their subject would be a very old man who wouldn't be able to walk to the OB studio. Ron's Lad had been observing Camp through a slightly ajar door at the back of the main hallway and had taken an instant dislike to him for treating the young nurse as though it was all her fault. He'd also decided to stay put for the moment and see what was happening, and, as the minutes ticked past, he could see Camp becoming more and more agitated.

Finally, Ron appeared, dressed in his brown 'shopkeeper's' coat, and certainly not looking like someone in charge of a nursing home; his nose was well out of joint when he saw the crowded hall now littered with cables, stands, boxes etc.

"What's going on here and who are you lot?"

To Camp, this was an insult. Had his manager not spoken to Springfields? "Now, look here. Where's Stock?" He hadn't even had the decency to introduce himself or answer either of Ron's questions.

"I'm not sure I can tell you that. Not until you let me know what's this all about."

With a 'Tut' and an exhalation of breath, Camp responded, "We are here to interview Colonel Stock. Look. We're here from the BBC. Didn't you get the call?"

Ron couldn't recall any phone calls, as he tried to fathom out what this was all in aid of. "Nope, nobody told me. Do you have an appointment?" Falling back on what little he knew about the protocols of Springfields.

"Yes, we have an appointment." Half-lied Camp. "And yes, we really are from the BBC and yes, this will be televised."

Ron was now uncertain, but also unconvinced since Mr Green had not told him about any interviews, even if it was the BBC. "Well, I'll have to contact Mr Green and ..."

He was cut short by Camp. "That's the name of the chap, if you must."

So, Ron went behind the desk to ring Mr Green's mobile. Meanwhile, the crew had been carrying out the preparations for setting up the links with the OB unit in the road, and cables now snaked their way across the drive and in through the front doors. A veritable trip hazard if there ever was one. They had even plugged into the mains socket behind the reception desk and flooded the whole room with a blinding white light.

Ron wasn't to know that Mr Green's mobile phone was in one of those 'black spots' where there was no signal, a frequent occurrence in the countryside, and after three attempts he gave up. "He's not answering his phone, so you'll just have to wait until he returns from the show this afternoon."

There ensued a heated argument with Ron standing still, his arms folded across his chest while Camp pranced up and down berating the inefficiency of all in Springfields.

Ron's Lad decided it was time to come to the rescue of Ron and quietly crept out through the kitchen door and around the side of the building.

Ron knew perfectly well that Colonel Stock was on the coach with Mr Green and just to get rid of the mob from the BBC, he offered, "He's not here anyway."

Camp stopped in mid-stride. "What?"

"He's not here anyway."

"Well, where the bloody hell is he then?" he snarled, almost adding 'you grotty little man'.

"He's gone to the show."

"What show?" Automatically thinking it would be one of the productions in London.

"The agricultural show, in Hassocks."

Camp had never heard of such a show. "Where's Hassocks?"

"Not too far, You'll find Mr Green there with Colonel Stock." Hoping that that would make everybody go away.

"Why didn't you say that earlier?"

"You never asked."

Camp's blood was getting near boiling point, and he took it out on his assistant hovering by the doorway. "Find Hassocks. We're leaving." Putting his head in the air with whatever composure he had left, he pranced out through the front doors. As if on cue and out of sight from around the corner, Ron's Lad turned on the garden sprinkler system. The first to suffer were the two make-up girls who had not had a chance to fit into the building and had opened their cosmetic boxes on the front steps. Water rained down from the sprinkler and started to turn their powders to mush. One of the micro water pipes feeding the hanging baskets on either side of the entrance had come adrift, and under the high mains pressure it now danced haphazardly in mid-air, squirting anyone who came within a few feet of it and getting Camp in the left ear as he exited. "Ooooarrrrgh." As he stepped smartly sideways, and inevitability tripped over the black cables and dislodged one of the rectangular connecting blocks. It didn't take long before the puddling water caused a short, which in turn fed back to Springfield's main fuse box, causing the safety breaker to cut off the electrical supply to the Home.

The rest of the crew inside the building were now packing up but still had to run the gauntlet of the errant micro pipe. It came as a bit of a surprise to them as, in turn, they exited with arms laden. Ron just stood and stared at the retreating army of technicians, inwardly smiling, and blessing his Lad.

*****

The coach was meandering through the country lanes quite slowly as Green carried out his duty of allocating which chaperone would accompany which patient, or in this case patients, as he was still several staff members short. He'd given Matron the most awkward to deal with and reserved the last two for himself. He peered over the last row of seats and was pleased with himself as he spotted Stock and Perry, then two small children.

"Who's this?" he aimed his question at the two gents, hoping that he had not managed to kidnap two children by accident.

"I'm Tom."

"And I'm Ann."

"And we're with Grandpa."

He now recalled the two faces that peered back at him and could see nothing wrong with their being there, it was just that he had not been expecting it. In fact, it might make his day easier but, then again, he really should have had something in writing from their parents, and he was just about to start asking some awkward questions when Stock saved him the trouble.

"Not to worry, Mr Green it is all my fault. I asked them to come along, and we are going to have a wonderful day out. Aren't we?" Stock had an arm around each child which he now squeezed them with.

"We're going to have candyfloss and ice cream."

"Yeah, and go on the rides. Yeeeehaaaa."

Mr Green gave in easily. At least these two weren't going to cause any trouble. Or so he thought.

*****

Wickes was having trouble getting hold of Camp, Jefferies was having trouble getting hold of Wickes, and Corston was having trouble getting hold of Jefferies. The foremost due to sporadic lack of phone signal. Jefferies, because the recently formed department had not yet moulded itself into the smooth operating machine one would expect from a government department, and the newly installed internal phone system had developed hiccups. The last because Corston could not find one of his mobile phones, the one that he kept all his important numbers on.

He had found his other two phones but, after rifling unsuccessfully through his desk drawers, he had pressed the intercom button to get hold of Jefferies only to be advised by a secretary that Mr Jefferies was out of the office, but at least she had given him Jefferies' mobile number. He had asked her to ask Jefferies to come and see him as soon as possible and within half an hour Jefferies had knocked on his door and entered.

Corston looked up from his desk. "Ah, there you are. You haven't seen my phone, have you? The green one issued to all ministers?"

"No, Sir John. How long has it been missing?" Jefferies was concerned as the green phone was very much restricted and was issued by MI5 solely to important personnel within the cabinet and the most senior ministers. They had been pre-loaded with their contact numbers and monitored calls were channelled through the GCHQ secure centre at Cheltenham. It also acted as a locater and it had been impressed upon the few recipients, including the prime minister, that the primary use of these phones was for national security. Should it ever go missing, it was to be reported at once. Corston had few faults but one of those was his ability to lose mobile phones and he had done just that a few weeks ago. It had resulted in all the green phones being withdrawn and everybody being issued with new ones, with new numbers. No doubt, Corston thought then, it will go down as a black mark against me.

He was therefore reluctant to be the cause of another such episode. "Er, not long. I think it's at home so don't call Security just yet."

"As long as you're sure."

"I'll let you know in the morning. Now," Changing the subject. "Can we go through those arrangements made for the Japanese delegation?"

He had not yet put two and two together as the upsetting event a few days ago in one of the BBC's store cupboards was now an insignificant memory. It was that same cupboard that some of the more dedicated smokers on that floor of Broadcasting House frequented to feed their habit, and it was quite a regular meeting place. In compliance with the countrywide ban on indoor smoking, it had been enforced rigorously by the BBC and salary would be deducted if any employee was found doing so. It was an unwritten rule that the last person to leave a session at the end of a day was responsible for emptying the tin foil ashtray. Had there been a spot check on the contents of that cupboard, nobody would have been surprised to see a cardboard carton that once held a thousand tin foil cupcake holders, but guessing as to their real use would have been difficult.

Julie Scargill was one of the assistant sound technicians who regularly popped in for a quick drag and on this particular day, in between puffs, she was chatting to her friend about the dreadful performance of her ex at the Apollo. Not paying full attention to how she was stubbing out her cigarette, she tipped the ashtray and its grey contents onto the floor and bent down to clear up what she could. Next to the bedecked ashtray was a green mobile phone that she brought up and showed her friend. "Not yours, is it?"

"Nah. Mine's on my desk. Open it and see whose it is."

The battery was flat.

"Go and charge it and see if there's an ICE number."

"ICE number?"

"In Case of Emergency. Dummy."

Julie was not the quickest person and hadn't heard that before.

Nobody in her office had lost a phone but one of her colleagues lent her the right charger and she plugged it in and turned it on while attending to a spreadsheet on her computer in front of her. Beep

Beep. Beep Beep. She flicked it open to reveal the screen that said there was one message. 'PM's @ 7'. She ignored it and went to the contacts window, searching for the ICE. There was not one but out of curiosity she flicked through the names in any case; some of them were familiar, but she was only half concentrating as she wanted to complete the spreadsheet before she left for the day, and she didn't make any connections.

Crofts Wine Bar just off Cavendish Place was a very trendy place for up-and-coming young executives and was the perfect place to meet a future wealthy husband. It came as little surprise to the owner that the early evening after-work crowd consisted of eligible bachelors and unmarried women, but he didn't care as long as he could keep charging well overinflated prices for dirt-cheap plonk. It was also one of the very places where freelance reporters gathered to pick up any gossip about the goings on in the upper echelons of society. Julie was a regular and definitely on the lookout for a husband so accepted far too many large glasses of Chablis from those who took her fancy. This evening was no exception and, perched on one of the barstools, she chatted away with two chaps vying for her company for the night.

"Excuse me." As the phone in her handbag rang, without looking she withdrew it and put it up to her ear; but it kept ringing, and it took her a moment to realise that she had the green phone, not hers. She put it on the bar and continued to ferret around for her own phone.

The chap on her right was one of those freelancers whose photographs had appeared in Hello Magazine and having had previous assignments in the company of some cabinet ministers, instantly recognised the pearlescent green shading on the phone Julie had left on the bar. Geoff was impressed. If it was what he thought it might be, perhaps Julie was more than she made herself out to be.

It was a short phone call from her sister to say that she would not be able to make it later that night, and he sidled up even closer to her as she finished.

"Two phones, eh? One for each boyfriend?"

She decided to flirt, "If I had one for each boyfriend, I'd have more than two phones, and besides which, what makes you think they're boyfriends?" She leaned over and whispered in his ear. "I have girlfriends as well, you know." She sat back. "How many mobiles have you got then?"

He was not embarrassed. "None with phones that colour."

She swivelled around on her barstool and picked it up to have a closer look. Under the bar lighting its cover seemed to be almost translucent, not something she had seen before. A wicked thought came into her head. "These are my special numbers that I reserve for my most intimate friends. That way I don't get caught making an idiot of myself."

Geoff decided he would try to get hold of her phone, even if it wasn't what he hoped it might be, there ought to be at least some names and numbers in it that he might be able to use.

"My round," he announced and, calling the bartender over, he cast his eye down the list of expensive bottles of white wine that ended in a three-figure sum. This better be worth it, he thought.

Some two hours later Julie was more squiffy than normal. Geoff had managed to sideline his competitor and they had retired to one of the more intimate alcoves at the back of the wine bar where he had managed to ply Julie with another just as expensive bottle while watering down his own without being caught. He had convinced her to try shots of the various types of *eau de vie* which she knocked back quicker than he could order the next, and without remorse kept plying her with enough alcohol to warrant a stomach pump to most normal people. The inevitable happened on her way back from the loo as she bounced off the empty coat rack, knocking it loudly to the floor.

"Shorry." She turned to where it had stood a moment before, mistaking it for a person.

Geoff was there in an instant, recognising that this was now the moment to strike. "You ok?" he said, picking up the wooden pieces of furniture and glancing at the barman to ward off any interference. "One for the road?"

"I fink I better go home now." She staggered towards the exit. Geoff followed right behind her in case she had trouble staying upright. He didn't want her to bring too much attention to them and certainly not pass out in a place as public as this.

Outside, even the fresh air seemed to be out of focus, and she had trouble avoiding the temporary bus stop sign but clung to it as though it was a life belt. "Can you get me a cab?" she managed in staccato. "I don't think I can stomach the tube."

You can't stomach any more drink either, he thought as he raised his arm to an approaching black taxi. "Where do you live?" and instructed the cabbie as he joined her in the back.

She had instantly fallen asleep once seated in the corner for the twenty-minute ride and Geoff had found her front door key in her handbag. Her flat was mercifully on the ground floor and, with an arm around her, eased her onto her sofa where he proceeded to remove her shoes with great difficulty before stretching her out on it and letting her fall back to sleep. There were no sexual thoughts in his mind, but he eyed up her shapely legs as he positioned them into a comfortable position for her.

He toyed with the green phone going through the messages and contacts and realised that this was indeed one of the phones issued exclusively to an inner circle of government ministers, royals, and other luminaries. He got on his own phone to a friend who he knew could help and fifteen minutes later a TV detector van drew up outside. Keeping her keys on him for the moment, he went outside.

"What you got?" asked the man who was getting out of the van. Mike and Geoff had helped each other out in the past, Mike more than Geoff, and a greeting was unnecessary. Geoff showed him the phone and explained what he thought it was. "It'll have a tracker on it so we can't be too long."

"OK. In here, "said Mike as he opened the back of the van and went inside. "Close the door."

Geoff had never been inside Mike's van before and was amazed to see that it was kitted out with electronics. There was one seat facing a bank of panels with knobs, switches screens and lights. Mike was proud of his creation "Good disguise, eh? Nobody ever queries what all this does, and it really can detect TVs if it has to." He plugged a lead into it. "Now, let's see what we've got here." He attended to a keyboard as the valuable information displayed itself on a flat screen in the centre of a panel. "Oh, yes. OH YES... This is your real McCoy. Look, here's the Queen's number... the Duke's.... etc. etc. Here's the PM's... Defence Secretary's, your bird's number's this one. Let's look at the messages." Mike went through them pointing out several items, before moving on. "Look, here's the instructions in case of nuclear strike - where to go and who to contact etc. What you want me to do with this?"

To Geoff, this was like opening Ali Baba's treasure cave; there was so much information he didn't really know where to begin. "Look. I've got to get this back to her before the spooks come down on us like a ton of bricks. Can you download everything and monitor it all from now on?"

"Now that I've got the frequencies and numbers, no problem." He played his keyboard at breakneck speed. "Even if they change the numbers, I ought to be able to keep tabs on it. Give me a couple of minutes. Who did you say she was?"

"I didn't recognise her, but her name's Julie and she told me she worked at the BBC. Very unassuming kind of person but there must be more than she's telling. Shame she's passed out."

Mike paused for a moment at his last comment. "If you've got one of the minor royals pissed and they find out what you've done, you're in for a shit load of trouble."

"What *we've* done, Mike, what *we've* done."

Silence for a few seconds while they both reflected on the consequences of their actions.

"OK. But handle like eggs, alright?" Mike continued his finger exercises. "Does she know who you are?"

"Not exactly. I told her I was a freelance photographer, and she hasn't got my number. Besides which, I doubt in her state she could remember what day of the week it is let alone what I look like."

"There, that ought to do it." He unplugged the phone and handed it back to Geoff. "Let's get out of here. I'll ring you when once I've gone through this."

They parted, Mike in one direction, Geoff back into Julie's flat to return the phone and her keys to her handbag. Julie was in the same position as he had left her, but before he left, he tilted her head to one side. He didn't want her to choke on her own vomit.

he could be better engaged elsewhere, but it had been an exhausting day, and he felt that the duty officer was probably correct. He also felt it unlikely that a one-hundred-year-old man with two small children would be likely to stay out for too long. His mind was made up by the officers' next comment.

"Why don't you wait at the bar and have a drink?"

The truth was that the duty officer didn't want to be seen carrying on a potential security problem in the lobby.

Wickes was ushered over to the bar where he took up station in one of the comfy chairs that adorned the front window and got his phone out so that he could continue his co-ordinations from there. He could have waited in his car, but the thought of a nice cool lager and a bowl of complimentary peanuts was just what he needed.

*****

The Show was enthralling; Osibisa were playing to their largest audience yet and revelling in it. Their performance had everybody dancing and was exactly the right tone of entertainment that the occasion called for and part of it included them taking their instruments on a walkabout among the crowd. This was not the main concert which was taking place in Hyde Park and included some of the most famous names in the music industry, but one of the many smaller ones that was there to cater for the masses who could not fit into just one single venue. Nevertheless, there were TV crews there to capture the moment, and the cameras followed the snaking line of drumming and whistling musicians through the audience which quickly resembled a conga, possibly a record breaker. It was getting late and there were still more acts to come on and, even though the management had been told to expect this, inevitably the schedule was running behind, but they were the only ones worried about timing as the atmosphere of enjoyment reached new heights. The mood was such that those officials on duty were caught up and readily joined in, all captured on camera.

"Can we join in? Oh, go on, please," cried the kids.

"Alright. But remember to come back here." Stock was also enjoying himself, but the minute they went, he started to feel a bit weary. It was almost half an hour before they returned, breathless, Osibisa having finished their performance to the loudest cheer the kids had ever heard.

"That was great."

"Yeah, such fun."

"Can we do it again?"

They had to shout to be heard.

"I'm hungry."

"Me too - and thirsty," added Ann.

Stock's spirits rose with the return of the kids, as though his energy ebbed and flowed with their presence. He didn't try to speak to them as the surrounding noise was still rather intense but instead he engaged his joystick and set off in the general direction of the hotel. About halfway to even more food stalls, the wheelchair started to slow down.

"It must be the battery," declared Stock to the waiting kids. He was about to ask them for a push when in unison they each grabbed one of the handles and pushed for him.

It was now well over two hours since they had left The Ritz. Approaching the same back door, it was opened for them by one of those on duty. The seated man by the lift had replaced Terry and, like him, had been briefed on those permitted to ascend to the upstairs rooms and he duly logged their return on his electronic device, which was linked to the Duty Officer's at his own desk off the Lobby. He had not however been passed the message to alert Wickes directly but considered the mere logging of their return sufficient.

"I've got the key." Ann barged her way in front of the wheelchair and flashed the card in front of the lock, the door opening fully automatically. This left Tom to finish pushing the wheelchair through the doorway on his own. "Where's the charger, Grandpa?

"Under the seat, I think. Can you do it for me, please?" He left

Tom fiddling about with it while he went off to the toilet and when he returned a proud Tom told him that it was charging.

"I think it is bedtime for you two. Which room would you like?

"This one. It's got a bigger telly," Tom volunteered.

"But we didn't pack my night dress and I haven't got my toothbrush."

"Nor my pyjamas."

Even though Stock was weary, he convinced them that they did not need nightwear and pointed out the toothbrushes and pastes that came with each en suite. The kids had not slept in just their underpants in bed before and it was a bit difficult to get them to calm down, ready for bed, but once they were in it, he sat on the edge.

"If I tell you a bedtime story, will you go straight to sleep?"

Both nodded their heads, but Ann pointed out that the sheets tickled.

"Have I told you the one about the phantom tiger?

He hadn't.

"Well. When I was in the jungle, the headman of the village came to see me one morning to say that the bandits had returned to their valley. These were nasty bandits and every so often they came and stole food and animals from his village, but they could not be stopped because they had guns. He pleaded with me to help them, so I agreed."

"Didn't you have guns?" from Tom.

"Oh, yes. I had my Sten gun and my heavy service revolver, but…"

"What's a Sten gun?"

"It is like a machine gun, only much lighter. Now listen. Do not interrupt me again or I will not finish the story." He left his threat hanging, then continued. "Now, where was I? Oh, yes. He said that there were as many as twenty of them and they had been known to kill. I was on my own as my sergeant had gone down to headquarters for more supplies, but we set off in search of them. There was only me, the headman and three of his helpers who carried short spears made out of bamboo." He paused while Ann adjusted the sheets around her.

"We walked through the jungle for hours, following an old hunting trail. It was very hot and humid and there were creepy crawlies everywhere." Unnoticed by either of them he had crept his hand under the fold in the top sheet which now moved upwards a few inches.

"We found their camp just as it was getting dark but there were more than twenty of them gathered around a bright fire. It was too many to take on by ourselves, so I came up with a plan and waited for nighttime.

"Now, everybody in the land had heard about the phantom tiger who would wait until midnight when the night was darkest. He would creep up slowly and silently, then wait a little, then move closer, and closer. His ears would be pinned back trying to catch any sound that was out of place. His big red eyes focusing only on his next victims. When he got close enough, he would start to let out a soft growl, then a bit louder." His imitation of a tiger growling was pretty poor, but it was more than enough to have the kids wide-eyed. "His deep-throated growl would gradually get louder and louder until it was heard by his victims. He wanted to let those know it was he who was going to kill and eat them, and he waited until all his victims were awake. It would be as black as black can be outside the ring of fire and nobody inside it could see out. His growling never seemed to come from any one direction, and he would wait until there was panic. Men would stand back-to-back, peering into the blackness and the growling would become so loud that some would cover their ears. He would suddenly pounce on his chosen victim." His hand now jerked forward so that the sheet covered their faces, and he was rewarded with a squeal from Ann while Tom merely took a sharp intake of breath.

"Nobody ever really saw the tiger, but those who did manage to get away said it was white all over and was the biggest they had ever seen and that is why it was called the phantom."

Ann was tucking the sheets back around her as though it would offer her more protection against the tiger.

"We quietly positioned ourselves outside the dying ring of fire so that the bandits could not see us and waited for midnight in the pitch blackness. I waited until all of them were asleep and started growling softly." His poor imitation this time took on a more realistic sound - at least, it seemed that way to him. "Just like the phantom. And the others who were with me took turns growling from the other side of the ring. Soon the bandits were all awake and shaking with fear because they knew one of them was going to be the phantom's next victim."

"Then, just as they were beginning to hope that the tiger might go away, the headman, who had placed his rope on the ground as close as he dared, pulled on it with all his might. It caught the nearest bandit's feet, and he was hauled away into the jungle." Stock's voice was triumphant. "The rest of the bandits just ran away in terror, and they left behind a large bag of gold. I gave the bag to the headman, and we took all the rest of their belongings back to the village the next day, but that night we slept under the stars by a waterfall, and do you know what? I had no pyjamas, no bed, and no pillow, but it was the best night's sleep I ever had.

"Why didn't you keep the gold?" Tom felt it was safe to open his mouth now that the story had ended.

"The headman told us that the gold was from the Temple of Rain and had to be returned there and that anybody taking it out of the village would drown… but that's another story I'll tell you about another time. Now, time to go to sleep." He turned down the bedside light and hobbled across to the door. "Good night and sweet dreams."

"Good night, Grandpa."

He was just about through the door when the small voice of Ann asked, "Will we see Mummy tomorrow?"

He pondered for a brief moment. "Yes, you certainly will."

It was his own bedtime, and it had been a while since he had had such an exciting day himself. Come to think of it, it had been a while since he had put himself to bed.

*****

Wickes was now bored, and his bottom was beginning to go numb. He had had three lagers and two bowls of peanuts and had visited the duty officer twice in the past half an hour. He went off in that direction again.

"Look, if he hasn't turned up, then he's obviously elsewhere. I can check his room for you if you like?" It had not occurred to him to check his computer that had already registered that the colonel had returned, but he had not heard from the usually reliable Terry. "But I don't know who he is or what he is doing here, and I don't really want to put myself in the awkward position of explaining what I was doing in someone else's room, uninvited at midnight. Do you?"

There was only one more thing Wickes wanted more than speaking to the colonel, and that was a bed.

"Why don't you leave me your mobile number, go home, and I'll call you the minute he shows up?"

Wickes was not a man to easily give up on a task, but he admitted to himself that he could do with at least some sleep before tomorrow. "Ok." Was about all he could manage as he handed over one of his cards. He tapped on his driver's window to wake him and take him to his apartment in Dolphin Square.

*****

Stock eased himself into the biggest bed he had ever been in after first making sure he could reach the light switch from within it, and almost immediately fell asleep. He had wanted to go through in his own mind what he was going to do tomorrow, but the sheep beckoned. One of his last conscious thoughts was that at least he wasn't likely to fall out of this bed. His foot was twitching in time with the memory of the African band.

Chapter 19

The Fairer Sex

Roger wasn't sure if he was happy or not; in fact, he wasn't sure of anything, especially after the amount he had drunk that evening. As Susan had predicted, he had met someone he knew and had hardly finished signing the register in the three-star hotel before he was whacked on the back by Freddy, an old chum from his motorsport days who had emigrated to the Black Mountains in darkest Wales to open his own Bed & Breakfast.

The jovial pair had not even bothered to go up to their rooms to leave their luggage but instead had gone straight to the bar mid-afternoon, and stayed there until a fellow hotelier reminded them that the reception at The Grand was in half an hour. They weren't pissed, but an alcoholic aura surrounded them as they sauntered down the road dressed in suits and ties to attend the opening of the conference. It was only 7 pm and the admission tickets stated carriages at 2 am; a long night lay in front of them, and they already had a good head start. At some point in the proceedings, Roger had won a bottle of 12-year-old malt whisky from the raffle and had joined Freddy and his guests on his table by unnecessarily bribing his way onto it with his prize bottle. The handsome Freddy was not a philanderer but always seemed to have an excess of beautiful women on tap, and that night was no exception. Freddy was more of a champagne person while Roger preferred his whiskies and ports, and the pre-ordered bottle of Dow's '88 now went clockwise around the table of eight, six of whom were female who also preferred champagne. It was therefore left mostly to Roger to do justice to the two bottles and consequentially the rest of the night was lost on him. He could remember dancing with two girls at the same time to the energetic disco and smooching with someone else later on, but he couldn't work out in whose room he now found himself.

Roger was a faithful husband and had no intention of breaking that oath he had given to Susan at the altar, but he wasn't so sure now that he had kept that promise. He couldn't remember and it was as simple as that. During his brief visit to his room the previous evening to change hurriedly into his suit he hadn't taken any notice of what it actually looked like other than it had a window and a single bed. This was definitely not it. For a start, the bed was about eight feet across and was round with a matching overhanging half-canopy with drapes, and when he focused his eyes further away, a lot further away in what seemed to be a cavernous bedroom with a polished marble floor, there was an Emmanuelle style chair facing an ornate full-length mirror with the outline of a curvaceous woman in it. Naked? He lay back and shut his eyes trying to figure out if he was happy or not. Susan was about that sort of shape, wasn't she? He felt down his body to check if he still had his underpants on and was relieved to feel elastic and material where it ought to be, but he had a bit of a wedgie and the more he tried to ease the cramping between his legs, the more it seemed to squeeze. He explored further and suddenly stopped, opening his eyes in horror. They weren't his underpants. He threw back the sheets and gazed down at a pretty pair of women's pink panties that were several sizes too small for him, but worse was that they seemed to be twisted. Pain shot through both his groin and head at the same time as he sat bolt upright, and then again as he flopped back down to relieve the pressure on his wedding tackle. "Aaaaarggghhh. Ooooogh." As he clutched his hands between his legs in a futile effort, screwing his eyes shut. He didn't dare move, but a sound from across the room forced him to open his eyes in the direction of the chair and he was rewarded with a wonderful sight that would have taken his breath away if he had had any left. Coming towards him was the picture of a perfect nude woman, her semi-curly shoulder-length blonde hair bracketed a youthful angelic face with a smile that would have made any dentist proud. Her tall classic hourglass figure emphasised by her perfectly formed breasts centred by nipples, cat-walked towards him on legs that seemed to end just below the armpits, her stilettos forcing her legs to swing her hips at just the right time. Still a few paces away, she stopped and raised her arms to adjust her hair, accentuating her perfect figure as she thrust her hips to one side in the classic pose. "Good morning, handsome." In a silky seductive voice. "Are you ready now?"

Roger was quite naturally dumbstruck, but a stirring in his loins and the consequent pain reminded him of his restrictive attire. He shut his eyes for more than a moment, not sure if when he opened them again, he wanted to see her still standing there or not. This was every man's dream come true, but at the same time he didn't want to think about the consequences. She was still there when he gingerly opened his eyes again.

"Well?" she asked as she lowered her hand to her hips. "After all, I am at your command." Her silken voice taunted him and the longer she just stood there, the more he felt like he was being gelded by his swelling.

"Please." He could only stammer in a higher-than-normal pitched voice; he dared not cough. She approached, her neatly trimmed pubes just above his eye level were all he could focus on until she daintily sat down on the edge of the bed. "How can I please you?"

"C-c-can you take these panties off me?"

She kept him waiting while holding his stare. "Of course, anything you say."

She leaned over him, her subtle perfume infusing his senses and raising his blood pressure further as her breasts swung across his line of vision. He shut his eyes and arched his head back in agony as she pulled the offending panties down his legs, revealing his injured manhood to her. He definitely needed time to recover and just lay there, relieved of the pain at last.

"Oh, dear." She said in a dulcet tone. "It doesn't look like you're up to much for the rest of the day, does it? Would you like me to massage it better?"

His eyes shot open immediately. "No." He couldn't bear the thought of anything going near his member for a long time. "I'm sure it will get better on its own." He put one of his hands down there to feel just how bad it was and winced. "How did they get there in the first place?" he asked.

She held the laced panties temptingly across her face as though they were her veil and giggled. "You asked me to last night. Don't you remember?" She placed them squarely on his chest, stood up and slowly walked around to the other side of the bed where her clothing lay.

He didn't want to admit to anything right now as she started to put on her half-length red dress without any underwear. She walked back around to him and turned. "Can you zip me up, please?"

He obliged. She held onto his hand before he could withdraw it and looked into his eyes. "You were wonderful last night, and I hope you recover soon." She was looking down at his excuse for a penis that was very gradually returning to its normal colour. "Perhaps tonight instead?" She stood and headed for the door. "You know where to find me." And then she was gone, leaving him with a hundred and one unanswered questions.

*****

Sitting on the edge of a leather sofa with her legs together, a naked Susan had a warm glow about her and, in the same room, several other women in various states of nakedness sat watching the large flat-screen television on the wall, laughing, and chatting about the evening's entertainment. Thirty seconds later, the blood drained from her face.

She had arrived at Victoria's a little later than she had planned, getting lost somewhere between the spa and Vicky's house around

Basingstoke, but it hadn't taken her long to catch up on the white wine front with the other female guests who were tucking into the buffet when she walked into the room. Their chat centred mostly around their husbands not being there to witness their glee at holding their own Ann Summers evening that was about to begin. Vicky had paid for one of the reps to come and demonstrate the latest from the sex-orientated firm, and Angie was almost finished setting up from the half dozen or so suitcases at the other end of the room. Alcohol was an essential ingredient to loosen the society-induced inhibitions on the group of thirtyish-year-olds whose excitement charged the atmosphere with expectations.

Being held in her own house and having been the prime mover of the occasion, Vicky was the leader and, until the drinks took full effect, the other girls expected her to be the first to do Angie's bidding. Angie had given a brief description of how the evening would unfold but had held back some of the more intimate goodies; they would become apparent later on. She had started the proceedings by modelling the latest provocative evening wear and then had the girls in pairs do likewise by changing behind the screen she had set up earlier, then parading across the room in front of the others. The dress lengths became shorter and the slits higher as the evening got going, and from past experiences Angie would judge when the best time would be to move on to the underwear and then the sex toys. To help break the ice, the screen was not particularly stable, and it wasn't long before it was knocked over revealing a topless girl in changing mode. The screen was dispensed with, and the lingerie came out. Angie would point out a particularly suitable item for one or another depending upon their shape, and always a winner was the see-through bodice modelled by one of the bustier ones. She got the taller ones to model the suspenders, the shorter ones night dresses, and the bras were usually better on the big bosomed. It was all part of the sales pitch and her commission depended upon it.

The girls posed for each other in front of their mobile phones, the poses becoming more daring, and all the while endless bottles of Chablis and Beaujolais maintained the alcoholic euphoria. Sex toys appeared with lotions that had to be kneaded into bodies and it soon became apparent which girls had more lesbian tendencies than others. There were shrills of delight as one held a particularly large vibrator against her face as its rubbery surface tickled her cheek and it initiated thoughts in their own minds of what was coming next; this was what most of them had really come for. Susan was not shocked and gathered from another that she was not the only first-timer as they re-filled their glasses but could hardly help herself being turned on when she glanced over at the far corner where Vicky and another girl were rubbing something into each other's breasts, the latter paying attention to Vicky's prominent nipples.

From Angie's perspective, the evening was a success and she had been picking up plenty of orders along the way, but now, before the girls either paired off or went to bed on their own, or even returned to their husbands, she produced the last items from the suitcase: the bondage and shaving kits. She had already picked out the girl it ought to be tried on, and Susan was her target, as she could see the state of arousal she was in by the way she wiggled her bottom amongst other signs.

As a neophyte, Susan had reluctantly had her pubes shaped in front of the others and when she had returned from the bathroom after drying off, found that the others had turned on the tv to watch the live concerts taking place in and around the UK. Fortifying herself with a glass of red wine, she sat down between two girls who congratulated her on being such a good sport. Four of the other girls were dancing to the music beckoning the other two and Susan to join them, but as she put her glass down on the table in readiness to do so, an image on the screen caught her eye. At the end of the conga, she could have sworn she had seen Tom and Ann, but surely not. So, she sat a few seconds longer to let the cameraman pan towards the back of the end of the line and, yes, it was Tom and Ann. She'd recognise his backpack anywhere by the way the straps held it against his back and Ann's handbag was definitely hers.

That was when the blood drained from her face. She couldn't understand how they had got there when they ought to be tucked up in bed and initially, she put her fist to her mouth in horror. The image on the tv lasted only a few seconds more but it was enough for her to be sure, yet it looked like they were certainly enjoying themselves, and perhaps they had been taken there by her babysitter. She closed her eyes for a few seconds just to make sure it wasn't a dream and by the time she re-opened them, the view had changed, but there in the background she thought she saw them again, still jigging up and down. Maybe she ought not to worry and her thoughts of phoning the babysitter at this very late hour would be exceptionally unsociable. She reached for her glass and decided that she would make an early start in the morning. The view of her two children had had a sobering effect on her, but she recognised that she was really in no state of either mind or body to do much about it right now.

*****

Early in the morning when most of London was still asleep and dawn was just about apparent, two workmen casually sauntered down a residential street as if they were off to work. The bespectacled older one with the flat cap and a roll-up hanging from his mouth appeared to be lecturing his younger counterpart who carried the brown tool bag. The passing milkman in his float didn't give them a second glance and neither did the jogger on the other side of the road and, if anybody was curious enough to be looking out of their window at that time of the morning, they would have thought nothing unusual. They stopped outside one of the properties while the older one consulted a piece of paper he had produced from his dungarees pocket and nodded at a front door up a few steps, before they both approached it, the younger one gratefully putting down the tool bag. From directly across the street an observer would have assumed that the older one had the key as he attended to the lock and, a few seconds later, he had the door open and the two of them went inside, closing it behind them.

Despite their appearances, they were the same age and both Stevens and Rogers were very good at their jobs: to work for MI5 one had to be. They had been dispatched very early to catch everyone asleep with instructions from their controller to locate Sir John Corston if he was there and ascertain if he still had his phone on him or retrieve it if he didn't. And all this without waking anybody. GCHQ Cheltenham had reported that Sir John's phone had spent most of the night in an unusual place and had advised MI5 of their concerns. If Sir John was having a clandestine affair, then they needed to know about it, and Julie's background had been dissected before the two operatives had been dispatched.

They knew within a couple of feet exactly where the phone would be from their handheld GPS locator and moved like silent spectres, quickly establishing which room it was in. Stevens attached the latest minuscule night vision monocle to his glasses as he softly opened the living room door, Rogers right behind him as they entered. They were too professional to laugh and had seen it nearly all before but had to see the funny side of what greeted them. Like a young Labrador puppy asleep, on the floor between the sofa and the coffee table, Julie lay on her back with her legs splayed as wide apart as possible, her skirt having ridden up during the night revealing her sodden knickers. Her head lay on a pillow of sick that was fast adhering her head to the shaggy off-white rug underneath and her mouth wide open with a trail of snail-like mucus that obeyed the laws of gravity.

Rogers consulted his handheld and reached into Julie's handbag to extract the green phone, while Stevens went and looked over the rest of the flat to see if there was anyone else like Sir John in there. One minute later they emerged through the front door, chatting nonchalantly and retraced their steps down the street.

Chapter 20

Gently Gently

April 1945

The cavernous room they had been left in was now occupied by just Stock, Corston, and Deeks. The two armed guards were over a hundred feet away by the door and could hardly be seen in the gloom. Stock considered that the need to locate Akiko was becoming more urgent; when the general returned, it was likely to be with a decision that would mean he may no longer be near her. The layout of the long room, with an anteroom at the further end from where the two sentries were, offered some degree of protection in the semi-darkness and Stock felt he was left with no other alternative than to seek help from his compatriots. They were already standing at the far end of the table when the general and his staff had left the room and he now lowered his voice to address them.

"I am afraid that I have some bad news for you."

"I don't think it can be any worse than what you have just told the general," remarked Corston in an attempt to regain some sort of superiority over Stock.

Stock ignored the relatively flippant comment. "Alfredson did not give me the authority to tell you anything, but please believe me when I tell you now that I need to get out of this room for a short while, straight away, and I need your help to do it."

"What are you talking about?"

"You remember when we were leaving Alfredson's HQ that he asked me to stay behind? Well, I cannot tell you why except he asked me to do something for him and I am now asking you to help me."

After a moment of the other two just standing there with incomprehension written all over their faces, Deeks acceded on their behalf, "What do you want us to do? He said they'd be back in an hour."

"I am sure there is another exit to this room. That chap who sat behind Keisuke - he left through that room behind me, behind that curtain. It is well in the shadows and if we all go over to the corner, the guards will think we are just trying to keep out of earshot." He let them ponder for a moment. "If I am right, I can get out that way while you two talk amongst yourselves. Pull up these chairs over there and I'll keep an eye on the guards to see if they look our way." There were a few questions but the three of them looked from one to another and nodded with approval and each lifted one of the heavy chairs to where Stock had indicated. Their location was not only deeper in shadow, but when seated with their backs to the guards they were almost invisible. Stock had noted that neither of the guards had turned to look in their direction as they had de-camped and even the scraping of chairs legs on the floor had not produced a reaction.

"I think we are ok here. I just hope I am right and there are no sentries this way. See you soon, gentlemen, and keep talking about the cricket back home while I am gone." He ducked down a little and peered behind the heavy curtain and, as he did so, a very slight change in the air confirmed that there would be another door or at least a window.

It was almost completely black, and it took half a minute or so before his eyes adjusted, but he felt more than saw that the chamber continued for some distance. Reflected firelight rippled through very high windows casting eerie shadows but it was sufficient for him to make his way across the half-sunken room to where the darkest shadows were. His hands slowly felt along the stone walls in the hope of finding some sort of aperture and he was glad he was doing the same with his feet, as the ground suddenly fell away. He had located a stairway and nearly bumped his head on an arch as his feet sought the next step. Another two steps and he could feel fresher air on his face. In the gloom, he could see the ground even out and the corridor turn to the right, then, without warning, he was outside. Now what? he thought, 'I did not want to go outside.' He no longer needed his limbs to feel the way forward and, looking around as he stood in the shadows of the high-sided building, could just make out another staircase inside the archway back from where he had just come, this one going up in the opposite direction.

Remembering to duck, he gingerly followed the uneven stone steps around two left-hand turns, counting them as he went, and emerged onto a landing. His hope that this was one of the galleries that led to the rooms he had seen on his way through the great hall and his sense of smell soon picked out the Japanese sentries. He couldn't afford to wait too long and being caught was not the preferred option, but he silently walked forward until he was against the wide stone rail that surrounded the balcony that stretched around the internal quadrangle and pressed himself against one of the large upright pillars. As far as he could make out, there seemed to be just one sentry on this level and had to assume that there would be another on the level above. They would of course become bored with staying in one place and, as like as not, occasionally saunter around the square balcony on their rounds.

He found that he could easily duck down to the same level as the stone rail and flitter unseen between the large uprights. /As he did so, he was looking for some sign of where Akiko was. There was nothing that helped him, so he returned to the stairway and went up to the next level. Poking his head around the corner, he nearly revealed himself to the sentry who was just a few feet away, walking at a leisurely pace in his direction. He recoiled back into the shadows of the narrow staircase and held his breath until he had passed. This was an opportunity not to be missed. Re-emerging from the shadows, he glanced to his right to confirm that the sentry was far enough away and walking away from him. He went to the left, clockwise around the upper balcony, glancing down to the lower level to see if the other sentry was visible: he wasn't. He stopped in the corner so that he could still see the fading sentry and looked down the next leg of the quadrangle, scanning for the giveaway sign that would lead him to his next problem. His ears pricked and eyes straining, he discerned a dim light coming from below one of the doors a few feet away and, glancing to his right before moving, he nearly missed that the sentry had turned and was walking slowly back towards him. He judged he had about 30 seconds or so before he could be seen and tip-toed over to the door and pressed his ear up against it; there was definitely someone inside, but who? He had to take a gamble. He drew back the two-sided bolt enabling him to open the door enough to go through and returned the bolt to its original position.

With relief that there was no one to challenge him he exhaled, taking a moment to steel himself for what lay around the corner in the adjacent room. The one he was in was like an antechamber and was curiously shaped to take in the design of the building. Now he could make out a woman's, no two women's, voices talking in hushed tones. Rounding the corner, he saw that there were two of them out on one of the external balconies, oblivious to his presence. The room he found himself in was a large bed chamber with two beds in it, one taking centre stage covered by mosquito nets, the other much smaller one up against the wall on his right. A dressing table of sorts lay against the external wall on top of which was balanced a slightly flaky mirror. His next problem was how to make them aware of him, without either of them crying out; after all, the unexpected appearance of an enemy colonel in one's bedchamber would most likely initiate just such a reaction. He made sure that the ring Alfredson had given him was in his palm and hoped that the mere sight of it would speak a thousand words in the blink of an eye.

He returned to the first room he had come through and softly called Akiko's name, repeating it louder and louder, occasionally casting an eye around the corner towards the balcony. He was about to give up on this course of action and just walk over to them when their voices stopped, and he could hear that one of them had entered the bedroom. He peered a bit longer and was elated to see that it was Akiko and not the other woman; a wave of relief engulfed him and for a brief moment he almost forgot why he was there. He withdrew as she looked around the room to see who had called her name. Stock opened the palm of his hand and protruded it into the dim light of the room and waited for a few seconds before taking a step towards her. He heard her gasp in surprise before he could see her, but at least she hadn't screamed, and he took another very slow step forward, then another as he put a finger up to his pursed lips. He stopped about twenty feet away from her, smiling to help allay her fears, and he could see the quizzical expression on her face. He beckoned to her as he returned to the first room, out of earshot of her companion and she followed the hand that held the precious ring in a trance-like gait.

Stock had been rehearsing, when he had had time, how he would introduce himself when the time came; it was nothing like what he actually said. "I am a friend and I need to talk to you alone." He still didn't know if she would understand him, so he gestured with his eyes to her companion in an internationally understood gesture. He was rewarded with the briefest of nods from her before she turned and disappeared out onto the balcony. Their conversation seemed to go on far too long and he was beginning to wonder what they were talking about and went to glance around the corner but was shocked to see her companion walking towards him. He looked around and backed himself behind a protruding wall a few feet away. Her companion went past his hiding place and out through the door leading to the internal walkway, closing it behind her.

Akiko silently entered the room and waited for Stock to reappear. "Who are you?" she said in barely more than a whisper as he approached her in the half-light.

"Your maid?" he questioned.

"I've sent her to go and feed herself."

He didn't want to sound pompous especially when referring to a member of a royal family, but he had to get her on his side in very short order. "I am a personal emissary from Ignatius, and I come with his blessing." He held out his hand again so that she could see the fine gold ring that clasped a large rectangular chamfered ruby, worth a king's ransom by itself. She hesitantly stretched out her hand and picked it up between her thumb and forefinger and held it to one side in more light. Her face began to crumple with the memories that came with it and tears began to run down her cheeks. Stock gave her less than a minute for self-indulgence, allowing her the luxury of reminiscence before bringing her back to the present. He took the opportunity to look more closely at her and saw that she was very much like the photograph he had seen of her. The taut skin across her face betrayed her youthfulness and the way she held herself indicated her quality upbringing. He was about to take advantage of her state of mind by reminding her of her Fiancée, but she beat him to it. "Did Ignatius send you?

He was on thin ice here as he had never met him and would probably never do so, but he believed that lying in general only led to unwanted repercussions. He chose his words carefully, "No, and I wish I could tell you otherwise, but I was given this ring so that you would know from whom it comes and that the message I bring is genuine."

She pondered. "How is he? I do miss him."

He had to take a gamble now and continued blindly with the very scant knowledge that he had. "When I left, he was well but recovering from a bout of influenza and I was asked to convey his heartfelt desire that he wishes you could be with him."

It seemed to satisfy her curiosity and she even managed the smallest of laughs. "He always was one for picking up the flu."

Stock's confidence was growing, and he continued, "There is more but I am afraid there is very little time."

She relaxed a little, wiping the tears away. "Please go on."

"I am here with an aircraft that is waiting to take you to him, but you must decide now if you wish to stay here or come with me. I am sorry I do not have time to explain, but I must return downstairs." He held his hand out for her to return the ring. "I must ask you for its return as I am charged with its safekeeping."

She had been caressing it with her fingers as if it brought her comfort and for a moment she considered keeping it, but finally, and with a precise movement, placed it back on Stock's palm. The tension within her returned and he could see the conflict taking place within her. He sympathised, but he remained focused on his task and prayed that she would volunteer to come willingly but had mentally prepared himself if she chose not to. He had seen that there were creepers that hung down outside the balcony that he could use to climb down, but it would be a tall order indeed to reach the bottom without dropping her. He had to hurry her.

"He was very insistent, and we have gone to extraordinary lengths just for me to be here to give you this message. It demonstrates his depth of love for you, and I think you would be in a better position if you were with him rather than under your father's wing."

She stalled further.

"I must have your answer."

"You are right, I would be better off with Ignatius but I cannot disgrace my family, especially my father. He knew of our love for each other and had forbidden me from marrying him until I told him of our engagement. Just before the war, I think he was resigned to having Ignatius as his son-in-law but after the war broke out, he cut me off from all outside communication. I did get one message from him; you are only the second in nearly three years." She paused to reflect on what might have been. "Does he really still love me?"

Stock didn't have time for a long-drawn-out debate on the merits of elopement, so he continued to lie. "Yes, he loves you dearly, and I do believe he will return to his old self again if you were able to be with him. Please, you must come with me."

It was probably this last point about his state of mind that turned the tide of her decision-making.

"Very well. But I will need a moment." She turned and disappeared back into the bedroom but returned in under a minute, carrying a small satchel. "These are all the possessions I have in the world. I cannot leave them." He didn't stop to ask what they were but instead turned to explain what they were about to do.

"We need to go down the back staircase but there is a guard on each floor. Just stay close to me and be very quiet." It was only then that he noticed that she wore no shoes. I hope she doesn't tread on anything sharp and cry out, he thought. "You go first and see where he is."

She opened the door while he stood directly behind and a few moments later she turned. "He's on the far side, walking east."

Stock had no idea which way was east but at least he wasn't right outside her door. "Come on, then." He led her up to the rail as had done so earlier, seeing that she didn't have to stoop as low as he did. He spotted the sentry nearing the far corner, and within a few seconds they would be directly in his line of sight. He took hold of her hand, and they went to their right, towards the staircase, then down the two flights that brought them out into the open.

"Stay here for a few minutes while I go and fetch my two friends." He had spoken quietly.

"Don't be too long."

"When we come back, we will need to get to the airfield quickly and quietly but there will be guards over the bridge. Do you think you can talk us past them?"

"I, I don't know. I haven't done this before, and I am not sure they all know that I'm here yet. I haven't been here very long."

Stock didn't like the sound of that. "Is there another way, avoiding the bridge?"

"I'm not sure, but I've seen lorries going in that direction." Stock could make out her outstretched arm in the gloom. It might be a better way in any case as otherwise they would need to go right past Haruko's marquee.

"Stay out of the way while I am gone." He turned and disappeared through the stone archway. Even though his night vision was now more adjusted to the night, he still struggled in the pitch blackness, but as he emerged up the steps, he could see light around the edge of the curtain on the other side of the room and silently headed for it. As he approached, he could hear Corston and Deeks waffling on in monosyllabic tones, nothing to do with cricket.

Before pulling back the heavy drape, he halted and whispered, "All clear, chaps?"

Deeks nearly jumped out of his skin. "Bloody hell. Didn't hear you coming." Stock took this to be affirmative and joined his colleagues by sliding onto the vacant seat.

"Any trouble?" he asked.

"Only that we got bored with discussing cricket. The twins over there haven't moved a muscle." He jerked his thumb over his shoulder. "We were just..."

Stock held up his hand to stop him. "We have not got long, and the hour cannot be too far away." There was an urgency in his voice that had the other two thinking. "Do not ask any questions, but we have to leave. Immediately."

This was too much for Corston. "Now look here, we've..."

"I am not going to argue with you. There is no time to explain. Either you leave with me right now or you get left behind." He was becoming tired of thinking and repeating that he did not have enough time, and for a fraction of a second he even thought to himself that he hadn't had enough time to think this through properly, but that would have to wait. "I'll tell you as much as you need to know en route."

"What about the guards? Don't you think they may notice we've gone?"

"We have to take that chance. Now come on."

Deeks looked compliant but Corston was not convinced. "No. I am not moving until you tell me why we should. After all..."

Stock got nasty. Any delay now would ruin everything. "Alfredson's orders after you left his room were for my ears only, and your brief here pales into insignificance compared to mine. If necessary, you get left behind." He let this sink in for just a moment before adding. "That is exactly what is going to happen unless you leave now." He showed Corston the small piece of paper that Alfredson had given him, Deeks looked at it also. He pulled back the edge of the curtain and added, "Go and talk to them about the cricket if you want, but do not get in my way." His tongue had a harsh enough edge to it and was enough for Corston. "Here, put your hand on the shoulder of the man in front and keep up."

The trio made their way through the blackness, Corston bringing up the rear. With Stock's guidance, they found themselves outside and caught up with a relieved Akiko.

"Tell you later," remarked Stock to the others. "Now, which way do the lorries go?" as he turned towards Akiko.

She led them across the coarse grass, the meagre moonlight allowing them to pick their way over fallen branches and other debris. Stock was hoping that they would pick up a path or the roadway she had talked about soon, as their progress was painfully slow. They circled around several huts and an animal compound when Akiko brought them to a mud road. "This way goes to the airfield, I think."

Stock had been keeping direction from the moon and had to agree that it made sense. He was becoming worried as it couldn't be much longer now before the two guards realised that they were gone and the luminous dials on his watch told him that the hour would be up in a few minutes.

"Run," he said. He had a vague idea that the airfield was about half-a-mile ahead, and he slowed the party as they approached the luminosity of Haruko's marquee, which cast just enough light for him to make out the tail fin of the Beaufort beyond. He was glad to see that it had been turned pointing towards the runway.

"Wait here while I check ahead," he motioned them to the adjacent shrubbery. "Wait for my signal, but if the plane starts, get on it."

He tucked his hat under his arm and marched towards the side of the plane where the hatch was. He considered that anyone seen running would be up to no good, and this way, in the dark he might just be mistaken for one of them; it would at least give him a few seconds' head start. Nearing, he could hear chatter coming from the command marquee and made out the two sentries on each side of its entrance with another pair guarding the plane's hatchway and thought he saw another patrolling the far side of the plane. A line of Jeep types and transport trucks was parked off close to one side, the nearest he could see was manned by someone behind the wheel. It was going to be impossible for them to walk, let alone run, anywhere near the plane without being challenged. He kicked himself for not anticipating this level of security but was glad he had gone ahead of the others. A military phrase entered his head: *Time spent in reconnaissance is seldom wasted.* He needed a diversion and just before he could be either seen or heard, darted behind the nearest truck. He was not used to this sort of operation and silently cursed Alfredson for putting him in this position. It would be no good for him to create a diversion if the pilots weren't ready for them and he racked his brains as he looked down the side of the truck at the plane no more than eighty feet away. As he did so, his foot turned on a stone and he nearly fell over, but he grabbed hold of one of the footplates to steady himself. It gave him an idea and he looked around for some smaller stones about half the size of a cricket ball.

He had managed to find only two and they would have to do. Recalling his cricket coaching, he drew back his arm and threw one of them towards the far end of the plane, hoping it would land somewhere on it near the cockpit. He was more or less lined up with the length of the plane and, unless it overshot, it was bound to be heard by the two crew. It would also likely be heard by the sentries, but he hoped they would assume that it had come from within the plane and not on it. He was rewarded with a 'clank' as it made contact and he cringed with the loudness of it, but he saw that none of the sentries had moved. Perhaps he ought to try a smaller one for the next throw, and he was about to look for another suitable missile when a head poked itself out of the hatchway and looked around. He couldn't make out which of the two of them it was, but if he could just repeat the same action, it would probably alert them that something was going on.

He found a rough marble-sized stone and lobbed it towards the hatch, being very careful not to hit one of the sentries. Such was his aim that he saw the head recoil as the marble silently hit him. They would be alerted now, and he turned back to fetch the others. He knew it would take them a couple of minutes or so to get the plane ready for take-off and that was just about all the time he needed. He found the others with ease and told them to follow him to the back of the truck where they assembled.

His voice was little more than a whisper. "I'm going to set fire to that jeep at the end and when I do, those guards ought to come running. When they go, so do you, even if one of them stays behind. Clear?" He paused for any questions but there were none. "Get that plane moving and I will catch up with you." He felt in his pocket for his handkerchief. "Anybody got a match?"

Deeks handed him his box of Swan Vestas. "Good luck. See you on the plane."

He glanced around to check that there were no wandering sentries in sight before running at a crouch around the back of the half-a-dozen vehicles before reaching the end one. On second thoughts, why not fire two of them? He had had some experience in blowing up vehicles from when he had been ordered to destroy all the equipment on an airfield in France, just before the Dunkirk evacuation, and he split his handkerchief in two, before unscrewing the fuel cap and shoving it in. With a final look around, he scraped the match against the box's striking surface and set the dangling handkerchief alight, hoping that the fire-hungry fumes would give him enough time to do likewise to the next, before igniting.

Still in a crouch, he crossed the few feet to the next one to repeat the operation, but this one's fuel cap was stiff, and it took him what seemed an age before it rotated. He was just about to strike the next match when he heard a far-off commotion in the direction of the General's headquarters. 'Time's up' he thought as he rasped the match and was just offering it up to the handkerchief when the first jeep's fuel tank exploded, knocking him off his feet. He was dazed and in a prone position on the ground when the second vehicle exploded, the handkerchief having caught fire from the first, searing him from head to foot right next to the inflammable fireball, but he was just far enough away not to be set alight himself. He knew not to gasp for air immediately as sucking in volatile fumes would destroy his lungs, and he managed to hold his breath until he had crawled far enough away before collapsing onto the ground. His head spun and throbbed and his jaw felt as if it was broken, but before he passed out, he caught sight of his party dashing for the aircraft.

He surfaced to consciousness and felt himself being manhandled to an upright position but being able to open just one eye, could not make out just who was rather roughly helping him to his feet. His one good eye told him it was no longer dark, but his arms were pinned up his back, preventing him from finding out why the other wasn't working. In front of him stood General Keisuke, barking orders to those around him and gesticulating with his sword in his right hand. He suddenly stopped shouting as he could see that his prisoner was now awake. Even though Stock recognised him from the previous night, it was clearly not the same cool and calm man now in front of him and he could make out the bulging veins running down the side of one of his temples.

Keisuke uttered a short few words and Stock was thrown forwards onto his knees by something that felt like a sledgehammer in the small of his back and his arms twisted until his head almost touched the ground. He saw Keisuke walk around to his left and he realised that he was about to be beheaded. Keisuke's feet spread apart in preparation for the downward stroke.

In the last few seconds left of his life, he didn't reminisce and didn't waste his precious time, but instead he gave Keisuke a parting shot.

"If you do that, you will never find your daughter." Blood dripped onto the ground in front of him.

The sword stroke was a long time in coming and Stock shut his eyes, clearing his mind of everything. A shout from Keisuke and unconsciousness took him again.

He couldn't tell if it was hours or days, but when he came round again, he was on the floor of a bamboo cage, his hands manacled behind him. His body ached all over, his tongue swollen so much that he could hardly breathe and a taste in his mouth that was rather foul. He tried to lift his head off the ground, but his hair pulled it back down, stuck to the dirt by the pool of blood that covered a sizeable area. He tried again and successfully sat upright to see what he could out of his good eye. It was dark again and there was little to see as he went through his senses, he realised that the only one that was fully working was that of touch and that was working overtime.

His thoughts turned to Akiko, Corston and Deeks, remembering them from what he had last seen of them, and prayed that they had all got away safely; perhaps he would never find out. He longed for some water and tried to cry out for some, but all that came was a very painful rasping noise. He tried several times to test the chains behind him, but they were so tight he could not even turn to see how they were fixed, at least, not with that eye. Whatever he tried either brought pain or discomfort, so he gave up and just sat there for hours, drifting in and out of sleep.

He was woken by a kick in the ribs from a Japanese soldier who was standing over him holding a bowl. He was shouted at again and again while he lay there until the soldier put the bowl down and sat him upright before leaving through a small cage door. He looked at the bowl half full of rice and wondered how he was going to eat it. Not only were his hands still chained behind him, but even if he could free them, he wasn't sure he would be able to swallow anything in any case. He couldn't even reach the bowl with his head. Now that it was daylight, from his very limited viewpoint he could see his bamboo prison was set apart from two others which were empty and a little further away were some huts beyond which he occasionally heard voices. At least he was not directly in the sunlight but underneath the jungle canopy and he presumed that the huts in front of him were those he had seen on his way to the Temple. Some hours later a pair of soldiers returned, and Stock hoped that the bowl that one was holding would be water. The other unlocked the cage door, kicked Stock to one side, un-manacled him and handed him the bowl. When Stock didn't respond, he lifted his head to the bowl and forced the water down his throat. It was very painful as he tried to let the water just trickle down his throat but needed to breathe at the same time. It forced him to cough; coagulated blood and spittle gushed over his chest, but the soldier persevered and waited until Stock was ready for another go. When the bowl was empty, the soldiers left him chained by just one hand to the cage.

Stock started to explore his wounds, and inspected the remnants of matted blood on his one free hand that he gingerly rubbed over his face and thought he felt a deep cut somewhere between his right eye and ear. He was grateful he could ease his body to shift position so that he could relieve the almost intolerable pain that came from his back when he moved, and his left manacled arm felt very swollen around the elbow. He thought he detected a broken rib or two when he tried to breathe in more deeply and there was pain in his groin. He wasn't feeling hungry but forced himself to eat some of the now rock-hard dehydrated rice that had been left from the first guard and recognised that he was in a pretty poor state, before drifting off to sleep again.

General Keisuke was standing over him outside the cage when he was woken by another kick from a guard, and he waited while Stock sat himself upright. The guard was dismissed, and he saw that the interpreter was with him. Not an interrogation then, thought Stock as the General started speaking.

"You are a dishonourable bastard and do not deserve to live but you have taken my daughter from me and that is the only reason why you still live. I want to know where she has been taken."

Stock did not have to feign his inability to respond; when he tried, more blood and thick dribble filled his mouth and his larynx felt as though it was on fire. It took him a while to gently cough enough mucus out of the way so that he could speak.

"If I tell you, I die." He shut his eyes and his face contorted in agony at the effort of uttering those few words.

The General stood there, his fists balled in anger. To him, this colonel was holding him to ransom in his own headquarters. Since the departure of the Beaufort, he had been preoccupied with trying to find where it had gone and although he had a suspicion which direction it had taken, there had been no trace. He had had to attend to the urgent matter of an advancing enemy and, from time to time, had received reports about Stock's condition. Although he wanted him dead in revenge, he needed him in a condition so that he could at least speak. He had been deciding whether to torture the truth out of him or just execute him, but his dilemma was two-fold. Stock was his only contact with his daughter, however remote it was, and he wanted to find out why Akiko had abandoned him in favour of this colonel. He was also very aware that he had divulged probably more than he should have to the other two Englishmen who would have by now reported what they knew. If he were to execute Stock and still wanted to pursue a course that would not see his country destroyed by a bomb, the English would be very unlikely to send another party to talk to him if they found out that Stock had been executed; He would have to go to them, and that was not something he wanted to do. His only option was to keep this English colonel alive - for the moment.

He barked orders at the interpreter, stormed off, and left him to re-lock the cage.

Stock's resolve strengthened from that point onwards and he assumed that he had succeeded in the task that Alfredson had given him. Left alone with only the infrequent visit from one of the guards with a bowl of mushy rice and occasionally another of water, he contemplated his position and that of the general. His cage was large enough for him to nearly stand up in and just long enough to lie down straight, but he was never allowed out.

He endured day-to-day, losing a little physical strength with the passing of each one as the amount of food and water he was being given was barely adequate. He thought he would die from his wounds and was concerned that the open cut would become infected, but it didn't and the pains in various parts of his body gradually receded, his eye eventually opening fully. His cage was also his toilet and he designated one corner for his ablutions but there was very little output from his body as everything that he ate or drank was used as fuel. He was not completely alone as the creatures of the jungle became his friends. A trail of ants had detected one corner of his prison and there was a constant stream of them that cleaned up after him. Above him the birds carried on as if the war did not exist and, in the distance, he often glimpsed a troupe of monkeys swinging from tree to tree. Some days they would come close to his cage and peer at him from the overhanging branches and he attempted to mimic them to entice them nearer and succeeded on just one occasion when a young one jumped onto it, but then ran off screeching in alarm. An occasional hog would pass, nosing through the undergrowth, and snakes that would taste him with their forked tongues, ignoring the boundaries of the bamboo. The only one that had him worried was a Banded Krait, but he managed to scare it off by taking off his boot and hitting the ground in front of it. He was startled from his sleep one night by the sound of a Bengal Tiger padding around and around his cage, looking for a way in. He smelt his breath and saw the ruby-red reflection of the eyes in the moonlight as the beast stood still and stared at him from less than two feet away, involuntarily raising the hackles on the back of Stock's neck. He did not know the name of the birds each with their own unique trill and he tried to name the different types. Daily, one lone bird with the loudest call almost spoke to him: "You're ill, you're ill."

The monotony of the daily routine was depressing and somehow he kept his mind active enough not to descend into becoming too morose.

He kept count of the days and weeks by using one of the bamboo splinters as a pen to etch onto a fallen branch. During the fourth week, he heard the sounds of heavy guns in the distance, and a few days later the Japanese camp was bombed. He hoped a bomb would come close enough to open up his cage so that he could escape, but the closest one that came only managed to disintegrate the two huts in front of him, showering him with bamboo and fronds that had been their roofs.

The sound of guns returned the following week, this time closer and a few days later he thought he could hear machine gun fire, praying that it was General Slim's troops doing the firing and coming closer. There seemed to be fewer and fewer Japanese planes coming and going, and then none at all and he wondered if it was due to lack of fuel. Still, he could not see the fuel depot from his position.

Early one morning, the general appeared with his interpreter, and he looked a lot older than Stock remembered. "I see you are still alive, and I am glad you are suffering but I can assure you, you will not leave here alive. No doubt you have heard your guns coming nearer and we will soon have to move, but before we do, I shall personally execute you. I give you one chance to live. Tell me where my daughter is."

Stock could see in his eyes that he was willing him to reveal what he knew. Perhaps he ought to tell him, as by now Alfredson would have her well and truly hidden and certainly beyond the reaches of the general; there would be little he could do about it. But then again, he wondered how much Keisuke did know and Stock felt he could not let him know the little Alfredson had told him. Besides which, there was probably more to it than what he had been told. In his own confined world within the bamboo, he had had plenty of time to mull over what was said in Alfredson's headquarters and he had come to the conclusion that Akiko would probably be used as a political pawn. It even crossed his mind that Corston and Deeks' part in all this had merely been a blind. There were several possibilities, and he would probably never find out what the real reason behind it all was.

Much as Stock craved conversation, he kept quiet, returning Keisuke's stare; he eventually turned and strode off and Stock thought he could hear him swearing.

Stock received no more food or water from then on and within a few days didn't even have the strength to stand up. He became delirious and unable to tell the difference between night and day, crying out for water, but none came. He shrunk further into his now ragged uniform. All but unconscious and hardly able to open his eyes, he felt himself being dragged from his cage but was unable to mutter anything or even realise that this was the end. The past few days had merged into dreams and perhaps this was another.

He opened his eyes but this time. Instead of the all too familiar view of bamboo, there was movement, circular movement. Voices he recognised, English voices. In a room, with walls and a ceiling fan. Then his eyes closed.

The next time he opened them, he could feel the rest of his body and it didn't feel too bad and his thirst had gone. He had trouble focusing but made out the shape of someone standing over him; a woman, no, a nurse, and with a smile. He could tell she was speaking to him because her lips were moving but it was rather muffled at first.

"Colonel, Colonel, can you hear me?"

He gently nodded his head and managed a very weak, "Yes."

"You're going to be alright."

He felt so feeble, and that small exercise drained him of strength. He closed his eyes, returning to the blissfulness of sleep once again.

Over the next few days, he continued to recover and discovered that he had been found in a cage by advance elements of the Fourteenth Army. Some days later he had been transported to the hospital in Putao, but nobody was telling him anything much, other than they were winning the war and that Rangoon had been re-captured. He had surprised the doctors and nurses with the speed of his recovery and had learned that when he had first been brought there, few of them had little hope of his living, but now, nearly three weeks later, he was able to walk unaided again.

Alfredson's adjutant had come and seen him for a short while, passing on the brigadier's good wishes for a quick recovery and impressing upon him not to talk about the events involving his actions. Stock could hardly remember much as his mind had been severely bruised by his experiences, or maybe it was that he chose not to recall and that he did not want to remember.

Stock state of mind was improving. Walking through the pleasant gardens one bright morning, he heard a great cheer go up from one of the buildings across the road and saw several people running about in all directions. It was August 15th and the radio had just broadcast Japan's surrender. A great sense of pride welled up inside him and he sat down on a nearby bench and wept. He had done his duty for King and Country and knew that the small part that he had played had contributed to victory, yet, just as important, he was alive and had kept faith with himself. He could go back home to his family and friends, hold his hand on his heart, and say to those who asked, "Yes, I was there, and I am proud of it."

Those who had served longest throughout the campaign in Assam were designated to return back to England but when Stock was summoned to General Stopford's Headquarters in Imphal, he learned that Alfredson had been sent to Borneo. He too was told that he was allocated to a ship back home along with most other officers, but they were short of general officers. And, in view of his most excellent results in building airfields in the most awkward of places and his intimate knowledge of the working of the corps, Stopford asked him if he wanted Alfredson's position as brigadier to oversee the logistics.

Two weeks later, Stock found himself staring over the handrail of RMS Strathnaver as it bobbed along the empty Indian Ocean, wondering if he ought to have taken Stopford's offer.

Chapter 21
Clink

A cold shower is seldom welcome and only those who recognise that they actually need one realise the benefits of it afterwards. It makes the skin glow in an invigorating way and is quite popular with the health fanatics of this world. Susan had never voluntarily had a cold shower before, but she now stood shivering in Vicky's state-of-the-art Nordic cubicle, suffering from the myriad high-pressure needle-like jets of what seemed to be ice-cold water that attacked her from every direction. Her skin could not have been more goose pimpled as she tried to get rid of the rouge around her very stiff nipples and she toyed with the idea of turning up the temperature as she attended to the rest of her body, which was reluctant to give up the last vestiges of the lotions from the night before. In the full-length mirror, she had seen that they had shaped her bush into a crude upside-down exclamation mark, and she worried about how she was going to explain that one to Roger, but right now her primary concern was her children, and she was now preparing to leave before the rest of the household was up and about.

She arrived back at The Twinings well before any of the B&B guests were likely to be stirring and let herself into the back door.

A chirpy Sarah greeted her. "Good morning, wasn't expecting to see you so early. Go on tell me. What it was like?" She had a wicked grin on her face but dropped it when she saw Susan's more closely.

"Oh, it was fine, but how are the kids?"

A non-plussed Sarah looked blankly back. "I thought you had them with you, I got your text, you haven't got them, then?" she asked.

They went over their predicament until Sarah reached for her phone and showed Susan the message she had received.

Just leaving. tom & ann with me

"But that's not what I sent...It's supposed to say '*melanie @ vill hall*.'" She compared the message with what she had sent from her phone and had to admit that it had been her fault.

"I saw them last night, on the telly at one of the concerts. Are you sure they're not upstairs?"

Two empty beds sneered at them as they entered their bedroom.

"Oh, shit! Where the hell are they, then?"

"God, I'm so sorry Susan. But what's this concert you saw them at?"

They stood looking blankly at each other for a moment and then in unison exclaimed "the internet." They raced downstairs to the computer in the office and began to trawl through the BBC's massive website, eventually finding the correct 'see again' section. It took them about ten minutes before Susan recognised Tom and Ann dancing at the back of the conga and they replayed it several times just to make sure.

"It's definitely them but how did they get there and where are they now?" Susan paused the replay and her eyes opened even wider. There in the background she could see a man in a wheelchair, and it looked like Bernard. She replayed the video again. Yes, it was him, in a uniform. She had never seen Bernard in his uniform before, only in black and white photographs from his war years, but there in the distance was her father-in-law. What was he doing there? How, what, when, did…? Susan was totally flummoxed, and she shut her eyes in despair.

She went next door and opened his wardrobe. She had been in there occasionally to clean but now noticed that there was an enlarged gap on the rail where his uniform had once hung. She returned to her house, commenting to Sarah on the way, "His uniform's definitely gone, I'm just going to phone Springfields. Perhaps he's there with the kids."

She recalled that there was to be a day's outing for the old folk and that was yesterday, but they were supposed to be going to the agricultural show, not London.

Natalie answered the phone to Susan.

"Well.... we've had some going's on here," she offered. "Mr Green is down at the police station with Matron, and the senior Sister is busy with the patients at the moment. Can I get her to call you back?"

"This is urgent, but what I really want to know is if my father-in-law Bernard Stock is still with you. You see, I think he's gone missing with my two children."

Natalie had to think about that one but then recalled the note she had been handed by Green that said that Colonel Stock and Captain Perry had not returned with the coach party yesterday. That was why he was down at the police station, and she told Susan as much.

"What about my children? Have you seen them?"

"Sorry, but I only came on duty a short while ago, and nobody's told me anything about anyone's children. Let me go and ask Sister and I'll call you right back. Oh, what's your number?" Susan gave it and hung up the phone. She started talking out loud to Sarah to help put her thoughts in order "Where were the kids Friday night if they weren't here? Bernard went to the show yesterday in the Springfields coach and the kids were with him last night, then that means they must have been with him on the coach, right?"

Sarah nodded, still feeling rather sheepish at having lost Susan's kids.

"That means that the coach didn't go to the Show but went to London instead, yes?

Another nod.

"But the coach came back without either Bernard or the kids, or some other chap, so what are Mr Green and Matron doing down at Horsham police station?

"Well, they definitely didn't come back from the Village Hall, and they weren't here last night. God knows what they've been up to. Why don't I phone Melanie and you keep on at Springfields? If we don't get any joy, we'll get in touch with the police. How about that?"

"OK," Susan agreed and reached for her cordless landline, while Melanie dug into her handbag for her mobile, and the two women paced around various rooms firing off questions. Sarah finished first and started boiling the kettle for some tea. When Susan got off the phone, she said, "Melanie didn't have them for a sleep-over and swears that she saw them walk up the drive about 8.30, but I was here then, and I didn't see or hear them. I really don't know where they went, and I am so sorry I cocked this up."

"It really isn't your fault. I should never have gone." Susan cuddled the cup as though it somehow alleviated her feeling of guilt and wondered when it would be a good time to let Roger know.

"Any luck with Springfields?"

"Not really. It only deepens the mystery." She was staring into middle space as she sipped her tea. "The coach did come back from the show minus Bernard, the kids, and this other chap. It never went to London." Susan shook her head in disbelief. "The sister told me that the other chap was taken to hospital by mistake but that there had been absolutely no sign of Bernard or the kids. She suggested I go down there as Mr Green is expected back shortly." Another sip from her cup. "What the hell is going on here?"

"I'd get onto the police if I were you; they're likely to know more than Springfields."

They stared at each other in silence for a moment before Susan made her mind up. "Can you hang on here while I go and find out what's been going on?"

"Of course, I can. I've not got anything on this weekend other than I was supposed to be meeting Barry down the pub this evening. You go but let me know if you need me."

Susan went through the B&B register and other matters with her before collecting her car keys and heading off to Springfields.

She met with the Sister in charge who didn't know much more than what she had already told Susan and her reassurances that Mr Green would soon be back from the police station to explain everything did nothing to alleviate her anxieties.

Susan's patience was running out. "You've lost my father-in-law, my two children are with him, and you haven't the faintest idea where they are. You've hospitalised another of your patients by mistake and you don't know when your boss is coming back. This must be the worst-run home in the country and I'll make sure the authorities know about it. I'm off to talk to someone who can help me: the police." She stormed out of Green's office.

Ron's Lad had been ear wigging from his usual spot under the window and didn't like what he heard one bit. If there was going to be any sort of investigation, he certainly did not want his name cropping up and his cunning mind immediately went into passing-the-blame mode. He didn't want to see Springfields closed down either as that would mean he would have to find somewhere else to live, but perhaps there might be an opportunity to get rid of the one person left who could still make his life uncomfortable: Mrs Weeks from the Council.

He went and retrieved her handbag from the Well Room and silently entered Green's office, which he quite rightly assumed would be unused until he returned. He ferreted around in her bag until he found her Council pass, photocopied it, and pasted the Council's logo onto another piece of paper before feeding it into the printer tray. He was not used to computers but had watched Green and copied the strokes that finally open the word processing window and typed.

Two children to accompany Colonel Stock on the coach.

He looked around the various pieces of correspondence on Green's desk for something appropriate to finish the note off with.

Authorised
Patricia Weeks

He was about to press print when another thought came into his mind. Why stop there? He flicked through more of Green's correspondence and found Matron's signature on an official requisition order and copied the same procedure. The note that printed out was not quite straight, but it would have to do; he had already spent far too long somewhere where he ought not to be, and getting caught now would be disastrous. He placed the note under the top page of Green's pile of correspondence in his 'IN' tray and left the office as he had found it, before spiriting Mrs Weeks' handbag back to the cellars. With any luck an investigation would point the finger away from him but towards those who could interfere with his comfortable life.

Susan used the precious time driving to Horsham police station to consider what had happened and what best to do next. She had also been on her mobile to Sarah who had looked it up on the internet and told her what she needed to know. When she arrived at the empty front desk, she knew exactly what to say to the desk sergeant.

"My name is Susan Stock and I demand to see Chief Constable Colin Taper straight away."

She was lucky it was Sgt. Stokoe she was addressing as he sauntered over from behind one of the desks to the front barrier. "You wouldn't have a relative under the name of Colonel Bernard Stock by any chance, would you?"

This was not the sort of reaction she had been expecting. It was more of a brush-off, and she hesitated before replying, "Yes. How do you know?"

"Well, there's not too many people around here called Stock and under the circumstances, even fewer who would be coming here announcing who they are. We were about to send someone out to you in… Yeastings." He looked down to consult from a folder. "But being the Bank Holiday, we're a bit short-staffed here today; every available man's in London today."

"That's what I want to talk to you about London. You see my children and their grandfather are...."

"Hold on a minute. Perhaps you ought to come round to one of the interview rooms and we can go through things properly." He paced off to a door on his right, and another security door on Susan's left opened. "This way please, Madam." He held it open for her.

During the next forty-five minutes, Susan was shocked at what Sgt. Stokoe told her but in return he was surprised to learn that there were now two missing children to add to the list.

"I think we had better get you up to London to help us find and identify them, but by the sound of things, it doesn't seem like they've been kidnapped. If he's, how shall I put it, rather vague, it's possible he has gone to attend the ceremonies and taken his grandchildren along for company."

"At an all-night concert?" queried Susan. "And how did he get there anyway? He can't walk that far and I'm sure his wheelchair would have run out of batteries long before he got anywhere near London. It certainly wasn't by coach either. And where did they stay last night if they are still there?"

"I think I had better have a word with my Super. Perhaps he can help. You see, I only came on duty about an hour ago and I haven't had a chance to go through the nightly reports yet. I'll try not to keep you long." He rose and opened the door to confer with the superintendent in one of the back offices. As he did so, Susan caught sight of Mr Green in the corridor through the open doorway.

"Mr Green, Mr Green." She hurried out of the room to confront him. "What have you done with my children and where's my father-in-law?"

Green was looking a bit shabby; not having shaved that morning wasn't helping his appearance. He had been at the station all night 'helping the police with their enquiries' and was looking forward to getting out of there. Being confronted with one of his patient's relatives who accused him of having done something with her children was a real shock to him. He managed to recall her name but not her children's. He told his story to her. "The last time I saw them they were heading off to an ice cream stall not more than a hundred feet away. My back was turned only for a minute or so but when I looked around, they were gone. I even gave them some vouchers."

"Sounds like you're the one who needs looking after. Do you know they were in London last night?"

His head had been hanging low as if in shame, but he now jerked it up. "In London?"

"Yes. At a concert. And now they've vanished again and it's all your fault."

"But how did..."

Sgt. Stokoe had not gone to his Super but had waited in the background in case Susan had wanted to vent her anger on Mr Green, and he now interjected, "I don't think Mr Green's in a position to help us any further." He grabbed him by the arm and lead him to the exit before ushering Susan back into the interview room.

"I'll be speaking to you as soon as this is over," she called over her shoulder as Green departed.

"I promise I won't be long," said Sgt. Stokoe as he left the room once again.

There was a great pile of statements on his desk from all of the BBC crew who had readily signed whatever had been put in front of them. Most of them said the same thing, but he hadn't had time to go through them all in as much detail as he would have liked. The crew were still all down in the cells now; all except Camp. It irked Stokoe that Camp had managed to contact his solicitor who had obtained his release the previous evening.

It had been like a scene from the sheepdog trials, thought Sgt. Stokoe, recalling the real sheepdog trial he had seen yesterday. When Superintendent Falls had put the some twenty BBC OB crew under arrest, he discovered that they did not have enough secure vans to transport them back to the police station, and so had commandeered the tour bus, which was now taking up much of the station's car park. He and two other constables had had to round them all up before any of them vanished, including two shifty-looking individuals who went by the names of Sam and Ham. He would be looking at their statements more closely in a while. The driver of the bus was the only one who was licensed to drive such a large vehicle and he had been coerced and directed by one of the constables back to Horsham police station, where they had all disembarked and milled around the car par until herded into the underground cells.

Camp had been particularly obnoxious when told to share the one big open cell with them, especially the bearded, padded chequered shirt type who seemed to have a swarm of insects constantly hovering above him. Horsham police station was one of several in the country that had still not been replaced by a modern one and had been built in a pre-Victorian era when it was not thought necessary to cater for crowds of prisoners, just the occasional villain. The influx of a score of prisoners all at the same time filled the large iron-grated cell to capacity. Camp had complained bitterly and had demanded to be moved to a more personal cell, much to the derision of his fellows. In order to keep the peace, Sgt. Stokoe had moved him to a solitary cell, where Camp had shouted even louder at being cooped up and had insisted that his rights were being ignored and that he was entitled to contact his solicitor. His solicitor was in fact a prominent barrister, a Sir Double-Barrelled something, who knew the chief constable and obtained Camp's immediate release. Boos and obscene comments from the crew followed Camp down the tiled corridor as he was escorted away to freedom, his one objective was to be instrumental on the nation's tv throughout the event of the century and to make contact with even more rich and famous glitterati.

Sgt. Stokoe was standing in front of Superintendent Andrew Falls' desk, having apprised him of Susan's presence, and watched him thumb through the Statements he had placed there. He knew better than to interrupt while he did this and waited while he opened and read through the overnight report folder. This dossier was circulated every night to all stations around the country advising them of the latest misdemeanours of criminal society.

"It looks like this Colonel Stock is very well connected. He's expected to appear on one of the podiums at The Cenotaph this afternoon." He had selected a piece of paper from the folder which he now held in both hands. "As he lives in our county, it instructs us to locate him if possible and deliver him up there by 1 o'clock today." He looked up at the Sergeant. "You tell me that you've got his daughter-in-law downstairs but that he's missing somewhere in London with her two children in tow. Have I got that right?"

"Yes, sir."

Supt. Falls considered the situation for a short while. If he was found to be responsible for locating the colonel for such a high-profile occasion, it would certainly do him well for his promotional career. "I think we ought to help Mrs Stock find him and her two children, then. Organise a car and we'll take her up there."

"Errrr, sir... We're a bit short-staffed this morning and I'm supposed to be on the desk today, and there aren't any drivers. Shall I ask the senior constable to take my place and I'll drive you?"

"As you like, Sergeant. We'd better go straight away. Time is short and we can use Mrs Stock's knowledge of him to help us find him."

"Errrr, sir... What about the crowd we have downstairs in the cells?" He knew the answer and knew what his Super would say but thought it prudent to ask in any case.

"I suppose we ought to release them, but not those two..." He looked down at the report sheet. "Ham and Sam. We may have to charge them with kidnapping. Have we heard from the hospital whether Captain Perry is going to be alright?"

"Only a preliminary report. He ought to live but it's still touch and go, and if he does die, we may have to consider a manslaughter charge."

"In that case, definitely retain Ham and Sam. Come on, then. I'll meet you downstairs in five minutes."

Chapter 22

The Search for Stock – Part I

Whether or not we realize it, the subconscious works better when we are asleep which is why the gurus of the world advocate a twenty-minute power nap in the middle of the day. The old expression 'sleep on it' is well founded; the mind, being freed of the conscious restraints of having to make decisions, wanders along not just those well-trodden paths it usually does but explores the millions of impossible dead-end scenarios. Few manage to remember their dreams, but a minority wake up with a solution to the problems they were thinking about the night before.

Stock didn't know why he had woken; perhaps it was the strange odour of the room or the unfamiliar smells that wafted in through the window or even the oblique sunlight, but it was probably the background noise of traffic. It could even have been that he was used to being woken up at this time, but whatever it was he gently opened his eyes as he lay on his back and stared at the blank high ceiling. Half in and half out of sleep he just lay there, only vaguely aware of which way was up.

He had been dreaming about the previous night's revelries and the wonderful atmosphere that went with it and how happy it made him to watch his own grandchildren dancing. But in the background emerged a more sinister figure weaving its way through the crowd that bayed for more from the big stage ahead of them, and it walked slowly through the throng and was now leading a line of men. But these men were not the same ones dancing in the conga, and they were heading in his direction, seeming to multiply as they got closer, eventually fanning out in front of him and cutting off his view of both the stage and his grandchildren. From the centre emerged a huge figure.

"You failed me, Stock." It was Alfredson. "You promised me you would bring her back to me and here you are malingering. Where is she?" he boomed.

Stock tried to answer but couldn't and now they were all shouting at him. "Where is she... where is she?"

"Bring her back to me. I need her... Your King needs her... Your country needs her... You must bring her back."

Staring up at the ceiling, he recalled Alfredson's demand. He knew where she was and all he had to do was go and get her. But where was Alfredson? Where... where? Hang on a minute, wasn't he in London? Churchill was in London. He could take her straight to him, couldn't he?

His confused state of mind had no concept of time, and he hadn't even fathomed out how or why he was in London, why his grandchildren were with him, and why... why... why...? But he had a purpose and his military training had engrained in him that every action had to have an objective. His was to retrieve Akiko and, if he couldn't hand her over to Alfredson, he would do so directly to the Prime Minister, from whom the order had come in any case.

His eyes focused and he knew what he had to do and went to jump out of bed, but his hip reminded him of his age and so he eased his feet gently onto the floor and went in search of the toilet, nearly tripping over his stick. He was confused by the spaciousness of the room and found himself in the adjoining living room faced with the problem of finding out which door led to it. Crossing the room, he entered the other bedroom and saw Tom and Ann sitting on the bed playing with some electronic gadgets.

"Hello, Grandpa." In unison.

"We're playing lemmings," volunteered Ann.

"And I'm winning," countered Tom.

Stock was non-plussed until he looked over at the large tv screen hanging from a wall to see cartoon creatures running in all directions accompanied by suitable noises.

"Do you want a go? It's great fun."

"Yeah. You've really got to look out for the cliffs… here we go." Dozens of the little creatures scampered vertically downwards.

"No, thank you, but you can tell me which door leads to the toilet."

"Yours is through your room on the left. Like ours only the other way around." Ann had paused the game. "When can we go for breakfast?"

"Let me get ready and we will see what we can find – it'll be downstairs I expect. Get yourselves ready." He turned to find his way back to his room.

Looking into the mirror as he cleaned his dentures the best he could, the face that stared back at him was a little unfamiliar, but it was definitely him; it didn't seem quite as old as he remembered. His neatly trimmed moustache hid some of the wrinkles around its edges and he ran his hand over the unshaven face. He found a wet razor and soap next to the basin. His hair was not totally grey, but the sideburns increased in whiteness the further down his cheeks they ran, and he delicately squared them off. He finished his hair off with the courtesy comb and brush, rubbing some of the fragrant oil over it to keep it in place.

He frowned as he bent down to pick up his uniform from the chest he had put it on the night before. The trousers showed signs of wrinkling and there was dust on the sleeves of his jacket, and he made a mental note to have a word with his Batman - what was his name again? He was just reaching for his shoes when Tom and Ann came in.

"Ready, Grandpa?"

"Yeah. I'm starving."

Stock was saddened by the state of his shoes as they no longer had that parade-ground shine on them. "Wish I could get these polished," he muttered to himself, but it was overheard by Tom who was standing next to him.

"I'll do it," he said as he picked them up. "There's a machine in the hall and it tickles your feet if you leave your shoes off."

He returned a few minutes later and offered them up to Stock for approval. "There you go. What do you think?"

Stock inspected his boots and although they were still not up to the standard he would have liked, he could see that they were shinier than before. "Thank you, Tom. Here, help me get them on, will you."

He stood in front of the full-length mirror and surveyed himself for a moment. Self-esteem and confidence welled through him as his reflection stood to attention. He didn't realize it but dressed in his full colonel's uniform complete with cap, Sam Browne, and medals, he exuded an air of authority.

"Come on then. Breakfast." He announced in a military tone, and strode off, limping slightly, towards the hall with Tom and Ann in line behind him. "We'll walk today, I think." Rather than turning right out of the door towards one of the lifts, Stock turned left and headed towards the main grand double staircase. About halfway down, he wished he had taken the lift instead since his hip was complaining but he wasn't the sort of man to give up that easily. The maître d' in the restaurant caught the trio heading his way across the marbled foyer and, without needing to look down at the restaurant's reservations page, showed them to one of the prepared tables. The kids had never seen so many pieces of cutlery before, and it wasn't long before they were positioning the various eating implements to create a run for the marbles that Tom had produced from one of his pockets. As one waiter produced a jug of water and filled their glasses and another offered them a selection of bread, they quick-fired questions at yet another who had given each of them a menu, asking what such-and-such was and other queries like what *flambé* meant and, all the while, their mouths watering at the descriptions.

*****

Wickes' breakfast was altogether different. He was dog-tired from the previous day's exertions and had struggled to open an eye when his first alarm went off. He had snoozed it in automation but had to stretch to silence the second bell a few minutes later which just about managed to bring him to his senses. Finally, the watch on his wrist buzzed and vibrated and he struggled to turn the damn thing off, loosening the metal strap by accident. Always an awkward waker, he had shuffled zombie-like into his bathroom and was going about his usual business when he realized what today was. Standing in front of the toilet pan, he managed to wet his feet while trying to focus on his wristwatch. This really did wake him up and he cursed as he stepped back, managing to wet the linoleum floor even more and the loose watch around his wrist scuttled off into the toilet pan. More expletives followed. Knowing he had to locate the colonel as soon as he could, he hastily made himself a luke-warm cup of tea and a marmite sandwich from almost stale bread while still getting dressed, and used his mobile to alert his chauffeur who ought to have been waiting outside in any case. He would need to return later to change into more appropriate attire for the afternoon's ceremonies.

There was an awkward scene outside The Ritz as his name had still not been added to the list, but fortunately for him the same duty officer as the previous evening had just started his shift and when contacted by one of the doormen, allowed him to enter and they met outside the same lift. Terry was also back on duty and back in his chair. "No sight of him yet." He commented as they waited for the lift to arrive.

Wickes was becoming worried "I don't have a choice. I need to find him, and we've got to see if he's in his room."

"Ok but let me go in first." He readied his electronic pass.

It soon became clear that the Stock entourage was not there. "Well, his wheelchair's still here and so's his walking stick so he can't be far."

"The beds have been slept in and there's the kids' backpacks in one of the rooms. Where the hell are they?" Wickes was now worried. "Didn't you say your chap would let us know if he saw them?"

"Let's go and have a word."

Terry stood up as they stood over him. "I wasn't on duty last night and have only just come back on like yourself, sir. Let me check the register." His handheld Palm revealed that the Stocks had returned around midnight but that they hadn't been seen since.

"He's like a ghost," commented Wickes. "But you say he hasn't come down here this morning."

"That's right. I've been here about half an hour, and he definitely hasn't come past here." Terry realized that the two in front of him were going to lay the blame at his feet unless he could divert them. "Would you like me to contact Martin who was here last night, or shall we initiate a 31, sir?"

A 31 was the call sign for a search and would mean that they had lost track of their target. This would be noted on the duty officer's record and wasn't something he wanted to do just yet. "

"Yes, contact Martin but no 31 yet. Let's just have a look around, shall we?" He spoke into his wrist-mounted mouthpiece, ordering all security staff to casually look for a colonel with a wheelchair. He didn't want a full security clampdown that was bound to be seen by the other important guests and possibly be responsible for causing an incident. He didn't realise that he had mentioned a wheelchair.

One chap did notice a man in military uniform serving himself from the buffet table in the restaurant but concluded that anyone standing would not be in a wheelchair, and besides which on today of all days, there were more and more people dressed in their national uniforms and it was therefore not worthy of a comment.

While the Stocks enjoyed a hearty breakfast, Wicks was developing an anxiety that he had not experienced since his school days, but he was still one of the more senior coordinators of the day's minor issues, mostly to do with who was doing what and when.

"Look. He's bound to come back here for his wheelchair and when he does, please, please contact me. You've got my number.

I'm off to Whitehall."

"Do you want us to restrain him?"

Wickes had to think about this one. "Yes. If he appears, keep him here. At least I'll know where to find him, then." As he was leaving, he added "And add my name to your list."

While the Stocks were finishing up their sumptuous breakfast, a worried Wickes was getting a grilling from Jefferies in Sir John's outer office. "He's vanished. Like a bloody ghost and even his children have disappeared, presumably with him."

"His grandchildren," Jefferies corrected as he replaced his phone on the receiver. He too was getting more than the usual number of phone calls. "That was the PM's secretary, and it seems Mr Keisuke wants to meet Colonel Stock and I've just assured him that he'll be there."

"Mr Who?

"Mr Keisuke… He's heading the Japanese delegation. I've met him on a few occasions and he's a very pleasant man. His father commanded their forces in Assam during the war but was killed just before they surrendered." His voice trailed off as the names of both Keisuke and Stock in the same sentence began to ring a bell at the back of his mind. He probably would have made the connection if his thoughts hadn't been interrupted by Wickes.

"It looks like we're going to have to initiate a full-scale search for him then, but I'll need your say-so first." Wickes waited for Jefferies to catch up with what he was saying, as the full implications of initiating a full-scale search would mean that the media would also be alerted and they would be asking questions, questions that may reveal that Wickes and his newly formed department had lost somebody. "The biggest problem is that we don't have a photograph of the man."

"Look, somebody must know what he looks like. Doesn't he have a family? He's got two grandchildren and their parents must be able to help. Your department's supposed to be coordinating this, so I suggest you get Jackman's lot and MI5 in on it. Time's running out so get a move on. I've got other matters to attend to." His phone rang and so did that of Wickes.

Two minutes later and off their phones, they were both breathing a sigh of relief, Wickes more so. "He's back in his room at The Ritz, with the two children." Before Jefferies could say so. "I'll go and see him straight away." He left with the intention of going directly to The Ritz, but getting into the lift, caught a whiff of his unwashed body and considered that while MI5 had Stock in their charge and were unlikely to lose him this time, he had time to go via his apartment, shower and change into cleaner clothes.

Jefferies, meanwhile, on his blotting paper pad, had jotted down Stock's name as a reminder to ring his aunt who he hoped may be able to cast more light on why he thought he knew that name. He felt sure his now-deceased father had mentioned him but couldn't recall in what context.

The Stocks were spotted by the security man from behind the reception desk as they crossed the foyer, and he immediately alerted his duty officer via his wrist mike. As they approached the lift, Terry stood up and waited with them, trying to look like an innocent bystander. His standing operational orders would have been to accost a target within the confines of something just like a lift, rather than in an open space. Any actions he might have to take may be seen by the general public, or in this case, high-profile diplomats, and this was exactly what his masters wanted to avoid. As the lift doors closed, he turned and briefly presented his security card to Stock. "Good morning, sir. Do you mind if I accompany you to your room?"

Stock was impressed with the service this hotel was offering. "Not at all." He hadn't had time to focus fully on the small card that the man had momentarily held rather close to his eyes other than the letters MIS and wondered what they stood for. Meanwhile, the kids had been scrambling to be the first to press the right button and then squirming with each other to be the holder of the room's key card, and as the door opened, they shot off down the corridor.

Terry followed Stock to his room and, as he went in, he said, "I'll be right here, sir." He took up station beside the door. Stock paused and looked at him before going in. "In case you need anything." He added with a smile. Once Stock was out of sight, he advised the duty officer that the Stocks were back in their room.

Tom beat Ann into first place to the toilet while Stock sat down in one of the comfortable armchairs and closed his eyes, instantly falling asleep after a most satisfying breakfast. It was a routine he had become used to lately although he didn't realize why. For about twenty minutes, Tom and Ann played with the controllers on their bed in front of the tv, until a fidgeting Ann had to go to the toilet and when she returned, Tom was scrolling through the options of other items on the screen. With the sound of the tv off, they could now hear the reverberation of the gathering crowds outside, and it drew them to the balcony where they now looked down on a riot of colour. The bunting and flags all responded to the gentle breeze and below it, hundreds of people meandered here and there, most of them dressed in vibrant colours. Their view had been restricted the night before by dusk but in the clear morning air they could see right across the park.

"Look, that's Buckingham Palace over there and the Queen's in," said Ann.

"How do you know she's in?"

"Miss. Cooper told us that when the Queen's in, the flag is at the top of the mast. When she's out, it's halfway down. That's how I know."

"I thought she lived in Windsor Castle, but I can't see it from here."

"Let's go and ask Grandpa. He'll know."

Stock was stirring in any case as Tom shook his shoulder and the trio went out onto the balcony and looked around while Stock explained some of the more famous landmarks. He didn't know very many of them but recognized Nelson's Column and in the distance pointed to the tall city buildings. "When my parents brought me to

London, we visited Hamleys.”

“What’s Hamleys?”

“Hamleys is the biggest toy shop in the world.” He didn’t know that it wasn’t the biggest any longer, but in his day it had been, and he recalled fond memories of it. Even now he could picture the front window when he had first seen it, and for his birthday he had been given a box of wooden toy soldiers which he had lovingly painted with his brother at home.

“Can we go there, can we go there, oh, please,” was the inevitable response.

Stock looked down at the eager faces and kept them waiting. “Well, alright then.”

“Yippeee….” Ann was pogo-ing again and jumped back through the balcony doors. In his excitement Tom upended his backpack from the bed, spilling most of the contents over the floor and Ann spotted one of the walkie-talkies. “Did you remember to bring the other one too?”

“Oh, yes. It’s in here somewhere.” He tipped out the rest to find it.

“Why have you got four torches?” asked Ann as she looked down at the different shapes.

“Thought they might come in useful.” Tom loved torches and, as the last of the contents of the backpack emptied on the floor, some dozen or so batteries followed. “Here you are.” He handed Ann one of the radios. “Channel 7.13.” A pair of ‘beeps’ confirmed that they were both on and they tested them.

Stock appeared at their bedroom door in his wheelchair. “Ready?”

*****

Statistics show that when world leaders meet, be it under the banner of the United Nations, G7, or some other body, there’s always one country that spoils the otherwise common accord by demanding some sort of oblique concession or insisting upon a rule change etc. before a unanimous agreement is reached. Like a schoolmaster addressing the assembled pupils and declaring 'It's always the same few that spoil it for the rest, isn't it?' In this instance, it was the French - again.

Under direct control from Paris, French Guiana is situated in the north-east continent of South America and part shares its borders with Brazil on one side and Suriname on the other, while the Atlantic Ocean breaks on its coastline. Not too far offshore live indigenous islanders who once came under the jurisdiction of the Brazilian authorities and before that the Spanish, and before them the Dutch and it came as no surprise to anyone that, because of their chequered history, the few islanders had recently been crowing for independence. The Island actually had no local name, it was that small, but was affectionally known as Serenidad and its only asset was that it had an emerald mine, and consequentially the few who lived there enjoyed the status of having an extremely high per capita 'National' wealth. Fish and coconuts were the abundant staple diet. When approached by the islanders to discuss the issue of independence, the French prefect appointed from Paris had firmly refused to even meet them by scribbling just one word on their well-presented letter: 'Non'. This naturally insulted them.

It was doubtful that there would ever be any conflict as the largest boat in their arsenal was an ancient twenty-five-foot fishing smack and the longest blade on the island was a mere 20" long. Undeterred, two of the islanders had been voted to go and plead their case before the UN and had been on a tour to bring attention to their plight to the rest of the world. The two individuals were staying at The Holiday Inn opposite The Ritz and seeing the delegation from French Guiana milling about underneath the arches which marked the front entrance to The Ritz, they went over to remonstrate. In a very short time, the passing crowd had faltered and grown in size to see what all the shouting was about and looked on as an argument developed between what looked like white security forces and subdued blacks. There was in fact no violence as that was not the islanders' way, but it didn't help that a passing press photographer started snapping away at very close range, elbowing his way between several security staff. The duty officer had called on all personnel to attend the scene to prevent any escalation, and consequentially Terry had had to leave his post. Shortly after, the Stocks emerged from their room and headed off towards the nearest lift. They were not seen exiting The Ritz by the same back entrance they had used the previous night as they obliviously set off for Hamleys in Regent Street.

A well-turned-out Wickes arrived at The Ritz a few minutes after the disappointed crowd had dissipated and this time had no trouble accessing the front door as the duty officer was still standing there. It had taken him much longer than he expected to return since the direct route was now barred to all traffic, and his chauffeur had had to take him initially in the opposite direction along the Embankment and through the back streets of Covent Garden. He and the duty officer approached Terry who was now back at his station beside the Stocks' door.

Wickes couldn't believe it. "I thought you said they were here."

Terry was made to explain why he had left his post and Wickes took it out on the duty officer.

"The PM's after him, the Japanese are after him and all you can say is that the bloody French are responsible. All you had to do was keep a defenceless old man and two children in a room three floors up with no way out other than through that door for an hour and you couldn't even do that." Wickes was beginning to rant in frustration but calmed down enough to think a little. He rounded on Terry.

"You, you saw him. Whatever else you are, you can be professional now. What's he look like? Describe him to me."

Once the duty officer had finished taking notes on his electronic pad, they left. Wickes was not looking forward to returning to Jefferies office with the bad news, nor that he would now have to involve Commander Jackman, but at least he would now be able to circulate a photofit once the Duty Officer had forwarded it. The description given by Terry was quite accurate and was now being circulated along the designated channels, but somehow on the electronic airways, someone somewhere had omitted the wheelchair. The focus was on the man, not the machine.

Chapter 23

The Search for Stock – Part II

Sgt. Stokoe had driven Falls and Susan to the police station in Belgravia and, even as they told their story to Deputy Superintendent Hodges, they were interrupted by a constable who produced a bulletin concerning Colonel Stock and his two grandchildren.

"That's them," piped up Susan. "But this describes Bernard as being about sixty years old. He's a hundred, or nearly."

The constable continued." It says here that they were last seen at The Ritz in Piccadilly but have now vanished and if found they are to be detained." He paused and briefly looked at Susan "A Section 31 Notice has been issued."

A silence descended while the implications of a Section 31 Notice sunk in.

Susan broke the peace, "Well, what's a Section 31 Notice?"

Falls and Hodges looked at each other but it was Hodges who broke the awkward news to Susan. "A Section 31 Notice is circulated to all police forces across the country as well as Special Branch, MI5, the Royal Protection Squad, and other such bodies and takes priority over almost all other notices. It means that we have to find and detain any person listed on that notice."

"That's great news," piped up Susan, but her elation was short-lived when she looked at the expressions on the faces of the policemen in the room. "Isn't it?"

Falls interjected. "In one way, yes. It means that your family is likely to be found in very short order indeed, but I must tell you that a Section 31 is normally reserved for terrorists and the like."

The previous silence paled into insignificance compared to the one that followed.

"I think it's about time you told us all you know about your father-in-law."

*****

Mike & Geoff had agreed to meet upstairs in one of the coffee houses just off Oxford Street rather than returning to Crofts Wine Bar which would have increased the possibility of running into Julie. It was a place they had met before. Geoff could hardly contain himself as Mike pulled up one of the tall chairs opposite him. "I've got to hand it to you, you've certainly struck gold this time. I don't know where you found her, but she's got it all at her fingertips and it seems she's very well connected. You want to keep her on your hook if you can."

"Come on. You didn't bring me over here just to tell me the bleeding obvious. What've you got?

"Ok. Here we go. First of all, I've managed to tap into all calls and messages to and from her phone. Nothing juicy yet but, better than that, because the RX and TX frequencies are the same for all the numbers on her phone, I can monitor them all and there's a hell of a lot coming and going, especially now." He paused to gingerly sip his coffee while it was still hot. "For example, and from what I've gleaned so far, it seems that the PM's got a double. Now that in itself is not too unusual, but this character - whoever he is, and I haven't had a chance to try to find out more yet - while he really does look exactly like Neale, may, in fact, be his illegitimate brother. There isn't a name I can give you yet as most transmissions are in code and I'll need more time to dig deeper, but it goes a long way to explaining why the PM's getting into all this philandering trouble at the moment." Another slurp from the large cardboard cup. "Now that's got to be worth quite something, isn't it?"

Mike was resting his elbows on the tall table, edging himself as close as possible in order not to miss a thing. "Certainly is, and once you get more, we'll try and get the timing right as to how and when we release it."

"Now, here's the really good news. As long as they don't re-encode the transmissions too far from the current frequencies, and there's no reason why they should deviate from the norm, I ought to be able to continue to trace them, but just in case we ought to move quickly."

"You got anything right now?"

"I'm not sure, but just before I left there was a Section 31 issued."

They were both aware that Section 31 was the highest form of alert for a potential terrorist which recently had ended in the shooting of said terrorists when found.

"Who's the target?"

"I've never heard of him, and he doesn't sound like one of those Middle Eastern types, but he could be a Merc." He looked at the palm of his hand. "A Colonel Stock. Know anything about him?"

"No." Mike shook his head. "But I know someone who may. He knows just about every mercenary from here to Timbuctoo."

"Perhaps it's a hit on someone but with the number of world leaders in town today, God knows who."

For a few moments, they just sat there, lost in their own thoughts, occasionally looking at each other across the table as well as watching those around them in case anyone was eavesdropping.

Mike made his mind up. "Look. You keep ferreting away at your end and I'll make a couple of calls. See if we can't find out more about Colonel Stock. It oughtn't to be too hard as a 31 has been issued. If it's a hit it'll probably be in the next day or so and with our inside intel we ought to be able to keep one step ahead of the rest." He was referring to the media fraternity who would descend on such a story like a pack of wolves. He got down from the high stool. "Ring me as soon as you can. I need to find a phone box."

"He's that sensitive, then, your contact?"

"Oh, yes. Invaluable. Say half-an-hour?"

*****

Commander Jackman felt that his attitude to Wickes was totally justified. Not only had the upstart tried to belittle him in front of the security committee but now he had the gall to demand the assistance of Special Branch in covering up for his mistakes. If it had been left to him in the first place, there would not be the need for a manhunt now, and to make matters worse there was very little time in which to find him. The Section 31 Notice had been received from the Home Office with explicit but unusual instructions not to shoot on sight, just detain. With increasing frustration, Jackman had demanded that all files and documents pertaining to Colonel Stock be brought in front of him immediately.

Usually attached on the inside cover there would be a single page of the basic details of the individual concerned, but in this instance the passport-sized photograph was shadowed with the letters *'N/A'* stamped over it; this meant that no photograph had been taken. He read over the rest of the file which had initially been compiled by a vetting officer when Stock had volunteered for the Royal Engineers in 1939 and had been added to at various points during his career in the Army. It contained all the usual descriptions about him and his family background, of his sponsors, commanding officers, postings, discharge, etc. but turning a leaf what caught Jackman's eye was that in 1945, the additions had been inserted by military intelligence, now MI6. There was a sudden cessation of information after he had been discharged in 1946, which he found extraordinary, as MI6 had a habit of keeping tabs on anyone right up to their final demise. To his suspicious mind, he felt that there was probably something that someone didn't want anyone else to know about and, annoyingly, he was one of those who didn't know.

Matters got worse when his head of surveillance told him that there was no CCTV footage from The Ritz as they still had a privacy policy regarding their most esteemed clients. *"Our guests are advised that we would not impinge on their privacy through the medium of any form of video recordings. "* In an age where CCTV was prevalent, he found their attitude rather archaic and very annoying in this instance, but the hotel operative Terry had been drafted into the video centre and was at the moment scrutinizing footage from the previous night's concert in an effort to capture a picture of him. There were in fact four special branch operatives looking at a bank of screens which relayed real-time footage of the major London streets directly into their hub. Gone was the age when a photograph of a wanted man was printed and then circulated via the police stations, by which time the individual was often long gone. These days it was all sent by electronic devices so that 'arrest' orders could be carried out far more quickly, and the Section 31 Order to detain Colonel Stock was already winging its way across London. It would normally be accompanied by a head and shoulders photograph, but in this case it was Terry's photofit description. There was still no mention of a wheelchair.

Out of the corner of his eye and not on one of his screens but one of those adjacent, Terry thought he caught the last remnants of a familiar entourage entering Hamleys off Regent Street and he called over to the officer in charge who was standing almost right behind him. "It could have been them, but I'm not certain. I wasn't really looking but concentrating on these screens and it could have been anyone, but there was something familiar about them."

The senior officer ordered a re-wind of screen eighteen and there in the far top right-hand corner for just a few seconds, the images of a man in a wheelchair, a small boy, and a dancing girl in tow, were seen going into Hamleys store. Although digital, the zoom in didn't really help as it was at the far end of the camera's range and the images blurred.

"Ok. I'll dispatch a couple of operatives to have a look but don't let up on what you're supposed to be looking at."

*****

Being founded in 1760 right at the beginning of George III's reign, Hamleys is one the world's oldest toy stores and their claim to sell *'The finest toys in the World'* is renowned. One could spend an entire day visiting the seven floors of traditional and modern goodies that have children squealing with delight and, given half-a-chance, Tom and Ann would have done just that had not Stock curtailed their visit. Buying smaller bits 'n' pieces, he had had to buy Tom a bigger backpack as when he tried to close his old one over yet another torch, the zip had broken. Tom was now the proud owner of a big brown bear backpack and Ann a larger Super Sophie handbag. Stock too was enjoying himself. As they threaded their way past the music department, Ann spotted a giant piano mat and they both charged off to try it out. Tom managed to find the volume control and the noise was considerable as they both tried to coordinate their own version of 'Chopsticks.'

They were too engrossed to notice a pair of dark suited men combing each side of the aisles. One of them spied the two cavorting children, but in his eagerness to verify that they were who he hoped they were, his foot caught the edge of a well-stacked pile of giant pandas which tumbled down around him. Normally, he would have just shrugged off this minor inconvenience, but the heaped pile of pandas was being kept upright by a sturdy pole in their centre. This was attached to the ceiling at one end and the floor at the other. His efforts to minimize the effects of flying giant pandas on the general public brought him into direct contact with the metal pole, and he knocked himself unconscious to the floor. Across the aisle from the pandas was a selection of the latest musical 'windballs' precariously balanced in a pyramidal shape, but the normally stable structure could not withstand the onslaught of half-a-dozen hefty pandas and the entire stack disintegrated. They scattered in all directions, some cascading down the nearby escalator, automatically turning themselves on with movement, and started their random musical repertoire. Along with everyone within earshot, Tom and Ann's attention was diverted to this mayhem that seemed to have taken on a life of its own. At first glance, it appeared that the pandas had attacked the neighbouring balls and were winning. Stock wasn't keen to be confronted by the store staff; although he knew neither Tom nor Ann was responsible, their mere presence right by the scene of the battlefield might be construed incorrectly so he beckoned them over and told them they were leaving. It was difficult to drag his grandchildren away as everyone around was laughing at the obscure sight and sounds but they headed for one of the lifts at the front of the building, unnoticed by the second dark-suited man.

They found themselves back on Regent Street. While he had been watching his grandchildren enjoying the delights of Hamleys, he had felt a growing feeling of anxiety within. He had had to concentrate on why he was here and what he was supposed to be doing. It was a struggle, but he remembered that he was trying to get to Mansion House to retrieve Akiko and complete his task.

Looking for the same type of taxi that had taken them to The Ritz, he positioned his wheelchair right next to the kerb, and after a few minutes stuck out his stick when he spotted one. This one was even more modern than the last and had a curved bubble-like dome that reminded one of a balloon of bubble gum about to burst. There is a peculiar breed of cabbies unique to London, but this one was small and well-dressed with a tie and jacket and had an educated accent. "Good morning, sir. And where would you like to go today?"

"We are off to Mansion House."

"Certainly, sir, I know just the right route to take us around all this traffic. Just position yourself here and we'll be off in a jiffy. If you two youngsters would like to sit up front with me, we'll be away in a moment."

In a little over a minute, they were on their way, the cabbie taking them through the back streets of Soho, through the narrow lanes around Covent Garden, across Kingsway and into the labyrinth surrounding Lincoln's Inn where the chambers of the country's leading barristers were centered. Their route took them across Fetter Lane and towards the oldest part of London below St. Paul's and then into the City of London where the Bank of England's building held majesty over the convergence of ancient trade roads. Almost opposite is the official residence of the Mayor of London, the magnificent Mansion House, but the vast majority of tourists were converging on the West End of London and were nowhere near the more austere business end of the City.

"We're nearly there, sir. The usual entrance for visitors is just around the corner in Walbrook. Would you like me to drop you there?"

"Fine, thank you."

Their disembarkation was observed by not just the usual bank security guard but also a member of the royal protection squad who, along with his colleagues in and around Mansion House, were keeping the Japanese entourage safe and sound. At the same time that the Stocks were approaching the entrance where he was stationed, his electronic beeper pinged in his ear, alerting him that he needed to look at the message on his screen and he decided to do so once he had seen to the strange party that were now in front of him. "Can I help you, sir?"

Some instinct helped him recognize the stoic tone and attitude and his response was just as official. "My name is Colonel Stock, and I am here to see Akiko Keisuke. See me in straight away, would you."

The RPS man was rather alert, and the previous evening had seen Stock's name on the circulated list of VIPs, but he hadn't had notification of the two children who accompanied him. "And who are they, sir?"

"They are my grandchildren and will be with me all day."

"Very well, sir. Please follow me." He reached for his radio and requested that the door be opened for him to allow entrance. "Mr Griffiths will take you from here, sir."

Once inside the coolness of the cavernous building, the sounds and smells of the metropolis instantly disappeared as though they had gone through a portal into another world. Stock steered his wheelchair between the marble columns across the polished granite floor. He had no idea where Akiko would be, but his thoughts were interrupted by a pin-striped suited man who had left his position behind a small wooden pedestal and met him in the middle of the reception hall. "Can I have your name please, sir, and please state your business?" Similar to the man outside, his electronic beeper also went off, but dealing with people took precedence over looking at messages.

Stock repeated what he told the man outside. "She is on the second floor, and you can take this lift, sir." He ushered them towards a wooden panel which slid open as they approached. "I will ask someone to meet you there, sir. Please press number 2."

Within a few seconds of the lift doors closing, both RPS men knew they had just made a very big mistake and the airways started chattering. Stock had been found.

Chapter 24

Confluence

While the recently released BBC's OB crew made their own way from Horsham by public transport, some via the local pubs as the coach driver had decided to go home, Camp had had a friend collect him and return him to his London apartment. As the Porsche sped up the A3 he vented his anger.

"Bloody officious police." He was quite naturally in a foul mood. "I've never had the indignity of being arrested before and when I am it's because of some insignificant person in the back end of nowhere while the real action is in London, and in the grottiest cell I've ever come across." He didn't add that it was the only cell he had ever come across. "Doesn't this thing go any faster?" He wanted to return to his apartment to change his now grubby clothes before confronting the BBC OB controller to obtain another crew. He knew it would be hard work as the crew he had left behind had been allocated to him for the weekend. There were other crews, but they had been allocated to his fellows. He smiled to himself as he knew he had a hold over the controller by way of an indiscretion he had found out about and would threaten to use it if necessary.

It was therefore a second-rate and mainly novice OB crew armed with dusty old equipment that had been earmarked for disposal that now accompanied Camp in a trio of mostly rusty old hire vans. In his forced absence he found he had been supplanted as lead reporter and the argument with the OB Controller had resulted in his being given the option of covering one of the numerous street parties or the Japanese delegation. When Camp learned that they were staying miles away from the central proceedings in Mansion

House, the air turned blue, but he reluctantly took the second option without having to recourse to blackmail. He didn't know anyone in the Japanese delegation and after all, he thought, it would be an opportunity to do so, and off he went to tap his sources to find out what he could before the main event.

Fortunately for him, most of his new crew held him in some esteem from what they had seen and heard about him, and although they had heard rumours about another crew being imprisoned, it didn't take Camp very long to convince them of what really happened in his own words. His pep-talk to the crew went along the lines of convincing them that, in order to obtain decent footage, they needed to follow him closely and not accept the usual brush-off given to their ilk by the security forces. "Where I go, you go," was one of his favourite phrases when initiating a new crew. By the time they arrived outside Mansion House, the crew had had a sense of importance instilled in them and were keen to follow their leader anywhere, and they went about their business of preparing for live transmission with a sense of pride, determined not to let down Mr Camp.

Camp was unused to failure, and it never entered his mind that he would not, once again, become their primary reporter to whom most agencies, and in particular the BBC, would turn to when it came to interviewing the high and mighty. He still harboured an inner rage against the security services of the world and in particular the English who he viewed as an unnecessary barrier that kept from him those in the seats of power and influence. He had already made his mind up that he was not going to brook any interference from those thugs who would no doubt be closeting the Japanese delegation in what they called a 'safe house'."

It had been estimated that there would be upwards of 3 billion people tuned in to watch the ceremonies and he was determined not to miss out. He would show the world.

*****

Terry was primarily a field operative used to the surveillance rigours of unsociable hours. On the odd occasion, he had even been found in the office, but today he was fast developing 'bug eyes' sitting in front of so many screens. He had a natural knack for picking out certain individuals in a crowd but had never before been sat in front of so many screens and asked to perform his magic. Across the corridor and through the glass walls of the corridor was the large communications room manned by just as many personnel and at the end of the corridor was the senior officer's desk, overlooking both rooms. Glass walls were necessary for several reasons but mainly so that visual contact could be made with one another much quicker than if otherwise. There were of course radios and phones but in addition there was an internal intercom system accessible by any and heard by all and activated by the mere press of one of the buttons adjacent to each workstation. When time was of the essence, this was an invaluable tool as it meant that one did not have to repeat things twice, and everybody was immediately up to date with whatever was going on.

After replacing his phone handset, the senior officer leaned over and pressed his intercom button. "I've just heard from our men at Hamleys and they're streaming some video footage from the store's CCTV. Pete, let me know the minute you get anything and Terry, you make sure it is him."

Some five minutes later, Pete beckoned Terry over to his computer where the downloaded video was being re-played. First, came the footage of the Stocks entering Hamleys take by the ceiling camera but that didn't clearly show their faces, but then the scene changed to the top of the escalators where it seemed that a selection of furry giant pandas were making a bid for freedom. In the background Terry saw a full frontal of Colonel Stock in his wheelchair, and he immediately pressed the intercom button. "Terry here. That's him. That's Colonel Stock."

*****

"But he's such an honest man. There's no way he would ever consider treachery and I refuse to believe he still conceals enmity against the Japanese to that extent. He put his life on the line for King and Country and has medals to prove that he almost did give his life for what this country believed in and, by the way, still does. That's what he fought for, so don't you dare even mention to me that he's off on his own to take revenge. That's just not him."

Susan had been in front of two senior police officers and another officer who took notes for nearly an hour, answering as many questions as they fired at her but was now becoming angry that they seemed to be twisting her answers to portray her father-in-law as a loose cannon with a sinister agenda that might end in the assassination of a Japanese dignitary. It was absurd and she could not - would not - believe that Bernard had somehow regained all his mental faculties and decided that they were still at war.

Superintendent Falls was a little embarrassed by the way his colleague was carrying out an aggressive interview and felt sorry for Susan. He had interrupted Hodges's lines of questioning on occasion just to soften the whole tone of their inquiry, but in the end, he had to see the justification of some very awkward questions and consequent conclusions. Hodges obviously felt there was more promotional mileage in continuing his lines.

"Mrs Stock," he paused to let what he was going to say next carry the gravity it deserved. "When a Section 31 Notice is issued, it is done so only by the Home Secretary and he wouldn't issue it unless a very senior member of the security services had recommended it; in fact, it is often endorsed by the Prime Minister himself. It is used only as a last resort. For example, the recent case of Michael Coombes the Irishman and, before that, Raoul Moat…"

"But they were both shot dead by you lot and you're asking me to believe that Bernard is in the same category… You're insane. Just think about what you are trying to do." It was clear that she was not getting through to Hodges. "Look, a one hundred year old man, an Englishman, who comes from a long line of ancestors all with brilliant military careers, who was recently put into a home, who is wheelchair-bound, who has to take medication so that he can understand the time of day, suddenly comes up with the idea and wherewithal to go and carry out an assassination of someone who he's not met for over sixty years. Whose hare-brained idea is that?"

"Please, Mrs Stock. I too find it incredible, but they wouldn't issue a notice unless they had very good reason to, and I'm…" He was interrupted by a knock at the door and an officer entered.

"They've found him, sir… over at Mansion House."

"Mansion House!" Hodges was dumbstruck for a moment. "That's where the Japanese are staying."

"Apparently he's managed to get through security and is inside now."

No words were necessary, and Susan bit the back of her hand as she pushed it against her mouth to help stop any utterance from coming out. If there was any time, it was now that she needed Roger.

Hodges almost leapt out of his chair. "Come on. We'd better get there soonest." And as he headed for the door he turned to Falls. "And bring her. She may be our only hope. And by the way, find her husband," he said to the officer who had brought the good news. "Where did you say he was going?" This to Susan.

*****

Roger was still in agony as he slowly ambled cowboy fashion down Blackpool's seafront promenade back towards his hotel and nearly tripped over on a slight protrusion of sand that had found its way across part of the pavement; the extra movement that forced his legs to keep him from falling over brought another shot of pain to his groin. His thoughts were miles away as he tried to understand what had just happened to him and he found that he had overshot his hotel. He hadn't even noticed the two armed policemen standing astride the hotel entrance, nor did he hear the lewd comments between them as he clutched one hand between his legs. It was only when a third officer emerged from the front door did anything really register. "That's him. Get him in the van - quickly." Before he could comprehend what was said, he was whisked off his feet by the by the two officers and dumped in the back of a Transit van. The twin doors slammed shut.

Even if he could have lashed out with his legs, which he couldn't due to the nature of his injuries, it wouldn't have done him any good; the officers were all too proficient at bundling people into the back of vans and had had years of practice from the usual high-spirited revelers who frequented Blackpool at the weekends.

"What the bloody hell is going on?" Roger shouted towards the sturdy panel that separated him from the front passenger compartment. "Hello. Is anyone there?" The movement of the speeding van should have answered his rhetorical question, and it certainly did so as he was thrown off his seat as it sped over a roundabout. "Where are you taking me? I haven't done anything. Aaaaaargh!"

His face squashed against the dividing panel as the driver braked sharply to avoid another motorist. Perhaps he had done something. A very short while ago, he had been musing over the past few hours' events and now he focused on what may have caused his arrest. Perhaps she was the police chief's daughter, and this was his revenge. Perhaps she was a policewoman and had lured him into a trap, but his heavily alcohol-fuelled mind couldn't cope with much more than trying to stay in his seat, despite bracing himself in a corner.

He had hardly had a chance to consider what else might happen when the van dived to a halt and the rear doors wrenched opened to reveal what seemed like a small army of armed policemen waiting outside. There was some sort of whining racket that refused to go away, and he was unceremoniously hauled from the van by a pair of burlies. As his feet hit the ground another shot of pain doubled him over, but this had no effect on his escorts who carried him over to the steps of a waiting aircraft where they handed him over to yet another pair who hauled him up the few steps, along the aisle and threw him into a seat. "Aaaaaargh." He re-screwed his eyes in agony as his nether regions contacted with the relatively soft seat swab. He was breathless with pain, but eventually registered that someone had buckled him up and that the plane was taking off. He couldn't even focus properly on what was happening outside the window as he sought confirmation that they were airborne, and he shifted himself to ease the dulling pain.

"Mr Roger Stock?" a bewildered man asked from the seat across the aisle.

He nodded.

"You don't look too comfortable."

"That's an understatement," retorted Roger as he unclasped the seat belt and eased his buttocks to the edge of the seat where there was nothing below his groin.

"Were the lads a bit rough with you?"

"Not sure what you mean, but they weren't gentle." He shifted his trousers so that there was no restriction and looked more closely at the man opposite. "They didn't kick me in the balls if that's what you mean."

The quizzical expression revealed that the man waited for further explanation which Roger was reluctant to give but felt that he had little choice. Besides which, it may provide an opening for him to discover what he was doing here, who the man was, and who the blonde was.

"There was this woman: fabulous blonde, and she…" He still wasn't exactly sure what she had done other than almost geld him. The man opposite held up his hand.

"There's no need to explain… You're not here for that."

"Well, what am I here for? And where are we going?"

"It concerns your father."

"My father? How could he know where I am? He doesn't even know what day of the week it is… Oh. Has he… passed away?"

"On the contrary. It seems he has resurrected himself. I take it that it is your father who, up until yesterday, was resident in Springfields Nursing Home?"

"What do you mean up until yesterday?"

The man had phrased the questions so that he could ascertain if Roger was who they thought he was and that he had little knowledge of what Colonel Stock was doing right now. There were a few more questions he wanted to ask before he revealed what was happening.

"Please answer my questions and I'll explain later. Was he living at Springfields?"

"Yes. My wife and I put him in there some weeks ago. He was becoming a liability and a danger to himself, as well as the public in the Frog and Hopper."

The man had previously read the scanty dossier on the Stock family and was now satisfied that he had the right person next to him.

"As his son, he must have told you a lot about his war days. Did he mention anyone specifically?

This was a totally unexpected question and Roger was nonplussed as to why this was being asked of him. "Oh yes, lots of stories, and there's several people who I can name, but it might help if you can be more specific."

"Any Japanese names for example?"

"Not that I recall." Roger was starting to put two and two together. "Has this got anything to do with the Japanese being over here for Peace Day?"

"You're quite bright for someone who's just been uprooted and, yes, it has everything to do with that."

There was a pause while the man allowed Roger some time to remember. "I'm sorry, but I don't think I can help you there. If you tell me what this is all about, I might be able to help."

The man revealed that they knew very little about his father and that somehow he had gone to London. They believed he might be about to assassinate someone from the Japanese delegation. He and Roger went over Bernard's history in the little time available, as the flight from Blackpool to London was expected to take little more than 45 minutes.

As the plane taxied to a halt next to a waiting car he added, "There's something else I must tell you. He's got your children with him."

A poised Roger, ready to get up from his seat, fell back into it and rather wished he hadn't. "But my wife was looking after Tom and Ann. Is she alright?"

"We believe she too is looking for them all, as are we, but we know they were at The Ritz last night. Do you know why he might have gone there?"

"The Ritz?" Roger mentally scratched his memory. "I think he told me once that his parents went there for tea sometimes, or was that The Carlton?"

The second pilot came down the aisle. "You can switch your phone back on now, sir. We received a message that Colonel Stock is at Mansion House, and you are to take Mr Stock there immediately. A car's waiting."

"Shall we go?" the man offered.

*****

In the rolling countryside of Hampshire and despite a habitual hangover, Victoria and her friends were pissing themselves laughing. Now that Susan had left, she could tell the others what had happened and was inwardly smug with herself that she had not let the cat out of the bag the previous night; it would have ruined the surprise.

They were sitting on bar stools at the large island countertop in her kitchen.

"Yes, Serena moved 'Up North' to shack up with this movie producer and took him to the cleaners when she found out he was already married to two other women, threatened him with all sorts. Anyway, I phoned her and asked her to do a little favour for me." She spun the laptop around so that the others could clearly see the screen revealing a middle-aged man trussed up like a chicken on a four-poster type bed and dressed in erotic lingerie.

"Who's that?" asked one of the girls.

Victoria was grinning with complete satisfaction and waited for more calls from the captive audience before letting on. "That's Roger, Susan's husband."

Howls of laughter and derisory comments followed.

"She doesn't know. Bit small, isn't he? Shame he wasn't here last night. Where did she get those cuffs? Are there any more shots? Not of *that*!" The girls were in seventh heaven with mirth. "Come on, tell us what happened."

"Well, Susan told me that Roger was going on some convention in Blackpool this weekend and how she completely trusted him on his own so I thought wouldn't it be great to have him set up. Serena owed me a favour, so I told her where he was and asked her to put him to the test."

"Not sure he's going to test much with that," commented one of the girls.

"No, no. Don't get me wrong. I didn't ask Serena to screw him, just tease him but she's surpassed herself with these photos. Emailed me earlier this morning."

"Is he actually conscious?" asked another as she crooked her head around to see better.

"If I know anything about Serena, she could raise the dead," piped up another.

Their jollity was interrupted by one of their party entering the kitchen holding just a towel across the front of her body. "Hey, everybody."

They all looked towards the doorway.

"This really does work well in the bath, just like Angie said. It's so… sensual." The others were not quite sure what the odd-shaped pink apparatus was that she was holding. "Come and try it." She grabbed one of the girls by the arm and led her out of the room. The others meanwhile returned their attention to Vicky's laptop to pan through the photos that Serena had sent but it didn't take long for their interest to wane. One filled the kettle in preparation for a cup of tea, while Vicky's eyes were drawn towards the wall-mounted television showing the pageantry of Peace Day and she turned up the volume with the remote.

*****

Geoff was perched on one of the bolted-down stools in the back of Mike's van listening to the pair of loudspeakers mounted on the inside of the roof panel. They had parked in one of the back alleys behind Abbey Road Studios just to the west of Regent's Park as Mike reckoned that it was a central enough location to be able to move around the traffic and temporary pedestrian areas without too much delay. It was also not far from a public toilet. He had several different radios tuned into various police and security frequencies and had asked Geoff to monitor those while he scanned the secure phone line with the help of a computer. Picking out what they wanted to hear was almost impossible as most of the airborne traffic was about mundane details and of course the inevitable plea for help from a member of the public who had lost their cat twice in the same morning.

"Probably forgot to put out enough milk. Here, talking of which, can you pass the flask behind you. Tea? Milk's in the fridge by your right knee."

They had been ensconced in the back of Mike's van for some hours and were beginning to lose concentration when Mike suddenly froze. "Sssshuuussshhh. I think I've got something. Turn those others down."

Geoff busied himself with twiddling various knobs, hoping they were the correct ones.

Mike was playing on the computer with his left hand while his right hovered in mid-air. "Yes, yes, yes! Right, here we go. They've found Colonel Stock and apparently he's broken through the security cordon around the Japanese at Mansion House. By God, we weren't wrong. Here pass that map and get in the front."

They both jumped into the front, Geoff fingering his mobile phone which also doubled up as a satnav and headed off around the north side of Regent's Park where there were no traffic restrictions.

"Ought to be there in about fifteen mins. according to Google but it depends on traffic. Left here, now right. My press pass ought to get us within spitting distance, but we'll just have to see how close we can get when we get there." It was stating the obvious as they had discussed such a scenario earlier but with any luck, they might just be able to pick up an exclusive.

"No problem with that. I've got today's password to get through the security cordon." Mike grinned. "With what I've got now, I reckon I could get us the Crown Jewels."

*****

Commander Jackman was one of the first to learn about a serious breach in one of his security cordons from one of his colleagues in the royal protection squad, and then only a few seconds later he had confirmation from his own communications officer. As was his nature, he wasn't distracted by the news, only very annoyed at himself for not seeing this coming. Using the microphone attached to his sleeve, he set in motion one of many pre-arranged anti-terrorist plans that would send covert operatives scurrying and set off from his headquarters with his driver in tow. It wasn't that he was worried about his job, which he would most likely lose if anything should happen on his watch, nor the loss of his privileges, pension etc., but it was the loss of pride that he would have to live with. He was fiercely patriotic and still considered Britain as one of the best places on earth and was ready to give his life for what his country stood for, yet that came second to his conscience. He guarded those thoughts very closely. As he raced for the garage beneath his offices, he automatically reached under his jacket with his right hand to check the weight of the Heckler & Koch 45 to confirm that it was loaded and felt a little further down to count the number of spare clips for the relatively small but powerful weapon. He hoped he wouldn't have to use it, but without it, he felt incomplete, especially on this occasion. Once ensconced in the passenger seat of his car, he continued barking orders through his microphone all the while listening to the latest developments on his earpiece and, at the same time, trying to fathom out exactly what Colonel Stock wanted with the Japanese and how best to counter whatever might arise.

Meanwhile, his communications officer had managed to contact Wickes who was now accompanying Sir John Corston in the back of one of the official black Daimlers and was already en route at a respectable sedate pace to Mansion House. A few minutes earlier, a very sheepish Wickes had had to accept his admonishment from Sir John as he stood in front of his desk because he had failed to locate Colonel Stock and it seemed to him that his career prospects had come to a shuddering halt. He signed off from his phone and with relief announced the good news.

"Sounds like we won't have long to wait before meeting the colonel," he announced to his minister who had been looking up at the passing London skyline out of the opposite window.

Corston was caught out by the surprising, good news but didn't want to show his pleasure to a man who he had virtually reduced to tears a short while ago. "Go on."

"It seems that Colonel Stock is already at Mansion House as they originally requested and not only that, but he's already in contact with the Japanese." Wickes tried to keep his answer short as he didn't know if this bit of news would reinstate him in the eyes of his employer.

"How can he be in contact with them when he doesn't have any security clearance….?" And then it dawned on Sir John just what a resourceful man they had been trying to find over the past few days. He had phoned his aunt who had been her usual helpful self; after wading through the requisite family greetings, had learned that his father had held Bernard Stock in high esteem and that they had often met up again after the war.

"They used to meet at The Constitutional Club at least once a year and I met him myself on a few occasions at The North Surrey Rugby Ball, I think it was. He was a very handsome and debonair man and, if he hadn't introduced me to Clarence, I'd have probably married him myself if he'd proposed. In fact, I think you met him when you were little, but you won't remember that. He saved your father's life, you know. I don't know the ins and outs of it, but from what I can remember it had something to do with airfields behind enemy lines and he got your father out just before the war ended. Come to think of it, it was all supposed to be a bit hush-hush. No, I don't know where he's living now -if he's still alive…"

Sir John now married up what his aunt had told him with the recent scanty information he had been given and the fact that someone from the Japanese delegation had requested Colonel Stock's presence at today's ceremonies. There just had to be a connection, but with whom? And why was the Colonel doing whatever he was doing today of all days?

He leaned forward and tapped on the dividing glass partition that separated himself and Wickes from the driver. "Get a move on, will you? I want to be there as soon as you can make it, ok? Quickly now."

They arrived in front of Mansion House a few minutes later and drew up alongside a small fleet of gleaming vintage Rolls Royces accompanied by extremely smart chauffeurs.

"That'll be their official transport," pointed out Wickes in the hope that Sir John would acknowledge another aspect of the organization that he had helped to set up, but he didn't. The Daimler had hardly stopped moving before Sir John jumped out and headed for the pair of oversized ornate double doors. But before he could take even two paces, he faltered as another car came into view and pulled up just in front of him with a screeching of tyres. Commander Jackman nearly knocked him over as he opened his door and the two men briefly stopped and looked at each other, not just in recognition but each showing their understanding of what the other was trying to do.

What happened next was something neither of them had been expecting. It seemed that the normally quiet courtyard in front of Mansion House had become Piccadilly Circus as first a pair of police cars appeared from the left, followed by a fleet of vans and yet more police cars from the right and, within a few seconds, people were getting out and running in all directions. Jackman groaned as he recognized that non-security personnel were also in the melee and, worse still, he caught a glimpse of media equipment through one of the van windows and his hesitation nearly cost him first place to the doors.

Ten seconds earlier, the security guard had been at his podium inside watching a peaceful scene of waiting cars on his monitor, and the next moment he glanced down and recognized a charging Commander Jackman followed by a horde. He didn't stand a chance as he opened one of the doors for an obviously worried superior officer and the flood of people rushed past him.

"Which floor?" shouted Jackman as he passed him en route to the left-hand staircase.

"Second."

Everybody now knew where they were going as the almost thunderous sound of some fifty running people echoed off the polished surroundings despite the three-quarter carpeted staircase.

Chapter 25
Questions Answered

The old-fashioned lift doors opened onto a spacious galleried landing beyond which stood four Roman columns. This, in turn, opened into a wider chamber and was flooded with light from four tall matching Georgian windows framed by ornate reveals. At each end of the room, a pair of proportioned Gainsborough oil paintings stared at each other across the polished mosaic floor which would normally have been empty but today their view would have been obstructed had they been mounted a few feet lower.

As if on a stage, three rows of Orientals were facing the columns with the windows behind them. Those in the front were seated in chairs while those behind were standing. Several yards to the fore, a photographer with his assistant attended to his tripod-mounted camera and reflection umbrellas. As Colonel Stock and his grandchildren left the claustrophobia of the lift, the scene in front of them may well have been a photograph. For a few seconds, the only muscles anybody moved were their heads as they all focused on the wheelchair whirring slowly towards them, its tyred wheels making a sucking sound on the floor, otherwise it was totally silent. Stock stopped almost in the centre between the photographer and his subjects. Tom and Ann now joined hands in reassurance behind him, as the sight ahead was indeed awesome.

Leaving his stick perched to one side on the chair, Stock stood up, took two paces forward before bringing himself to attention and casting his eyes over the assembly. Nobody coughed in the complete silence and, if anyone was bothering to notice, there was hardly a blink as they all waited for what was to come next. Un-noticed by

Stock, behind him and blending into the background beyond the four columns and the furniture were several heavily built Japanese security personnel; they too did not move a muscle.

"Akiko Keisuke," he called out in a clear voice but there was no reply. "I believe there is one here who answers to that name." Stock's tone of voice was firm and full of resolve, but it was several moments before anyone responded.

"I am Akiko, and I once went by the household name of Keisuke which is still my…. Koseki… my given name" A lithe-like lady had stood up from near the left-hand wing of the front row and stepped forward. "And you, Colonel Stock, are a very brave man." Her English was perfect and without a trace of an accent.

He looked down at the clearly elderly female that stood opposite him. Up to that point Stock had envisaged Akiko as a young girl in love, barely out of her teens. He struggled to assimilate his depiction of her in her bed chamber from many years ago with the old woman who now filled his entire vision. He stared at her for some time, picking out the similarities with what his memories had engrained on him and compared them to the facial features, behind the heavy makeup, of the person who claimed to be the one and the same. He had come ready to rescue a petite and innocent daughter from the clutches of an evil enemy but instead here was an old woman who seemed entirely at home with her surroundings. His concentration did not waver as he struggled to reconcile the two different images, but her voice carried the same intonation as he remembered. He pictured the scene in Alfredson's headquarters and could hear their conversation:

"You are to bring her here…. to me. We must succeed at all costs."

"What's to happen to her once I bring her back here?

"Please don't ask me; I don't know."

He needed to ascertain exactly who this was in front of him.

"If you are who you say you are, when did we last meet?" Surely only the real Akiko would know the answer to that question?

As if weighing up the quality of an inquisitor, Akiko looked directly into Stock's eyes and delayed her response long enough for Stock to begin to wonder if he had asked the right question.

"I'm not sure that everyone here should be privy to that, but I can tell you that this building is much easier to get out of than another one in Burma."

Stock recalled the clandestine efforts he and Akiko had made to evade the guards. But surely others would have known how they had got out and he decided that he needed more.

"Well, tell me this: when did we first meet?"

"Really, Colonel, you must not let your eyes deceive you. That was a long time ago when we were both a lot younger and more beautiful." She was purposefully being a little evasive still testing his qualities but quickly realized that such an answer would not satisfy him, so she continued, "A bed chamber is not the best place for a first meeting in the eyes of a high society which would scorn a girl for accepting a ring."

The ring. Stock had forgotten about it, and he now raised his hand and displayed the magnificent signet ring that Alfredson had given him. He stared at it, considering the implications of her answer. This had to be Akiko and he had at last found her, but what now?

For the first time he could remember, Stock was unsure of himself. On the one hand, he had orders that still needed to be carried out. To deliver Akiko, and why not directly to Winston himself here in London? On the other hand, the circumstances seemed to have changed beyond recognition as this was not the Akiko that he remembered. He faltered with indecision and could not comprehend the effects of time, and it was like a blow to his logic that had so far never failed him. If Akiko was older, then so was he, and what of his friends, his colleagues, Alfredson, Winston, Ignatius? When? When? It was time that was his main concern and he started to take in the rest of the ensemble. They were all Japanese and Akiko was with them. There was thunder in his ears, far off at first, but it was getting closer. He felt himself trying to concentrate on what he was doing here but couldn't fathom it. He fell back on his military training; always achieve your objective. He had to get her away from them.

"Please come with me." He opened his hand beckoning for her to take it, but she just stood there.

"Colonel." She was almost dumbfounded by his offer and replied with a modicum of laughter, "I think you ought to know that Ignatius passed away some years ago now." She could see he was struggling with events, and it was clear to her that the man who had rescued her all those years ago had come to rescue her again, like a knight in shining armour. "We were happily married but his illness got the better of him and he passed away over twenty years ago. This is my family now." She turned and waved her arm at those behind her.

While Stock tried to take in the consequences of what she was saying, he also cast a more critical eye over the assembly which varied from large children to those of a similar age to Akiko, all dressed somberly in immaculate and fine clothing. There were no smiles and still no movement, but all eyes were fixed on him. Looking around at his surroundings he noticed the photographers behind him and, beyond them, the several security men standing like statues in between the columns. He then noticed his own glum-looking Grandchildren who were holding hands on one side of the wheelchair, looking back at him quizzically. He finally returned his gaze to Akiko, and it began to dawn on him that there had indeed been a considerable passage of time that he had been missing. Time had not passed him by but somewhere between his meeting in Alfredson's headquarters and now, an awful lot had changed, and he suddenly felt his real age, and his logical mind tried to cut through the muddle of what had happened. Like the cogs of a clockwork timepiece reaching midnight, when the smallest of movements from the second-hand starts an unstoppable series of motions that heralds in the onset of a new day. The cam of the biggest wheel, released from its constraints, clicks round to release the minute wheel which in turn releases the hour wheel which automatically advances the day and date settings. Just like such a watch, Stock's mind was going through a similar unseen metamorphosis.

Taking in the scene in front of him and what Akiko had said, his mind started to work backwards like a video in rewind. He could first picture the past few hours, then the past few days, weeks, months, years. The video was going faster and faster and bringing with it sounds, smells, feelings and all those small details that are all too easily forgotten. In those precious few seconds, time was chronologically ordered and with it came clarity, clarity about what he was doing there and why. He had no remorse, only regret that he found himself unwanted and making a nuisance of himself, but the thunder would not go away and, if anything, it was becoming louder.

He focused on Akiko once again and she returned his stare as if in understanding but it was she who broke the silence first.

"I believe you now understand but please do not rebuke yourself. What you did for me and my family is almost impossible to reconcile. I have been kept informed about you and your family ever since I returned to Japan. When I was told that you had been committed to a home, I did not envisage seeing you up and about again, yet here you are, come to rescue me once again."

Stock's mind was by now in overdrive. 'Was it possible that she did not know what the instructions given to him by Alfredson really were? By Christ, he had better keep that one to himself. Nobody must ever know. The thunder was now becoming a roar and seemed to be on top of him making it more difficult to concentrate. Was there something else he had missed?

Akiko continued, "I believe that in your old age, you have become disorientated and unaware of my circumstances, yet in my old age, I can now understand the confusion that surrounds you. I too have trouble recalling when something took place, but as you can see, I am here with my family headed by Hideo Keisuke, my cousin." She turned and made a small traditional bow to the man in the centre of the front row. "It is only by your gallant actions that united me with Ignatius so that we could spend the best years of our lives together and it has been one of my deepest wishes that I would one day, and once again, meet the man who made it all possible.

Stock just stood there without showing any emotion although inwardly he was beginning to flinch.

"When we arrived here a few days ago, I asked our head of security to keep an eye on you and it was my intention to come and visit you in Springfields in the coming days, but I should have realized that, for a man with your special talents for finding his way into secure areas, it would not be a problem for you to appear here before us now."

She was laughing as she spoke, and it produced a similar reaction from the rest of the assembly. It also had the effect of turning what was a previously tense situation into one of ease as it dissipated the 'us-and-them' atmosphere.

The recent exertions he had demanded of his body, the smell and sight of his old uniform, the intensity and grandeur of the occasion and now coming face-to-face with Akiko, together with the Razadyne II, had concentrated his mind to an extent where it was as agile as it used to be. He could see it all now, and a flush of foolishness flooded through him; he hadn't felt this wrong or as small, since he was a child. The enmity towards all Japanese which he had felt over sixty years ago somehow evaporated in the presence of Akiko and he realized that he was being acknowledged by her, and indeed the rest of her family who now looked at him as an actual living character from the past.

He felt that a suitable response to excuse himself from them would be appropriate and was about to speak when the thunder broke.

The hoard had been sprinting up the twinned staircases and along the corridors, their efforts to reach Stock first spurring them on. Footfalls and elbows echoed off the walls and ceilings of the enormous, chambered gallery that surrounded the reverberative stairway terminating in front of the four Roman columns and the breathless leading echelons went to rush forwards. The large security guards were now joined by others who appeared out of nowhere and now barred the way forwards between the columns, holding their hands out wide; the impassive look on their faces dared anyone to go any further. None did. Neither did they say anything as they gawped at the unusual sight in front of them. The thunder Stock had been hearing now subsided as the hoard crowded around each other to see and hear what was going on. Almost last to join the throng was a panting Nicholas Camp who, resting his forearms on his knees, motioned more than directed one of the cameramen to start rolling as the other technicians connected up cables to boxes and battery packs. A live feed was now being relayed to the BBC.

Stock's composure returned as he addressed the Japanese ensemble, "I may be nearly one hundred years old now, but it seems that I have been a little hasty.

This anomaly produced a ripple of laughter and served to lighten the atmosphere further.

"Wars are inevitable but, once over, those who survive them spurn them and all the terrible events that go with them. I think this is perhaps why I chose to forget much of my involvement. It is not just our duty to our lords and masters that drives us to these conflicts but fear for our families, our standards, our way of life… It is but mere human instinct that wells up and urges us to protect them. Although not part of my family, my particular duty in this instance was to reunite a young lady with her fiancée and I must apologise if my actions here today have caused any offence. I can only put it down to my ignorance and drive to see decency prevail over the madness of war. I have as much right to exist in this world as you do, but that does not give us the right to impose our wills on each other. That is human nature. I will not bend to your will nor you to mine, but one thing we have in common is the ability to recognise the difference between right and wrong. Living with ourselves in the knowledge that we are in the wrong is like a cancer and it will eat away at us until it eventually turns us into ignominious individuals. Living with the right ethos gives us hope and we all thrive on that hope. I think I have been a decent man in my life and have tried to uphold the right kind of principles and perhaps that is why I have lived for so long; or perhaps it is time I passed on.

He shifted position to lean more heavily on his other leg and focused on Akiko.

"I am overjoyed to learn that you found your husband and managed to spend some pleasant years together, yet you hold me responsible for this; in that case I am guilty. The sheer joy of husband and wife in each other's company is often enough to provide the necessary strength to us to live out our days in serenity but I have known those who have literally died of a broken heart through being parted for whatever reason. You have lost your husband and I, my wife, but our spirit is strong enough to overcome these losses. O once we do, we become stronger for it; those who do not, wither and die. Because of our inner strengths, I believe we will survive and pass that same strength on to the next generation. The saying 'The strong survive and the weak perish' is as relevant to the mind as well as the body but most of us do not realize this. You and I are fortunate people.

Stock shut his eyes for a moment, reflecting on his dubious circumstances and removed the ring from his finger.

"Here, I think you ought to take this; it belongs to you, not me." The large jewel sparkled in the photographic lights as it sat in the palm of his hand. "I hope it gives you the comfort you deserve."

Still there were no sounds coming from either the Japanese or the hoard as they listened to Stock's oration, but Camp had now regained his breath and he went to push one of the cameramen forward.

"Oi, you! Get this on camera and… oooooof!" He never finished as one of the security guards simply lowered his hand quickly into his nether regions. Camp doubled over and fell onto the floor.

For a moment nobody moved until Akiko took a few small paces forward and stood directly in front of Stock, all the while, holding his gaze.

"I think you are an exceptional man, Colonel, and you have a good heart; in your own idiom, a *right* heart. I certainly do miss my husband and I draw strength from my memories of him, but I also draw strength from my family. This is as much the Japanese way as well as the English way and probably the world over." She looked down at Ignatius' ring. "Thank you for your considerate words and, yes, I will take this as one of our memories." Tears were beginning to well up in her eyes, but in the presence of such company, she held them back as she returned to her seat with a lowered head.

It had not been a burdensome task keeping the ring these past few decades, but he felt relieved that he was now released from his duty. His shoulders sank as he waited until she was seated before turning around to look at his grandchildren, oblivious to the throng of people in the background. "Come on, kids, it is time to leave." He went to sit in his wheelchair.

"Colonel," an assertive male voice called out behind him. "Now you really *are* being hasty."

He turned back to face the Japanese ensemble and saw that a man in the centre front row had stood up and was walking towards him. He was a tall, elegant man in formal regalia with a starred emblem over one breast and a red and white sash crossing his torso supporting a decorative sword by his side. His English was almost as good as Akiko's, but the slightly clipped words betrayed oriental origins.

"I am Hideo Keisuke and I understand you came across my father in Assam."

Stock remained impassive yet he could now detect that same hereditary tone in Keisuke's voice: like father, like son? Could his offspring have the same cruel tendencies as his father and why was he being beckoned? What did he want? A hundred and one questions agitated him and deeply buried memories surfaced, but he held his composure. He decided that diplomacy would be more productive until it became clear what this man wanted with him, but foremost of these questions was 'How much did he know about Akiko?'

"The Assam jungle where I met your father was a most confusing theatre of war. Once within its vast confines, it was often impossible to gauge which way was north, which way one's own lines were, which way the enemy's lines were, and which way was the best to go. Yes, I met your father, but I cannot say it was a pleasure. It was one of those episodes in my life that I prefer not to recall, and I think you too must be like-minded otherwise you would not be here. Surely, we are not here today to expose all those mistakes from over half a century ago?"

Keisuke took another two paces forward. "My age precludes me from having experienced that particular war and I am not here to revive its memories. As my cousin, Akiko has told me a lot about her father. It is one of our ways of handing down history. She also told me of your actions and how you stole her away from my uncle to reunite her with Ignatius, which otherwise may never have happened. There is obviously a lot I do not know, but one thing I am sure of your selfless acts displayed the characteristics of a person whose heart is full of courage and what you have done here reveals that you are an honourable man. You are quite correct to maintain your beliefs, yet they are coupled with the rare ability to see them through to the end but without imposing them on others. That is for them to decide for themselves.

He paused in thought for a brief moment.

"You are aware that we are participating in the global Peace Day ceremonies today, and it is most unfortunate that my Emperor cannot be here due to ill health, but he has given me the authority to act on his behalf. We shall shortly be meeting your Queen on a world stage and on his behalf I shall be apologizing for the maltreatment of those prisoners of war that were in our care. There are still some in my country who believe this reconciliation ought not to take place because it might degrade our nation in the eyes of the world, but that is an old world and one that this generation does not subscribe to."

It was clear to Stock that this Keisuke did not have the same traits as his uncle but why was he now being lectured by him? Some sort of mitigation perhaps?

Keisuke continued, "Those of us in powerful positions in my country, and that includes my Emperor, would see that your attributes are those that we can all aspire to, and you have reinforced my belief that today's apology is the right thing to do. You have suffered by the hand of my uncle and for that I must give you my personal, and my family's apology."

Without taking his eyes from Stock's, he unclipped his sword from his belt and held it out at full length in front of him.

"Please, take it with my humblest apologies." He lowered his head just enough so that Stock could not see his eyes.

It was a highly decorated piece from which a small golden tassel dangled and was shaped in the traditional style of a full-length Samurai sword. The last time Stock had seen such a similar shape was in the hands of General Keisuke and he had almost been on its receiving end. Now he was being offered it in peace, in reconciliation. It was being offered in such a gracious manner that to spurn it would give the impression that it was insufficient, but to accept it would not right the wrongs, not even part of the way. He suddenly realized that this was impromptu and was coming from someone who had little else to submit there and then. He may have been Japan's First Minister with all the power anyone could ever ask for, but this offering was personal. Stock was not used to ceremonies, certainly not as high-level as this one, and had had no training in the necessary protocols but he slowly brought the sword to his chest with both hands and gazed along its length. Keisuke's head was still bowed, and it dawned on Stock that it would probably remain bowed until he said something.

"What would you say if I told you this is not necessary?"

Keisuke's head shot up, his inquisitive eyes fixing Stock's in horror. He had just offered one of his family's heirlooms and it was now being rebuffed. To him, it was a total insult.

Stock saw and understood the look in his eyes, probing for the effect that his words had on him. In that moment, there was an understanding between them, one that existed between two adversaries trying to outthink each other.

"Our Spirit endures within us all and it ultimately dictates who and what we are, and it is with one's words and actions that we are measured by Society. From that perspective, words only would have been sufficient from a man in your position, yet you have chosen to make restitution from your family as well. I think it is a most magnanimous gesture and it would be coy of me if I did not treat it as such. I will accept your gift and your apology with my deepest sincerity as I believe it comes from your heart. I hope it is a precursor to things to come.

A wave of relief swept over Keisuke as he recognised that Stock's statement honoured him in a way he had not been expecting, but then again, he was learning that there were several facets to this man that were unexpected. He spoke again.

"Now, I think you can return to your family in peace and with our gratitude. I certainly must as the rest of the world will be waiting." He gave a short bow before walking back towards the waiting delegation who now stood up and headed for a door to one side of the room.

Stock didn't know what to do with the sword; he had never had to hold one so sheathed before. He looked down at his grandchildren who had taken up residence in his wheelchair. "Come on. It is time to go."

As the last of the Japanese were leaving the room, the security guards lowered their arms and the hoard pressed forwards to encircle Stock and his grandchildren, but it took quite a while before the voices diminished. There were endless questions from all quarters fired at him and questions between policemen as to who and what they were doing there, and questions between the civil servants that would not be answered fully until later. Unanswered questions from the media but one question was more pressing than all the others as Ann tugged at Stock's arm.

"Where's the loo, Grandpa?"

Eventually, they all went their own ways as the centre of attraction that day was some way across London, and they all had their own agenda.

Roger sympathized and recognised that Camp had still not recovered sufficiently enough to walk, and he was helped back down the staircases by a pair of techs and into a waiting ambulance whose driver had followed one of the motorcades of rushing vehicles on the off chance. Camp learned that the camera op. had caught the entire episode clearly, helped by the photographers' bright lights, and that the BBC had broadcast it all live. He was aghast that he had not managed to feature in it and was turning the air blue with his language as he was laid out on a stretcher in the back of the ambulance, the nurse quickly fixing an oxygen mask over his face, while opening the nitrous oxide gas tap to quieten him down.

Geoff and Mike went to sneak off quickly, eager to sell their side of the story to as many editors as they could contact but they got no further than the first flight of stairs before being apprehended. While Stock and Keisuke had been engaged with each other, typically Jackman had been eyeing up those around him and recognised Geoff from one of his files. He had quietly contacted his base through his sleeve-mounted microphone and mentally rubbed his hands with glee as the information came back through his earpiece. He managed a rare smile as he was told that their van had been found and, if these two were who he thought they were, he would enjoy 'talking' to them later. Much later. Let them sweat for a few days in isolation. After all, he could hold them legally for 28 days under the Prevention of Terrorism legislation. As he joined Hodges and Falls at the edge of the encircling throng around Stock, in his mind he was arranging their accommodation in the nastiest cells that could be found.

Sir John and Wickes were being berated by Susan once she found out who they were and her vicious tongue lashed their ears for being 'inadequate, soulless functionaries…….' Corston no longer saw the need for the colonel to attend the official ceremonies that were already underway as he seemed to have already done his bit, but he would certainly have a lot of explaining to do to the PM tomorrow. His bleats about their families being intertwined fell on Susan's deaf ears and, for the first time that day, Sir John was really grateful for Wickes as his arm was grabbed and he was led away by him with murmurings of having to be elsewhere.

The grandchildren returned under the watchful eye of a non-descript dark-suited man. Ann was in the lead and now relieved of a full bladder, was hopping again. "You should see the loos here. They're bigger than our house."

"And there's gold everywhere. Even the soap's gold." Tom caught up. "Can I hold the sword?"

Stock sat back down in his wheelchair and placed the sword across its cushioned arms and saw Roger in front of him now that the hoard had all but disappeared. "There you are, Son. Fortunate you were here otherwise you would have missed this."

"You never told me any of this," said Roger. "What else were you up to?"

"Oh, I think that can wait a while; let's talk over one of Susan's nice cups of tea."

Susan grinned at the compliment. "Talking of what else has been going on, what have you been doing?" She had noticed that Roger's gait was not its usual self.

Roger immediately flushed a little. "Errrrmmm, like Dad said - over one of your nice cups of tea." He hoped that, by emulating his father, the flattery would come to his rescue, even temporarily.

Commander Jackman broke into the family reunion, "I must also apologise to you, Colonel. It seems that I underestimated you."

"How so?" Stock did not know who this man was and was not sure what he meant.

"I am a commander in Special Branch and responsible for the security and safekeeping of our Japanese friends. Despite all my efforts to track you down, you managed not only to elude me but break into a most secure area." He managed a sarcastic laugh. "It seems that I must come to you for lessons. When you have the time, would you mind if I call on you and ask you to fill in a few gaps that are missing from your file?" He was being polite as he recognised that Stock would be more likely to respond positively.

"You might have to put up with Matron's tea."

"I'll take that as a yes, then." And for a second time that day, Jackman managed a smile and went to go but returned. "Just one small item left, I think. It would probably be for the best if you let me have your revolver. Safer for everyone." He pointedly looked at Stock's holster. Any other person found with such a weapon would instantly be put in prison for several years, but the circumstances dictated otherwise.

Stock leaned over, unbuttoned the webbed holster, and withdrew his Webley revolver. He hefted it in his hand, feeling its weight for the last time, before reversing it in his other hand and offering it to Jackman. "It's not loaded."

"Thank you, sir." Jackman broke open the chamber to make sure it was indeed unloaded. "Goodbye for now."

Susan called after him, "Commander, do you think you can get someone to take us back home?"

Chapter 26

Slippers

Returning to The Twinings in a little short of two hours was a bit of an anti-climax for the Stock family, despite them being chauffeured in a posh limousine supplied by Jackman. They were escorted by a pair of motorcycle out-riders through the South London suburbs towards Sussex and, as they reached the opening fields on the edge of the metropolis at Coulsdon, their escort peeled off to return to more important duties. Roger and Susan were catching up with each other as well as Bernard as to how, where, when, and what had been going on over the past few days, but there was a lot still unsaid that would be answered over the forthcoming days. The kids were eventually told off for fiddling with the various gadgets after Roger burnt his ear on one of the gooseneck map lights.

As they entered the sleepy village of Yeasting, the chauffeur asked, "Can you direct me please, sir?" and it simultaneously dawned on Roger and Susan that they could hardly take Bernard back to Springfields, not now that he seemed, well, capable of looking after himself once again. Roger went indoors while Susan and the kids accompanied Bernard to his bungalow to see that sheets were on beds, lights worked, keys where they ought to be, etc. Returning from the toilet, Bernard 'ooofed' down into his favourite chair, aided by his stick and went to shut his eyes.

"Grandpa, Grandpa," the kids interrupted his 'nap'. "Someone's been in your room."

"Yes, and they left the wardrobe door open. Mum says it must have been burglars, but they haven't taken anything."

Bernard was a bit non-plussed until he remembered retrieving his uniform from there a few days earlier. "Have you looked to see if they are still here?"

Their eyes widened as they shook their heads but before they could ask any further questions, Susan appeared in the doorway. "Bernard, do you want help getting out of your uniform? I've got some of your old pyjamas ready."

"Now, that's a good idea. Here, can you two start with my bootlaces?"

"What about the burglars?" asked Ann.

"He can fight them off with his new sword if they come back," added Tom.

Once the kids had removed his boots, he went to change in his own bedroom and they were still there when he returned, dressed in his stripy pyjamas.

"Look what Mummy found," blurted out Ann as she held out a pair of worn leather slippers at arm's length. Bernard immediately recognised them as his favourites and as he slid his feet into them; they brought back fond memories. Memories of Mary. He had an urge to go to sleep dreaming of her and the gaiety she had brought into his life, but he did not want the kids to see him crying. She had bought them for him as a birthday present a long, long time ago and he had taken great care of them ever since. "I feel rather tired, so I am off to bed now."

He was just getting into bed when Susan and the kids came into his bedroom to say goodnight.

Susan had stated that Bernard was too tired, but the kids persisted, "Oh go on. Please. Just one quick story."

"Just one quick one only, then you two come straight back home. Good night, Bernard. It's really nice to see you back to your old self again." She bent down and kissed him on the forehead while the kids cuddled up to each other at the end of the bed.

"Tell us a story about a sword," piped up Tom.

Bernard thought for a while. "No, but I will tell you one about your grandmother." He shut his eyes as the pictured the scene.

"Not too long after the end of the war, I had asked Mary to the North-East Surrey Rugby Ball. It was a grand occasion and there were hundreds of people there: the Mayor of Guildford and his wife, the Commissioner of Police, and lots of dignitaries. At one end of the ballroom was a loud seven-piece band. We danced and danced all night on that highly polished wooden floor. I was really fit in those days, but Mary had trouble keeping up, and just before the final waltz she had to take her shoes off. Can you think why?"

There was a shaking of heads from the other end of the bed.

"We had danced so much that she had worn a hole in one of her new shoes." Giggles from the kids as Bernard wiggled a worm-like finger through an imaginary hole in his other hand.

"The next morning, I took her shopping and bought her a new pair of shoes, and do you know what she bought me? A brand-new pair of slippers and she said I ought to wear them instead of wearing out her feet." He reached down and brought up the pair of slippers that Susan had found. "These slippers are older than your parents."

A "Wow" from Tom as he reached forward to finger the faded leather.

"That same afternoon, I proposed to her, and we were married."

"They must be really old then," volunteered Ann.

Bernard just smiled as the kids continued to feel the quality of the slippers that meant so much to their grandfather. "Time to say good night. Here. Come and give me a hug."

"Good night, Grandpa." He held a child in each arm, squeezing them affectionally, and slowly closed his eyes. As he did so, his grasp weakened, and he drifted off to sleep dreaming of Mary.

The kids had the sense to turn off the bedside lamp and close the door behind them as they left.

*****

Susan found that Roger had given up tidying the guest sitting room and was channel-hopping on the TV with the remote. Most channels seemed to be covering the ongoing Peace Day ceremonies, not just from London but also from around the world.

"I've left Bernard telling them one of his stories and they certainly seem no worse the wear from being up in London, Oh look, go back a channel, there's Bernard." Roger flicked back to one of the BBC's which was showing the previously live broadcast from Mansion House. "Turn it up."

By the time Roger had found the volume buttons the scene had changed to the front of Buckingham Palace. "We weren't going there in any case but somehow we seem to have been part of it, and how did Bernard and the kids get up there without you?" asked Roger.

There had been so much to talk about in the limousine on the way back from London that they had just skipped over some of the very basics. Susan had been so relieved to be reunited with her family again and knew this moment was coming, but she hadn't yet had the chance to work out what she was going to tell him, nor indeed how much. She really needed to talk to Vicky first and was wondering how quickly pubic hair grew back. "It's a very long story, and I'll tell you all about it over supper."

"Was it the kids who took Bernard or the other way around? And you still haven't told me why you left Sarah in charge." Roger wasn't being fobbed off quite so easily.

"Look. I'll tell you what. Let's swop stories over a nice steak and kidney pudding." She calculated that an appeal to Roger's stomach would hopefully defer what she had to say. "And you can tell me all about your trip to Blackpool." She was oblivious as to the real reason why he now wanted to stall, and it had nothing to do with his stomach. Roger too was wondering just how to broach the subject and how much he ought to tell her.

"OK. I'll go and dig out one of those bottles of that Chianti I've been saving."

Unbeknownst to each other, they each breathed a sigh of relief. Susan had made her mind up that the best time to reveal her indiscretion would probably be in bed. Roger had similar thoughts.

Just as they entered the kitchen, the phone rang and they both paused by it, but let it ring.

"Let's not answer that," volunteered Susan, catching the same thoughts as she looked into Roger's eyes.

"Good idea."

But just as they went to go about preparing their evening's meal, they remembered that the answerphone loud-speaker would kick in, and it was too late to stop the recording as the cyber voice asked the caller to leave their message. It was Vicky.

Only the kids ate supper that night before bedtime, but Roger and Susan managed to get through almost three bottles of Chianti before taking the stairs, hand in-hand.

Chapter 27

Amor omnia

Normality had returned to Springfields after several days: normal for Springfields, anyway. Mr Green was sitting back in a chair, kneading his un-stockinged right foot that rested on his left thigh and paying particular attention to his big toe. There he was walking along the corridor to one of the Day Rooms, when from around the corner he heard Ron's Lad pushing the tea trolley at his usual breakneck speed. He had sharply sidestepped against the wall to avoid being run into again, but he had gone the wrong way. The trolley was taking the perfect racing-line and a wobbly wheel jammed his foot against the corner of the skirting board and, before he could berate the bloody oik, he had continued out of range. Bloody little Lad would get a real talking to this time, he thought as he hopped to the nearest chair in the Day Room; this time it had broken the skin.

There was not quite as much venom in his thoughts this time, though, since that same morning, he had received a letter from the board of trustees confirming his status as Administrating Manager of Springfields. It had come as a complete surprise as he had expected to have been replaced after all the recent mishaps that had taken place, but he was certainly overjoyed at his official appointment. What he didn't know was that whomever else the trustees had asked, the position had been turned down by all the applicants.

He would save his good news for when Matron next tried to belittle him and hoped he wouldn't have to wait too long. No sooner had the police investigation cleared him of any wrongdoing, than the Council-led enquiry had begun, but what came as a bit of a shock was that their findings also absolved him. This may have been something to do with the fact that Eve was one of those Inspectorates, but once again, he had been oblivious to this. There had been a tricky time when some of the staff had queried his decision to move Mrs Freeman back into her original room and one even claimed that she was not the same person, but after a while nobody had kicked up a fuss. Ron's Lad's habit of sometimes carrying around a pet or two in his pockets paid him an unexpected dividend. One day he had brought one of the wee baby ferrets in his trouser pocket and, when he had a hand free, would comfort the tiny animal by stroking it, and it would poke its head out to receive his fingers. Standing beside the tea trolley he found himself next to ex-Mrs Weeks and the idea of seeing her reaction came to him. He slowly lowered his hand towards his pocket and out popped an inquisitive rodent-like head in full view of Mrs Weeks.

"R-r-r-raaaatshhhhh!"

The ear-piercing shriek caused one nurse to launch a full cup & saucer through the air and onto the lap of a previously docile patient, who knee-jerked his leg into the middle shelf of the trolley, sending a handful of clean crockery crashing to the floor. Ron's Lad beat a hasty retreat, satisfied that Mrs Weeks was definitely not on the road to recovery.

In between his trolley racing, he went about his usual tasks that kept him busy and among them was his once, or sometimes twice, daily visits to the pear tree where he had laid his traps. Disappointingly, other than the flattened fox faeces which could have been done by a badger or rabbit, there had been no further signs that anyone had come close. He had received one or two odd looks from the staff as he would go around sniffing people in odd places, particularly their knees if possible. He reckoned to himself that the autumn would produce a good crop from the orchard, and he started thinking about ways of turning the sweet fruits into alcohol. *That* would liven up Christmas. He had also been asked by Ron to attend to the livestock in his room and he reluctantly agreed to make a lean-to shed to house his pets and went about the locality collecting all sorts of stray bits of timber and board. Mistakenly, the inhabitants of Yeasting thought he was doing a good turn by tidying up their Parish, and word soon got around that if there was any timber that somebody wanted to get rid of, all they had to do was leave it outside their house on the side of the road and it would disappear. Most of it was of such poor quality that it ended up in the annexe wood-burning stove, but long before the arrival of winter, there was a considerable surplus that would see them through.

He was being given more and more work to do by Ron but enjoyed the extra responsibilities and was even asked to use the motor mower after being given a stern lecture about not racing it around like the trolley. If anything, his prowess at mowing exceeded Ron's high standards and the lawns shimmered evenly in the dappled sunlight, but to spice things up a little, he had removed the silencer from the exhaust; until told to put it back by Mr Green.

Ron's reasoning for this delegation was soon clear to the Lad as he was spending more and more time with Eve; it also explained why Ron had asked him to move his pets from the Annexe to the shed. Eve found another excuse for calling into Springfields one Friday afternoon so that she could utilize the free taxi service from Horsham and then spend the rest of the day with Ron. They sat holding hands under the shade of a plum tree on one of the oak benches, accompanied by faint clipping noises from the unseen Lad's shears.

"Tell me how you came to be here," she asked Ron, kicking her feet out in front of her as a small child would in embarrassment.

"No one's asked me that before. Ever since I left school, I've been gardening for people...." He went on to explain how he had been working for someone who was employed in the Council's maintenance department and that a permanent position had become available at Springfields. "That was several years ago. I don't get paid very much but at least I've got a roof over my head and I'm well fed. These old folk come and go, but the staff are a nice bunch and I enjoy their company."

"I enjoy your company." Their eyes met. "You're the only real friend I've got down here. Everyone at work is either married or too busy and it's a bit depressing going back to an empty flat. You've got lots of friends here and I really envy you."

Ron's gaze dissipated as he considered his next words carefully, but it didn't make any difference. He wanted to say a hundred and one things but in the end all he said was, "You can move in with me if you like."

"Can I? Can I really?"

"Of course, you can, otherwise I wouldn't have asked."

She leaned over and gave him a great big hug. "Oh, thank you. You've made me the happiest person on earth." And then she kissed him on the cheek. Separating from their momentary embrace, the gap between them at first widened, and then closed and brought them closer together as their lips joined.

On that same bench one week later, Ron proposed to Eve.

*****

An official communiqué to Mr Green by the manufacturers of Razadyne II for the withdrawal of the medicine advised that there was a very remote possibility of some minor side effects when given in conjunction with some other medication. It went on to say that when taken within 48 hours of Aspirin derivatives, the patients may experience slight hallucinations, but in its place, they would shortly be producing Razadyne III. This got Mr Green wondering about Colonel Stock and some of the others and it went a long way to explaining why his patients seemed more lucid of late. He went to the Day Room to quietly observe Captain Perry and General Bristow and after a while decided that they were both more aware now than they had been when they had first been admitted to Springfields. They weren't sleeping as much and had started taking more interest in the news channel on the tv. He sat unseen on several occasions and watched them commenting on the latest reports from around the world but there was no sign of any hallucinations.

On one occasion, the newscaster introduced Nicholas Camp who was reporting from outside The Old Bailey on the trial of two men caught phone hacking.

"That chap looks familiar," volunteered Perry.

"Of course, he's familiar. That's Nicholas Camp and he's on tv every day, sometimes twice a day," retorted Bristow.

"No. I think I've met him, but I can't place exactly where."

"Interviewed you about your bunions, did he?"

Mr Green also recognised him and knew exactly where Perry and Camp had met, but he hadn't told them; he had no intention of telling them either.

The newscaster went on to the waning subject of the world Peace Day reports. It had initially been a resounding success as conflicts around the globe faded away, but nobody really thought it would last very long. The butterfly effect that brought the utopian atmosphere to an end was brought about by the independence issue of Serenidad and inevitably the intransient French were considered by many as the bad boys on the block. The angst of increased taxes to Paris spread to nearby Islands and eventually involved the European Commissioners, but in the meantime, violence had broken out in French Guiana, and this had set an example to other under-trodden peoples around the world. Luminaries being interviewed all advocated that the various factions revert to peaceful methods of resolution, and some had already started talking about the following year's Peace Day.

*****

Nearer the centre of the village, The Twinings household was adjusting to the re-addition of another member; Bernard had moved back into the bungalow and the kids were preparing for the new school year that was due to start all too soon. The imminent annual village fete was in the forefront of conversation in The Frog &

Hopper as this was where the organizing committee met. All too often, those outside this elite inner circle who closeted themselves in an anteroom next to the main bar were interrupted by other regulars who overheard the various proposals. Alarm was raised when one member offered pets from his nearby reptile zoo as a display.

"Alligators aren't dangerous if you know what you are doing."

"Rubbish. Have you seen the size of their teeth?"

"No, no, no. These are baby ones and my wife and I hand-reared them ourselves."

"Have you counted how many hands your wife has lately? I'd heard that she was being pretty liberal with them myself." A guffaw followed this comment.

"Whatever my wife does in her spare time has nothing to do with my alligators, and in any case, it's a lie. Just because one ripped off her blouse when a thread got caught in its mouth when she was showing some people around, it doesn't count as adultery." What had actually happened was that the local newspaper photographer had been snapping away with his camera, just as his wife had hefted a juvenile alligator out in front of her in a perfect pose. Its teeth had indeed ripped her blouse and bra away, revealing a pair of breasts that would have made a page 3 girl proud. Decency prevailed, and the editor had not published the photographs, but somehow, they appeared on the internet and most of the village had had a good look. Even the alligator seemed to be smiling.

"How about we electrify the fence on that display and ought we to consider moving it away from next to the marsupial compound? Alligators eat them, don't they?"

"But if we do that it will interfere with the Punch & Judy Show."

The chairman of the meeting had come to a decision: "We'll stick with the original plan as it's almost too late now to do anything about it. Now, moving on, I had a word with Colonel Stock, and I am pleased to report that he has agreed to open the fete."

Discussions continued well into the night, accompanied by

plenty of wine and beer but it was just as well that minutes were being taken as the next day few could remember exactly what had been resolved.

Bernard had visited the Frog & Hopper briefly just once since his return. He had been accompanied there during lunchtime by one of his chums from The Constitutional Club and they had enjoyed a fine crab salad together. It had been a quiet affair and very unlike the lively evenings of not so long ago, and out of politeness, those who knew him did not interrupt but only glanced discreetly.

He was no longer on any drugs and, although the withdrawal of Razadyne II did not cause any symptoms, he was beginning to revert to his natural state. His memory was going but before it went completely, he, Roger and Susan had discussed the options available and had concluded that he would not return to Springfields. His bungalow was smartened up and Bernard had sat back in his chair as Roger had put two screws high into the wall to hang the decorative sword.

"It's not level," he said just as Roger got down from the step ladder and stood to one side.

"Yes, it is."

"It is down on the left a little."

Roger squinted trying to make the image easier. He had to agree that his father was right but didn't want to admit it. "It's your glasses that aren't straight."

"I thought I taught you to measure twice and cut once."

"You did, but this is an optical illusion. The ceiling's straight but the sword is curved. And the tassels on the left just make it look wonky. I'll get some gum and wedge it up a little if you like."

"No. I am sure it will do."

A knock at the front door terminated the conversation, and Roger went to see who it was. Bernard was still looking up at the sword when Roger announced the Reverend Huw Lister as they came through into his sitting room.

"So that's it, is it?" He stood next to Bernard before approaching the sword to get a closer look. "Never seen one close up before. Are the ceremonial ones as sharp as the real ones?"

"Oh, yes, they are very sharp. Aren't they, Roger?" Roger had asked the same question not more than an hour ago and had run his thumb along part of the edge, but not for long as blood oozed out from it before he had covered not much more than an inch.

"I can vouch for that. It's safer on the wall… Ask the reverend here if he thinks it's not straight. I'll leave you two to get on with whatever you're getting on with."

As Roger closed the front door, Huw sat down opposite Bernard. "You've been a busy fellow… Seen you on the news quite a bit but you don't seem any the worse for wear." Huw was referring to Bernard's celebrity status after his replayed appearances on television. "In the words of Shakespeare 'some are born great, some achieve greatness, and some have greatness thrust upon them.' I suppose you qualify for the latter."

"If there has been any greatness, it has been this nation's dignity that has been upheld, and, yes, I have to admit that also of the Japanese to a certain extent. I doubt I will be remembered for very long and I do not wish to be. From when we are old enough to think for ourselves, we realise that there will be one crisis or another in our lives and to some, this is something to look forward to; to others, it is abhorrent. I have been fortunate enough to survive them but have very little to relish now."

"In other words, your ten thousand days are almost up." Huw was blunt with his comment as he knew Bernard would appreciate directness.

Stock leaned forward and retrieved a white envelope from under a leather-bound book on the table between them.

"No doubt it will be you who will bury me despite my agnostic beliefs, and I have no objection to being interred in a Christian graveyard, but I will be damned if you declare me one in the name of God. You must promise me this: neither a prayer to God nor a mention of anything to do with the Trinity in your church. If there is life after death, then I will live with it and, if not, then I am right, and you are wrong."

Huw had half-expected he had been asked to call to discuss such a matter but, even so, he was still shaken at the demands that were now being put on him. It was likely that with someone of Stock's stature that the bishop himself would want to conduct the service, but as it was his parish, he knew he could insist upon himself in carrying out that duty. If he did accede to Stock's demands then he would probably find himself in deep trouble with his ecclesiastical superiors but, then again, his first responsibility was to his parishioners. He decided he could take the fine line between the church's doctrines and Stock's beliefs; after all, they both had the same agenda up to the final reckoning.

"I'll not swear on the bible, nor by God, as this will not have as much gravity as my word in your own eyes. So, this I will do. I promise to accede to your wishes and make sure you rest in peace."

Stock's emotions nearly overwhelmed him; the knowledge of being able to pass away as he wanted to brought great joy. "In this envelope are some of my wishes which you may like to read out at the right time, and I have also made some notes for you in case you have second thoughts." He handed it to Huw who accepted the burden. "I am sure you will know when to open it."

Nothing that Stock had said to Huw even hinted at a threat to him should he not carry out his wishes; it was plainly unnecessary. The only threat was to damn himself and he considered that this indeed summed up the man to a t. "If I had a parish full of people like you, I would probably tear my hair out."

"If they were all like me, I doubt that there would be harmony either." They both laughed at his comment, but their eyes met after a moment's silence, Huw trying unsuccessfully to see further through the windows into the mind of this dying man,

"Any last comments?"

Stock lowered his eyes. "None that spring to mind straight away and in any case it has probably all been said anyway. Where we go after death only matters to those who are still alive and, to my knowledge, it is not a reciprocal arrangement." He closed his eyes and dozed off.

Chapter 28

Robin

At The Twinings, Roger was serving old-fashioned Sunday morning cocktails from behind a low, white-clothed table he had positioned under the roof of the loggia outside the guest's sitting room. From his vantage point, he could shout a hearty welcome to newcomers as well as oversee those whose glasses were becoming empty. The kids were diligently passing between the chatty throng with trays of mini sausages, canapés and the like, eating much more than they really ought, while Susan did her best to make sure she had spent enough time with everybody to be at least polite; this was an impossible task in the given time. The warm end-of-summer's day brought with it the usual plethora of flying insects attracted by the scent of the gathering but still, there were those who considered the wearing of a tie appropriate, despite the increasing muggy humidity that is often the harbinger of a thunderstorm in England.

In his wheelchair and dressed in his uniform, Stock enjoyed the attention of those who could get close enough to him; he was after all the star of the show. Roger had gathered together as many of his surviving contemporaries for a belated celebration of his 100th birthday and it was surprising just how many there were, but there were more relatives than friends. It was almost sad to see that there were so few in uniform, mainly those whom he had met at The Constitutional Club, but it underlined the military theme that went with the occasion. The convivial atmosphere was interrupted by an exploding soda siphon that Tom had been investigating. It extinguished the pipe of a bespectacled man next to him, but also created an outburst of mirth from those not too close by. Somehow

Roger was the main recipient of the fizzy water mid-way through pouring another Pimms and he huffed off to change his shirt.

The formalities of this middle-class English family required respectful silence during the speeches, and in traditional manner, there was the occasional outburst of humour from the crowd. Stock stood up when it came to his turn to respond, all ears and eyes expectantly waiting on what words of wisdom would be forthcoming. He had no notes and, as usual, spoke from the heart.

"How nice it is to see so many of you, I mean it. There are not many who reach one hundred and who are still capable of seeing that far." There was a ripple of laughter. He was referring to those at the back of the crowd, and he now had their attention even more as they craned their necks. "I understand that there are more and more of us who are living to this ripe old age so either the doctors are becoming cleverer, or we are learning to outsmart them. We are also told how lucky we are to live this long, but I say it is you and the next generation who are lucky to have had people like me to show you what the benefits of a full life can bring. I am not grateful for you all being here as that implies that I am beholden to you, but I am glad you are able to join my family to celebrate the first of us to reach one hundred years old." He leaned down a raised his glass high. "Cheers, everyone."

His audience retorted with a rousing "Cheers. Cheers, Bernard."

He continued once relative silence returned. "When one becomes old and infirm, one becomes a burden on society, but by our own methods in bringing up our families, we have instilled in them a decency to care for us. This compassion is a relatively recent development in human nature and has been forced upon us by society's demands. If I had not received this compassion from my son Roger, his lovely wife Susan, and my greedy little grandchildren, I would not be here today enjoying your company." It had not escaped Stock's notice that Tom and Ann were tucking into the 'goodies' instead of listening to him.

"I am a very happy and content old man whose dreams have

somehow all come true. I am still surrounded by a wonderful family and some generous friends and with the recent ceremonies in London, I expect you will all be able to live long enough to be able to appreciate what is best in our lives."

Responses of "Hear, hear, well said, first class, etc."

Stock was beginning to feel his years, but he felt he still had more to say. "I have but one regret today: that my wife Mary is not here to enjoy your company. Many of you knew what a fine, upstanding, and, yes, long-suffering, woman she was and although it has all been said before, many years ago, it was her resolve that helped me to reach the inner peace that I continue to rely on. I think I need to sit down now."

The entire audience clapped and cheered as Stock gratefully reposed back in his wheelchair and closed his eyes.

*****

Some three months later he ironically passed away on Christmas Day, and a few days later, in the presence of Roger and Susan, Huw had opened the envelope given to him. Sadly, but faithfully, he had followed the instructions but there was in fact relatively little for him to do. There was no church service, and he was grateful that Bernard had stipulated that as an agnostic there would be no need for one. There was no notice put in The Times and hardly anyone in the village even knew of his passing for some weeks. It was as though Bernard's every wish had indeed come true.

Soon into the New Year on a typical English winter's morning, the family gathered around to scatter his ashes in the church graveyard. Huw carried out the last request and read one of Bernard's favourite poems out loud to the twenty or so assembled.

There's a breathless hush in the Close tonight --
Ten to make and the match to win --
A bumping pitch and a blinding light,

An hour to play and the last man in.
And it's not for the sake of a ribboned coat,
Or the selfish hope of a season's fame,
But his Captain's hand on his shoulder smote --
'Play up! play up! and play the game!'

The sand of the desert is sodden red, --
Red with the wreck of a square that broke; --
The Gatling's jammed and the Colonel dead,
And the regiment blind with dust and smoke.
The river of death has brimmed his banks,
And England's far, and Honour a name,
But the voice of a schoolboy rallies the ranks:
'Play up! play up! and play the game!'

This is the word that year by year,
While in her place the School is set,
Every one of her sons must hear,
And none that hears it dare forget.
This they all with a joyful mind
Bear through life like a torch in flame,
And falling fling to the host behind --
'Play up! play up! and play the game!'

They stood under the dark branches of an ancient yew tree and, as
Huw held the brass urn high to press the release lever, a small robin
came and landed on the handle momentarily, blinked at them before
flying away. It brought a smile to their faces and compounded their
thoughts of a very dear man.

The last Full Colonel from the Second World War was dead.

Author's Notes

I have of course changed the names of the main characters and invented some others, based on people I have met, but some of the more minor ones did actually exist, such as Digby and the Matron. Stock of course did exist and indeed excelled at most things he set his mind to. I had the idea of writing a book about my father at his wake soon after his death on Christmas Day 1999 just as we were about to serve out Christmas dinner. The number of further stories that came out then brought mirth to the occasion and in particular ones about how he continually managed to escape from the secure home. But that is another set of stories.

At one point or other in our lives, most of us will have the need to visit a home either to call on a relation or prepare for our own parents, and they really are not interesting places; dull is hardly a sufficient description of these places but that is what they are. What is worrying is that one day it is likely to be you and I sitting mindlessly in a chair until our own passing. For those that are still mentally capable, these people are worth listening to as they are a fountain of stories. Prompted they will ramble on until they fall asleep or are interrupted by a visiting nurse with the next set of pills. There are some very good homes out there but occasionally one comes across one that is as ineptly run such as Springfields and these are too good a target to avoid writing about.

Peace Day is obviously a utopian invention but acted as a focus for the later plot of the story. How Stock managed to get to London is not inconceivable as old folk have been known to end up in the most unlikely of places; I should know as I often had to retrieve my father from remote places across the southeast of England before we put him in a good home.

Stock's characteristics are quite accurate in that he was a very athletic man who loved his cricket, rugby, tennis, etc. and had the ethos of 'work hard, play hard' and in that order. He volunteered for the Royal Engineers now known as REME (Royal Electrical and Mechanical Engineers) before the outbreak of the Second World War and was involved with the Dunkirk evacuation before being posted to India and Assam. There he built twenty-two mainly forward airfields to support Major-General Wingate's Chindits' campaign across the Irrawaddy River. One such airfield was so far forward it turned out to be behind the battle lines and it was here that Stock shot down a Japanese Zero fighter. He cut a piece of the wing away and kept it. On one side, one can clearly see the markings of the 'Rising Sun' while on the other, he painted on small aeroplanes, each one representing either a single or double runway. He also took the pilot's sword, which still has traces of blood on it.

My father actually finished the war as a decorated lieutenant colonel and, once the war ended, he was offered a brigade overseeing logistics, which he turned down. His promotion to full colonel suited this storyline better.

I have the fondest memories of listening to his stories, many of which I have forgotten, and I regret not having paid closer attention to him. Always present in him was his lightning speed of wit and a wonderful sense of humour, but I am almost sorry to say that I seem to have inherited mainly the latter.